THEY WERE AFRAID
TO SPEAK...

Their bodies were in perfect harmony, when too often they'd gone wrong with words. Laurel lay, her legs twined with Morgan's, her cheek pressed against the damp warmth of his chest. She could hear his breath steadying at last, feel his fingers idly stirring among her tangled curls.

For a timeless interlude they basked in the firelight, content just to be...until he broke the spell. "Well, I guess it's off."

"What?" she replied absently, her attention on the sensuous play of muscle across his bare midriff.

His answer was a fraction late in coming. "Our annulment."

Numb with dismay, Laurel gazed at Morgan, suddenly a stranger to her. Was that triumph in his tone? Had he used last night to make sure she couldn't escape him so easily?

JOCELYN GRIFFIN
is also the author of
SUPERROMANCE #8
BELOVED INTRUDER

London life offered Penelope a tempting
proposition. Theater designer Nigel Burnett
wanted her beside him as he skyrocketed to
fame. Only his terms struck Pen as immoral.

So she escaped to her peaceful Lakeland
cottage to think. Soon all she could think
about was her next-door neighbor,
Alistair Heath.

Some dark secret had rendered Alistair
incapable of love. But beneath his bracing
insolence, Pen could sense strong passion.
Longing to ignite the hidden fires of his
heart, she vowed that her love would be
strong enough for them both.

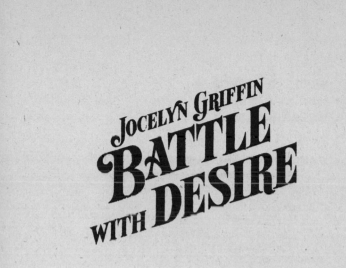

Jocelyn Griffin

BATTLE WITH DESIRE

A SUPERROMANCE FROM
WORLDWIDE

TORONTO · NEW YORK · LOS ANGELES · LONDON

In memory of J.B.
with thanks
for his interest and encouragement

———————◆———◆———————

Published June 1983

First printing April 1983

ISBN 0-373-70069-5

CHAPTER ONE

"EXCUSE ME...."

Not having heard the office door open, Laurel was caught doubled up behind her desk, trying to retrieve the one sandal that seemed to have vanished since she kicked it off after lunch. At the sound of a deep, slightly harsh voice she reacted automatically, coming up so fast she banged her head against the desk.

Controlling a definite urge to swear, she blinked watery eyes that gave her only a hazy impression of the man before her. But her tone was coolly professional as she asked, "May I help you," wondering whether he could see the errant sandal from his side of the desk.

"Forgive me for startling you, Miss... Andersen." The owner of that voice suavely read her nameplate into his apology and added, "I'm Morgan Hamilton, and I believe my grandfather is expecting me."

He let the last words hang inquiringly, and she murmured, "Yes, of course, Mr. Hamilton," and promptly forgot her place in the standard introductory ritual they'd been going through.

As she spoke his name, his image finally sharpened

into detail—and into the most attractive man she'd ever seen, crossing the room with long unhurried strides while the image of every other man she'd met seemed to fade out of her memory. Above his broad shoulders in a soft gray suit of immaculate cut, this man's skin gleamed like bronze over his strong features, as clearly molded as a new coin, and his thick hair had the sheen of a blackbird's wing. He looked as though he'd spent his life under the Mediterranean sun, except that the eyes under his straight dark brows were a clear light blue.

One of those eyebrows rose slightly at her silence, however, and she rushed into speech again. "Just a moment, please, while I let him know you're here—"

She reached for the intercom, but he cut her motion off with a gesture. "Don't bother—I'll just let myself in."

"Oh, but—" Trying to stand up so that she could at least show him to the inner door and announce him from there, she teetered to get her balance, since the leg without its sandal was three inches shorter than the other. And by then he had neatly sidestepped around her desk to reach the door behind it.

"The other one is by the left front corner," he observed, deadpan, and vanished into the office that lay at the heart of the Hamilton Corporation.

Just beyond the door, she heard his distinctive voice say, "Granda, your orders have been obeyed; you called, and I've come. Now what is this all about?" Then it receded as she sank back into her chair and reached with stockinged toes for that miserable sandal. Slipping it on, she was torn between irritation and amusement, embarrassment and admiration.

So *that* was Morgan Hamilton, heir apparent to the family firm and terrifically handsome besides! The society page photographs really hadn't done him justice, she thought as appreciation won out over annoyance and her lips puckered in a silent whistle. No wonder he had always been shown escorting Boston's most spectacular society women. Even without the Hamilton fortune, breathtaking looks like that would certainly make him attractive to them—as they would to any woman in neither her cradle nor her grave, Laurel decided.

When she'd first come to work here four years earlier, he'd been a favorite topic of discussion at the coffee machines and in the washrooms. But never having seen him for herself, she had been inclined to doubt that anyone could possibly be as good-looking as the other women claimed he was. He rarely visited the company's headquarters during those years, and the office grapevine had it that he and his grandfather often quarreled. By the time she was promoted into her present position as his grandfather's executive assistant, Morgan had gone to Europe, supposedly to study innkeeping and restauranteuring on the Continent. According to more rumors around the company, he'd also found time for a variety of other activities.

She had known he was due home, of course. She'd been handling most of the paperwork involved in the proposed transfer from elder to younger Hamilton of the chain of luxury hotels that stretched down the Eastern seaboard. The older man had decided to retire from active control of the firm he had built, to retain only a seat on its board of directors and management of a small group of country inns he'd begun to buy in the past few months.

Laurel had been on hand when most of those decisions were made, and although her opinion was irrelevant, she approved of them. In the eighteen months since her promotion to replace his previous assistant, she had worked closely and continuously with Adam Hamilton and grown genuinely fond of the old man. Shrewd, he had begun with nothing but the name of an old and impoverished Boston family and built up a hotel empire worth millions. Kindly, he had given away millions as well, in donations recorded in the private files only he and Laurel ever handled. And if he demanded much of people in hard work and dedication, then he paid them well for it. If he sometimes seemed to manipulate them, again and again she had seen them ultimately better off for his interference in their lives. Indeed, sometimes Laurel thought with wry amusement that the phrase "benevolent despot" could have been invented for Adam Hamilton. Certainly, working with him had been an education in itself!

Lately, though, she'd sensed a change in him.

Decisions came more slowly from the office behind her desk, and the fierce vitality that had always motivated him and kept his employees moving, too, seemed to have ebbed. Once or twice she'd caught him slipping a small tablet into his mouth, and the faint bluish tone that worried her would fade from his skin. A doctor's daughter, she'd recognized that Adam had a heart condition. But the few times she'd tried to protect him from trivial demands on his energy and attention, he found her out immediately.

"Don't you try to coddle me, my girl," he'd barked the last time, and she had drawn herself up stiffly as he fixed her with a stern gaze. Then it softened as he added, "You're a sweet child, though, and I appreciate your concern, even if I don't need it. Just finish up with those papers for the transfer, Laurel, and send word to Morgan about coming home. He's in Biarritz, I believe. But once he takes over here, I can have time off to tour those old inns of ours and maybe even indulge myself in a few games of horseshoes and old men's chess, with a cap on my head and my pipe in hand."

That last had been said with a chuckle, and Laurel had smiled as she went back to her own desk. Even over a chessboard, Adam Hamilton would be a master strategist, maneuvering the players as well as their pieces and somehow contriving to make everyone feel like a winner in the end. With a flash of insight, she guessed he would enjoy that every bit as much as the larger campaigns involved in running his corporate empire. On a swift wave of affectionate comprehension, she had reached for Morgan Hamilton's latest address.

That had been on Tuesday, and on Friday here he was in his grandfather's offices. Laurel's indignation at the way he had surprised and then evaded her began to melt into approval that he had responded so quickly to Adam's summons. Before the last of her annoyance could vanish completely, however, she became aware that the murmuring voices in the office behind her were now shouting. She was on her feet and hurrying toward the door before she admitted to herself that the head of the Hamilton Corporation hardly needed her to protect him from his own grandson.

Irresolute, she hesitated, her hand already on the brass doorknob, and then she heard the grandson's voice say furiously, "Just the fact that he managed to find a girl fool enough to marry him so he could father a couple of homely brats doesn't make Paul any less an incompetent than he always was! I warn you, Granda...."

The rest of the words were lost, as if the speaker had turned to pace in the other direction, and from farther back in the room Adam's reply was inaudible, too. Then someone approached the door with rapid strides. Before Laurel could move away the knob had been snatched from her slack fingers, and Morgan appeared in the open doorway.

She had an instant to notice that even someone

who didn't know him could tell when Morgan Hamilton was angry by the forbidding angle of his eyebrows and the flare of his nostrils, before his enraged expression evaporated as if it had never been. His light eyes narrowed, and by what must have been an exercise of sheer willpower he suddenly looked pleasant and composed again as he gazed into her startled face.

"Ah, Miss... Andersen," he said in a voice that was now perfectly modulated, "would you do me the honor tonight of joining me for dinner, to celebrate my return to Boston, the home of the bean and the cod?"

As disconcerted as the last time he had addressed her, Laurel blinked, then pulled herself together. "I think—" she began, and he interrupted her.

"Thank you. I appreciate your fitting me into your schedule and I'll pick you up in the lobby downstairs at half-past five. That way I can give you a lift home to change, and we'll decide at the same time where to go. Until then, Miss Andersen."

And with a brief nod he strode lithely from the room before she could finish a sentence that had been going to end, "I'd rather not, thank you." Fuming, she glared at the outer door he'd just shut with excessive care. Gorgeous as he was, she hadn't the least intention of going out to dinner with him, either now or at any other time! She might have been fresh from the Missouri farmlands four years earlier when she first joined the Hamilton Corporation, but even then

she'd known employees—even executive assistants—
don't go out on dinner-dates with the grandson of the
firm's founder. That came under the heading of mix-
ing business with pleasure—if going out with so arrogant a man could be classed as pleasure—and she
was a whole lot too professional for a mistake like
that!

"Laurel." A voice cut across her interior tirade.

"What?" she snapped.

"Would you come in here for a moment, my dear?"
the voice on the intercom said with a slight chuckle.

She arrived in front of Adam Hamilton scarlet
with embarrassment.

"I beg your pardon, sir," she said to the man behind the fine old desk. "I didn't mean to be rude."

"You weren't, my dear. Only a trifle abrupt, and
my grandson has been known to have that effect on
people. Sometimes they even raise their voices," he
added dryly, giving her a humorous look over the top
of silver spectacles that, as usual, seemed to be ready
to slip off since they perched so daringly close to the
tip of his nose.

Adam Hamilton, even at seventy, made a striking
figure. A fringe of fluffy white hair around his head
gave him a deceptively cherubic appearance. Laugh
lines edges his eyes, but those eyes were penetrating
enough to make an errant employee think him anything but angelic. Now, however, they looked mildly
at Laurel over the tips of the fingers he had placed
precisely together.

"Morgan left the door open behind him, Laurel, so I couldn't help but hear his invitation to you." Morgan's grandfather went straight to the point, but Laurel hastened to forestall him.

"Yes, of course, Mr. Hamilton, but I assure you I don't mean to go out with him. I know that would be unsuitable, but he didn't give me time to say so."

"He didn't intend you to have time for that, my dear—an old and devious tactic, but one that has been known to work." The words were accompanied by a sudden grin that made Adam look younger than Morgan, but Laurel opened her mouth indignantly. "No, Laurel." His grin faded and he waved one hand in a delaying gesture. "I know you're going to assure me that you won't go out with your employer's grandson, and before you say it I'd like to ask you to reconsider."

"What?" Laurel was reduced to a monosyllable for the second time in only a few minutes.

"If you're really busy this evening, Laurel, then don't let either of us interfere with your plans, but if you're not...."

He paused and Laurel admitted, "No, I'm not. My class was just canceled."

"In that case, I'd be grateful if you'd change your mind and go to dinner with Morgan tonight."

On the surface it wasn't a particularly unusual request. A number of times in the past year or so, she'd acted as Adam Hamilton's hostess for a company party or joined him to entertain important business contacts. But going out with his grandson wasn't the usual business situation.

"Yes, of course, if you'd like me to," she agreed slowly. "But may I ask why?"

"Certainly you may ask, my dear. Shall we just say bluntly that given the fact my grandson left here in a somewhat reckless mood, I'd rather know who he's with than not?"

That hardly answered her question—in fact, it raised several more—but Adam had joined his fingers together again and was smiling blandly at her over them. Clearly, he had nothing more to say on the matter, and Laurel's training took over. After all, she was paid extremely well to assist Adam Hamilton, and it didn't really matter whether that meant working with company business or company personnel. Besides, arrogant as he was about commandeering her time, Morgan Hamilton *was* a devastatingly handsome man!

"All right, sir, I'll be happy to oblige."

"Thank you, Laurel. Now why don't you let me demonstrate my gratitude immediately by giving you the afternoon off? You could go shopping, if you have a fancy to, and be back in time to meet Morgan here—or you could just gather your strength for what may be a difficult evening with my grandson."

That last was said with a twinkle, and Laurel reacted to it automatically, as she was meant to do. Five minutes later she was poised on the sidewalk in front of the Hamilton Building. Impulsively she decided she really *would* go shopping. The clothes she'd bought for business entertaining didn't seem anywhere near spectacular enough for going out with Morgan, so she retreated from the bustle of the sidewalk to the welcome peace of Boston Common's wide tree-lined paths, cutting across them to the new boutique Fran had been raving about.

Three hours later Laurel came back to the Hamilton Building, having first dropped off her various packages at home in the apartment she shared in the Back Bay district. In spite of his peremptory invitation and the fact that she was only out with Morgan because his grandfather had asked her to, she certainly wasn't going to let him known she'd be doing it in a new dress!

With that thought in mind, she whisked into her own office and worked on the transfer papers Morgan's entry had distracted her from, getting caught up with the schedule she'd set herself by working as busily as if she had been gone a week rather than a few hours. In fact, she was so busy that she successfully kept both Morgan Hamilton and the new dress out of her mind for the rest of the afternoon. Promptly at 5:25, however, Adam appeared in the doorway between their offices.

"Laurel, dear, I thought I heard you come back." From his considerable height he looked brightly down at her through intrepid spectacles. He didn't ask specifically how she had spent her time off but only inquired, "Did you stay away long enough to rest and recreate yourself to face your evening with my grandson?''

There were few tactful answers to that, so Laurel took refuge in simplicity. ''Yes, thank you,'' she smiled, and Adam Hamilton awarded her an answering smile for her diplomatic response to his provocation.

''In that case, my dear, I'll send you on your way. Whatever else he is, Morgan is unfailingly prompt, and he'll be waiting for you downstairs. All teasing aside, I trust he'll make sure your evening is pleasant whatever his mood, but thank you again, Laurel, for agreeing to spend your time with him.''

Her sense of the ridiculous suddenly made her smile as it occurred to her that she was being thanked for going out with the most spectacularly handsome man she'd ever seen—no matter who he was or what his moods might be—and she protested with a laugh, ''It really isn't anything.''

''Perhaps, perhaps not,'' her employer answered a bit enigmatically. ''But be off with you now and I'll see you on Monday.''

A brief pat on her shoulder, and he had gone back to his own offices, leaving her to collect her things and go. After getting off the elevator, she started across the wide lobby at the base of the building, and as she went the heels of her sandals seemed to tap out a rhythm on the glossy marble floor. Under her breath she began accompanying it with words before she realized what they were.

"And here's to good old Boston,
The home of the bean and the cod,
Where the Cabots talk to the Lowells
And the Lowells talk only to God."

She finished the satirical little rhyme with a
chuckle. Years ago, before her mother died, she had
entertained her three children in Missouri with tales
of growing up very differently in Boston. Laurel's
favorite part of those story-telling sessions had been
that rhyme, always spoken by her mother in an impossible accent that she swore was "proper Bosto-
nian," but that Laurel had never yet heard anyone
use since she came east to find out for herself.
Morgan Hamilton had borrowed some of that mocking verse for his high-handed dinner invitation. Surely no man who did that could be all bad!

On the contrary, he seemed to be anything but.
The suave man who met her at the far side of the lobby had nothing in common with the angry individual
who had erupted from Adam Hamilton's office and
only controlled himself with an effort to ask her out.
If it made any sense for a man like Morgan Hamilton, she would have said he had deliberately set
out to make himself overwhelmingly and absurdly
charming.

On the short drive to Laurel's apartment, after she
agreed to his suggestion of a restaurant, he entertained her with farfetched accounts of his experiences
in Europe learning his grandfather's trade, and while

she changed he amused her roommates, Fran and Sally, in the same vein. When Laurel reappeared, she was wearing a silky clinging dress of pale cream that was the most daring thing she'd ever owned—long sleeved, but with a narrow neckline that plunged nearly to its waist—and she'd chosen it in a surge of recklessness. Even though Morgan Hamilton might never realize she was going out with him simply because his grandfather asked her to, at least he'd have a chance to discover that a working woman could be as glamorous as the society beauties he was usually seen with!

Whether or not he caught the point, however, she couldn't really tell. Those crystal eyes unreadable, he just surveyed her from her flimsy bronze sandals to the smooth chestnut braid across the top of her head. Then he drawled exaggeratedly, "Charming, fair damsel! You are fit indeed to grace the halls of Castle Rackrent. First, however, I shall ply you with food and wine until you are helpless to resist my wiles."

Fran and Sally had already succumbed to his obvious charms, and making them an elaborate stage bow, he took Laurel's arm in a warm firm clasp and swept her away while they were still laughing. He did ply her with food and wine, too, taking her to a famous harborside restaurant that was even better known for its cuisine and its cellar than for its spectacular view. He kept up his nonsensical banter throughout the meal and an evening of dancing, when he gathered her close to the hard length of his body so that they moved as one, and when he returned her to the apartment long after midnight Laurel was happily exhausted from the long day and an exciting evening.

She was also more than a little way toward falling in love with the dark and devastating Morgan Hamilton, and the fact that he proceeded to monopolize all her free time quickly sealed her fate. And perhaps she fell in love with him so quickly just because she was finally ready to love and be loved.

The truth was that she'd never really been deeply in love before; she'd always been too busy—at first trying to take her mother's place and keep things going at home for her two younger brothers, and then later taking classes at night for a degree in business administration and overworking by day to earn her present position with the Hamilton Corporation. At any rate, she'd buried herself in work and studying right up until this year, when she had finally let Fran and Sally persuade her to accept invitations from a few of the persistent men who kept calling and calling.

"For heaven's sake, Laurel, you can't spend your whole life shuttling between Northeastern and the Hamilton Company, vaguely assuming that someday you'll get around to looking and Mr. Right will magically present himself!" Sally had scolded in exasperation.

"Especially not when going out with Mr. Wrong can be such fun!" Fran had added impishly, and Laurel had finally given in.

"All right, all right! Bring on these marvelously charming and debonair gentlemen, and we'll see what happens."

But what happened was nothing. Maybe because they weren't marvelously anything, but only ordinary mortals—not princes but just friendly peasants— Laurel's dates always became her friends and never her lovers. She appreciated their time, enjoyed their company and never realized any one of them would have been delighted to mean a great deal more to her than that. Fran and Sally had both virtually despaired of her before Morgan Hamilton entered Laurel's life, and everything changed.

Together she and Morgan took advantage of an unseasonably warm March, taking early picnics to the Arnold Arboretum and watching the first of the boat races on the Charles River, while he wrapped her in his coat to keep the sea winds off. Walking hand in hand, they visited small galleries and exhibitions that Laurel would never have found for herself, stopped at sidewalk cafés in parts of the city she had never seen and explored the market district, finishing up with enormous bowls of clam chowder served on red-and-white oilcloth in the friendly boardinghouse clamor of the old Durgin-Park pub.

They toured Old Ironsides at her dock on the harbor, too, and Laurel kept her eyes fastened on Morgan's clear profile as he looked out to sea and into memory to describe the Bicentennial, when the historic old ship had left the harbor for the first time in fifty years.

"The fireboats came back in first," he remembered, ebony hair ruffled by the wind and eyes narrowed to a Viking stare, "arching streamers of water from every hose as if it were liquid confetti, and behind them came the Tall Ships, heading down an east wind and led by the *Constitution* herself."

An arm around her shoulder, he drew her to his side so that she could follow his gaze, gesturing with his free hand while she fitted her body to his and tried not to be distracted by the contact.

"She came under bare masts, powered by tugs at her side and firing cannon salutes as she swept into the harbor. In her honor, all the other ships behind her suddenly shook out acres of square white sail until they looked like a dream armada, sailing down the centuries."

He paused, letting his hand drop, then added almost to himself, "And from all of us watching on the harbor a cheer went up, rolling back from the crowds on shore but ragged because tears were running down nearly every face."

He fell silent, and Laurel blinked away a mist from her own eyes. The dark face above hers was curiously undefended, though, and some instinct kept her silent, content to stand touching Morgan at hip and shoulder and reliving the gallant pageantry he'd brought to life for her, while he looked off into distances she didn't see.

In a few minutes he stirred again, releasing her and saying, "And now, after that voyage through memory, you must be starved. Where shall we eat?"

Light self-mockery laced his tone, and his face had taken on its usual hard angles, almost as if denying the emotion she'd sensed in him. She felt the sea wind cut into her, too, where his body had sheltered her a moment before.

"How about somewhere with seafood?" she answered at random in the same light tone, while she tried to conquer an odd feeling of loss. But then he took her cold hand in his warm one, and the inexplicable feeling faded, leaving only the faintest echo. She clung to him, and they left the ship.

When night came, they went to the theater or the symphony, to cabarets and jazz clubs, sitting in the shadows with their hands linked. By day and by night, they roamed and laughed, dined and danced, and through it all Laurel found more and more to like about Boston—and to love about Morgan Hamilton. After years of concentrating on her career, after years of being businesslike and rational, she finally let herself be something else as well. In Morgan's company, in Morgan's arms, she reacted with her heart and body as well as her mind, so passionately she hardly knew herself.

The only cloud on her happiness—a wisp when she was with Morgan, a thunderhead when she was alone—was her lingering surprise at their relationship. Gossip-column photographs, company rumors and even his own grandfather's concern about his companion that first evening—all suggested that Morgan Hamilton was the sort of man who appeared with a different social butterfly every time he went out. But here he was spending all his free time with just one woman, and a responsible working one at that.

Certainly the brunette they met one evening in the interval of a concert seemed to emphasize the contrast between Laurel and Morgan's usual companions. Having gone to the ladies' room while Morgan ordered a glass of champagne for each of them, Laurel had to weave her way back to him through the noisy throng that had gathered in the lobby of Symphony Hall. She could see his sleek black head, well above nearly everyone else's and partly turned away from her, but she couldn't get to him. As she edged and excused her smiling way through the crowd, smoke and sound, voices and laughter rose around her in a shifting mosaic.

"Did you hear Dorati last year at Tanglewood?" one voice asked, and another nearby quipped ruefully, "Do you know, I spent the summer so tangled up with work I never even got as far out of town as the Berkshires?"

"I'm sorry—was that your foot?"

"Apparently not. I can't even see my feet in this mob, but I didn't feel anything, either!"

"Domestic or imported?"

"Mmm, must be domestic. Support your local winery and all!"

"Excuse me...."

"Anytime!" That one came with an appreciative

grin, and Laurel couldn't help an automatic answering smile, even though her eyes were still fixed on Morgan's bent head.

"Isn't he soloist for the Haydn in the second half?"

"Sorry. . . ."

"But I have seen you so little these past weeks. . . ."

"Sure beats staying home and trying to escape from my kids' stereo!"

"I've got to see this through—you know that. Then when it's all settled. . . ."

"Sorry to be so long!" Laurel finally reached Morgan's side and gratefully claimed his glass. "Thank you! Now I understand that phrase about 'a sea of humanity.' I must have just swum at least a day's voyage!"

Throwing him a laughing look of mock exhaustion, she raised the champagne to her lips just as another billow swept the people around her. Someone jostled her, and catching her off balance, made Laurel splash the front of her dress.

She gave a little snort of disgust, and Morgan handed her a handkerchief from the breast pocket of his well-cut suit. "Here," he offered and added smilingly, "Try this for a parting of the waters!"

Patting the silky folds of her skirt, Laurel chuckled at the fractured reference, but then glanced up again in surprise as another voice commented on her mishap.

"Ah, *quel dommage*! To spill champagne is bad luck—and on such a sweet dress."

It was a black velvet voice, and its owner wore a black velvet gown that clung to her rounded hips and swooped low over her full bosom. On a sweep of soft flesh, an ostentatious collar of diamonds blazed with every breath. And above it was a face as striking, if as hard, as the gems.

The face belonged to a woman standing on the other side of Morgan, and his handkerchief turned into a soggy ball in Laurel's fingers as they clenched reflexively. But she declined to answer in the same tone and just murmured noncommittally, making a wry note to herself that "sweet" could be a remarkably insulting word. And as for bad luck—she had a primitive urge to wish the woman in front of her a lifetime of broken mirrors, spilled salt and the black cats she resembled.

But that velvet voice was purring again. Looking past Laurel now, the woman was gazing limpidly at Morgan. "But at least there is still the good luck of having such opportunities as this to meet others. It is always so interesting, is it not?" she breathed huskily.

Silently he nodded his head once in acknowledgement. His dark face was bland and his blue eyes as unrevealing as agates, but for a second as she watched them, Laurel seemed to feel her throat closing up. Before he could introduce the two women to each other—as Laurel intuitively knew he could—a bell chimed to indicate the end of the interval, and Morgan slipped one large hand into the crook of her elbow to lead her back to their seats, while the other woman swayed gracefully out of sight. Behind her she left only a drift of heavy scent—and a churning jealousy in Laurel's heart, wordless because there was no way she could possibly ask Morgan any of the questions about that woman that sprang, Hydra-headed, to life. The most she would allow herself was to say brightly as he seated her, "What a beautiful woman that was!"

Her voice must have been a few notes higher than usual, though, because he gave her an intent look from those opaque eyes. "On the contrary, my dear," he drawled exaggeratedly in a Rhett Butler voice, "that was a very beautiful cat—beautiful, calculating and self-interested." Then the accent faded and he went on, "She's an old acquaintance from my misspent past—before I met you—and no one you ever need think twice about."

She would have, of course—she would have thought about that diamond-decked brunette all evening—except her mind was overruled by her body, the way it always was with Morgan. Lifting the hand he'd kept in his, he kissed her palm, so that the warmth of his breath flowed softly across her skin, then folded her fingers in on the kiss as the conductor returned to his podium. The audience fell silent, as did the niggling voices of Laurel's doubts. While the pure notes of a Haydn trumpet concerto soared around her and her hand still rested in Morgan's, she was deaf to all the whispers that asked how far forward his past reached and why he had suddenly abandoned that sort of woman in favor of her. It didn't matter. He was here beside her, his kiss was warm in her hand and his thigh lay along hers, radiating a heat that seemed to rise slowly through her whole body. That was all that mattered—that and the fact that she loved him more each day, even though they rarely spoke of it in words.

But lying in his arms that evening in the firelight that warmed the cool luxury of his bachelor apartment, she didn't bother to analyze her feelings in words. Words were for the mind, and for the first time in her life she was letting herself be swept away by her heart. In his arms she could study the flickering shadows that revealed a thousand new facets of his dark face, each one instantly beloved. She could run the tip of a gentle finger over his strong slashing eyebrows, across his high cheekbones and down his straight nose to trail it across his firm lips, learning new wonders of human architecture in the strength of a man's features. Slipping her hands shyly into the collar of his shirt, she could investigate the joining of his neck and shoulder, the smooth buttress of his collarbone, the throbbing pulse that crescendoed beneath her touch in the hollow of his throat. And beneath his touch she, in turn, was discovering new realms of sensation that she had never dreamed could exist. He guided her into kingdoms of delight, and his hands and lips mapped in flame regions no one had charted for her before.

He searched her mouth with his, one breath serving them both until she grew dizzy, and he released her lips to wander elsewhere, grazing her throat with the slight sandpaper roughness of his lean cheeks. Then, as his lips flared across the scented hollow of her neck his breathing, too, came raggedly, and he murmured incoherent phrases she didn't need to hear. As their clothes seemed to melt away, cool air brushed her heated skin that shivered from inner fires of his igniting. She arched taut breasts to his lips; his hands cradled their satiny fullness. While his mouth tugged her nipples with sweet insistence she cried out brokenly with the pangs of joy and forgot the different worlds they'd come from to meet in this enchanted timelessness.

Several moments later, his voice stirring the tendrils of hair at her temple, Morgan spoke her name as they lay cradled together in the deep billows of his sofa. "Laurel."

"Mmm?" Dreamily, dazed with happiness, she'd been watching the surge and ebb of the embers that glowed in the fireplace beyond his dark profile, her head in the hollow of his shoulder, and her answer was only a contented murmur.

"Will you marry me?"

The question rumbled beneath her cheek, and as it penetrated her mind she stirred against the bronze warmth of his skin. Raising her head, she looked at him in the firelight while her fingers slipped through a mat of fine hair to brace against the firmness of his chest as if it were the most natural gesture in the world. And as if it were the only natural response in the world, she said simply, "Yes."

Turned to her, his face was shadowed so that she couldn't see his expression, but she didn't need to. Every look, every movement was so memorized and beloved she couldn't have given him any other answer. She knew their backgrounds were radically different. She couldn't help but see that their life-styles had little in common. She realized they'd only known each other a few months. She admitted he caught her up in flames of passion that seemed to burn away the levelheaded career woman she'd always been. . . .

All those things were true, and she didn't care, couldn't care, because his lips were igniting hers again almost before she finished shaping her answer. Everything would work out, she thought hazily, and none of those possible problems really mattered anyway when the fire on the hearth seemed to have blazed up to consume them both. . . .

CHAPTER TWO

So on a Saturday in the middle of June, when the air was soft and honeyed, she married Morgan Hamilton in his grandfather's Beacon Hill house, while Adam beamed on them both.

Two hours after the ceremony Laurel drifted across the beautiful bedroom that had been hers for the past two weeks and slipped onto the brocaded bench set before an antique dressing table. She'd left a letter there, and alone for a few minutes before she went downstairs for the last time, she reached for it, smoothing the page so she could reread with the ease of long practice her father's quick illegible scrawl.

I'm sorry we can't be there, baby. My firstborn hasn't had a wedding day before, and I really fancied myself as the proud father of the bride! The boys were looking forward to their first trip east, too, but I'm afraid this fool leg of mine just isn't up to that kind of travel yet. I feel like a grade-A idiot—and an uncomfortable one at that—for managing to break it now, of all times. But evidently bad luck is no respecter of schedules.

But even if I can't be there to tell you in person, Laurel, I want you to know that I'm deeply proud of you, and your mother would have been as well. Not because you're marrying a man whose name will apparently give you social position as the world sees it, but because you've already earned a business position of trust and responsibility entirely on your own merit.

I've always been sorry that after your mother died you had to step in and look after the boys, doing the job of an adult without having had time to be an ordinary teenager, and it still grieves me that I couldn't give you a chance at a college degree. But you've trained and educated yourself to be a capable and efficient businesswoman, as well as the thoroughly satisfactory daughter you always were. Now be a happy wife, and you will have made your old father completely content. I love you, baby, and I'll be there on your day in spirit if not in body.

Dad

With fingers that were especially gentle, Laurel was folding her father's letter again when Adam's big Irish housekeeper tramped back into the room.

"Are you still here, dearie? I've tended to your wedding dress, checked that the food is holding out and nipped at the heels of those catering people, and when I get back you're still just where I left you!"

Laughing, Laurel stood up, and Mrs. O'Reilly

helped her into the coral pink coat that went with her going-away dress. "There you are." She patted it into place and added with a teasing look, "I've got you into this pretty outfit, but your new husband will have to be getting you out! He'll be waiting for you, too, and I've never yet known a man who wasn't impatient on his wedding day once the knot was tied!"

Eagerly, uncontrollably, Laurel blushed—as she was meant to.

"Eh, now, I'll stop plaguing you," Mrs. O'Reilly chuckled. "Be on your way, though, before everyone starts thinking you've had a change of heart and abandoned the poor man."

"Yes, Mrs. O'Reilly," Laurel said obediently and pantomimed sudden haste. The two women smiled at each other, and the younger one reached up to give the older a quick hug. "Thank you for everything! You've been so kind."

Now it was the housekeeper's turn to color revealingly. "Pish, girl," she said gruffly, "I've done little enough, and you're a pleasure to have about the house. Now do be off to young Morgan. Enjoy that deserted island he's taking you to and be happy."

A minute later Laurel had reached the foot of the heavily carpeted stairway and stood hesitating. She really had been upstairs longer than she'd intended. This was one time when Morgan, always so prompt himself, wouldn't be impressed with her efforts in that direction. The sounds of their wedding reception in the rooms this side of the central hall were still loud, and she paused to decide whether to just go and find Morgan wherever he might be—and risk attracting all those guests who fancied showering newlyweds with rose petals and rice—or try to find some way of letting him know she was ready, so they could make their escape unnoticed.

She'd just made up her mind when Fran and Sally came into the hall, Fran carrying a champagne glass and Sally still clutching the bride's bouquet Laurel had tossed neatly into her hands before going upstairs to change.

"Laurel!" They met her with joyous hugs.

"We were hoping to have a chance to say goodbye before you left," Fran said.

"Yes, and I wanted to thank you for this," Sally caroled, flourishing the bouquet. "I'll tell Tom his time is up!"

Laurel chuckled. Lanky Tom had been pestering Sally for months to name the day. Apparently the excitement of her own wedding had finally persuaded Sally to make up her mind.

"Lovely, Sal!" She hugged her friend in return. "Be sure to let Morgan and me know when it is, and we'll come with bells on. Meantime, though, does either of you know where Morgan is? If I can get to him without alerting everyone, we might be able to go on our way with a bit more dignity than most couples manage."

Sally grinned understandingly. Although they'd kept the guest list relatively small, Laurel had already had more than enough attention from those society-page photographers she wasn't used to. Fran said thoughtfully, "It seems to me that I saw him a while ago, heading toward that beautiful library of his grandfather's. He'd been making himself charming to all the guests, and I suspected he wanted some peace and quiet for a breather."

"Thanks, Fran. You're a dear—you both are, and I'll miss you."

"But not much!" Sally amended dryly, and Laurel had to agree laughingly over her shoulder as she turned toward the library.

It was on the far side of the house, enough removed from the buffet in the dining room and the spacious living room beyond so that it would be a quiet retreat from the well-meaning hubbub. No wonder Morgan had chosen it! But how like him to have made a point of speaking to everyone who'd come to wish them well.

Her lips curved in a happy smile, Laurel sped across the soft Oriental rugs in the hall and quietly opened the heavy library door. That way, in case Fran was wrong and someone else was here instead of Morgan, she might be able to close it again without being discovered.

She wasn't discovered either. But someone else was there, not instead of Morgan but with him. On the far side of the room, a dramatic woman Laurel had seen once before was poised in front of him, her body arched so that she could press against him teasingly as she undid his tie with heavily ringed fingers. Her black head tilted, she was looking up at him through thick dark lashes, and he seemed utterly absorbed in meeting that provocative gaze, his arms loosely around her.

As Laurel stood paralyzed and unnoticed at the door, he started to say something.

"Renee—" But the woman raised one hand to lay those glittering fingers across his lips.

"*Non*, Morgan," she purred throatily, "you shall say nothing. I have decided how it is to be. We will simply plan more carefully when we shall meet, *n'est-ce pas*? Nothing needs to change because of this foolish marriage of yours."

She lowered her hands to caress him, and he made no further attempt to speak, simply bending his head to begin sliding his lips down the side of her throat while she gave a small triumphant laugh. She murmured, "So come, the door locks, and the time is enough. After all, there is a little while before you must leave...."

She let the words trail away, and Laurel's paralysis evaporated. Before either of them could turn toward the door, she swung it closed.

One remote corner of her mind wished it had been lighter so that she could have flung it into the doorframe with enough force to shake the walls down, but the only sound it made was a muffled final thud. The rest of her brain was filled with an icy rage as she swept over to the narrow Sheraton table that stood in the hall and took out a pen and pad from the drawer where they were always kept. Without hesitation, stabbing the paper so hard it tore once, she wrote a brief note to Morgan. Then, folding it, she stopped a caterer passing through the hallway.

"Excuse me," she said in a voice she didn't recognize as her own. "Would you deliver a message for me?"

The caterer, a middle-aged man with a creased kindly face, agreed. "Yes, of course, ma'am. I'd be happy to. And may I congratulate you, Mrs. Hamilton, and wish you and your husband the best of luck?"

"Thank you," Laurel said in that same unfamiliar voice, and handed over her note.

"Who would you like me to take it to, Mrs. Hamilton?" the man asked.

"To Mr. Hamilton, please."

He looked puzzled for a moment before his face cleared. "Oh, Mr. Adam Hamilton, of course," he said smilingly.

"No, Mr. Morgan Hamilton, please, whenever you see him next," Laurel specified, and the strange voice rang in her ears.

As he finally caught its tone, the caterer's smile faded. A look of concern spread over his fatherly features, and he seemed about to ask something, but another glance at her set face changed his mind. Slipping her note into the pocket of his white jacket, he just picked up the tray he had put aside and nodded politely. "Right, ma'am. I'll take care of it for you."

A moment more and he had gone toward the back of the house, and Laurel, still moving with a kind of icy purpose, walked in the other direction, out the front door and down the street to the car she'd left yesterday, parked at the end of the block. A much-loved Rabbit, it leaped to life and then raced off with a furious grinding of gears.

STORMING AWAY FROM BEACON HILL, Laurel didn't see Morgan come out of the library only a minute or two after she left. Nor did she hear anything of the muted commotion that, a little while later, began to seep through the old house. She didn't know when Morgan asked for his wife so that they could leave on their honeymoon, didn't know when he checked her room for her and found no one, or when he asked the servants and caterers if they'd seen her. And she had no idea how alarmed he was becoming before the man she'd entrusted with her note handed it over, and—after a brief stupefied pause—Morgan's worry passed into anger.

Coming from the spacious living room, where the guests were beginning to murmur among themselves about the delay, Adam found his grandson in the center of the downstairs hall, an instant after he had crumpled Laurel's note in one furious fist. Seeing the look of black rage on Morgan's angular face, Adam's own genial expression faded.

"Morgan, what is it?" he demanded. "Where's Laurel?"

"Gone!" Morgan gritted through set teeth, his harsh voice harsher than ever. "She's had a change of heart and left me on our wedding day." At the hiss of Adam's indrawn breath, he thrust out the wadded paper in his hand. "Here."

Adam took it, pushing his wandering spectacles up into position, and smoothed the scrap of paper enough to read. Then the brief message leaped up at him.

Morgan—I'm leaving. I never should have married you, and now that I know it for sure, I'm going. Don't ever try to contact me—I don't ever want to see you or talk to you again!

Laurel

He read it through twice, but when he looked up his face was still uncomprehending, and his glasses slid down again without him noticing. "I don't understand," he said suddenly seeming old and vague.

"What's to understand?" Morgan snapped. "That little missive seems brutally clear to me!"

Adam's usual decisiveness returned. "Well, it isn't to me! This doesn't sound like something Laurel would do—at least not voluntarily."

At his altered tone, Morgan shot him a swift glance, and his furious expression faded some. "What are you saying? Do you mean you think she might have been forced to write this?'' Then his black brows knitted into a look of concern. "Kidnapping?'' he asked tersely.

Adam nodded wordlessly, and for a moment Morgan considered the idea. It seemed unlikely, but possible. He reached out and took the note from his grandfather's hand, rereading it intently. But when he looked up again, his dark face was twisted with fresh anger, and he handed the note back with a bitter little flourish.

"No, I don't think we need to concern ourselves on that score,'' he said bitingly. "I don't believe a kidnapper yet has dictated a note in which his victim said *not* to try to contact him!''

Adam nodded thoughtfully. "Yes, there's that. It doesn't sound right for a ransom plan,'' he agreed slowly. "Well, then, Laurel wrote it of her own free will, but I still don't understand why. She'll have to tell us for herself. We've got to find her.''

"Oh, no!'' Morgan flashed. "We have our orders from my vanishing bride, and I for one intend to obey them!''

"Nonsense,'' Adam began briskly, but his grandson cut him off.

"Not at all. If my wife,'' he gave the word a nasty twist, "has so little respect for me that she abandons me virtually in front of our wedding guests, without even having the decency to explain herself in person, then she's undoubtedly right—our marriage was a mistake.''

Adam's protest took on an edge of irritation. "Morgan, you can't simply write it off that way, without trying to find out what's wrong!"

At that last phrase, something flickered at the back of Morgan's eyes, almost as if he'd asked himself a question and got no answer—or no acceptable answer.

"Indeed I can," he grated, "and I intend to begin immediately."

"Do you really have so little commitment to your marriage?"

"I have exactly as much commitment to our marriage as Laurel has trust in me!"

He swung away toward the outer door, but Adam's voice followed him, mingling anger and command now in a measured tone.

"Morgan, you can't do this! I forbid it."

For a few seconds his grandson paused, his back rigid with fury. Then he turned around, his face a mask.

"Excuse me, sir," he said punctiliously, "but this is one of those times when I'm afraid I won't be able to obey an order."

"Then what will you do?" Adam demanded, finally as enraged as Morgan, but by old quarrels flaring again between them. "Go back to Europe and practice being the playboy of the western world once more?"

If anything, Morgan's expression became even less human as he answered in a voice that was devoid of

all the emotion that had filled it earlier. "Perhaps.
I'll let you know through the company. Meanwhile, I
leave you to make my goodbyes to our guests."

"I swear, if you leave here this way you won't be
welcome back again!"

"Paul will be pleased," Morgan said detachedly.
And with a small salute that was utterly artificial in
its studied grace, he let himself out the fanlighted
front door, even as Adam's last furious call rang
after him. "Morgan!"

By now several miles away, encased in her own
fury like a suit of armor, Laurel heard none of this.
Unfortunately, the wedding guests had no choice but
to hear almost all of it. And so for the next half hour
Adam, in turn, had no choice but to put as good a
face on things as possible and bid his guests goodbye.

It wasn't, in fact, until Monday morning that he
even learned Laurel was still in the state. He'd just
reached his office when a call from her came through
the main switchboard. Lifting the receiver, he heard
the echoing of a long distance line. Then Laurel's
voice said, "Mr. Hamilton—" and broke off.

"Laurel! Where are you? Are you all right? For
heaven's sake, what happened?"

"I'm down on the Cape, and I'm fine, thanks,"
she said unsteadily, drawing a deep breath. "But I
had to call you and tell you that I'm sorry but I won't
be able to finish the transfer papers for you next
month—"

Now she spoke rapidly, trying to get through a

speech she'd rehearsed, but he cut in before she could finish giving him her resignation from the company. "I understand—but Laurel, I want you to do one other thing for me right away."

His tone was commanding and she responded automatically, "Yes, of course." Then she added more equivocally, "If I can."

"You can," he said flatly. "Come up and meet me at Merton's for lunch today at noon."

She didn't answer immediately. He added, "Laurel... we'll be alone. Please come."

His tone had shifted, adding a request to the command, and she wasn't proof against the combination.

"I'll be there," she said quietly, and hung up.

A FEW MINUTES BEFORE NOON he was waiting for her in one of Boston's oldest and most conservative businessmen's restaurants, a place she'd never been with his grandson. And promptly at twelve, she slipped into a chair across from him in the dignified quiet of the private dining room.

"Laurel." He just said her name in greeting as he surveyed the face across from him, confirming his guess that whatever had made her leave his house that way had evidently been no foolish whim. Her eyes had lost their usual golden color and turned the flat tan of pebbles, and there were blue shadows on the translucent skin beneath them. But her chin was high. The laughing radiant woman he had last seen before she went to change out of her wedding gown might never have existed.

"My dear, I'm so sorry," he said simply.

"So am I," she returned, her voice breaking on the last syllable. But then she steadied it and turned her answer in a different direction by adding, "I'm afraid you must have been in an embarrassing position when I left that way."

A waiter silently brought the first course Adam had ordered for them, and when he was gone, Adam asked quietly, "Why did you, Laurel? I saw your note, but it didn't really say why."

She met the shrewd kindly eyes across from her and hesitated as an instinctive kind of loyalty stopped her. Then she recognized how misguided that sentiment was and angrily rejected it. Loyalty—why be loyal to Morgan! He'd hardly been loyal—or decent—or even honest with her, and she owed a good deal more to this old man that she'd grown to love! Certainly, she owed him an explanation, even an ugly one.

Her face tightening, she looked away from Adam and said succinctly, "Because I saw him in the library, making love to his girl friend."

Because she'd fixed her eyes on a point beyond his shoulder, Laurel didn't catch Adam's immediate response to those bald words. If she had, she would have seen a look of utter rage and revulsion cross his face. He was aware that Morgan had had lovers before; the two men's last encounter was not the first time they'd quarreled bitterly on that subject. Nevertheless, even Adam was shocked to think that Morgan had been with another woman on his wedding day, if Laurel was right—and Adam assumed she was.

But then his shrewd old eyes narrowed thoughtfully, and his own feelings were swallowed up as he remembered the depth of Morgan's fury at finding his wife gone, having abandoned him in front of their guests. Simple possessiveness was not a trait he'd ever seen his grandson display. Nor, he knew, did Morgan generally give a damn what other people thought. What then, Adam wondered, could account for the strength of his reaction? Both the anger and disgust faded from the old man's face, to be replaced by an expression of renewed determination, quickly masked in turn by a bland calm.

Laurel well knew the kinds of thoughts that went on behind that look, but this time she didn't catch it. His thinking had taken only a few seconds, and she wasn't really aware of any pause before he inquired, "And did he see you, my dear?"

"No."

Seeing the remembered shock and resentment reflected again in her face, Adam nodded a silent confirmation to himself, but only said, "All right, Laurel, I understand," and picked up his fork.

Bringing her gaze back from the far wall, Laurel looked at him, a weary tide of dismay rising inside her. She hadn't thought she could feel anymore, but as she watched Adam methodically begin his meal she had a sudden fancy that his side of the table was a million miles away and she was seeing him tiny and faraway through the wrong end of a telescope. Didn't it matter to him that his own grandson was a liar and a cheat!

Learning that in Adam's house on her wedding day had made her learn more about disillusion and loathing and hurt than she'd ever guessed she could. When she'd left that way, she'd abandoned a man who was too despicable to be worth fighting for, or even explaining to, but her pain had come with her, because nothing could change the fact that she'd loved him. It had taken her endless miles of walking on a gray and foggy beach and her own ocean of tears before she could begin to cope with her aching heart—but Adam could sit across from her and eat as if nothing extraordinary had happened?

Pushing her own plate aside, she looked at him as if he were a stranger, and said abruptly, the words almost bursting out of their own accord, "How do I get an annulment?"

For an instant Adam didn't comprehend what he heard. Then, setting his knife and fork together precisely on the plate, he said carefully, "My dear, let me take care of that for you. The family lawyer is also an old and trusted friend, and I'm sure he can tend to that with as little fuss as possible."

"All right," she said stiffly, but as she spoke she searched his face. It was unreadable, and she began to wonder in growing horror if she'd been as wrong about him as about his grandson. Didn't he expect honesty and decency from his own family? Or was he only concerned about making sure the annulment was handled discreetly?

She was still staring at him with dismay when Adam began to fumble at his jacket. His movements were usually so sure that she tended to forget his age, but now his hands groped shakily until they came up with a small bottle from his breast pocket. Every other thought fled from Laurel's mind as he clumsily shook out a tiny tablet and put it under his tongue. She recognized his heart medicine and knew that it was effective. In seconds it would take action and he would be his usual self again—yet he had never before taken a tablet so openly. Was the attack so much more serious this time? Frightened for him, she leaped to her feet and hesitated, unsure if she could call for help or take action herself—

"Sit down, my dear, and don't look like that." Adam's voice sounded perfectly normal, and his face had flushed, giving an impression of good health. "I'm fine now."

She looked at him anxiously, but he just smiled at her in his usual way, and she dropped back into her seat, clasping her hands under the table to stop their shaking. Before her, though, Adam's reassuring smile faded, and he met her eyes for a long moment. Now she could see the aftermath of anger, as well as grief. . . and loneliness?

"Don't give up completely on the Hamiltons, my dear, please," he said quietly.

"Oh, granda—" she began impulsively, and stopped. Not sure what she wanted to say, she just shook her head and didn't notice that she'd used Morgan's name for him for the first time.

Adam recognized it, though. Saturday's ceremony had given her the right to call him by that name. His lips compressed momentarily and then released before she could see, turning up instead in a slow warm smile to echo the look in his eyes.

But all he said was, "Thank you, Laurel." Then he cleared his throat and asked more briskly, "Now what, my dear?"

It was a question she had begun asking herself through the long drive up from Cape Cod and the small beachside hotel where she had blindly taken refuge Saturday when she was too exhausted to go any farther. It was also a question she had no answer for yet, and the strained look returned to her face, telling him clearly what she would like the first step to be: to blot out forever anything to do with the memory of that scene in the library. But both of them knew that was impossible. "I have to leave," she said slowly.

Her eyes dropped and then came back up again quickly. "I'm sorry—" she began.

"Never mind, Laurel," Adam interposed. "I'd love to keep you with me somehow, but I understand why that's impossible. Where would you go— home?"

Home. The word instantly summoned up her
father's loving arms, but Laurel shut her eyes against
the thought. "No," she breathed. When she was a
child her father had been able to patch and soothe all
her scrapes and hurts. But now she was a grown
woman, and even he couldn't set a broken heart;
he'd only suffer with her. Not home.

"Then where?" Adam persisted gently, and now
she opened her eyes again to look at him, still at a
loss and only able to shake her head slightly in
answer.

Oddly, her uncertainty seemed to please him.
Leaning forward across the table, he asked, "In that
case, will you listen to a suggestion I have to make?"

"Yes, of course," she answered, puzzled.

"As well as being my assistant, my dear, you said
words yesterday that made you legally my granddaughter, with or without Morgan." On that final
phrase she flinched, but his grandfather went straight
on. "And I don't intend to let you vanish into thin
air in either capacity. So if you have nowhere else
you'd rather go, Laurel, I'd like to send you up into
Maine on business for me."

He paused and noted that her face had relaxed a
little. A faint look of curiosity had crept into her expression.

He went on. "The latest of those old inns I've been
buying is near Fryeburg, about halfway up the western border of Maine, on the edge of the White Mountains. It's remarkably beautiful country up there, and

the inn has a splendid location, but I understand it's been almost completely neglected for the past few years.

"My idea, Laurel, if you agree to it, is to send you up there as my representative, to look over the inn and evaluate it—see what repairs are needed and whether or not it could be reopened any time in the reasonable future. In fact, I'd give you a free hand to do as much or as little as you liked toward putting it into operation again."

He had her full attention now. This had nothing to do with the wretched mess of her marriage, but only with a possible future. By putting his suggestion the way he had, Adam had appealed to both his trained assistant, who was in the habit of carrying out his suggestions, and his new granddaughter, who wanted nothing more in the world than somewhere remote to launch herself into a new project that would use up every ounce of her energy and keep her too busy to think.

But still.... "It's very kind of you to think of it—" she began, and the hint of tension left his face before she ever noticed it.

"No, my dear," he corrected her calmly, "it's very practical. I'd thought of asking you to do it for me weeks ago, long before Morgan ever came home. It's a job I can't rush up there and do for myself, but it has to be done. Even the real-estate agent who sold it to me admitted that if someone doesn't take the old place in hand very quickly there'll be nothing left to salvage!"

Suddenly Laurel was sure this was exactly the sort of thing she wanted desperately, but it seemed reckless of Adam—and the Hamilton Corporation—to entrust so much responsibility to someone without any training in the area. Wild to agree, she still tried to give Adam a chance to change his mind.

"But the only experience I've had with old buildings is the farmhouse where I grew up. What makes you think I could do a decent job for you?"

"The fact, my dear, that I've watched you work for almost two years and learned that you can do virtually anything you put your hand to. And also the fact that you're my granddaughter, whom I love and trust."

That resounding vote of confidence brought a lump to her throat, and she was silent for a moment. Then she said softly, "Thank you."

"Then, my dear, if you'd like to be on your way this afternoon, I think we'd better finish this neglected meal." His tone was gruffly practical, but they shared a long smile. On the far side of the room their waiter sighed with relief as they turned to the food at last. He'd about decided they weren't ever going to eat.

THREE HOURS LATER Laurel drove away from Boston again. She'd snatched up a few practical clothes from her apartment and wrote a brief note to Fran and Sally that she was fine and going off on a new job; she'd tell them all about it later. Meanwhile she could just disappear, as she longed to do. And as for the headlines that were probably still on the society pages of today's papers, or the public embarrassment that her disappearance had already caused Morgan—they were unimportant compared to the private misery his appearance in the library had caused her.

But at least this time she wasn't just bolting blindly out of the city. This time she was going to, not just running from. And so she wound her way carefully through the narrow streets of the city, then to the central artery where she could climb to the Mystic River Bridge and turn northward—away from Boston and her wedding, away from Morgan and misery—as she concentrated solely on driving in a state where all too many people seemed to consider it a contact sport.

Instinctively, in some far corner of her mind, she knew that sooner or later she'd have to come to terms with everything that had happened. Grieving wasn't a process a person could finish quickly, even if that grief was as much for a loss of faith in someone as for a lost love. But for now, because she was a good driver, she was able to go through the motions automatically and limit her thinking to Adam's directions on the slip of paper she'd taped to her dashboard.

CHAPTER THREE

THE EXPRESSWAY that had taken her out of Massachusetts and up the New Hampshire coast now came to a major junction, and Laurel turned left onto the smaller highway that would take her inland. Soon the oaks and elms of southern New England gave way to increasing numbers of pines and birches in the colder north as she drove along a road that rose into the foothills of the White Mountains.

Yesterday in Boston the air had been soft and balmy, melon sweet and scented. But today she was driving north, and here the season was several weeks behind, still tenuous and uncertain. Yesterday the sun had shone and the trees had spread rich full canopies of green. But today the clouds were low and the spring leaves only lace, their furled shapes just embroidering the branches. In the distance, their delicate early green misted into varying grayish blues, blending together as they climbed the lower slopes. Among those slopes, deep in the glacial valleys, lay Alpine lakes, scattered like burnished pewter plates.

All of this was new to Laurel, and so beautiful that for a while she forgot everything else, even why she

was here, and longed only to be sharing it with—
Momentarily her hands tightened in distress on the
steering wheel, and then they clenched still more in
alarm.

Lumbering toward her along a shallow curve on
the wide two-lane road was a large tanker truck, pon-
derously leading a long procession of cars that had
probably followed it for miles. Just as they neared
her, one of the cars darted out into her lane, intent on
finally passing the truck and unable to see her against
the diffused silver brilliance of the lowering sun
behind her.

Driving at this speed, rational thinking would have
taken fatally long, and after a split second's paralysis
instinct took over. Laurel saw the driver of the oncoming car catch sight of her at last and waver, saw,
too, that the other cars had closed up so there was no
room for him to dodge back into his own lane. It was
the action of an instant, then, to turn her wheels
slightly and pass the tanker so closely that she could
almost have touched the horrified driver, while the
oncoming car swerved far over into her lane and
drove along the shoulder, passing her simultaneously
on the other side like a bit of beautiful and daring
choreography.

In seconds it was all over. The road ahead of her
lay clear and empty again, and safely behind her were
the tanker and all the other cars. The danger was
passed, but adrenaline still raced through her body.
Her hands began to shake, and with difficulty she

pulled over to the side of the road and stopped her car. Stiff fingered, she turned on the emergency lights.

She was sitting motionless, her hands lying helplessly along the steering wheel and her head bowed into them, when a deep voice sounded beside her.

"Are you all right?"

Very slowly Laurel lifted her head and looked at the man who had spoken to her through her partially opened window. At first she simply stared at him, while her brain, in contrast to its lightning speed a few moments earlier, laboriously catalogued long-fingered hands resting on her door and a man's broad face, kindly and concerned, framed by a mane of unruly brown hair and a luxuriant reddish brown beard. He looked ever so slightly like her early childhood's image of God, and abruptly she croaked, "I didn't know people saw You on near misses, too," and began to giggle.

The giggle rose rapidly into laughter that had a hard hysterical edge to it, and with a muttered exclamation the man she had greeted in that extraordinary way wrenched open the door of her car and half urged, half lifted her from her seat. With one arm firmly around her, he led her past the front of the car to the grassy verge of the road and sat her down there. She was still laughing, however, in a breathless desperate kind of way.

Taking both her arms, he shook her, and her hair, bundled into a knot at the nape of her neck, tumbled down onto his hands in a soft cascade. But her laughter only sounded more shrilly. Finally, as a last resort, he struck her once, sharply, across the cheek.

The laughter stopped immediately, and Laurel raised her left hand automatically to her reddening cheek, while her startled dull gold gaze met his worried gray one. Then her eyes filled with tears, and suddenly she was sobbing wildly on the stranger's broad chest, her face buried in an old tweed jacket that smelled faintly of pipe tobacco.

It was a long time before she cried herself out, weeping away most of her fears of the near crash and some more of her grief for a marriage that had been a mockery before it had ever really begun. At last, though, her sobs subsided and she raised her head. Discovering she'd somehow come into possession of a large white handkerchief, she dried her eyes and finally sat up to look apologetically at the man in whose arms she had spent so much time.

"I'm sorry," she said with a watery smile. "I don't ordinarily fling myself at complete strangers and then ruin their clothes by behaving like a sprinkler system!"

"After that moment of telepathy on the highway, my girl, I don't really feel as though we are strangers," he corrected her in that deep voice, adding in a wryly fervent tone, "And anytime you save my life, you may feel perfectly free to cry all over me in reaction."

Taken out of herself, she looked at him more carefully and realized there was something familiar about him. "You were—" she began.

"The idiot on the highway who nearly got us all killed," he finished for her in tones of disgust. "If you hadn't correctly read my mind and understood the desperate move I was going to try, then you and I, that gas tanker—yes, *gas* tanker—" he read her appalled glance correctly "—and I knew that—and probably most of those other cars would be nothing but a fiery mass of wreckage now."

He took a deep breath and ran one of those long-fingered hands through his hair; she understood why it looked rumpled. Apparently he did that when he was thinking, and he was thinking out loud now, still castigating himself.

"And, of course, if I hadn't delayed leaving for North Conway until the last possible minute, I wouldn't have been trying to break the speed limit. The irony of it all is that the second movement still isn't right, and now I'm going to be late for the woodwind sectional I called. I hope they have the sense to go on without me."

None of this made a great deal of sense to Laurel, but that didn't matter. His words didn't seem to be addressed to her anyway, and he was giving her time to pull herself together a little more. For that she was grateful. But she tucked her disheveled hair behind her ears and arranged her expression to look politely attentive, just in case. In a minute he noticed her reaction and laughed, a deep hearty laugh tinged with self-mockery.

"You see my great flaws immediately, I'm afraid. I talk to myself—even in company. I procrastinate about appointments when I want to finish something else, and then I take reckless chances trying to make up for lost time. Since you've saved me from the consequences of the most recent chance, allow me to introduce myself: Giles Thomas, at your service." Still seated, he waved a hand in a gesture that managed to suggest a graceful bow. "Composer, conductor and highway menace."

Laurel's answering smile was steady now, and as he cocked one bushy eyebrow at her inquiringly, she responded, "And I'm Laurel—" for a fraction of a second she hesitated then finished evenly "—Andersen, sometime farm girl, executive assistant and eventually maybe even innkeeper."

With an unobtrusive movement she covered her ringed left hand with her bare right one as she spoke, but Giles Thomas seemed to notice neither that nor the tiny break between her two names. He kept his intent gaze on her, and now his eyebrows had taken on a decidedly skeptical tilt.

"To farm girl and assistant, I'd be inclined to add vehicular telepath—but innkeeper? That one surprises me. You don't look anything like the traditional plump jolly host, or even the forbiddingly upright old party who owned the inn near me until her death about a year ago. Are you sure it's really innkeeping you mean to tackle?"

"Well, inspecting and maybe renovating for now, at least," Laurel conceded the difference, and Giles pounced on it.

"Aha!" he crowed triumphantly. "Now that one

I can see. You can tie your hair back in a bandanna, put on a pair of jeans and an old work shirt and scrub, polish and paint up a storm, all the while looking deceptively demure. Where is this inn you're going to transform?''

Briefly she gave him the directions and told him her employer had bought it and sent her up to look it over. She did not, however, tell him how she had been chosen to do the job. He couldn't have noticed any omission, anyway, because he was already reacting to her directions.

''Well, Laurel Andersen, since that is, in fact, the inn standing just up the hill from my place on the lake, let me welcome you officially. It'll be a pleasure to have another face around the village. The regular summer people are just starting to arrive, now that the mosquitoes are getting over their first ravenous hunger of the year.''

With a frankly interested stare, he looked over the new face, and he was so direct about it that Laurel had to smile again. At that, he gave a quick self-congratulatory nod, as if eliciting that smile had been his real aim all the while. Then, glancing away, he conceded, ''If you're really thinking of opening up the old inn, though, I'm afraid you've got your work cut out for you. It was almost empty and none too cheery the last time I was inside, and it's stood completely empty for more than a year since then—but I wish you luck.''

''Thanks,'' Laurel murmured a shade dryly, and

he flashed her a quick grin that acknowledged her tone before leaning back on both elbows and narrowing his eyes thoughtfully to add, "Still, it could be beautiful again, even though it is rather a blot on the landscape now, if only someone enthusiastic took it in hand. As a matter of fact—" He looked at Laurel again with even more interest but then cut himself off as he caught sight of something behind her.

"Hold on a moment," he said. Surging to his feet with an agility that was surprising in so large a man, he strode out into the roadway in front of an approaching car, one that had made no apparent attempt to compete with modern machinery.

Laurel remained where he'd left her, sure that she was about to witness a fatal accident after all. At the last instant she wrenched her eyes away, but she couldn't cover her ears fast enough, and sick with distress, she waited for the sound of impact. There was an urgent screeching of brakes but no dreadful concluding thump, and after a blank wondering pause she looked back.

Giles Thomas was walking calmly across the highway again. On the far side of the road, skidded onto the shoulder at an angle, was a venerable station wagon of some indeterminate age, and scrambling from it was a girl of much less age. With short carroty hair scraped into stubby pigtails and a dusting of golden freckles, she looked about fourteen, but she had to be a bit older to be driving.

"Giles, I could have killed you!" she was saying

in a slightly husky voice as she caught up with him.

"Yes, infant, and since you've undoubtedly wanted to do just that many a time, I'm surprised you muffed your chance," he answered blandly, and she gave him a look that said perfectly clearly, both that she'd like to murder him right now and that the rest of the time she'd sooner die for him.

He didn't see it, though. They'd reached Laurel, and he held out a hand to her. She took it automatically and he swung her easily to her feet.

"Laurel, this is Peggy Martin, local child and member of the North Country Symphony that I direct. Peggy, Laurel Andersen."

The two women clasped hands while Giles beamed impartially at them both. But only Laurel was aware that Peggy's lively face was filled with curiosity. Giles seemed well acquainted with her and he had, after all, not added to her name the sort of explanatory tag he'd given to Peggy's own name.

Doing it for herself, Laurel said, "Hello, Peggy. I envy you living all your life in this lovely country. I've only just come up to see if the local inn can be reopened."

It was the briefest of explanations, but it satisfied Peggy's curiosity.

"Yes, and I've nearly seen to it that she never reached the place," Giles added dramatically, bringing their attention back to him.

"She just saved me from a fiery crash with a gas tanker," he explained, and while Peggy gasped gratifyingly he went on, "and so I'm going to send you on to North Conway, infant, with a message to Frank that I'd like him to take over the sectional and then the regular rehearsal. He can earn his keep as concert master, and I can escort Laurel the rest of the way to the inn. Seeing that she finally arrives there seems like the least I can do."

Laurel protested—after all, she had perfectly good directions, and it wasn't completely dark yet—but not too long or loudly. Subconsciously, she felt warmed by the vibrant presence of these two people, and consciously, she knew she really would rather not arrive at the inn alone for the first time. Peggy's bright head was nodding agreement to Giles's plan too, so Laurel let herself be persuaded. In a few minutes the old wagon was disappearing down the road in one direction, with a fanfare on the horn and a last flourishing wave, and Laurel was following Giles's battered orange Volvo in the other, on through Fryeburg and beyond it to New Suncook.

The shadows of night deepened rapidly as they drove the last miles to the inn, and Laurel gratefully followed the cheery red beacons of Giles's taillights as they sped through the darkness. She was more than glad of his company, too, when they pulled up in front of a ghostly white blur, Giles in a flurry of gravel and Laurel more sedately.

That blur, according to a peeling and barely legible sign Laurel discovered when she stepped out of her car, was the Mountain View Inn. There was no view visible at this hour, though. The mountains had vanished into deep blue twilight, and the only thing to look at was the inn itself. Certainly, it was quite a sight, even in the dimness.

It began directly in front of the half circle of rutted dirt where they'd parked. Stretching away to the right, a large ell had been added onto the main building, followed by an open woodshed containing a few lonely sticks of wood and a huge old barn attached to the woodshed. All together it seemed to stretch away into the gloom forever, and as Giles walked back from the Volvo to stand beside her, Laurel blurted out, "It's so long!"

He laughed, and the infectious sound echoed back to them from the shadowy face of the building. It almost seemed as if the old inn were chuckling, too, and in that moment it suddenly became less forbidding.

"That length, my girl, is explained by the fact that when it was built upward of two hundred years ago, shrewd settlers around here had figured out that if they built a house and all its outbuildings connected, then in the worst of winter they wouldn't have to go outdoors and struggle through deep snow to feed their livestock."

"That does make sense," she admitted, gazing at the old place with a dawning respect.

"Of course it does," he agreed emphatically. "Those old Yankees were a canny lot. They always built to get the maximum benefits from the minimum labor. Now let's have a look at what you've got to work with inside. You have a key?''

''Mmm-hmm,'' Laurel nodded and burrowed in her bag for the key Adam had given her. She handed it to Giles, who took it with a cocked eyebrow that told her he knew why he was being given the honor of going first—Laurel rather liked the inn so far, but she saw no reason why the one who knew the building shouldn't lead the way in.

As they picked their way over the uneven ground that lay between their cars and the inn's wide front porch, she had a fancy that the dark windows before them watched their approach with a sort of weary hopefulness, and that when they stepped cautiously across the sagging porch its tired old boards sighed. At any rate, she knew why hope would be necessary when, after fumbling with the stiff old-fashioned lock, Giles heaved the front door open with a grunt of satisfaction and groped his way to a light switch.

''At least someone's turned on the power,'' he muttered as the entrance hall to the inn leaped into sight under the merciless glare of a huge bare bulb dangling over their heads.

''Oh, no,'' Laurel said faintly as they looked around them, and Giles half reached out to switch off the too-revealing light before he conquered the reflex and let his hand fall heavily to his side. He said nothing, although he hadn't struck Laurel as the sort to be at a loss for words.

For several minutes they both simply stared—at

the old bulb swinging on the end of a frayed length of black wire, at the ceiling so cracked that its plaster looked like a road map for ants, at the ugly and water-stained wallpaper that had begun to peel back from the damp walls, at the stair carpet that was so threadbare that only loose horizontal strings remained to trip the unwary, at the wide pine floorboards buckled and heaved to different heights, and in the all-encompassing dust, at the numerous traces of insects and small furry creatures that had obviously been the inn's most recent tenants.

At last Laurel swallowed audibly and stepped across the hall to a doorway by the stairs. Vanishing from Giles's sight, she flicked on another light. There was silence again until the light went off, and she reappeared. Her face was a study—complete with a gray smudge along one cheek—but she wasn't saying anything as she crossed the hall again to another doorway on the opposite side. This time he went with her. Together they peered around a long room whose haphazard assortment of broken tables and chairs suggested that this had once been a dining room. Beyond it lay a huge antique kitchen, and still farther into the ell were pantries and storerooms, with another staircase ascending into the dark like a narrow tunnel.

Their eyes met wordlessly. Then they turned and retraced their steps to the front hall, climbing the wide staircase to the second floor. There they found two ancient and cavernous bathrooms whose fixtures should have been in a plumbing museum, and one after another, forlornly empty bedrooms, each with its own water-stained ceiling, peeling wallpaper and small rust-marked washstand.

Only one of the rooms upstairs was different from the others, and that was the last bedroom in the ell, at the top of the second staircase. It was reasonably warm, instead of cold and dank. Better yet, this one was filled with fine old furniture whose beauty shone even through the dust that covered it. A handsome antique block-fronted chest of drawers stood between the room's two windows, and across from it was a four-poster bed whose softly faded hangings still gleamed a dusky rose. A fireplace stood to their right, flanked by two graceful chairs, and the last wall held a small washbasin and a massive old cherry wardrobe whose plain lines accentuated the beautiful wood.

Looking around this room, Laurel suddenly had a picture of its previous owner, the "forbiddingly upright old party" who had owned the inn until last year. She might have been uncompromising, but she had certainly loved beauty. Her room said clearly that it had been her final refuge. Here were gathered the familiar and lovely things that had comforted her in her old age when the inn itself became too much for her to keep up with. She had obviously given up on the other desolate rooms, which at the end must all have been uninhabited anyway, and retreated to this last beloved place. Even after a year of emptiness, it still had the look of a well-loved room, and Laurel was warmed and drawn to it.

Giles must have felt its appeal, too, because he finally broke the long silence to say with an explosive sight of relief, "Thank God! Everything else is even worse than I remembered, but here's a haven finally. I've been feeling guilty I didn't warn you more, but at least this offers some hope."

Laurel turned to smile at him absently, still caught in the room's gentle spell, and he accurately read her expression. Moving to the wardrobe, he turned the key fastening the doors. They opened easily, and the delicate scent of lavender stole out like some hospitable ghost as he investigated the drawers. They weren't all empty.

"Good," he said with satisfaction. "There are sheets and quilts here that don't seem to have suffered from being unused. Now we know you've got somewhere to spend the night anyway."

Laurel agreed. Adam had made her a reservation at a motel in Fryeburg, but now that she was here, there was no question in her mind that she meant to spend the night at the inn. It would be silly not to use this lovely room that seemed to welcome her so.

"And speaking of night," she added, "I feel as though I've monopolized your time for half of it already, but I really will be fine on my own now."

"My dear girl," he answered expansively, "you saved all of my time this evening on the highway, so you may have as much of it as you like! But on the other hand," he added candidly in an entirely different tone, "if you *are* all set for now, I'll be off to my second movement. It's what started all this, and if I leave you now I can be back to it sooner than if everything had gone as usual and I were coming back from rehearsal in North Conway."

He looked at her hopefully, and Laurel nodded in grave agreement. "Yes, of course," she said diplomatically, before the sudden change in his manner proved too much for her composure, and she laughed out loud. Noting the faint surprise in her expression, Giles gave her his sudden broad grin that made him look absurdly like a bearded child.

"Do you remember the list of my failings I was giving you when we first met?" he asked ruefully, and she nodded again, her eyes still smiling. "At this point I think it only fair to add another item to it: I tend to be deplorably single-minded when I'm working on a new composition."

She chuckled again, raising her hands in a dismissing gesture, and he caught one to give it a mocking but graceful kiss. "And so, having your forgiveness, I shall bid you good-night and return to my recalcitrant symphony."

Swinging away from her and starting back along the hall that led to this last room, he turned to give her a jaunty wave as she called after him, "With my thanks for taking time away from it to bring me here!"

He disappeared around the corner at the top of the

steps then, and Laurel gave the beautiful room that would be hers one more look before she followed him down the creaking stairs. She went more slowly, though, feeling less sure than he that the staircase would bear their weight again, so that by the time she reached the front door he was starting his car. Silhouetted in the light of the bare bulb, she stood with her hand lifted in farewell, and with a brief toot of his horn and a grinding of gears, Giles shot away from the inn. The black-cat night swallowed up the sound of his asthmatic engine and the sight of his bright taillights, and Laurel was alone.

Her hand dropped to her side. Closing the heavy old door, she stood leaning her forehead against it. Very slowly her smile vanished. For the past hour she had felt like a new person—someone completely different from the woman who had married Morgan Hamilton on Saturday. The near accident and Giles's exuberance had taken her out of herself, so that she could behave, for a while at least, as if she were nothing but what she'd said, an employee trusted to come here and evaluate this property for renovation.

But now the adrenaline from the near crash was gone, and the removal of Giles's vitality left her suddenly free to remember everything that had happened. Those memories pounced on her, and unconsciously she ducked her head against them. The movement brought her blurred gaze to rest on the worn rug at her feet and, staring at it, she made a mental note to mend its torn binding before she caught a heel in it and fell.

Improbably, the thought was a lifeline. She was alone in this old inn, and there was nothing left of the hopes and dreams she'd awakened with two days before. One way or another, she was cut off from everything familiar—her family, her old friends and apartment, her work and most of all her heart. She was like someone in a science-fiction adventure who finds herself reborn as an adult in a strange place. She had no choice whatsoever but to accept the situation and go on. Adam had given her this one chance, at least, to *be* reborn, partly for his sake, but mostly for her own. And for the inn's.

Giles had gone, but the inn was still here, needing her evaluation if it was to survive. She would concentrate solely on it. If she was lucky, in fact, it might occupy her thoughts so fully that there would be little room left in them for Morgan—or the woman he obviously knew so intimately.

Suddenly, the innate stoicism she'd drawn on since this morning was replaced by a fresh surge of anger, and she stood bolt upright. How could he? How *dared* he! Once she began to let it out again, the anger rose like a tidal wave, washing away both loneliness and grief—for now, at any rate. How dared he lie about his relationship with that woman, and lie so easily, so blatantly? How dared to sneak off with her like that at his own wedding reception. Two hours earlier he had promised to love and honor *her*, and that was how he did it!

Literally shaking with rage, Laurel slammed an open palm on the doorframe beside her over and over again, until she was exhausted and loose flakes of paint rained down on her fingers. Somehow that, more than the pain in her hand, finally penetrated her fury, and she focused on the peeling pathetic wood. It had stood there patiently under her attack, and subconsciously she made a judgment about the faithfulness of people and the faithfulness of things.

So Morgan Hamilton was lost to her. In fact, he'd never belonged to her at all. She'd let his devastating physical appeal overwhelm her common sense and distract her from the career she'd built with such care. In the long run she'd be better off without him anyway. But the inn was hers, in a way. Adam had given her free rein to go as far with it as she chose. Understanding now why he'd made this particular suggestion when she'd told him she had to get away, Laurel felt a flash of renewed gratitude. Resolutely her eyes swept the decrepit hallway. All around, signs of neglect and damage called out for her time, her care, her thought, and taking a deep breath, she yanked the door open again and charged across the rickety porch, unafraid now of its warped and sagging boards as she hurried to her car.

Sliding into the driver's seat, she opened the glove compartment and rooted around in it for the large pad she always kept there. Obviously, the first thing she'd need to do would be to inventory the present condition of the inn. The pad finally came free of a tangle of maps and scraps, and her searching fingers turned up a pencil, too. As she pulled them out with both hands, her eyes fell on the ring that she had thought symbolized Morgan's feelings for her and their commitment to each other.

For a long time she just looked at it. Then she put the pad and pencil on the seat beside her, pulled her wedding ring off with steady movements and dropped it into the farthest corner of the glove compartment. Someday she'd take it out and send it to Morgan via his grandfather—as soon as the annulment came through, that was—but for now she let it slip into a heap of change, subway tokens and string. Neatly latching the box with a final-sounding click, she gathered up her pad and pencil and walked back to the inn that would be her distraction from everything Morgan's ring should have meant.

It was midnight before she came back to the car, walking wearily now, to pull her suitcases from the trunk and take them upstairs. She had surveyed the entire second floor of the inn, room by room, and made notes on the contents of each, the damage she could identify and the amount of work she could estimate each would need before the old building could ever house guests again. Her notes went on for pages and pages, ranging from the water stains on the ceilings that probably meant a leaky roof to the holes in the woodwork that might mean insect damage—and she was all too aware that she hadn't even glanced at the heating, the plumbing or the wiring, because she wasn't sure what to look for.

Even without those major systems—or the first floor and cellar, the barn and exterior—she had an imposing list of problems. It could have been a terrifying one, but Laurel found herself almost welcoming every item on it, just as she welcomed her present mindless exhaustion. With all these problems and whatever else turned up, the old inn would occupy her completely for days to come. Already it had tired her so thoroughly she barely had enough energy left to struggle upstairs and get herself into a haphazardly made bed. In the last seconds before she fell asleep, she was grateful that exhaustion would keep her from lying awake and thinking. She wouldn't have to fight to forget what had brought her up here.

She was only partly right about that, however. Sometime in the middle of the night she awakened from a dreamless sleep, after her first fatigue was gone. Cold moonlight poured into her room between the shadowy curtains, and a draft stirred the hangings at the head and foot of her bed. Around her rose a faint scent of the lavender her mother used to love, and still only partly awake, Laurel sniffed it, rubbing her cheek against the soft fragrant sheets. Through her half-open eyes, the dim shapes that moved back and forth across the walls caught her attention, and she sat up abruptly.

Disoriented, she looked around the unfamiliar room. This wasn't her own room at home, no matter how it smelled, and even that hadn't smelled of lavender in years, since her mother died. She shook her head, bewildered. Her mother—was that why she felt this heavy sense of loss?

But that had all been years before, and miles away. Confused and chilled, she caught at her quilt that had slipped down from her shoulders and gathered it tightly around her, taking a deep breath. With it, paradoxically, came the thought of the Caribbean, and the memory of how she came to be here instead of in the islands with her husband.

Then the cold slashed through her quilt as memory slashed through her mind. For now the heat of her anger at Morgan had burned out again. Her heart was turning to ice, because she was alone, because her brand new husband preferred a lover to a wife.

Her wedding night had come and gone, and Morgan wasn't beside her. His lips weren't searching hers, his hands weren't caressing her into sensations she had only begun to learn, their bodies weren't sharing the ultimate joys of loving. He didn't share this big empty bed, and he never would. Tonight he was probably sleeping with Renee, and at that thought Laurel writhed frantically, torn by anger, jealousy, loneliness, and by hungers she couldn't control.

CHAPTER FOUR

FINALLY SHE SLIPPED BACK into exhausted sleep, and when she awakened again the experience was much different from her earlier waking. This time she knew immediately where she was and why, and this time there was a kind of empty calm in her mind. For a while, at least, she was completely drained of emotion, and she was grateful. She'd probably cry herself to sleep other nights in this big bed, but this morning, anyway, she had gained a kind of hard-won peace. And so she eased herself out from under her quilts, trying not to groan as each muscle complained of her miserable night.

A few steps seemed to work out the worst of that, though, and they brought her into a patch of sunshine that lay like liquid gold spilled across the wide old floorboards. Her bare toes discovered the sun's warmth, and she padded along it to the nearest window, swinging it open. Air that was mild and laden with the scents of new life and damp earth billowed in immediately, setting the lace curtains astir, and she leaned out into it—into it, and into the sight of the view for which the inn was named.

From her vantage point here at the back of the building, she saw an uneven meadow sloping gradually downward, patchy with the green and gold of new grass and old straw. At the far edge of the meadow was a stretch of woods, where evergreens and the graceful trunks of silver birches predominated. A narrow track led into the trees, but soon disappeared from sight in a slanting tunnel of sun and shadow. Its destination was obviously the lake, which lay still farther below her, with its etched glass inlets and coves visible here and there, a delight to her eyes. On the lake's farther shore stood a few rustic cottages and summer homes, tiny at this distance, clustered among the trees Then the forest went on, losing its pine and silver and leaf-green detail as it rose into remote blue mountains, cool and serene in the fresh morning air.

It was spectacularly beautiful, but Laurel's awe turned into a gasp of astonishment as a flat voice twanged, "Morning, miss."

Startled, she followed the sound with her eyes and discovered that an old blue truck had been pulled up beside the building; that might have been what had woken her up. Its owner was standing below her now, a lanky brown man in worn work boots and corduroy trousers that showed evidence of much mending. A plaid wool jacket hung open from his narrow shoulders, and an old hunting cap was pushed to the back of his head, which he tilted to look at her. And Laurel suddenly and appallingly realized she was wearing nothing but one of the deliberately revealing nightgowns she'd bought for her trousseau.

Diving back behind the curtains, she called down breathlessly to the stranger below, "I'll be down in just a minute—don't go!"

He just nodded; and galvanized in a way she wouldn't have believed possible when she first crawled out of bed, Laurel hauled a pair of navy slacks and a pullover from the nearest suitcase. As she scrambled into them her mind was racing. Who on earth could that be down there? At this hour of the morning, he probably wasn't looking for lodging, and even if he was, last night's inventory had made it all too clear that any guest trying to stay at the inn just now would be taking his life in his hands! And he really didn't look like a tourist, but more like someone who might live in this area himself. But then why was he here?

She raked a brush through her hair and quickly tied it back in a scarf, noting with a groan that the mirror reflected a face still scarlet with embarrassment. Hanging half-dressed out of windows definitely didn't seem appropriate for the official representative of the Hamilton Corporation. And if half of the stories people told about reserved and proper New Englanders were true, then she certainly hadn't created much of a first impression on this man!

Anyhow, that was clearly the feeling he gave her when she hurried out to join him behind the inn. When she came up to him, he was standing with his jacket pushed back and his thumbs hooked under his suspenders as he stared expressionlessly off toward the mountains. Hearing her quick steps, he turned his head and fixed her with the same farsighted, narrow-eyed gaze.

"Good morning," she offered with a bright smile, trying to start over and not be unnerved by his steady appraisal.

"Morning," he repeated tersely, but without an answering smile, giving her the distinct impression that he hadn't forgotten that frivolous nightgown—and in fact that he somehow knew of every foolish, inept or thoughtless thing she had ever done.

His manner was definitely intimidating, and she suspected it was meant to be, so she raised her chin defiantly and started her own inspection. Under a thatch of untidy gray hair, his face was tanned and weather-beaten with networks of lines around eyes and mouth. High cheekbones under tautly stretched skin and a beaky nose completed a face that looked stern, but still somehow intriguing.

She had got that far, the two of them silently studying each other, when she realized how ridiculous this deadlock was. Her earlier smile came back as an engaging grin, and she stopped trying to stare down the man in front of her and introduced herself.

"I'm Laurel Andersen," she said without yesterday's hesitation over her name, adding, "The new owner of the inn asked me to come here and see what kinds of repairs it would need before it could open again.''

"I know." Her opponent of a moment ago shifted his gaze away, too, looking off to the mountains again before turning back to add, "I'm Nate White. I was caretaker here for Mrs. Moore.''

It was the briefest of explanations, and his tone was still almost grudging, but there was a very slight change in the expression of those deep-set eyes, and Laurel knew he understood why she had been amused.

It wasn't much to go on, but it *was* a tiny piece of encouragement, so she said warmly, "Then you must be the one who turned on the power and water for me.''

"Eyah.''

"Eyah"? What on earth was that, she wondered hastily, flashing her companion a quick inquiring look. His leathery face told her nothing, so she went on tentatively, "I was grateful to be able to see my way around last night.''

She meant that as thanks, if he was the person who'd at least offered her that little bit of welcome, but at her words Nate unhooked his thumbs from his suspenders and muttered, "Nothing much else to be done.''

His eyes were on his feet now, but with quick insight Laurel guessed that elliptical remark had to do with the awful condition of the inn. But before she could decide for sure, or think of anything tactful and reassuring to say about it, Nate was in retreat. At the door of his truck, he paused long enough to say, "I'll send Abby over," then swung into the old cab, slammed the door and rattled off, clattering around the corner of the building.

Laurel called "Thank you!" after him, but she couldn't tell whether or not he heard her. She followed his truck around the corner, but by the time she reached the front of the inn, Nate was almost at the bend in the road. A minute later he was out of sight, and she was left standing in the dusty driveway, her arms akimbo and her lips still curved in amusement and wonder. For now, Morgan and all the turmoil that had brought her here stayed in the background of her thoughts.

While she was still standing there thinking about her first visitor, her second drove in. With a horn fanfare Giles skidded his Volvo to a stop in front of her and unpacked his large bulk from the small driver's seat with surprising ease.

"Good morning, O savior of reckless composers!" he greeted her exuberantly, catching both of her hands in his to give each one a theatrical kiss. The one on her left hand landed where she had worn Morgan's ring yesterday, but she was so distracted by the impact of Giles's boisterous personality that she didn't notice.

Laughingly she played back to him in his own style. "And good morning to you, guide to dark old inns!"

At that, he glanced over her shoulder at the decrepit

bulk of the inn and shuddered melodramatically, still holding her hands.

"I woke up this morning with pangs of conscience for having left you here last night," he confessed. "I had unnerving visions of you stuck with your foot through a rotted floorboard, or trapped by a giant spiderweb, or held at bay by a pack of savage mice and squirrels."

"Thanks," she returned dryly, "for your reassuring pictures of what may yet happen to me tonight!"

At her tone a wide grin spread across his face, but he dodged her complaint. "But my conscience is clean for today, at any rate," he pointed out, adding unrepentantly, "and my second movement is done as well!"

The severe expression Laurel had tried to assume crumbled into laughter again at his frankness. "Congratulations," she chuckled. "For an achievement like that, my possible sufferings would be small payment!"

He opened his mouth to respond to that, then realized she'd left him no room for an answer that would be even remotely tactful and shut it with a snap, dropping her hands to wet one finger and mark off an imaginary scorecard in the air. That done, he went off on a tangent.

"Was that Nate White I passed on my way in?" he asked, glancing down the road and looking back at Laurel with one eyebrow raised.

She nodded and then frowned in concentration. "Giles, what does 'eyah' mean?"

"That, my poor ignorant outlander," he lectured her with mock sternness, "is the taciturn New Englander's all-purpose answer. Used particularly in conversations with 'furreners,' it does the job when some answer is obviously expected, but the wily New Englander doesn't want to commit himself. It is generally said with absolutely no inflection and can mean 'yes,' or 'maybe,' or 'you've got a point,' or 'I'll think about it'—or nothing whatsoever!"

He eyed her, and she obediently mimed taking notes until he grinned again and dropped the pedagogue pose. "And the fact that you asked already means you have indeed met Nate White!" he confirmed. "Nate's refined the use of 'eyah' to an art form."

Remembering how her brief conversation with Nate had pivoted on that cryptic word, Laurel nodded ruefully, then thought to add, "And who's Abby? Nate said he'd send her over, but he didn't say why!"

"Of course not," Giles agreed. "Why should he waste his breath explaining what you could find out for yourself?"

He paused, but she refused to concede the practicality of that, thinking what a struggle it was talking to Nate. Instead she prodded Giles. "Well, then, are you going to help me find it out?"

Giles laughed, acknowledging his omission. He

did, however, finally cooperate. "As well as being erstwhile cook around here, Abby is Nate's wife, and a less likely pair I defy you to find."

Turning, he walked over to the edge of the porch and leaned against it. The rickety old boards squeaked a protest, and Laurel, following him, decided to stay standing as he continued in a warmly amused tone, looking up at her.

"You've got a pretty good idea now of Nate's measure as a conversationalist—"

"Don't I just!" Laurel interjected, but Giles cocked one eyebrow and went on.

"And Abby is just as extreme."

"Oh, no!" Laurel groaned, wondering what she was going to do when Abby arrived. "You mean I'll practically have to read her mind, too?"

"Not quite," Giles amended dryly. "Abby will be perfectly happy to speak it to you."

Laurel looked confused, and he explained, "She's as extreme as Nate, but in the opposite direction. Nate almost never talks, and Abby almost never stops talking!"

Laurel sighed with relief. Abby sounded a good deal easier to communicate with.

Giles went on musingly, "I've always wondered whether Abby started out that way, or whether she just took to babbling because she hated the silence and Nate wasn't going to break it. Anyway, he probably couldn't now if he tried! I doubt if Abby leaves him room anymore to get a word in edgewise."

He shook his leonine head in affectionate amusement. "She sounds like fun," Laurel decided.

Giles slanted a look up at her. "Unless you've got a headache, she is," he agreed. "In fact, they're both good people and a joy to know—even if they do always make me wonder if there isn't some fable about the magpie and the ant!"

Laughing, Laurel didn't have to guess which one would be which in Giles's fable.

"And now, my girl, you have had your introductory lesson on the quirks and customs of the area, so I'll leave you and take myself off to Fryeburg and the supermarket, since I seem to have forgotten about food lately in the throes of composition, and I'm starved. If I stoke up now, I'll be able to survive the third movement! Meanwhile, can I bring you anything?"

"Thanks, Giles, but no. I don't really know yet what I need, so I'll go for myself when I decide what my immediate plans are."

"You *are* staying? Last night's discoveries about this old place haven't scared you off?"

"No." Laurel shook her head, adding lightly, "I always did like a good challenge!"

"Well, you certainly have it here!" His sweeping gesture took in the whole sagging front of the building that seemed to watch them like an aged but hopeful bloodhound. "But it's good to hear the inn has a chance again, and that there'll be one more charming face around here."

And with another of those improbably graceful gestures, he swept her an elegant bow, strode back to his car, inserted himself in it and drove off with the grinding of gears she began to suspect was characteristic of his attitude toward machinery. One long arm waved her another farewell out his window, and he disappeared, leaving Laurel to smile over the contrast between her two morning callers as she picked her way up the steps and across the porch again, to go on with her inventory of the inn's disasters. .

Nearly overwhelmed by them, she was sitting on the floor of the kitchen an hour later, her notes in a sizable heap beside her, when she heard a knock. With a stifled groan she scrambled to her feet and hurried through the dining room to the front door, to find on the threshold a tiny woman with rosy cheeks and thick dark hair just beginning to be streaked with white.

"Good morning," Laurel offered, opening the door—and then said nothing else for the next few minutes, because there wasn't any chance for her to speak.

"Good morning, child—I'm so glad to see you're all right, after a night on your own here! This old place has gotten bad enough to give anyone nightmares, and I worried about Nate leaving you no better welcome than the power on and a bit of food. And when I think of how it was in the old days, when we used to keep a horse and buggy to bring guests out from the village in style! And then there would be a cup of tea or a cool glass of juice for them on the porch while their things were being taken to their rooms and unpacked. After dinner, if the weather was fine, the buggy would take them down to the lake and they'd have a tour by boat at sunset—''

She broke off with a regretful shake of her head, and Laurel made a small understanding noise, but before she could say anything her visitor was off again, having gained her second wind.

"*That* was a proper sort of welcome to give folks, and I wish you'd had something at least a little like it, child. The trouble was, we didn't know quite when you'd be in—or even what kind of person you'd be. Nate had the notion you'd be some sort of high muck-a-muck from this big company that's bought the inn, and you'd probably just want to look it over for an hour or two and then be on your way, without trying to sleep in such an old place or to squeeze in with us at our house. So I just made sure there were sheets for Mrs. Moore's bed and a bite of food, in case, and let it go at that. You're sure you're all right?''

The steady flow of words eddied, and Laurel smiled reassuringly at the little woman's concerned expression. For an instant she thought of those bitter tears she had cried in the night. But that would have happened wherever she'd been, and all she said was, "I'm fine, thanks, really. The bed was lovely and warm, and I had a glass of that good orange juice a little while ago.''

Last night it had never even crossed her mind to look and see if there was anything to eat in the inn, but this morning after Giles left, the juice had tasted wonderful. Her current visitor didn't seem impressed, however.

"That's all you've had, child? Good heavens, you're likely to fall over in a heap if you don't have more to sustain you than that! Wouldn't you like at least a cup of coffee and a bite of toast?"

Suddenly Laurel was ravenous. "That sounds lovely, but to be honest I haven't figured out how to cook anything at all on that stove yet," she admitted, shrugging her shoulders in a rueful gesture.

"Well, now, you just let me at it, and I'll have you something in a jiffy." Closing the door behind her, she added, "There is an art to operating one of those old wood cookstoves, but you'll catch on to it soon enough. Just let me give you a hand right now." She turned and started through the bleak dining room, then looked back on an afterthought to add with a warm smile, "I'm Abby White, by the way— Nate told you I'd be over?"

"Yes," she nodded—and Giles had told her exactly what to expect! Abby's chatter flowed like a brook and was just as pleasant. Laurel returned the smile and introduced herself. "And I'm Laurel Andersen. I work for the Hamilton Corporation. Mr. Hamilton asked me to come and see whether or not it would be possible to fix up the inn so it could reopen."

She followed Abby's small round figure into the

kitchen on the words and, obeying the other woman's gesture, seated herself at the bare wood table while Abby shrugged off her coat.

"And now that you've seen it, child, what will you tell him?" she asked, rolling up her sleeves over plump capable forearms. There was no particular inflection on the question, but a crease had appeared between Abby's eyebrows, and Laurel knew her answer was important.

"I'll say that it needs a lot of work, but that it deserves to have the time and money spent on it," she said steadily, and saw the crease disappear from Abby's forehead.

"That *is* good news, Laurel," was all she said at first, walking to a wood box by the back door and taking out a yellowed newspaper and a few bits of dusty kindling. When she turned back, though, her dark eyes shone with tears of pleasure. She dashed them away with her fingers and busied herself crumpling the paper and then laying a fire in the firebox of the ancient stove. When she'd lighted it and was satisfied it would catch, her eyes were dry again, and she came to sit facing Laurel after setting a kettle of water on to heat.

"There, child, that should do the trick in a bit."

She glanced back at the hulking stove and smiled reminiscently. "I was just a bride when I learned how to cook on that contraption. Nate and I had been married in September when I was due to go back to Providence at the end of the summer—" She backtracked with a chuckle. "I'd come up to stay with my aunt and recuperate after a bad bout of flu, and Nate proposed when I told him I was going home. I don't think he's ever quite gotten over his surprise at himself for marrying an outlander!"

Chin in her palm, Laurel responded with an infectious smile, and Abby went on. "Anyway, he'd been trying to set up a small hardware business, but when old Mr. Moore died he sold out and came to help Mrs. Moore run the inn. He took care of the building and the garden, drove the buggy and ran the boat, and I came along to do the cooking.

"It was quite a chore at first, too. Luckily, at that stage Mrs. Moore was still well enough to help me learn how, because that confounded thing had me bamboozled for weeks. It wouldn't light, or it would go out silently while I had a cake baking, or it would roar along twice as hot as I expected. It was a real challenge!"

Her smile faded now, and she went on more slowly, "Mrs. Moore kept saying we'd get a new one sometime soon, but somehow 'soon' never came. I'd finally gotten used to this one, of course, so I managed fine, but it was hard to see her getting frailer and frailer and spending more and more time in her own room. Nate and I kept things running as best we could, but our older guests got fewer every year, and there didn't seem to be younger ones coming to replace them. And then there wasn't any money coming in to replace anything that wore out or needed fixing, so we just had to watch the inn lose ground every season."

She sighed. "It grieved me because I'd gotten to love this old place, and it nearly broke Nate's heart. He never said anything, of course, but he took it personally that he wasn't able to keep things going by just plain hard work."

Laurel remembered the way Nate had looked when he'd said, "Nothing else to be done" earlier that morning and knew she'd been right to think he was referring to the condition of the inn.

Sympathetically, she leaned across the old table and patted Abby's clasped hands. "But he was able to keep the inn from falling apart completely, so that even though there's a lot to be done, it can be," she reminded Abby, and the other woman smiled at her again.

"Yes, child, that is true, isn't it? So we were able to accomplish that much, anyway. Well, then, what will the next step be, after you make your report?"

Sitting back again, Laurel answered honestly. "I'm not sure, but I was told I could go as far with the whole project as I wanted, and it would be so fascinating to be in on fixing things up!"

Abby smiled understandingly. "I know. It really would be wonderful, wouldn't it, to see the old place come back to life?"

Laurel nodded. Besides being a refuge for her, this inn was also a beautiful building that still showed traces of the charm and elegance it must have had once, and bringing those qualities back would be both worthwhile and exciting—almost like being able to make a lovely old woman young again. And without any more thought than that, she knew she wanted to stay here and do it.

Abby added encouragement, too. "If you do decide to take it on, Laurel," she promised, "you can count on me to work alongside."

Sure that Adam would approve, Laurel agreed wholeheartedly. "I can't imagine managing without you!" she said fervently, already conscious of how much Abby's practical good sense—and distracting chatter—would add to almost any project. "Will Nate be able to come back, too?"

Abby looked thoughtful, weighing her husband's reactions, then made up her mind—and perhaps his as well. "Yes. The truth is he's been at loose ends ever since Mrs. Moore died. This place was everything to him, and he hasn't been able to find anything much else that he wanted to turn his hand to. So, yes, Nate will come, too."

At that moment the kettle shrieked, and both women jumped as it shattered the quiet around them. Abby chuckled, saying, "Looks as if that old thing's burning hotter than usual again, just by way of welcoming me back! But since it's got the water ready, shall we have a cup of coffee before we get down to work?"

Smiling agreement, Laurel stood up and went to fix the coffee while Abby stoked larger logs into the firebox, so they would catch and could be banked to keep the room warm and the stove ready for later use. Then, old cracked cups in hand, they started working together on the inventory.

AND ALTHOUGH LAUREL'S INVENTORY of the inn was a long exhausting project, at least she had companionship and laughter. Morgan's inventory of his life was a good deal more unpleasant. It began when Tuesday's morning paper hit the front door of his apartment with enough of a thump to make him lift his head from the sofa. Raising it very slowly, he began his inventory with the discovery that his body was in complete rebellion. Both his head and his stomach were battle zones, and there seemed to be heavy artillery firing behind his eyes.

With a muffled groan, he eased his way into a sitting position and cautiously levered himself onto his feet. Hauling the door open, he began to bend over for the day's paper—and Monday's, and Sunday's—but the resulting vertigo was so overwhelming that he was forced to clutch the door for balance and kick the papers in with one foot. When his eyes focused properly again, he looked with loathing across the room at the empty bottle on the sideboard. There had been others, too, he remembered with distaste, and faces of people he didn't know in places he didn't ordinarily go. With a grimace that started another small skirmish in his head, he walked carefully into the bathroom, peeling off the clothes that had reason to look as though they'd been slept in and turned the shower on full force.

An hour later he had confirmed to himself that his private life was in a shambles. All the time he was in the shower he had held off the memory of his reason for turning the past two days into a blur, simply letting the water wash all those misspent hours away. Now, however, he was back on the sofa with an empty coffee cup beside him, his head in both hands and the newspapers scattered at his feet, except for the society section of Sunday's paper, which lay wadded on the far side of the room.

When the doorbell rang, the sound seemed to knife through his eardrums, and he swore, determined to ignore it. There was absolutely no one in the world he cared to see. It rang again, though, a second and then a third time, and he finally got up and wrenched it open, to find Renee de Beaumont reaching for the button again with one elegantly manicured finger.

"What do you want?" he asked disagreeably.

She let her hand fall and made a quick assessment of the man before her. His dark face was newly shaven and his hair still damp, but his broad shoulders were hunched, the pale eyes narrowed and the harsh voice harsher now than a November gale.

Stepping in past him, she shut the door behind her, latching it with exaggerated care and softening her face into an expression of affectionate concern.

"Only to see you, *mon cher*," she murmured soothingly. "To see you and know that you are well."

He was still standing near the door, eyebrows lowered and arms folded discouragingly across his chest, but she ignored the hostile stance. Catching sight of his empty cup, she picked it up gracefully and headed for the galley kitchen, taking care to brush softly by him on the way.

That little ploy had no apparent effect. He just strode across the living room and dropped into a leather wing chair on the far side, thrusting his long legs out in front of him and closing his eyes—all in silence. It was not a silence that expressed any particular interest or belief in her statement, but she went on preparing a fresh pot of coffee and humming quietly to herself. A few minutes later she set a steaming cup on the small table beside him.

She'd poured herself a cup, too. Stirring it as she perched casually on the arm of his chair, she went on speaking as if there'd been no lapse. "After all, I have not seen you since Saturday, and without you the time drags on so slowly."

She slanted a hasty look at the hard profile by her left shoulder, but it was as informative as an iceberg. She went back to gazing thoughtfully into the vapor rising from her cup and added, "And we had not finished our planning, when you left me so quickly...."

She let that remark trail away without referring to what took place immediately afterward in Adam's house, but it seemed to dangle unspoken in the air. Scowling, Morgan stood up abruptly, and while he walked away from her she quickly shifted some weight onto her right foot, striving to maintain her graceful pose on the chair arm without tipping over. She smiled very slightly to herself.

Morgan, turning suddenly on the far side of the room, caught the flicker of that private smile, took in the perfect face and figure, the seductive clothes and postures. But as if the smile were a window, he saw through it more clearly than ever before to the calculation behind every move, the strategy behind every response, the artifice behind it all.

He studied her intently for a minute more before he finally spoke. "On the contrary," he said with a note in his voice that she was coming to recognize, "we *had* finished—as you well know."

Another minute more and he had the last item for his disastrous inventory. Renee had flung out of his apartment, but a messenger had brought a large manila envelope in. Tipping him and shutting the door, Morgan slowly opened the package and took out the thick sheaf of papers that were to have transferred control of the Hamilton Corporation to him. They were all blank, and Morgan had no difficulty whatsoever in understanding his grandfather's unspoken meaning: they would stay blank, at least as far as he was concerned.

Like his body and his private life, his career, too, had been disrupted by the past few days; the inventory was complete. Morgan stood motionless for long minutes. Then, swearing fluently and fervently, he laid the papers aside and, walking to the closet, took out a set of leather suitcases.

CHAPTER FIVE

LAUREL HAD BEEN AT THE INN for four days, and Nate and Abby had taken the truck off to Fryeburg to shop, when she heard the sound of tires in the ruts in front of the building. Lifting her head from the linen list she was working on, she realized it couldn't be Giles coming to see her—he wouldn't stop his poor car that quietly! And he was probably at work composing again, since he hadn't been by after that first morning. So who could this be? Not. . . .

Setting the list aside, Laurel leaped to her feet and ran her suddenly shaking hands through her hair to smooth it back from a face where all color had ebbed. Then she straightened the old wool jacket she'd borrowed from Abby to wear—even indoors in this drafty old place—and walked to the front door—to see Adam getting out of his car. Adam, not Morgan.

For a moment she sagged against the doorjamb, then straightened and walked into his outstretched arms for a long silent hug, before he held her away from him so that he could look intently into her face. And Laurel, meeting the gaze that was so like his grandson's yet so different, wondered what she would have done if he had been Morgan. Would she have thrown herself into his arms, to have them close around her while he said her name, to feel his breath on her skin and smell the lime after-shave he used as his slightly roughened cheek pressed against hers, and to savor his lips as they brushed, then clung to her own, cool at first and warming under the contact?

Her own breath caught in her throat. No! Even if this had been Morgan, he wouldn't have held and kissed her. He was the man who'd promised to love her and then gone to another woman on their wedding day. She hadn't even meant enough to him to prevent something that despicable.

"Granda," she said in a voice she fought to make steady and welcoming as she released her hold on him, "how good to see you! Have you come to check on your inn?"

"And on you, Laurel," he returned warmly, those shrewd eyes observant behind his spectacles.

"You drove up alone?" The question ripped its way out of her, each word a ball of knives, as she confirmed that Morgan hadn't chosen to come after her.

"Yes, my dear," Adam quietly answered the question she was really asking. "I haven't seen Morgan since Saturday. We quarreled after you went, and I understand he's left the country."

"And my annulment?"

"Our lawyer is in California just now, but I've left a message that I'd like to see him when he's back in town. Then we'll set about dissolving this marriage of yours."

She wasn't looking at him, but when his old face tightened on the words, she heard the unhappiness in him that echoed her own. After all, his grandfather had to feel the same bitter disillusionment with Morgan that she did. And so she forced back her own feelings and didn't ask any more. Morgan had gone, and their marriage would be annulled. What else was there to know, anyway?

Swallowing hard, she said in a bright determined tone, "Come in, then, and let me fix you some coffee in the kitchen."

Half an hour later, their first cups of coffee were gone, and Adam had an accurate idea of the horrendous state of things at his inn. He knew about the roof leaking, the wind whistling through closed windows, the antique plumbing and wiring and the furnace that could barely keep any heat in the radiators, even when it clanked and groaned with the strain. And that list didn't include what he learned about the rest of the inn's furnishings and failings. But he also noticed that when Laurel spoke of it all the shadows that darkened her gold eyes seemed to lift and lighten, for a while at least, and her voice gradually took on some genuine warmth.

To test that impression, he challenged her, "And in spite of all this, you still think the inn would even-

tually pay back the money we'd spend on moderniz-
ing and restoring it?'' he asked skeptically.

"Yes, I do," she returned.

"Then you'd be willing to take charge of the whole
thing—take on the job of opening up the place when
it was ready?" he shot back.

"Yes," she repeated promptly, reacting only to the
bright-eyed look he was giving her, his spectacles for
once firmly in place, so that his eyes seemed larger
than ever. Then she paused as she registered exactly
what he'd said. "But...."

She'd promised Abby she would recommend re-
opening the inn and ask to stay with the project. She
had told Giles she liked challenges. She had been
eager to come here when Adam first suggested it,
because it had sounded like a haven. It had been that,
all this week, and she loved this decrepit old place
now. But still, what she'd just agreed to do suddenly
sounded impossible.

Thinking hastily, she realized it wasn't the first half
of Adam's dare. Overseeing the repairs the inn needed
would be fascinating, and so would refurnishing the
place to get it ready to open. But to open it herself—to
run the inn, even for a few months until Adam ap-
pointed someone else to take charge permanently—
that was the problem! Surely the first months had to
be terribly important in getting an inn's reputation
established, and what could she possibly know about
the practical details of providing the kind of lodgings
the Hamilton Hotels were famous for?

All her second thoughts ran across her face while Adam watched her. He took note of the way her high cheekbones thrust against skin that seemed almost too fragile to contain them, the way her lowered eyelashes lay in pools of blue shadow under each eye, the way her mouth drooped wearily when she wasn't consciously tucking up the corners. She'd been through so much this week, and now he had added another burden by daring her to take on this job. But if she had the courage to do it, he thought, then perhaps something could still be salvaged. . . .

She looked up again. "I think I could handle refurnishing the inn and getting people in to make the repairs it needs, especially if you'd let me hire Nate and Abby White officially—"

He nodded, and she went on honestly, "But I'm afraid I wouldn't live up to Hamilton standards, trying to run the inn when the time came. I just don't know enough about the technical parts of innkeeping to do a good job."

Adam smiled broadly at her, which made him look more cherubic than ever. What he said was purely practical, though. Placing his fingertips together to form that neat familiar triangle, he gazed at her and pointed out in gentle reproof, "I wasn't going to throw you into this, sink or swim, with no water wings, my dear."

She smiled at the image but still looked worried as he began explaining. "Once you and the Whites had contracted out the major repairs, you wouldn't have to stay on hand. I gather Nate and Abby would be up to handling the supervision of things here while you went off and got a bit of training?''

"Yes, definitely."

Her concerned expression starting to fade now, she sat up straighter as he went on, ''One of the very best schools of hotel administration in the country is at Cornell University, in upstate New York, and their summer session is underway right now.''

"But—"

He peered sternly over his spectacles at her, and she subsided. ''The dean of the school happens to have been a friend of mine since we were a pair of foolish young men, and besides that, his students have been coming to us for years. That being the case, I suspect he'd be able to find me a last-minute niche for one more summer student who needed some preparation for the specialized job of running an old-fashioned country inn.''

By now Laurel was incapable of speech. He went on, gazing blandly at his steepled fingers.

''The salary the company is paying you would cover your costs, naturally; we often pay for on-the-job training ourselves. Then when you've completed your session at Cornell, you can finish up with a *cordon-bleu* cooking course in Paris.''

So far he had sounded very businesslike, but now Adam pushed his chair back from the table, folded his hands on one knee and smiled at her again. ''With that much training, my dear, as well as the good sense I've always known you to have, I think you'd be more than ready to run a small inn.''

He paused for her reaction, and Laurel finally managed, ''Granda—''

Then she stopped abruptly and just looked at him. How could she tell him how she felt, when she couldn't even tell herself?

Her eyes fell, and she stared unseeingly at the table while she tried to sort out her emotions. Three months ago, before Morgan appeared in her life, an opportunity like this would have thrilled her. Ever since she'd left home she'd been trying to get as much training and experience as possible, trying to learn everything she could and build her career in any direction it could go. That had made her a superb executive assistant for the company; she knew it without false modesty.

But now, because she'd fallen in love with Morgan, what his grandfather was offering her wasn't just a new career opportunity. It was a chance to get her whole life back on some sort of even keel.

She drew a deep breath, conscious of Adam waiting patiently, and made herself go on thinking it all out. In loving Morgan, she'd evidently been a fool, letting her heart and body overrule her head. The only thing left for her to do about it was to forget that mistake and go on, pick up her career and dismiss all the emotion that had interfered with it. She'd been content enough in the past to focus everything on her work.

Below the edge of the table, she was twining her slender fingers together as she thought, lacing and knotting them as she forced herself to figure out a pattern for her life to replace the one Morgan had shattered in those few minutes with another woman. The past four days at the inn had been a kind of hibernation; after that first wretched night she'd thought of nothing but the present. But she'd known that eventually she would have to come to terms with her past and decide about her future. And now it was done.

Relaxing her hands in her lap, she finally finished her sentence, her voice husky. "Thank you, more than I can say. I'll justify your faith in me."

"You always have, my dear," Adam said, and added briskly, "All right, then, Laurel, we're in agreement about the inn's immediate future—and about yours. Now let's work out the details."

And before their second cups of coffee were gone, he had done just that. She was amazed when he sat back and said with satisfaction, "There. Now when I get back to the office, I'll turn this all over to my new assistant, who, by the way, isn't a patch on my old one—" Laurel caught the twinkle in his eye "—and let her handle the mechanics of this.

"In the meantime, my dear, I'm going to leave you and be off to catch up with an old friend who runs an inn in North Conway." Folding the lists, he pocketed them and grinned at her with a small boy's relish. "I keep trying to buy him out, but so far he won't have any of my palaver, and the truth is that we're both having more fun negotiating month in and month out.''

"I hate to have you go—" Laurel began.

"I know, my dear,'' he cut off her protests and eyed her sharply, seeing in her open face shades of grief and resolution, excitement and apprehension. "But I think you've had enough of my company for one day—and besides, *his* inn doesn't need renovating!''

"Oh!" she fumed, but he went on unrepentantly.

"By my calculations, I should be there just in time for a leisurely drink before dinner.''

There wasn't much she could answer to that last piece of provocation. Here she'd be hard pressed to find him a bed, much less dinner or a drink before it, so Laurel contented herself with making a disrespectful face at him. "Well, will you at least plan to have your next inn evening here?''

"I will, Laurel. I'll be here to enjoy this one when it opens. . . say, for Thanksgiving?''

"It's a bargain.'' She smiled at him lovingly, then grew serious again. "But before you go—''

She broke off, having so much to say that she could say none of it. The questions swirled through her mind. *Are you sure you have to go? Are you sure everything's taken care of? And beyond all the rest, are you really sure you want me to take charge of this inn?*

Adam must have read her mind. "Yes, my dear,'' he answered calmly and simply, standing up. Laurel rose, too, and came around the table, placing a hand on each of his shoulders and steadying herself to kiss him. Holding his granddaughter close, he could see with satisfaction that her changeable eyes were light again, nearly their usual gold, and the trembling that had shaken her earlier was gone. She would be all right, he told himself. She was strong, and his plan would work out in the end.

He left then, and half an hour later Nate and Abby rattled into the driveway in their truck. Without giving Abby a chance to start her monologue about what they'd done and who they'd seen in Fryeburg, Laurel greeted them with the news the renovation of the inn was to start immediately, and that the papers putting them in charge of it would be in the mail immediately, too, if they were willing. Abby's response was instantaneous and delighted.

"*Willing*, child? You'd have to tie me up at home to keep me away!"

Laurel chuckled, knowing that was probably the exact truth, and glanced past Abby to her husband.

"Nate?"

His answer was slower in coming, and Laurel was beginning to wonder if it would come at all when Abby sighed gustily, and Nate withdrew his gaze from the far mountains to meet his wife's speaking look.

"Eyah," he answered finally, and added slowly, "I'll be here, too."

Laurel found herself letting out her breath in relief. Nate was far from predictable.

"But, child, if we're supposed to tend things here, where are you going to be?" Abby demanded.

Laurel made her voice elaborately casual as she evaded a direct answer. "Oh, I'll be around," she said briefly, but her eyes gave her away. Abby caught the laughing glance she threw Nate and the conspiratorial twitch of his lips that meant he knew what she was up to.

And now Abby knew, too. "Laurel, how could you!" she wailed aggrievedly. "As if it isn't bad enough having to wring every bit of information out of Nate! Now behave yourself and tell me where you're going to be!"

Laurel hung her head repentantly, and when she lifted it again her eyes were a clear gold that Abby had never seen, her usually pale cheeks faintly tinted with color as she gave up any pretense of casualness and answered clearly enough even for Abby.

"Starting right away, I'll be at Cornell University studying innkeeping, and then I'll be in Paris studying gourmet cooking!"

With a whoop of pleasure, Abby pounced, kissing her soundly, and it wasn't until late that night that Laurel was alone again to consider the new direction Adam had given to her life. But he had been right to suggest that she'd gone through a great deal that day. Before she could even review everything in her mind, she was asleep.

As she slept she dreamed, a consequence of learning from Adam that Morgan had gone, a mirror image, reversing the reality that it was she who had left Morgan on their wedding day. She dreamed that she was in her husband's arms again at last, and all of this week's anger and grief were fading away as though they had never been. His arms were linked around her; she could lean back and feel their solid strength behind her. She could lean forward, too, and rest her face against his chest. Under her cheek the soft fabric of his shirt was warmed and scented by the heat of his body. She burrowed joyfully into the fabric and breathed in a blend of citrus and starch, mingled with the faintest sensual trace of perspiration. Aroused by his nearness, she clung passionately, slipping her hands under his shirt at the back until she could clasp the reassurance of skin that lay over his muscles like velvet over iron, and stroke the hills and hollows of his body.

She felt him react to her touch, and above her bent head his breath suddenly stirred her ruffled hair. Straightening slowly, she met his lips as they searched for her own. He took them tenderly, then with a rising passion that probed the sweetness she opened so willingly to him. His hands slid down from her shoulders, too, in exploration. As he reached her breasts they swelled to his touch, and she responded with murmured cries of delight while the hot wild tide welled up inside her to meet the desire she felt in him and be consumed by it.

Then suddenly he was gone from her arms, and she stood, aching and empty. Her skin cooled rapidly, deprived of the heat generated from touching his. But unslaked desire flamed within her. She felt like a husk of embers, burned but not consumed, aroused but not satisfied. Hungrily she looked for him—and found him, standing a few feet away from her at an airline check-in desk. The light caught on his obsidian-black hair as he bent his head to hear what the clerk had to say to him. Then he reached out to pick up two tickets and slip them into the pocket of his suit jacket. Above him, the Eastern Airlines departure board listed flights bound for Nassau and Montego Bay, Port-au-Prince and San Juan, Antigua, Barbados and Curaçao, while beside him, a dark-haired woman waited.

As Laurel stood there, the woman kissed Morgan possessively before turning to look straight at Laurel with triumph in her eyes. Morgan, too, turned and saw her, his face blank and incurious. His expression sent an icy stab of pain through Laurel, and she cried out wordlessly, soundlessly against it in her dream. He looked her up and down as if she were a stranger, and she realized she was wearing her wedding dress. Linking arms with the glamorous woman beside him, he strolled off in the direction of the airline gates.

Laurel tried over and over again to call them back, but she had no voice, and they sauntered ever farther away from her. Furiously she tried to run after them, but each step she took was an agonizing effort as she struggled to free her legs from some cold transparent cloud that enveloped them and restricted her to slow motion.

The same cloud seemed to rise and swallow the rest of her up, too, so that she knew she was invisible to Morgan and the dark-haired woman, as well as to everyone else moving calmly through the terminal. Yet she could still see all around her with bitter clarity, until the two figures on which her attention was fixed finally dwindled in front of her and disappeared entirely.

She was alone in this nightmare now, the walls of the airport terminal dissolving around her, melting away into her cloud with all the other irrelevant people as she floundered to an exhausted stop, her whole body leaden from her terrible and futile effort. She could hear her heart pounding ferociously as it battered her chest, seeking escape—could hear her breath rasp in and out. But the sobs that tore their way up from her soul were still soundless. She could feel the hot acid of tears scalding her cheeks, but her eyes were blinded by the miasma that had thickened into a solid gray wall around her. Exhausted, she sank down into oblivion, where her only remaining thought was that she would never see Morgan again.

WHEN SHE DID SEE HIM, on a brilliant day at the beginning of August as she sat in a sidewalk café along the Champs Elysées, watching to see if all the world would pass by, as the old saying claimed, she refused to believe that he was behaving far differently from the way he had been in that nightmare she'd never quite forgotten.

By the time she met Morgan again, six weeks had passed since the wedding. Her session at Cornell was behind her, and with it days full of the excitement of exploring an entirely new subject. She had studied tourism and public relations, hotel accounting and the theories of innkeeping, restaurant planning and food management. Now she was studying fine food and wine, learning more about how to prepare the one and select the other. With the welcome knowledge she'd gained, she'd also lost the strongest and most painful of her memories of Morgan Hamilton. Now she could revel contentedly in the summer sunshine, taking a rare break and idly watching the comings and goings at other small, bright yellow tables around her as she sipped a glass of cool white wine. Then suddenly the glass slipped from her fingers, and wine spilled across the table, soaking her other hand and dripping down onto her lap.

"Ah, *mademoiselle*, such a pity," murmured the attentive waiter who'd been keeping one dark eye on this young woman, who sat alone in spite of the way her hair flamed in the sunlight and her golden eyes sparkled.

Immediately he offered her a napkin to dry her skirt and removed the offending glass, going to fetch a replacement. He was back in a minute to find Laurel mechanically swabbing the tabletop, her eyes wide and fixed on another table at the far side of the

café. Her face had completely lost its delicate color,
and the golden gaze had gone a dull light brown.
Even the sun's aureole had left her hair as a cloud
moved across the sky.

It had been days since she'd last dreamed of Morgan, or thought that every black-haired man she
glimpsed from a distance must be him. But this time
it was, and she was completely unprepared for the
strength of her reaction. True, much of the old anger
had burned out, but her comforting belief that this
meant she had finally got over the disaster of their
brief relationship was stripped away from her in an
instant.

Her body made that very clear. She had always had
an overwhelming physical response to him, and even
now, after so much pain and at such a distance, it
was still true. Even now, her hands shook, her breath
came hurriedly and her heart pounded as if it wanted
to draw his attention from all those feet away.
Clenching her hands together, she fought to control
her body, which craved the fulfillment he had promised and then never provided.

Struggling against the civil war within her, Laurel
fought down a wave of desire that made her want to
rush over and throw herself into Morgan's arms.
After all, she reminded herself urgently, she had last
seen those arms linked around another woman on
their wedding day, when he had made it plain that he
felt no love for—or even loyalty to—his wife.

Her wide eyes finally focused on Morgan's companion, a woman who was as glossy and brittle as a lacquered vase, from the top of her ash-blond head to the toes of her sandals—but wasn't the woman Morgan had been with in the library. She had assumed weeks ago that the woman he'd turned to on his wedding day must have been his real love all along. That way his treatment of his wife hadn't seemed quite as loathsome, but now he had apparently abandoned even her.

The desire that had flamed in her a minute before dwindled to ashes in Laurel, and the taste of ashes seemed to be in her mouth, as well. He might have grown up with every privilege, but he hadn't learned loyalty, any more than honesty or decency. He was utterly faithless, this man she had loved, and she felt shaken with revulsion as fresh anger rose inside her.

Preoccupied with this final disillusionment, Laurel missed seeing Morgan start suddenly, move to stand up, then hesitate and slowly sink back into his seat. Running his long fingers through his black hair, he shook his head as if to clear it. Obviously, it needed clearing. For an instant he'd thought he'd seen Laurel in a woman seated at a table on the far side of the noisy crowded café. The way her long hair caught the sun, the turn of her head, the graceful curve of her body in the yellow chair all looked like Laurel—but then the shifting crowd hid her from sight, and he realized it couldn't possibly be her anyway.

"And, of course, paying me the courtesy of at least

pretending you care about your own mother is a good deal too much to ask.''

The petulant voice cut across his thoughts, and Morgan looked at the woman seated across from him. Even though she had never been any kind of a real mother to him, he still felt obligated to see her whenever he was in Paris. They were never pleasant visits, however, and this one was obviously going to be no exception to the rule.

Now, just reminded of Laurel, he had her image fresh in his mind, and it made the woman across from him stand out in harsh contrast. Although at a distance Vanessa still looked soigné and attractive, under the blond hair, bleached so many times that it was dry and lifeless, was a face that might have been molded from plastic. Thin and tanned, it was carefully tinted at cheeks and lips and eyes, giving it a hard shiny surface. But skillful and time-consuming applications of makeup couldn't conceal the way time had consumed the beauty that had once been there. Time and personality had creased the forehead and pinched the nostrils into a grimace of perpetual dissatisfaction, had drawn deep lines at the corners of her mouth, which drooped in a pout.

Vanessa's thin fingers tapped irritably at the table top, and Morgan said with tired good manners, ''I'm sorry. What was it you were telling me?''

''I was telling you that Raoul is gone. Without so much as warning me, he sold the yacht we'd been living on, and the first thing I knew of it was when the new owner's crew came on board and asked if I would move out. The barbarian! He didn't even have the guts or decency to tell me himself what he was up to. I had to find out about his marriage to that silly little heiress from the society pages.''

"I'm sorry, Vanessa," Morgan repeated mechanically, and at his tone her lips tightened.

"You couldn't care less what I know or don't know!" she contradicted him. "I found out about *your* marriage from the papers, too, because you couldn't be bothered to let me know yourself—much less invite me."

With anyone else, Morgan would have heard loneliness speaking, but Vanessa had driven him away so long ago that now that old pain of his own deafened him to hers. His face remote, he said without inflection, "I've told you how suddenly everything happened."

"Oh, yes," she agreed scornfully, "you told me how sudden it was, but not why it ever was at all! The last time I saw you, you had that Renee in tow, hanging adoringly on your every word and gesture."

He bowed his head in acknowledgement but remained silent, and it was clear he still didn't intend to explain his surprising marriage.

Looking sharply at him, she snapped, "You can stonewall it if you like, Morgan, but I see Adam's hand in this again. Whatever happened, he had something to do with it, just the way he's had something to do with everything that's gone wrong in our lives!"

At her accusing tone, Morgan raised his head to look at her, again with that weary expression she ignored. Rushing on, she dragged out all the old grievances and flung them at him for good measure. "He was behind all the trouble between your father and me—he was against our marriage from the start, and he poisoned Simon against me. And now he's done the same thing with you."

She glared across the table, but her son was impervious to the familiar attack. She altered her approach.

"But he's overreached himself this time, hasn't he? Somehow he got you into that hasty marriage of yours, but it's obviously not working out the way he planned, or you wouldn't be here on your own. Now, what was that fascinating tidbit from the papers someone was telling me about?"

She pretended to search her memory, and Morgan went rigid. She registered that with satisfaction before continuing in the professionally arch tone of a gossip columnist. "Is it true that a certain young hotel tycoon misplaced his own wife on their wedding day? Can it be that the playboy has been played for a fool?"

Picking up the drink in front of her, she sipped it thirstily and gazed at Morgan over the rim of the glass, obviously enjoying having got under his skin at last. But he wasn't even aware of her triumphant gaze; she could still have been speaking for all he noticed. Face hard, he was remembering the column she'd quoted and all the others. He was remembering the murmurs among the guests when the bride vanished. Most of all, he was remembering his own rage and humiliation at the way Laurel had abandoned him.

Against Adam's orders, his fury had driven him out of the house on Beacon Hill, so that he was cut off from his grandfather and from the company. Alone, he had come back to Europe. And for all these weeks here he had fanned that anger, telling himself that the only thing he felt for Laurel was contempt—that, and perhaps dislike. The irritable restlessness he'd known, the surprising dissatisfaction with his old haunts, the loneliness even with old friends—those feelings he attributed to the isolation that this entire marriage fiasco had caused. But a few minutes ago he had thought he'd seen Laurel, and what he'd felt in that instant before the woman disappeared from view had been neither contempt nor dislike.

Suddenly her image rose again in front of him, replacing Vanessa's petulant one, and he saw Laurel in a hundred different moods at a hundred different times. He had barred her from his thoughts for weeks, but here she was more vividly than if the wedding had been only yesterday. He saw her as she raised her face in church before he put the ring on her finger; as she'd looked the night before the wedding when she'd clung to him, drugged with desire before he'd sent her away to her own room; as she'd looked when they dined, danced, talked, laughed in those early weeks of discovery; as she'd looked, ruffled and indignant, when he'd first seen her and side-stepped her businesslike interference on his grandfather's behalf.

Then, he had thought she was just a capable assistant, efficient but otherwise no more remarkable than the office furniture. Frowning in concentration, he remembered he had casually underestimated her beauty. When had he finally realized that her eyes were genuinely gold and set in a feathery fringe of gold-tipped lashes? That her hair was the same color as horse chestnuts on a brilliant fall day? That her fair skin was so fine he could almost see the blood rushing beneath it? And that she moved with a liquid grace that made her smallest gesture ballet? When had he realized how truly beautiful she was? And why hadn't he realized until now—

Vanessa set her empty glass down with a snap that nearly broke it, her myriad bracelets jangling against the table. Morgan had lost the stiff look of irritation. In fact, he seemed to have lost all contact with their conversation, to be off in his earlier abstraction.

"Obviously, the whole marriage is a disaster, and a deplorably public one, as well," she purred provocatively. "Between you, you and Adam have botched the thing completely, haven't you?"

"Mmm," Morgan responded absently, and his very obliviousness goaded her on.

"Well, I for one am glad of it!" she lashed out.

"Do you hear me—glad! You ruined my life, the two of you, and Simon's as well, and I wish to God I'd never laid eyes on any of you Hamiltons! You're a bloody icicle, and Adam is a meddling old prig. Simon was the only halfway decent one of the lot of you, and you killed him!"

Her voice rose shrilly, and on her face the painted colors stood out lividly as she glared at him, trying once more to make him the cause of all her woes. Morgan looked at her with seeing eyes again, and for the first time he could pity her for the misery that made her strike out at him, because she was dimly aware of how hollow her own existence was, but was too spoiled and self-centered to take responsibility for the results. For the first time, too, her bitter accusations didn't have their old ability to sear him with grief and guilt, any more than her example had its old power to keep him from commitments and caring. As he finally realized this, his pity for his mother was swallowed up by something even stronger.

Reaching hastily for his wallet, he put down money for Vanessa's drink and his own unfinished one. Then he rose, unfolding his lean height from the spindly café chair.

"Excuse me, Vanessa," he said as he came to his feet, "but I need to check on the next flight home. I'll see you whenever I'm in Europe again."

"Damn you, don't put yourself to the trouble," she muttered.

For a moment more Morgan looked at his mother with a compassion she had never seen before. Then he strode off, weaving his way among the crowded little tables, almost running into Laurel just as she stood up from her own table.

As startling as it was for them both, she at least had had some warning in the glimpse she'd caught of him earlier—and some chance to conquer her desire for him by whipping up fresh anger and dislike. Now she stepped back, well out of reach of the hands he'd raised automatically to steady her before he even realized who she was. She kept her own hands firmly at her sides.

"Oh, hello, Morgan," she made herself say in a tone of elaborate unconcern.

"Laurel. . . ?"

"The same."

"My God, what are you doing here?"

"Having a drink," she answered matter-of-factly, ignoring the real meaning behind his question. Her response was weak. But in spite of her contempt for him, her impossible heart seemed to have switched to a syncopated rhythm, and thinking of something clever was beyond her.

But he didn't seem to have caught her tone yet; he was still staring at her with those sky-blue eyes. "I was just thinking about you."

"Oh, really?" she asked lightly, sarcastically. "I'm sure I'm flattered."

This time he noted the artificial way she spoke, and

his slashing eyebrows lowered a notch. But then he brushed the impression resolutely away. Moving closer, so that she was forced to sit abruptly back down in her chair to put more distance between them, he spoke rapidly. "As a matter of fact, I was going to find you. I have to talk to you, Laurel...."

She was simply staring at him, so he reached down and gathered her hands into his, holding them as if he were about to pull her up into his arms. "Come with me, please—somewhere quiet and private where we can talk. Whatever went wrong between us doesn't even matter—just come and listen to what I have to say!" The intent warmth in his face warmed even more as he smiled deep into her widening eyes and added softly, "Please come!"

For a moment she let her hands rest in his. For a moment she felt his touch seep into her skin and begin to heat her blood as the old physical alchemy between them began to work again. But that was how she'd let herself love him in the first place, in spite of all the differences in their backgrounds, in spite of all the stories about his past, in spite of all the cautions her mind had tried to whisper to her. That was how she'd let herself in for the hurt of finding him with someone else on their wedding day.

And now he was trying to use that tactic on her again? Violently she wrenched her hands away. "No!"

The word was almost a shout. "Why not?" he asked, the intimate smile fading.

"Because I don't want to!" she exploded, her voice cracking. "I don't want to go anywhere with you. I don't want to talk to you. I don't even want to see you! Why don't you just leave me alone?"

Awkward in her anger, she swept up her purse from where it had slipped off her shoulder to the ground, and didn't see the flash of unfamiliar emotion reflected in his eyes. "Go on back to your new girl friend—" jerking her head violently toward the other side of the café, she spat out the word "—and tell *her* whatever lies you decide to use this time!"

"My girl friend?" he repeated blankly. "For God's sake, I haven't got any girl friend!"

Then, as she stared in the direction she'd indicated, comprehension dawned, and he looked back at her. "Oh, no," he began, disbelief in his tone and expression, "you can't possibly think—"

But with a strangled sound of outrage, Laurel leaped to her feet before he could finish inventing the story that was supposed to reassure and pacify her this time—just the way he'd done that evening at the concert! Even now, when it couldn't possibly matter anymore, he kept trying to blind her with the perilous attraction between them.

"Wait!" he commanded, reaching for her hands a second time. But she shook him off wildly, her breath catching on an unexpected sob, and rushed away, fighting tears she didn't understand. Morgan, going to follow her, found his way blocked by a waiter with a slip of paper; after all, someone had to pay.

"The bill, *m'sieur*," he said, and watched dispassionately as, with a muttered oath, Morgan dragged out his wallet again and flung down some francs. Taking his time, the waiter pocketed them and finally stepped aside.

But by then Laurel had vanished completely, and Morgan was left to sink heavily into the chair she'd left, his dark face growing slowly darker as he relived the past few minutes.

CHAPTER SIX

IT WAS NEARLY A MONTH LATER and toward the end of summer when Laurel came back to the Mountain View Inn, winging home to a place she longed to see and people she was eager to greet. The inn—how would it look, she wondered as the miles between Boston and Fryeburg rolled away beneath her wheels. And Abby—Nate, too. Would they be as glad to see her as she would be to see them? Rounding an all too familiar curve, she tensed reflexively, but found no battered orange Volvo darting out into the path of destruction. This time, anyway, she'd be able to say hello to Giles without so terrifying an introduction!

She willed her hands to relax their anxious grasp on the steering wheel and gazed around her as she came close to the border between New Hampshire and Maine. Through a broad valley, the course of the Saco River was marked by a meandering line of trees growing along its banks. In the distance, the White Mountains reached up unhindered to a clear sky, at this time of year not white, but darker blue on light. Looking past pines and birches to the graceful

lumps, worn smooth by ages of ice and erosion
Laurel experienced a sense of kinship and homecom-
ing that had nothing whatsoever to do with birth-
place. Missouri was her family and her past, but
Maine, she promised herself, was going to be her
future.

Pulling up at last in the driveway of the inn, she
parked beside the newly painted Mountain View Inn
sign and stepped out, turning eagerly to look at the
changes that had been made since she was last here.
A new roof of shingles gleamed in the sun, the wood
still light and unweathered. Below that, fresh white
paint shone on the clapboards, and new leaf-green
shutters edged every window. The driveway where
she stood had been freshly graveled, too, and the
barn opened up, braced and cleared out so that cars
could be parked in the old horse stalls.

Delighted, Laurel gazed around her. It looked so
good! For a ridiculous moment tears stung her eyelids while she rejoiced to see the old inn made young
again. Some things really could be restored.... A
moment later the mist in her eyes vanished, as did her
thoughtful mood and the inn's air of tranquillity.

There was a shout from a front window of the old
building. Then the door burst open, and Abby and
Nate rushed out to meet her. Nate, longer legged, arrived first, his face rather less impassive than usual.
Only two steps after him puffed Abby, speaking
breathlessly before she even reached Laurel's side.

"Laurel, child, you're early! We'd meant to have

everything tidied up for you, but Mr. Hamilton sent word you wouldn't be here until tomorrow—''

"I'm sorry about catching you off guard," Laurel said with a laugh, taking Abby's round body in her arms for a hug, "but I couldn't stay away any longer! I'd had a good visit home and checked in with granda—Mr. Hamilton—and I had to come see how you were doing."

Kissing Abby soundly, she added, "And you've obviously been working miracles! The place looks marvelous."

"It does, doesn't it?" Abby admitted, returning the embrace and trying unsuccessfully to conceal her pride.

Even Nate suddenly chimed in, "Yep—looks right nice."

Laurel couldn't help glancing at him in surprise— this was the longest sentence she had ever heard him volunteer, and without an equivocal "eyah"—and Abby caught the look.

Twinkling at Nate, she explained to Laurel, "He's just relieved it didn't end up all glass and chrome! It turned out he'd had some addled fear that was what would happen when the Hamilton chain bought it."

A dull red seeped up into Nate's leathery cheeks, and he looked sheepish while Abby teased gently, "It took him a while to realize you don't get to *be* a big hotel chain by making mistakes like that! A glossy place along those lines would have been all wrong here."

The sheepish expression on Nate's face deepened, but he stood his ground and met Laurel's smile with a slight one of his own that could almost be described as friendly.

Nevertheless, he managed to think of some job that took him away a minute later, leaving the two women to stroll into the kitchen and fix themselves a pot of coffee, Abby proudly demonstrating the new institutional-size stove that had been installed.

"There, now," she concluded proudly, "isn't that more like it?"

"Oh, I don't know," Laurel teased, remembering its late and unlamented predecessor. "It doesn't seem anywhere near as challenging as the old wood stove!"

Abby gave her a mock ferocious scowl before she commanded, "Now tell me all about the exotic things we're going to be cooking here. In fact, tell me all about *everything*—Cornell and Paris—everything!"

Smiling, Laurel obeyed. There was only one thing she didn't tell her.... When she'd finished, she looked around her again and added, "But it's so good to be home! Oh, Abby, everything really does look absolutely wonderful, and I can't imagine any better welcome back!"

"We meant it to be a good deal more dignified. We were going to be out there waiting to greet you in our best bibs and tuckers," Abby allowed a shade regretfully, "but otherwise things were pretty much on schedule when Nate and I took stock this morning.

We'd been wanting to have all the major jobs finished before you got back, and I think we made it. You saw the roofing and painting, and Nate says the wiring, plumbing and heating are all set now, ready to handle guests whenever you're ready to have them.''

She paused on an inquiring note, and Laurel answered, ''I don't know for sure, Abby, but I'd like to be open by Thanksgiving, since that's the bargain I originally made with—''

Abby had set her coffee cup down, and now she looked keenly across the table. ''Granda,'' she finished Laurel's sentence, and then waited.

At first Laurel didn't respond, just gazed at Abby blankly.

''You said it outside just now, child,'' Abby explained, ''and then corrected yourself to 'Mr. Hamilton.' I couldn't help but wonder about it.''

The uncomfortable look in Laurel's eyes didn't fade. She had never meant to tell Abby the whole long story of how she came to be sent up here for the Hamilton Corporation; it was something she preferred to think of as rarely as possible. Irresistibly, the picture of Morgan as she'd last seen him in Paris flashed through her mind, and she shook her head slightly to drive it away.

''Never mind, Laurel,'' Abby said hastily. ''It's none of my business anyway. As well as talking too much, I must have started getting nosy besides.''

There was a harsh self-critical note in Abby's

pleasant voice that Laurel had never heard before, and it cut through her own abstraction. Laying a hand on the other woman's arm, she said, "You could never talk too much for me—I like to hear you. And you're not being nosy to wonder what someone my age is doing being put in charge of a whole inn. After all, you're involved in everything here at least as much as I am, and you have a right to know."

She paused, and Abby shook her head as a disclaimer, opening her mouth to say something, but Laurel went on, "I guess I just didn't tell you and Nate before because I wasn't ready to tell anyone. But it's all right now."

Taking a deep breath, she said without inflection, "Adam Hamilton is my grandfather by marriage, as well as my employer before that. When my marriage broke up on our wedding day, he sent me up here because he understood how badly I wanted to get away and lose myself in something that would take up all my time and energy."

Laurel was beginning to look tense for all her efforts to seem unemotional. A wild-rose color was seeping into her face, framed now by a mop of short silky curls. Setting her own hand on top of Laurel's, Abby clasped the cool fingers.

Then with a last pat and deliberate change of subject, she said, "Well, child, it certainly has done that so far—and I don't think there's any end in sight! We seem to have things generally in working order, but there's hardly a stick of furniture in the place. Now, what do you want to do about that?''

The red herring worked. In a few minutes Laurel was deep in discussion on the possibilities for refurnishing the inn. They decided that the most logical—as well as the most fun—way to make the inn look as it once had, was to try to find old furniture to replace what had been lost or sold or ruined. And that, of course, could best be done at auctions and antique shops. Getting approval from company headquarters in Boston, they set out enthusiastically to scour the area.

For the guest rooms they found a wonderful assortment of beds, so that each room's furnishings would be unique—a heavy old brass bed, several Jenny Lind beds with their turned wooden spool frames, four-posters and two antique field beds with high arched canopies—and also Windsor chairs, blanket chests, lowboys, a tallboy, and even a huge old Dutch *kas* with drawers and hanging space for the one room whose large closet had been turned into a private bathroom. For the parlor, they collected a Victorian rosewood sofa and matching chairs with velvet upholstery and ornate carving, along with a tea table and a pair of china dogs to guard the hearth. A massive grandfather clock with Whittington chimes was the finishing touch for that room. Low wooden settles with thick cushions, deep comfortable wing chairs, a cobbler's bench, a wide trestle table and a corner cabinet furnished the living room.

Over the next few weeks, each discovery was hauled home triumphantly. Once at the inn, every piece was unloaded by Nate with the requisite expression of long-suffering skepticism, followed by a good deal of grunting as he lugged it into the barn. Then Abby and Laurel would take over again, cleaning and polishing or sometimes even refinishing. And in spite of Nate's avowed disinterest in the whole project, whenever small repairs were needed somehow they were made, although he never let the women catch him working on a piece of furniture.

Abby and Laurel certainly worked, though, on the days they stayed at the inn. Whenever Abby wasn't making lists of the lamps and dining-room furniture they'd need, or the bed, bath and table linens, the kitchen equipment and staples, the curtains, carpets and even cleaning supplies, then she was out in the barn, shining old chairs to a soft patina—or dragging herself home to collapse. And whenever Laurel wasn't wading through order forms, licensing and logistics, permits and publicity photos, using the company channels Adam had set up for her, then she was in the barn, too, learning how to restore old wood that had been neglected for years—or hauling herself upstairs to drop into her own four-poster for a few hours of exhausted dreamless sleep. Or she was out with Giles.

He reappeared three days after Laurel came home to the inn and tracked her down in the barn, where she was using a solvent to strip layers of discolored shellac off a beautiful cherry corner cupboard, the first treasure she and Abby had bought. Dressed in faded jeans with her sleeves rolled up, she was wearing huge pink rubber gloves and scrubbing the old finish off the wood with steel wool, when he spoke behind her.

"Aha! Just as I predicted," he said triumphantly, and she spun around to find him surveying her with his arms crossed on his broad chest and one of those mobile eyebrows raised consideringly. "You make a charming inn renovator."

He appraised the smudge of sawdust on her cheek, the narrow braided headband keeping her curls out of her eyes and the way those eyes, pure gold now, sparkled at him, while she smiled back in welcome and amusement at having him pick up in the middle of their first conversation, as though it had happened only hours before, instead of more than two months.

"Giles! I didn't hear you come."

"That, my girl," he said loftily, "is because I walked up from the lake instead of driving that infernal machine of mine."

Then his tone changed abruptly. "And by the way, speaking of infernal—" he caught sight of a young cocker spaniel, lying contentedly at her feet and gnawing at something she hadn't wanted to look at too closely, in case it really was one of her good shoes "—isn't that Nate's and Abby's pup, the one who wandered down the hill to pay me a call last week and ate the entire second trumpet part of my symphony?"

Laurel acknowledged his accusation with a guilty grimace. "I'm afraid he must be the same one, but he seems to be mine now—although he wasn't last week!"

Giles snorted at her hasty disclaimer, and she explained, "He's adopted me, and Abby says she's delighted to get him off her hands. But he's keeping me so busy just apologizing for the mischief he's caused since I got him that I'd rather not answer for whatever else he was into before then! But did he really ruin it completely, Giles?"

"You could certainly say so," he answered disgustedly. "Most of the parts are already difficult enough to play without asking a musician to read one off seventy-seven irregularly shaped scraps of paper, each and every one of which is embossed with tooth marks and muddy paw prints."

"Oh," Laurel said in a small voice, and Limb—for Limb of Satan, Abby claimed—looked up at her changed tone. Finding Giles scowling fiercely at him, he dropped the anonymous item he'd been chewing on and came over to jump up and put his paws on Giles's leg, panting confidingly, while Laurel gazed at the composer in wide-eyed apology.

Faced with all that charm, Giles held out for only a moment, then ruffled the spaniel's silky ears, meeting Laurel's appeal with a reluctant grin. "Luckily, that wasn't the only copy in existence," he conceded, "and I wouldn't have been so appalled if this beast had been a music critic. After all, you expect them to make mincemeat out of most of your work!''

Relieved at his change of mood, Laurel suggested tentatively, ''Maybe this is an omen, anyway, that the public will find your symphony as much to its taste as the puppy did?''

For an instant Giles just looked at her. Then all pretense of anger dropped away and he shouted with laughter, while Laurel grinned sympathetically, feeling pleased with herself for wiling away his annoyance.

There was no doubt that he was pleased with her, too. When he had sobered slightly, he reached out and took her steel-wool pad, tossing it away and peeling off her rubber gloves. ''For that superb vote of confidence, my girl,'' he said with a chuckle, ''today I'll not only forgive that teenage hellhound of yours for anything, but also reward you both by inviting you down to the lake for a swim. Set aside your toils and come play in the water.''

Briefly she looked at her steel wool. She really ought to finish up the cupboard now that she'd started, but Giles was bowing her out of the barn with his usual flourish.... Less then five minutes later, Laurel had a towel and bathing suit in hand and was setting off down toward the lake with Giles, Limb racing ecstatically ahead of them.

The path to the lake passed below the inn, down the dirt road that Laurel had noticed her first morning here, months ago. But she had never followed it until now, and as it wandered through the back field and down into a green tunnel of trees, she felt as though she were stepping into some magic kingdom. Here under the trees the air was cool and slightly damp, scented with a blend of spicy pine needles and rich leaf mold. The sun slanted down into the woods on both sides of the road, dappling patterns of gold and green and brown. Invisible birds called overhead, and below them one very visible squirrel sat on a branch right by the road and watched them with bright eyes and twitching tail, announcing to the world what he thought of people who brought dogs into the forest. His displeasure didn't keep Limb from crashing happily through the undergrowth, though.

Eventually they left the irate squirrel behind, and the dog's rustling faded off ahead of them. The only other sounds Laurel heard were an occasional insect and the crunching of small stones under their feet. Hands in his pockets, Giles strolled beside her in silence, content for now to let the woods speak for themselves and watch Laurel's expressive face as she listened.

Half a mile below the inn, the road suddenly became much steeper, so that she had to watch her step. Then all at once she was in sunshine and on level ground again, and raising her eyes, she saw the lake up close for the first time. The water, lapping gently at a sandy shore that shelved off into small pebbles, was so clear that four feet out she could easily see the flicker of tiny translucent minnows. Farther still the water slowly changed to golden green and then deepened into blue, crested with a few small whitecaps. She saw a bay dotted with islands, most of which seemed, at this distance, to be made up of clusters of rock and a pine tree or two. On the far shore, granite ledges cascaded down, dropping twenty or thirty feet into the lake like petrified waterfalls. Atop them stood birches and more pines, and she could just glimpse a few wooden roofs, indicating cabins nestled, nearly invisible under the trees. The smooth slopes of the mountains rose behind and above the entire scene, dark green by the lake and misty blue in the distance.

"Oh, Giles," Laurel breathed, entranced.

"Oh, Laurel," he teased gently. "I gather our lake meets with your approval."

Dropping her towel and suit, she shook her head at the understatement and marveled, "How can it be so beautiful?"

She hadn't really expected any response, but Giles moved forward to stand beside her at the water's edge and said, with none of his usual foolery, "I don't know." Looking out over the bay, he added quietly, "I've been coming here ever since I was a child, trying to figure that out so I could capture it in music. But I don't think I've got the answer yet."

He hunched his wide shoulders in unaccustomed frustration. But then the puppy abruptly reappeared, his fur soaked, his tongue lolling happily. Loping over to them, he reached up to poke his nose against Laurel's hand and then spraddled all fours and shook himself energetically. The shouts that greeted him didn't deter him a bit. When he was finally done, he moved away to roll in the sand.

Sputtering indignantly, Laurel mopped herself off and glanced up to find Giles doing the same. Catching her eye, he asked thoughtfully, "Did I say I'd forgive that beast of yours for anything today?"

At her nod, he added with a lugubrious shake of his head, "I was afraid you'd remember that. Worse yet, he obviously remembers it, too." Giving the dog a jaundiced stare, he inquired on a faint note of hope, "But then maybe he just figures he'll get it all out of his system today while he's guaranteed amnesty?"

Laurel tried to look encouraging—and failed miserably. Three days' acquaintance with Limb had already been more than enough to convince her that he wasn't going to mend his ways in any hurry, and certainly not by tomorrow, when Giles's rash promise wouldn't be binding anymore. Sensing her dilemma, Giles laughed infectiously, and she joined in.

"Oh, well," he finally commented, "now that we've both had a bath, let's go for a swim. Come on over to the boathouse and change."

Scooping up her suit and towel, he tossed them to her and led the way to an old weathered building she hadn't noticed. Crouched under the trees, it actually reached out into the lake, standing in water up to its stone knees at the front while anchored to shore at the back. Inside, on the lower level, a space big enough for two large boats housed only a dented aluminum canoe now. A flight of wooden steps led to two bedrooms, a bath, a galley kitchen and a big airy room that served as both living room and studio—especially the latter.

It had huge west-facing windows and walls of beautiful natural pine, but almost nothing else was visible because of the enormous concert grand piano that stood majestically in the center of the room and books, old programs, photographs, recordings, stereo and tape equipment scattered everywhere. Music, sheets of it, printed or in manuscript, perched in untidy stacks all over the desk in the far corner, draped over the arms of the battered sofa and leaned against the wall behind the table. A few crumpled refugees lay near the impressively big wood stove. One even lurched out drunkenly from behind the picture frame that pinned it to the wall.

Laurel gazed at it all with wide eyes and a dawning smile. Somehow this was just the sort of place she would have imagined for Giles!

"What a fascinating room," she offered diplomatically, turning to where Giles stood in the doorway, looking around him.

Catching her smile, he returned it with a sheepish one of his own. "I was going to say 'welcome to my kingdom,' but it comes to my attention that this place looks as though a civil war's been happening here," he admitted. "Oh, well, that far bedroom is behind the lines, so you can go there to change in safety."

When she reappeared a few minutes later, he was sitting at the piano in nothing but faded cutoffs, looking more than ever like an amiable bear, idly picking out a wisp of melody. Laurel was wearing the minute bikini she'd bought in a defiant mood in the south of France as part of a deliberate effort to change the self Morgan Hamilton had known. It consisted of two tiny scraps of orange fabric.

Padding back to the studio, she wondered what Giles would think of a suit that might be more appropriate in Monaco than Maine and resisted an urge to wrap her towel around her. But when he looked up and saw her in the doorway, a tall slim woman with russet hair and fair skin flooded with color, his reaction was perfect. Pursing his lips in soundless admiration, he let his fingers ripple out a perfect wolf whistle on the piano keys. Then, eyebrows wiggling, he gave her such an exaggerated leer that she dissolved into laughter, threw her towel at him and was forced to race to the water with him in hot pursuit.

They played in the lake all the rest of that afternoon, the first of many scattered ones, as summer lingered into September, when Giles would appear at the inn looking for company as a break from the solitude of his composing.

At first redheaded Peggy Martin joined them, and the three of them swam in the bay, explored by canoe as far as the beaver dam in one of the inlets, picnicked on an assortment of rocky islands and searched for arrowheads in low green fields, where the coastal Indians used to have their summer encampments. But gradually Laurel became aware of a tension building between them, in spite of the friendship and fun, laughter and teasing—or maybe because of those things. Slowly she began to realize that Peggy's mobile heart-shaped face grew tight by the end of each outing. Finally, one afternoon, she recognized why.

They'd taken Giles's old canoe down the lake, idly exploring along the shore, and by the time they were within sight of the boathouse again, they were all sunburned and tired. Even Giles had lost his usual nonsensical flair. Laying his paddle sideways across the stern of the canoe, he announced, "All right, that's it—the rear engine of this thing is out of steam. If you two want to get the rest of the way home, you're going to have to stop being idle figureheads and supply a little motivating force." And with that ultimatum, he folded his arms across his chest, shut his eyes and dropped his chin, evidently for a nap.

Glancing over one pink shoulder from her position in the forward seat, Laurel found Peggy, seated in the middle between her and Giles, daydreaming, her hands dangling over both sides so that her fingers could dabble in the cool water. Feeling Laurel's eyes on her, she looked up and managed a faint smile. It turned into a genuine grin as she watched Laurel pick up her own unused paddle, dip it in the water and reach back to let it drip on Giles's bent head.

He didn't react at all. The droplets simply slipped down his hair and ran into his beard, so Laurel dipped the paddle again while Peggy scooped up water in both hands and started flicking it at him.

To their disappointment, he ignored them until he was nearly soaked. Suddenly opening his eyes then, he roared, "Aha! So it's rain instead of work you're wanting!" and used his own paddle to shoot a tidal wave in on them. Laughing and sputtering, they both responded in kind, and in a minute all three were soaked.

The silly water fight could have gone on, but both Laurel and Peggy stopped when Giles paused, holding himself perfectly still, his paddle raised. The women traded curious glances. When he had their attention, he slowly lowered the paddle and his eyebrows as well. Staring fixedly at Laurel, he growled threateningly, "And now as punishment for that bit of insubordination, *you* had better paddle so fast your end gets home before I catch up with you! And *you*—" he shifted his gaze to Peggy "—had better put on your water wings, infant, before I throw you overboard!"

But Peggy, instead of laughing or pretending to obey or even giving him another splash, just stared back at him while her own face went still. Then suddenly she leaped to her feet and dived over the side, and the canoe, rocking from her first move, capsized at her second.

It didn't matter all that much to Laurel and Giles, of course. The canoe had already been nearly swamped, and they were easily able to push it to shore to right it. But all the while they were doing it, Peggy was swimming home, and by the time they beached the canoe she'd vanished.

"What on earth—" Giles began, but gave up on the question, leaving Laurel with an uncharacteristically subdued goodbye.

Laurel could have answered him, though. Walking back to the inn, she recognized what he'd missed— that what had set Peggy off was the contrast in the way he treated the two of them. Even though he was only teasing, he'd threatened her but talked down to Peggy.

In fact, come to think of it, that was the way he always treated them both. Frowning a little, Laurel realized that she escaped entirely from the avuncular sort of teasing he offered Peggy. Yet he never seemed to notice the way it bothered the younger woman— not today, not the first day that Laurel met them both, when she'd seen the blend of irritation and adoration on Peggy's face, and not any of the other times they'd all been together.

After that afternoon, they were all together a good deal less. When Peggy joined them, Laurel tried to bracket herself and the younger girl, so that Giles would treat them equally, but her efforts didn't seem to have any effect. The problem wasn't anything she could ask him about directly, either. She couldn't think of anything to do, and Peggy began to use the end-of-September flurry at the camp where she was music counselor as an excuse not to go on outings with the other two. More often than not, then, Laurel and Giles were on their own.

Wherever they went, whatever they did, he was absurd, flamboyant, unpredictable. And perhaps he was also more observant than Laurel knew—at least with her—because he offered her the kind of undemanding friendship that combined with time and work to make Morgan Hamilton seem remote and unreal.

Even so, the scars from her brief marriage hadn't healed as well as she thought, and she and Giles both found that out on the last humid cloudy afternoon of the year. They'd been out walking, climbing the fire tower on a nearby hill, so that Laurel could get a bird's-eye view of the lake. As they headed back to the water for a swim to cool off, Giles told her the saga of his very first date, when as a nervous teenager he had taken a girl up that same hill "to look at the stars," and his so-called friends had scared them both into running for their lives by making bear noises in the woods.

Whatever terror and embarrassment he might have felt then, he told the story now with a wry self-mockery that had Laurel speechless with laughter by the time they reached the last steep stretch of road. Her gold eyes, dancing with amusement, were fixed on his as he looked back to talk to her. She was paying scant attention to the placement of her feet and suddenly they shot out from under her. With only a startled yelp for warning, she slid forward in the gravel on the seat of her jeans until she collided with Giles and knocked him off his feet, too, so that they skidded on down together.

Finally coming to a stop another three or four feet along the track, they were tangled together in a jumble of flailing arms and legs. Laurel didn't help much, either, by continuing to laugh instead of trying to extricate herself. Giving up, too, Giles looked at the flushed and beautiful face so near his. Without warning, he leaned closer still and kissed her.

Her laughter was cut off by his lips, and instantly all thought of laughing fled. Utterly still in astonishment, she simply received his kiss at first, her own lips barely parted, her cheeks brushed by the softness of his beard. The embrace continued, and Laurel gave herself up mindlessly to the warmth and pleasure of the moment, beginning to respond instinctively. Her eyes closed. One hand slipped behind his head to rest in the springy hair at the nape of his neck. Her lips opened beneath his, and they savored each other's nearness. He was a friend and companion, and she hadn't kissed anyone—

Then, appallingly, the man who held her was no longer Giles, but Morgan. She wasn't sprawled on a sunbaked dirt road in Maine, but lying beside Morgan on a deep pillowy sofa in Boston. It wasn't September but June, the night before their wedding, and she was imploring him not to send her away to bed alone, to let her stay with him. Her reason, her thoughts, her scruples were forgotten. The only thing that mattered was the magic he was working on her body. His tantalizing mouth and hands were arousing her until she seemed to be filled with rivers of fire. Awash in the flood, she lay quivering in his arms, aching for release from the throbbing desire that racked her. She couldn't bear this sweet torment until the wedding—the wedding, and a bitter torment.

With a strangled cry she wrenched her lips away from Giles's and yanked her tangled legs free, leaping wildly to her feet to run so far and fast that she would finally outdistance her body's memory of Morgan's touch. But at her first frantic step, she landed in a deep narrow gully that the rainwater had washed in the road, her ankle twisted under her weight. She collapsed as agony shot up her leg, exploded in a shower of light and left only darkness.

When she came to, her first fuzzy thought was that she was lying on something much softer than the road. Whatever was supporting her had lumps of its own, but they were flexible lumps, not gravel and pebbles. Cautious without knowing why, she turned her head only an inch and discovered faded plaid fabric on this thing, a sofa, and heard papers rustle faintly at her movement.

Still not certain where she was but not unduly curious, either, she looked beyond the edge of the sofa to the oversize windows close by. Outside, heavy clouds rushed across a darkening sky struck by a lightning glow—gray on somber gray propelled by a northeast wind. Rain slanted down into the lake, water striking water like a thousand tiny hammers beating pewter into form. It wasn't raining here. She was dry, but she felt as if those hammers had beaten her, too, and becoming aware of discomfort, she stirred in protest.

The action sent a wave of pain up her left leg, tearing away the last anesthetizing remnants of confusion, so that she moaned softly to herself. At the sound, a man in the shadows, bent over the piano and picking out muted melodies on its keys, raised his head and looked over at her, then straightened and came closer, materializing into Giles as he sat down on a stool by the sofa.

"How do you feel?" he asked quietly.

"Awful," she whispered. "What happened?"

One eyebrow quirked, and he said, "I was going to ask you the same thing, but you can go first. You stepped into a hole and twisted your ankle, then fainted with the pain. I've got it strapped up and I think it's only a bad sprain, but we can have it X-rayed over at the hospital in Bridgton tomorrow."

Having answered her question, he waited for her answer to his. Silence fell between them while memory reluctantly awakened in Laurel. It all came crashing back—the kiss, Morgan, her fall. Her eyes darkened, and she turned her head restlessly from side to side.

"I'm sorry," she said thickly.

"So am I," he returned. "I can't help thinking all this had something to do with my kissing you."

"It wasn't really that—"

"I hope not! Women haven't always welcomed my advances, but this would be the first time anyone's actually hurt herself trying to escape my clutches." He spoke in a gently teasing tone, and she tried to respond to it. But her smile flickered and vanished almost before it appeared.

"It wasn't you. It was me," she managed. He didn't say anything more, just waited in case she wanted to go on.

She didn't really, but somehow she felt obliged to explain to Giles why what had happened wasn't his fault. He was a dear friend, and he deserved an explanation. His silence was receptive.

"Kissing you reminded me of kissing someone else," she finally said abruptly, then realized how unflattering that sounded. "I'm sorry," she repeated.

"Don't be. My dear girl," he assured her with a trace of amusement in his deep voice, "that's one of the few things I'm not egotistical about. Everyone has to love my music, of course, but not everyone has to love me."

"I do, but not—" She broke off, and after a longer pause she backtracked with difficulty. "It made me think of my husband."

His surprise was evident in his expression, but he just murmured an encouraging, "Oh?"

Taking a deep breath, she brought it all out. "We were married the day before I met you on the road, and at the wedding reception I found him making love to someone else."

Her voice had gone flat, and as she finished Giles recalled, half to himself, "Then you *were* wearing a wedding ring when I first met you."

"Yes."

"But not the next day."

"No." The monosyllable said everything, and his fingers moved to touch hers in warm sympathy.

"Laurel, I'm sorry," he said quietly.

"Thank you." Her voice broke on the reply, and eyes closed, she turned away. He sat back on the stool. At its protesting squeak, she opened her eyes again and looked back at him. "There's another thing I'm sorry about," she added, and in spite of the pain shooting up from her ankle her voice was under control now. "I didn't mean to alarm you with a performance like that."

He smiled slightly at her attempt to return to the present. With an uncharacteristic sigh he stood up and turned to stand looking out the windows at the pouring rain. For a time the only sound was its muffled patter. Then, with the ghost of a rueful laugh, he turned back into the shadowy room. His broad shoulders silhouetted against the racing clouds outdoors, his face only a pale gleam, he said, "We're a fine pair, my girl, you and I."

At her questioning look, he tucked his hands in his

pockets and answered, "Kissing you reminded me of someone else, too. It made me think of the only time I ever kissed Peggy. She was sixteen years old, and she was so shocked she slapped my dirty old man's face and flounced away."

A twisted smile crossed his lips and faded, and Laurel, drawn out of herself as he might have meant her to be, carefully pushed herself up from the cushions so that she could see him more clearly. "Peggy?" she repeated.

"Peggy." His hands still in his pockets, he wandered slowly around the room as he continued. "Although it's crossed my mind once or twice to complicate our lives by falling in love with you, too—" with Peggy's vivid face in her mind's eye, Laurel made an instinctive negative gesture, and he shook his head slightly, going on "—I've loved her for years."

The last word brought him near Laurel again, and he dropped back down onto the stool, his hands clasped loosely between his knees. "That single kiss happened one day when I got tired of waiting for her to grow up," he explained with a shrug, "and it was such a disaster that I had to go back to waiting."

"But she isn't sixteen anymore," Laurel protested, remembering the expression on Peggy's face when she'd looked at Giles that night they'd all met.

"Granted, but she isn't thirty, either, and I am."

"Can't you tell her anyway?"

"No," he returned with quiet firmness. "She's got to have a chance to look around a bit before she ties herself down for life to someone eleven years older."

The shadows fell across his face again, but Laurel didn't need more light to see his expression. In it love blended with a stubborn generosity that meant he would risk his own happiness to make sure Peggy came to him only when and if she was ready. In the meantime he'd only hope and wait for love to come, while Laurel waited for it to go.

Struggling into a sitting position, she shook her head and asked regretfully, "Oh, Giles, now what are we going to do?"

Coming to sit beside her on the sofa, he slung a long arm around her shoulders, and they both looked out the window into the stormy world beyond. "Wait," he confirmed quietly. "I can't think of anything else *to* do."

Neither could she, so they sat there in silence, lost in their own thoughts and watching the raindrops slide down the glass until it was finally too dark to see even those.

CHAPTER SEVEN

FINALLY THE INN WAS READY for visitors. Laurel was off her crutches now, no longer limping on her sprained ankle. It was early October, but since she'd promised Adam that the inn would be habitable by Thanksgiving, she was well ahead of schedule. It had received plenty of advance publicity, too. Hamilton company spokesmen had appeared on travel shows, and advertising brochures had been liberally distributed.

It was a practically perfect time to open. The autumn leaves were at their best, and every major road brought more travelers on color tours. In the last few days before the opening, Laurel watched them pass by with understanding eyes. Each morning she awakened to a world that was more beautiful than the day before. Bounded by the blue of lake and mountains, the birches and elms, beeches and poplar trees had turned a hundred different shades of saffron, amber, maize, copper, russet and sepia. Along the roadsides, fallen leaves drifted like fragments of summer sunshine, broken by the first frost. And best of all, around the inn the sugar maples kindled slowly until they were like towering torches, flaming against a perfect autumn sky.

The night before their first guests were to arrive, Laurel and Abby walked one last time through the rooms. As they went, they occasionally caught each other's eye and smiled, but otherwise Laurel was still wrapped up in last-minute planning, and even Abby was uncharacteristically silent. One by one they checked the seven guest rooms, one with its own bath and the others sharing the two remaining oversize bathrooms. In each room soft floral patterns and the patina of mellow old wood combined to create an atmosphere of warmth and welcome. Downstairs, too, beautiful antiques, gay braided rugs and faded hunting prints gave the inn a timeless quality of repose. Gracing the narrow table in the hall was a magnificent arrangement of asters and chrysanthemums that Adam had sent to celebrate the inn's opening and add the finishing touch to its decor. Finally ending their inspection at the foot of the stairs in the broad front hall, the two women let the total effect seep into them, looking at each other again with satisfied eyes.

"You did it, child," Abby said softly, "and Nate and I couldn't possibly tell you how pleased and proud we are."

"We all did it," Laurel corrected her, and broke the tranquil mood when she swooped Abby into a bear hug and twirled her exuberantly around the hall. "Oh, Abby, I'm so *glad*!" she caroled, her eyes dancing as much as her feet.

Caught off guard, Abby squeaked a protest at this undignified behavior, then gave up and turned Laurel's impromptu dance into a polka. Twice they charged back and forth along the hall before they collapsed by mutual consent on the lowest step and sat there catching their breath, while Limb slunk out from under a nearby chair when he was sure their insanity was safely over.

Breathlessly Laurel laughed at the startled dog, fondling his long silky ears, and Abby panted, "Well, child, now that we've managed to shock even that disreputable dog, I'm going to go collect Nate and be off home—at least, as soon as I have enough air to get that far."

She patted back one brilliantly white lock that contrasted sharply with the rest of her black hair and tried to look responsible and proper again. She wasn't particularly successful, red cheeked and puffing as she was, but she did give Laurel a stern look and say, "And you take yourself to bed, too. Starting life as an innkeeper tomorrow is probably going to take plenty of energy, so see that you have it." Laurel grinned at these maternal noises, but when Abby and Nate had left, she did in fact go to bed after only one more tour through the inn.

When her first guests arrived the following day, they were housed and fed and entertained as if the inn had been open for years, instead of only hours.

Over the next weeks the early trickle of guests turned into a steady stream, and even when the fall colors faded, travelers kept finding their way there, attracted by its growing reputation for comfort and elegance. The inn was full as often as not. The townspeople came to its restaurant, too, with family or out-of-town company, to celebrate birthdays or anniversaries and eat the meals Laurel and Abby prepared with the help of Betsy, Nate's quiet niece from the village.

Giles often dropped by in the evenings when he wasn't busy with a rehearsal or working on a new project, and even Peggy came frequently, although always by herself, as if she was determined to meet new people. Her leggy figure and bright hair were a familiar sight, and one Laurel always made note of, even though she also noticed how little time the young woman was spending anywhere near Giles these days. Laurel occasionally wished she could have fallen in love with him herself. Yet at other times, exasperated, she considered locking him and Peggy up somewhere and leaving them until they worked out their feelings for each other!

In spite of her concern for them both, though, Laurel loved running the inn—loved greeting her guests and making them welcome, cooking for them and seeing that they were comfortable. Most of all she enjoyed meeting an endless variety of people: salesmen, businesswomen and foreign tourists, travel agents and government officials, retired couples and younger ones on runaway weekends without their children.

But the guest who appeared in mid-November didn't fit into any of the categories Laurel was now used to. She was seated at her wide reception desk in the hall one blustery afternoon when the outer door opened and someone blew in. Busy finishing a column of figures, she didn't look up immediately, so that when she did raise her eyes, the woman who had come in was already in front of the desk, pulling off her driving gloves and slipping her fur coat off her shoulders. Then she lifted one beringed hand to smooth her windblown hair impatiently from her face, and Laurel recognized that face. She recognized the woman she had last seen with her husband in the library of the house on Beacon Hill.

"Good afternoon," an appallingly familiar accented voice was saying. "My name is Renee de Beaumont, and you have a reservation for me, *non*?"

Laurel choked down an overwhelming desire to shriek, "No!" The present faded away, and she sat rigid in her chair, feeling again the shattering disillusionment of that moment when she'd first heard this woman invite Morgan to betray his new wife. Face to face with the one woman in the world she had cause to hate, Laurel was flooded with primitive emotions.

But the woman in front of her apparently did not sense her resentment. She might have attended Laurel's wedding, but now she showed no reaction to Laurel's face. Her eyes, cold and rather bored, sharpened for an instant when the young woman first looked up, but then recognition seemed to elude her, and she missed the connection between Morgan's vanishing bride, who had worn her long hair in a smooth coronet, and this innkeeper with a jumble of short feathery curls. Brushing away the faint sense of familiarity with a shake of her head, she looked down her nose at Laurel. Obviously, to her this girl at the desk was simply a hireling, and one who ought to be serving her more quickly.

"Well?" she demanded imperiously, her voice losing its throatiness. Renee was snapping her driving gloves against one palm, and Laurel realized she'd been staring.

"Yes," she said tightly, trying to conquer instinct with training, "of course we have your reservation."

Renee de Beaumont nodded in a hard little gesture of satisfaction, and Laurel turned the register around to her. "If you'll just sign here...."

While Renee wrote in angular black letters, Laurel kept her eyes averted from the other woman's face, her mind racing madly, her thoughts barely coherent.

That woman, here. How could she have guessed that Renee de Beaumont would be the same Renee she had seen locked in her husband's arms? How did she come to be here, of all the places in the world where she could have gone! Here, at the inn. How dared she invade even that? Hadn't she and Morgan done enough already? True, it had been Morgan's decision to cheat on her; Renee was merely the instrument. Yet just looking at her filled Laurel with distaste.

Suddenly her training gave way, and Laurel was on her feet so abruptly that her Chippendale chair squealed across the floor.

"Excuse me," she said through stiff lips. "I'll send someone else to show you your room."

Leaving Renee with her eyebrows raised, Laurel hurried away before she lost control completely and told Renee de Beaumont what she thought of her—or just tore her to shreds! In the dining room, however, she stopped, realizing she'd been about to go to Abby. But if she turned up in front of the older woman looking like this, perceptive as she was, Abby would be only too apt to figure out who Renee de Beaumont must be. And Laurel's affection for Nate's garrulous wife gave her a perfectly clear picture of how Abby would treat their latest guest then. At the very least, she was likely to be offered a room in the old coal cellar, and what would that do to the inn's reputation!

With a stifled sound that was part rage and part bitter amusement, Laurel swept out of the dining room, going to the barn in search of Nate.

She found him way in the back, past the other guests' cars and a new one, a silver Porsche with Massachusetts plates that undoubtedly belonged to Renee. Sitting on a rickety milking stool in the last of the old horse stalls, where he had a habit of retreating, he was reading the paper and absentmindedly gnawing the stem of a battered pipe. At the sound of her footsteps, he looked up over the top of his newspaper and watched her hurry toward him.

"Nate, could you find Abby and have her finish checking in the new guest who's waiting in the front hall?" she asked, hoping he would put the odd quality in her voice down to breathlessness. "I'm suddenly feeling a little sick." Heaven knew that was the truth—sickened by the sight of Renee de Beaumont!

He looked at her keenly, then folded the paper and slowly removed his pipe, setting them both neatly aside. Only when that was done did he take those far-sighted eyes of his off her and say, "Eyah."

Rising, he strode away, and when he was gone Laurel leaned against the side of the stall. Now that the immediate problem was being taken care of, her thoughts were free to simmer over that woman coming to her inn—and simmer they did, at a considerable temperature! She couldn't very well stay there, though, and after a few minutes she straightened and walked out of the barn, cutting across to the back door so that she could take the back stairs to her room.

She was standing at the window, staring out rather fixedly, when Abby knocked at her door five minutes later.

"Laurel?" she said softly at the doorway.

"Mmm?" Laurel answered without turning immediately.

"Are you all right, child? Nate came and said you

weren't feeling well.'' She walked quietly across the room, and Laurel looked around to meet her concerned gaze.

''I'll be fine now, Abby, thanks,'' she said with an attempt at a reassuring smile. ''I just felt ill all of a sudden, probably one of those quickie stomach flus that just last a few hours.''

''You seem a bit pale still,'' Abby pointed out, reaching up to lay a cool hand on Laurel's forehead. ''But at least you don't have a fever.''

No, Laurel thought wildly, definitely not a fever, but the thought of having Renee here, of all places, certainly turned her stomach!

Abby was still speaking. ''Why don't I take care of the desk, anyway, the rest of the afternoon? Then if you're really feeling well enough, you can come down and put the finishing touches on dinner. Or if you're not, Betsy and I will just do the basics for ourselves.''

''Oh, no, you won't,'' Laurel contradicted her firmly, pulling herself together. ''I'm fine now, and I'm not going to stay here any longer, malingering while you two do all the work.''

Stepping over to the mirror, she ran a brush through her hair, fluffing her curls, then touched a deeper rose shade to her lips and cheeks. Abby watched the process with a doubtful look at first, but when Laurel turned from her mirror and said brightly, ''There, am I presentable?'' Abby was convinced.

''You're a good deal better than presentable,

child,'' she smiled fondly. "You always are. All right, then. If you're sure, I'll go back to the ordering I was doing in the kitchen.'' She started out the door, then poked her head back in to add as an after-thought, "By the way, I put that new guest in the brass bedroom.''

She was gone again, and Laurel's careful smile vanished. The brass bedroom—the two of them always referred to the rooms by their furnishings—was the largest one and the only one with its own bath. Abby had given Renee the best room in the house, instead of the coal cellar. Nate's wife was a good deal too feisty to have let Renee's supercilious manner intimidate her, but she was also pragmatic enough to head off, whenever possible, any complaints before they could come.

Although Renee had little to complain about! After all, she wasn't the one whose marriage vows became a mockery before they were even three hours old! Without warning, the anger Laurel had just mastered before Abby appeared rushed back, with reinforcements. She was angry at darling Abby for giving Renee courteous treatment, furious with Renee in advance, in case she did find something here to complain about, and most of all enraged at herself for even caring what Renee said, or thought, or did!

That woman was nothing more than another guest in this hotel. She might once have been Morgan's lover, and that might have mattered a great deal to Morgan's wife—but it was all a long time ago now. It didn't matter anymore, because Morgan didn't matter. Adam had said there was some sort of delay with the preliminary paperwork for her annulment, but it was only a technicality. As soon as her annulment came through, Morgan would be nothing more to her than someone she had once known. So for whatever reason Renee de Beaumont had come here—even if it was to meet some new man, Morgan's successor—Laurel didn't care and wouldn't care!

She had, however, been pacing furiously up and down her room again, and now she forced herself to stop. Taking a couple of deep breaths, she shook off the tension that had built up inside her while she thought. Checking her mirror, she saw that all signs of her anger were firmly under control now. She looked like a properly self-possessed innkeeper. And as such, she'd better get downstairs to her desk, as she'd promised Abby.

In a minute she was back in her chair, working out where she'd been with those figures when Renee had appeared. It was a quiet afternoon. Renee didn't reappear, and except for Abby peeking in from the dining room to see that she really was fine, Laurel didn't see anyone else. Several of the other rooms were occupied, but the guests were out on their own. No one else was expected.

But someone else came. Laurel was about to set the bell on the desk, so that if more guests came while she was in the kitchen helping with dinner they could ring for her, when the big front door opened. Already on

her feet, Laurel looked over that way immediately—
and felt as though she'd had the breath knocked out
of her at the sight of Morgan Hamilton.

She must have gasped, but he apparently didn't
hear her. She ducked her head right away, standing
frozen to listen as he swung the heavy door closed
behind him and shut out the wail of a rising wind.
She heard small tugging noises and the slap of leather
gloves against one palm, followed by the sounds of
him shrugging of his coat. Finally he came toward
her.

His footsteps were rather slow and heavy, but
Laurel didn't notice. She was reminding herself
fiercely that he was nothing more to her now than
another traveler looking for a room. Come to think
of it, he was one without a reservation.

He spoke at that moment, addressing the top of
her bent head. "Good evening," he said in that
slightly harsh voice she had once loved, a thousand
years ago. "Do you have room for one more?"

Looking up at last, she found him gazing around
the hall while he waited for an answer, and so she had
an instant to imprint his image on her mind. There he
was, the man she had thought the handsomest she'd
ever seen. He seemed taller and more broad shoul-
dered than she remembered, even from Paris. But his
clear blue eyes were the same, the exact shade of the
far mountains on a sunny day. His face still had that
tawny gleam, too, under the thick black hair.

He seemed so much the same that immediately her

mouth went dry, and her eyes wet. She blinked away the ridiculous tears angrily, tears that prevented her from seeing that Morgan wasn't exactly the same as the last time she'd seen him. She missed the new lines that etched his broad forehead and the corners of his eyes, just as she missed the weary set of his shoulders. She didn't see at first, and then she was too preoccupied to see.

"No," she said smoothly in her best professional tone of regret. "I'm sorry, but we're all booked up."

At the sound of her voice, his gaze jerked away from the graceful stairway he'd been admiring and flew to her face, while his whole lean body seemed to straighten. With an expression of disbelief, he hastily catalogued the trim skirt and sweater, the elfin curls, the creamy skin, before he raised his eyes to hold hers.

"My God...Laurel?" he said on a rising note of what sounded like wonder.

Meeting that blue stare, she felt her heart start to pound unaccountably, and she had to fold her hands on the desk top to conceal the way they'd begun to shake. But she didn't care one iota for Morgan anymore—not one! It was just too bad she even had to be polite to him, but, then, he was her employer's grandson. Drawing a deep breath, she said with cool courtesy, "Yes, Mr. Hamilton?"

He didn't seem to hear her, though, as he tossed his coat and gloves on a nearby chair. "Laurel," he said a second time, more softly and with a warm intimate note in his voice, while his eyes kept searching her face. How dared he look at her like that...those beautiful eyes, and one square hand seemed about to caress her cheek as he bent toward her....

"I've looked so long," he was saying, his voice low. That must be why she was leaning toward him across the desk, just to hear what he had to say.

But he didn't finish the thought, because just then another voice from the stairway cooed, "Morgan, *mon cher*! You are here at last. I have been waiting all afternoon to see you." As she spoke, Renee swept gracefully down toward them. Morgan's hand dropped to his side, and Laurel snapped upright away from him.

Fool, she berated herself—nitwit, idiot and lunatic! How could she sign Renee into the inn and never guess that Morgan might be coming to join her? How could she practically fall into his arms herself as soon as he spoke to her? And how many times was this man going to work his old dark magic on her before she learned what he was like? After all this time, all he had to do was appear and say her name, and she forgot everything—forgot Renee was here, forgot he meant nothing to her anymore, forgot what she'd learned so painfully about not letting him coax her body into overruling her head. Thank God Renee had come along when she did to make the situation crystal clear and keep her from making the same old passionate mistake.

The cheek he had almost touched felt cold, but she

knew both were flaming, and awash with anger she
sat down in her chair. Snatching up some papers at
random, she began shuffling through them, her
head lowered so that she wouldn't have to witness
the reunion between Morgan and Renee. It would be
a loving one, of course; Renee's delighted trill had
indicated that. Obviously, she didn't know he was
two-timing her! He really was despicable, abandon-
ing her for Renee on their wedding day, moving on
to someone else in Paris, then setting up a rendezvous with Renee here—under her own roof, as it
happened!

This was, in fact, Morgan's first meeting with her
in months, and an unexpected one at that. Laurel
didn't see the glance of cool surprise he gave the
other woman as she swayed toward him on slender
heels, looking stunning—if out of place at a country
inn—in a clinging red jersey dress that revealed every
voluptuous curve. She might as well have been wearing burlap for all the tribute he paid to her appearance. Still looking down, Laurel didn't see his
evident indifference, any more than she saw how
neatly he diverted Renee's hands from encircling his
neck. Laurel didn't even hear what they said to each
other, because her own thoughts clamored so loudly.

But Renee certainly saw his reaction and heard the
neutral way he said, "Renee, how nice to see you."

A spasm of irritation crossed her face, but then it
was gone. Moving in on him slightly, so that her
hands rested intimately against his broad chest, she

peeped up at him through her heavily mascaraed lashes.

"Nice," she repeated huskily, giving a low sensuous laugh. "What a charming way to describe it! But then, you have always been charming, *mon vieux*. Now come, have you signed yourself in the big book yet?"

She glanced mockingly at the register that lay on Laurel's desk, but following her eyes, Morgan looked past the book to the top of Laurel's head.

"No," he said, stepping away from Renee, "I've just been informed the rooms are all taken."

"Oh, but mine is—" Renee began, but something in his expression made her break off. With a laugh that wasn't quite as seductive as her last one, she tried to recover herself. "But this is ridiculous!" she said hastily, throwing an irritable look at Laurel. Deliberately speaking more loudly, she added, "This one simply does not know. The noisy little woman who finally gave me my room said that this place was half-empty tonight."

Her tone added, "naturally," but Laurel didn't even bother with the implied insult. Her attention was riveted on the predicament the other woman had just presented her with. Oh, why did Abby have to tell Renee there were plenty of available rooms! For the first time Laurel began to feel that it really might be true that Abby talked too much.

Angry and dismayed, as well as disgusted with herself for being caught lying—was it contagious—she stretched out her right hand for the register, to turn it away from Morgan before he could check it for himself. It was a futile attempt, however. His eyes had been fixed on her with a peculiar expression in their depths ever since Renee spoke, and now at her slight movement he leaned forward and stopped her, covering her hand with his own.

In Paris she had been able to shake off his touch almost instantly. A few minutes earlier, Renee had come along before her cheek could feel his fingers. But now he had her pinned against escape, and her loathing for him began to seep away. The pressure of his palm across her fingers was like fire against ice; the sensation seemed to sizzle all the way up her arm. She felt as though her skin were seared and her bones beginning to melt. But there was no pain, nothing but a sudden sweet lassitude that meant she couldn't possibly withdraw from the contact. Instead she sat motionless, while he used his free hand to slide the register out from under her slack hold, all the while maintaining the pressure on her fingers.

Turning the book so that he could scan it rapidly, he confirmed what Renee had said. Including hers, only four of the inn's seven bedrooms were taken, and there were no other names in the reservation column until tomorrow.

"Ah, good," he said quietly. "There does appear to have been an error. Now may I have a room, please?"

Their gazes locked, his hooded and uncommunicative now, hers wide-eyed and almost mesmerized. Laurel couldn't have broken that stare any more than she could have pulled her hand away from his. But her mind was racing. If only she could answer him with a flat uncompromising "No!" If only she could force him to go away—anywhere—and take Renee with him. They probably deserved each other anyway. Then she could go back to building a new life here and forget about them both—and remember what she really thought of Morgan, even though he stood so near and touched her with his hand and his eyes— Oh, why couldn't her traitorous body obey her mind?

Not that knowing in her mind that Morgan was beneath contempt was going to do her any good right now. The infuriating truth was that now he knew there was a room for him, she would have to give it to him. Even her suspicion that Adam would probably forgive her if she tried it didn't really alter the situation. He *was* the grandson of the owner of the Hamilton Hotels, and this was a Hamilton hotel.

Renee finally became impatient over the delay in Laurel's answer—and over the way her hand lay beneath Morgan's. Stepping forward to stand very near to him, she asked fretfully, "So what is now the problem? Of course he may have a room, *n'est-ce pas*?"

So saying, she slid one hand down his arm to the fingers that rested across the register book, gathered them up and stroked them with her other hand, holding them close to her body. At the same time she looked at Laurel, still without recognition but with an expression of challenge and dislike. Laurel met that look squarely, and suddenly she was blazingly angry. If they were going to. . . .

"Oh, yes," she answered at last, her rage betrayed only by the slightest tremor in her voice, "of course Mr. Hamilton may have a room. In fact, he may have the one next to yours, Miss de Beaumont. They share a connecting door."

Her lassitude gone at last, she yanked her hand from under Morgan's and spun the book around to write down the number of his room. Then she jerked it back around and stabbed with the pen at the line where he was to write his name and address.

He gave her a long look but didn't immediately take the pen she was shoving at him. Although Renee was pratically purring her pleasure beside him, he asked, "Isn't there another room available? I wouldn't want to disturb Miss de Beaumont if there was somewhere else that wouldn't be as likely to interfere with her privacy."

Disturb Renee? Interfere with her privacy? Is that what he called sleeping with his girl friend? Nearly choking on her disgust at his hypocrisy, Laurel slapped the pen down and grated, "No. The other rooms aren't prepared for guests."

She was staring past him at the far wall of the hallway as she spoke, but she sensed that Renee's expression of satisfaction, which had wavered for a moment, was firmly back in place. Morgan was probably looking satisfied, too, of course. For the sake of propriety he had made a token protest against the room she offered him, and now he could relax and enjoy it, as well as enjoying Renee!

Revolted by them both, Laurel felt as if she and the inn were degraded by their presence. All she wanted to do now was to get away from them. Spinning on her heel, she snatched a key from the board behind her and dropped it on the desk in front of Morgan, still without looking at him. "Your room is number four," she said distantly. "It's at the top of the stairs and then along the hall to your right; Miss de Beaumont can show you the way. I'm afraid you'll have to excuse me. I'm needed in the kitchen to help prepare dinner."

As she spoke, she sidestepped clear of her desk and walked across the hall and into the dining room. Her steps were hasty, but she still heard Renee say with a silvery laugh, "*Mon Dieu,* she is as quaint as this place!"

Despite the laugh, her tone made it quite plain to Laurel, as it was undoubtedly meant to do, that she wasn't paying either the inn or the innkeeper a compliment. Morgan's answer to this piece of cattiness was inaudible over the sound of Laurel's own heels as she charged through the doorway into the kitchen. She had no doubt, however, that Renee would see that Morgan did indeed find his way to his room, and to hers, as well!

Back in the hall, Morgan watched her go with that same intent expression he had given her when Renee exposed her lie about the rooms. The swinging door stilled, and he eyed it thoughtfully for a moment. Then with an almost imperceptible shake of his head, he turned away toward the stairs and his room, while Renee slipped ahead of him so that she could lead the way. His lips twisting slightly, Morgan watched the exaggerated sway of her hips as she climbed the first steps. He decided it was high time he got his luggage.

Hearing both sets of footsteps fade, Laurel found she was breathing as though she'd just run a race instead of simply crossing the dining room. The hectic sound brought Abby's eyes up from the menu she'd been studying.

"Laurel, what is it?" she asked as Laurel dropped into the chair across from her. "Are you feeling sick again?"

Laying cool fingers on the younger woman's flushed face, she found no fever and gave her cheek an encouraging pat. Then she pushed aside the menu and clasped her hands lightly together, elbows on the table, in a receptive position.

"Stomach flu?" she asked, a gently skeptical note in her voice.

"Yes," Laurel muttered and then, "No!"

Abby let the silence extend between them for a minute or two, then asked quietly, "Do you want to tell me about it?"

"Yes, I guess so, but...."

Wildly, she wanted to pour out the torrent of emotions rising within her, but a natural reserve was damming them up. After all, why should she swamp poor Abby with her private fury and unhappiness?

Abby must have guessed the reason for her hesitation, because she prompted gently, "Did I hear another guest arriving just now? And does that have something to do with whatever's wrong?"

Laurel nodded mutely. Then she realized how futile it was to try concealing from Abby why their latest guest's arrival had upset her. As soon as Abby checked the register next, she would see Morgan Hamilton's name there and remember what Laurel had told her about their marriage. At that thought, it all began to flood out.

"He's here," she said baldly, growing more agitated as she went on. "Of all the places in the world he could have gone, he had to come here!"

"Your husband?" Abby interpreted shrewdly as Laurel broke off and leaped to her feet to pace angrily around the room.

Momentarily speechless with indignation, Laurel nodded vigorously. But Abby, instead of immediately sharing her dismay, was struck by some other thought.

"Well, well, well," she said slowly, and at the change in her tone, Laurel spun around to look at her again. Her chin in one plump capable hand, Abby smiled slowly. "So he's come after you, has he?" she murmured thoughtfully.

"Abby!" Laurel cried, aghast, and darted over to kneel by Abby's chair, gripping her hands so that she had to pay attention. "That's not it at all—that's the last thing on his mind!"

Her thoughts arrested by Laurel's urgent tone, Abby looked into the tense face below her own, and what she saw there made her smile fade. "Then why has he come?" she asked, puzzled. "He isn't here on business, is he?"

Struck by the thought, Laurel released Abby's hands and straightened up, considering that hadn't occurred to her before. Running her fingers abstractedly through her curls, she tried to calm down enough to think clearly. It was possible—but then, wouldn't Adam have called or written to let her know in advance that Morgan was coming? Probably, but what if he'd guessed she might be so revolted at the prospect that she would leave the inn? She would have done just that, she realized, if she'd been warned in time. She would have found business of her own somewhere else for at least as long as he stayed. But maybe Adam had been afraid she would vanish completely. He'd said once that he meant to make sure she never did that.

Besides, that wouldn't account for Renee's presence here—not unless Morgan had sunk so low that he traveled publicly with his girl friend when he was on company business. She couldn't believe that of him, or that Adam would tolerate it, even if Morgan weren't still legally married.

No, she decided as rationality dissolved into anger again, there was no logical explanation other than that he had set up a private meeting with Renee, and some horrible coincidence had seen to it that they chose this particular hotel. That being the case, she didn't care how much Morgan tried to cover up the situation by asking for a room farther away from Renee, or even if they never went near each other now, because nothing could change the fact that they had meant this to be a secret tryst.

"No," she answered Abby briefly at last. She was pacing furiously again, her skirt swirling around her legs with each stride, her hands unconsciously clenched. And Abby, far too observant not to see all this and draw conclusions, watched her with an expression of growing incredulity.

"Then that woman, that high-and-mighty type I signed in when you first felt ill this afternoon..." she began, her usually placid voice starting to rise.

Laurel swept back to the table and dropped into the chair facing Abby. "Yes," she confirmed flatly.

"*That's* the one he was with on your wedding day?" Abby still couldn't seem to take it in.

"That's the one."

"Well, of all the—" Words failed her, and Abby surged to her feet like some small avenging angel.

"Abby, wait!" Laurel called as the other woman charged across the kitchen to the door. "Where are you going?"

"To put her out on the street!" Abby snapped. "That's where her kind of alley cat belongs."

This was even more drastic than the prospect of the coal cellar. "Abby, no! You can't—"

"Watch me," Abby interrupted fiercely. "In fact, maybe I'll put him out there with her—he's certainly no better than she is."

She tried to pull free of Laurel's restraining hands, but Laurel held on tightly. "You can't do it, Abby," she repeated hastily. "You can't simply throw people out of the inn like that."

"I can when it's your husband and his—" She choked on whatever word she'd been about to call Renee, then raged on. "Here he is with a lovely wife of his own that he doesn't even hang on to, because he's too much of a fool to know what a good thing he has—"

Such partisanship had to be a comfort, but Laurel still didn't dare let Abby go, especially since she was sputtering furiously again.

"And then he comes and brings that *woman* here, right under your nose, as if this was some sort of cheap dive where he could meet his...*trollop*!"

She brought out the old-fashioned term viciously, her black eyes sparkling with rage, her whole body bristling with indignation, and tried again to yank free.

But Laurel held on, and suddenly she giggled. At the unexpected sound, Abby stopped dead, looking at Laurel as if she were demented. Laurel, laughing aloud now, lost her grip on Abby, but it didn't matter anyway because the little woman was too astounded to do much of anything. She stood motionless, gazing in bewilderment at the other's merry face.

"I'm sorry," Laurel gasped, trying without any success to stop laughing. "But it was just—"

She was off again, laughing delightedly as Abby continued to gaze at her with concern. Her own lips began to twitch involuntarily, but her eyes were worried.

In a moment Laurel's laughter subsided to a soft chuckle. She slid her arm around Abby's shoulders to pull her away from the door. Completely confused now, Abby didn't resist.

"It's all right, Abby, dear," Laurel insisted, amusement still echoing in her tone. "I'm not hysterical, and I haven't lost my mind—but you're a major reason why not."

She directed Abby back to the table and leaned against the edge herself, looking affectionately into Abby's mystified face. "It was just hearing you call Renee a trollop—" Her voice quavered again, and a reluctant answering smile began to curl the older woman's lips.

"She is one, though," she insisted stoutly.

"Yes, I know," Laurel agreed, "but I never heard anyone actually say that word before!"

Abby smiled fully then, but pointed out, "Well, I'm not very knowing about the words to call her sort."

"Thank heaven!"

"But I know one when I see one."

"I'm afraid I do, too," Laurel said on a slight sigh, before adding in a lighter tone, "But somehow I don't feel quite so wild about it now, thanks to you. It's as if Abby's anger for her sake had somehow lessened her own, Laurel added to herself.

She shrugged slightly, and Abby grinned sympathetically. "I'm not sure I quite see how, but I'm glad if it's true." At Laurel's nod, Abby went on, "But what are we going to do? That is, if you really won't let me toss them out," she concluded on a faintly hopeful note.

Laurel shook her head with a regretful smile. "I really won't, Abby," she confirmed. "We can't."

Abby continued to look a bit rebellious, so Laurel pointed out the impossibility of giving in to that temptation. "It might feel good, but we couldn't do it. First, they've already been given their rooms. Second, even though we might get away with putting Renee out if we only had to deal with her, Morgan would certainly stop us. Third, if we tried to be rid of him, we'd be insulting the grandson of the head of the company."

Convinced in spite of herself, Abby snorted in disgust, while Laurel realized she'd convinced herself, too. But she certainly would rather have got Morgan and Renee out of here instead of having to tolerate them for as long as they chose to stay.

They sat silently for a minute, each one lost in her own thoughts, until Abby said, "Well, then...."

She paused, and Laurel glanced at her in surprise; her tone had been suspiciously bright. Abby was gazing off across the kitchen, her eyes fixed on nothing in particular, a look of utter deviltry stealing over her friendly face. Laurel had a glimpse then of what a trial she must have been to her family as a little girl, and suddenly she was able to read Abby's thoughts as clearly as if they'd been printed on the air between them—although they weren't the kind of thoughts anyone would dare commit to paper, for fear of having them produced later as evidence!

With complete certainty, Laurel knew Abby was planning to see to it that Morgan and Renee stayed only a short time at the inn. She intended to make them so uncomfortable they'd go, and that would be easy for anyone as ingenious as Abby to arrange. At mealtime, their orders could be mixed up and their food cold when it finally reached the table. A few "mistakes" with the spice jars would make the dishes virtually inedible anyway. As far as their rooms went—Laurel shuddered. Their beds could be lumpily made up and their bedclothes insufficient for this cold weather. Their windows could be left slightly ajar so drafts would blow through.... Why, given half a chance, Abby could probably persuade their plumbing to jam and their beds to collapse! And all of this could happen without inconveniencing any of the other guests, as long as no one cared about the report that Morgan would take back to company headquarters!

It would almost be worth it, of course. To have Renee gone would be a relief, and to have Morgan go, too— Laurel would do almost anything to avoid contact with him, the contact that seemed to make sense take second place to sensation. But this she couldn't do, or allow Abby to do.

Slipping off the edge of the table to stand directly in front of Abby, she said firmly, "Abby, don't you dare!"

Abby's eyes left the far wall and focused on Laurel, and the conniving look left her face, replaced by one of bland innocence. "Do what, child?" she asked.

"Do any of the evil-minded things you're planning!" Laurel said clearly, and Abby's innocence evaporated.

"Whyever not?" she demanded. "I'd make sure no one could tell what happened wasn't accidental—"

"You might fool Renee—she already thinks we're well below her standards—but Morgan would figure it out."

"So let him," Abby answered cavalierly, "as long as he went away anyhow."

"No," Laurel said flatly, and with a fleeting trace of regret, the mischievously childlike expression left Abby's eyes.

"Why?" she asked quietly. Laurel didn't know. It was her turn to stare off across the room while she tried to figure it out.

Abby was probably right. Renee and Morgan could be made uncomfortable subtly enough so that they could never be sure it was deliberate, and not just the result of ineptness. Laurel couldn't care less if Renee de Beaumont thought she was incompetent, but for some perverse reason she did care about having Morgan draw the same conclusion, as well as caring about her own sense of professionalism.

She was entirely capable of running this inn. With the help of Abby and Nate, she had brought it back from the edge of ruin, and now she was running a pleasant and comfortable hotel that was already building a reputation. Morgan was Adam's heir, and thus would someday be in a position to fire her. But although it might be years before what he thought of her mattered officially—loving Adam as she did, she sincerely hoped it would be—even now she was reluctant to do anything that would lower his opinion of her.

If it was possible for him to have any less respect for her than his infidelity already indicated! Oh, why did she give a tinker's damn *what* a man like that thought!

She shook her head, having come up with no answer to Abby's question. "I don't know," she said with a shrug. "I just know I don't want to do it. In fact, I'd rather make sure they're incredibly well treated while they're here."

Studying her a moment longer with a thoughtful expression, Abby finally stood up and said briskly,

"All right, child, we'll do it your way. We'll make those two so darned comfortable they'll decide this is the best inn in the north country."

She didn't look as though the prospect filled her with enthusiasm, yet giving Laurel's shoulders a quick sympathetic squeeze, she added, "But if we're going to do it, we'd better get started with tonight's dinner, or none of our guests is going to think much of us!"

And Laurel, knowing Abby was right about that anyway, had no choice but to put away her own thoughts, jumbled as they were, and concentrate on cooking.

CHAPTER EIGHT

SHE DID IT SO WELL that the first meal Morgan and Renee ate at the inn was superb. Because she was rarely feeding more than twenty-five or thirty people, counting guests at the inn and anyone else who came to eat, Laurel limited the selection. Each evening she offered only two entrées, along with appetizers, salad, vegetables and rolls, wines and a choice of several desserts. But the advantage of her system was that it left her free to concentrate her talents on producing a few things spectacularly, with Abby's and Betsy's capable help.

That evening they prepared hot stuffed mushrooms, melon wrapped in thin slices of prosciutto and a thick creamy New England clam chowder, followed by a choice of either hearty Beef Wellington or salmon served with a delicate sauce of baby shrimp in cream, with wine to complement either. There was also a fruit salad and a selection of vegetables cooked only until crisp, to retain their texture and vitamins. Light fluffy dinner rolls and fresh date bread were offered, too, and the meal ended with crème caramel, Victoria torte or fruit and cheese.

It was a sumptuous meal for a country inn—or almost anywhere else—and as course smoothly followed course, Morgan couldn't help but notice it, whether or not he was visiting the inn in an official capacity. Renee had seated herself at his table and, preoccupied, he hadn't bothered to make an issue of it. Instead, he let her order first and deliberately chose a different meal. When both arrived, he saw that hers looked as beautifully presented as his and probably tasted as delicious. But he didn't see Laurel, even though his dark gaze nearly pierced every new entrant into the dining room.

Abby served their meal, as she served all the other diners, coping easily with the orders at six different tables. But while she chatted and laughed with the other guests in a way that was warm and natural, if not in the least "properly" subservient, whenever she came to their table she asked only the bare minimum of questions. She was meticulously correct, but her very silence was eloquent, even though Morgan was too abstracted to notice.

Renee did note Abby's manner, but it didn't displease her. On the contrary, as the meal went on she deigned to smile at their waitress in cool approval; this was obviously the sort of service she was accustomed to. And reluctantly, mindful of Laurel's strict orders, Abby kept on behaving herself.

She did, however, give in to the temptation to listen in on their conversation whenever she was near enough.

"*Mon cher*," Renee was pouting at one point, "you have not said one thing about the way I look, and I have dressed so carefully to please you—as always."

Morgan's glance in her direction was perfunctory, but he murmured, "You look spectacular, of course."

Another time Abby heard her say, "It was easy when I called your secretary to ask where you were." And she saw Renee peek seductively up through her lashes to add, "You see how determined you make me." To that one, Morgan's only response was a steady appraising look.

And a third time, as Abby came to set their desserts before them, Renee was sighing pathetically, "But it's been so long—" She broke off when she realized Abby was there, and from her black frown— hastily smoothed over before Morgan could see it wrinkling her skin—Abby gathered she had just lost some points as a perfect waitress. She certainly didn't care, though.

She didn't tell Laurel what she'd overheard, so it wasn't until a good deal later, when the kitchen was closed up for the night and Abby and Betsy had gone home, that she learned anything about Morgan's dinner. And then she found it out from Morgan himself.

Striding out of the parlor at the sound of her footsteps crossing the hall, almost as though he'd been waiting to catch her alone, he stopped her in the hall.

"Laurel," he said, and reached out to catch her arm.

She paused, moving slightly away from him. It had been the same this afternoon. The least contact with him seemed to sear her flesh. Although she had every reason to shrink from his touch in anger, still her rebellious body urged her to throw herself into his arms and feel them close around her. She had to fight temptation.

Morgan must not have noticed. His eyes seemed to flicker, but what he said was so ordinary that it caught her off balance.

"I wanted to thank your chef for an excellent meal. I looked for you during dinner to give you the message for him, but you weren't there."

"I was lending a hand in the kitchen, but I'll see your message is delivered," she murmured, forcing back a sense of anticlimax. She wondered fleetingly why she hadn't told him she was the chef.

Perhaps it was because she didn't want to prolong this conversation. Her instinct for self-preservation was shrieking a warning at her. He was here with Renee, and she had to tolerate their presence as long as they chose to stay, but seeing as little of him as possible would head off more of these interior battles with desire.

Without meeting his gaze, she added, "Now if you'll excuse me, please," and looked up the stairs. Automatically he followed her glance. Then she felt those blue eyes on her again as he switched from the polite to the personal without warning, catching her off guard a second time.

"I'd rather not," he returned softly, and smiled at her warmly and seductively, a smile he must have practiced many times. But still Laurel's body began to respond. "I'd rather keep you here, so I can say in private all the things I didn't say in public this afternoon."

In public this afternoon. The phrase was like a shower of cold water, reminding her of exactly how he came to be here and dousing the tiny sparks that he had lighted against her will.

Wrenching herself away from that smile, she said coldly, "I'm sorry—I have to go."

She whisked around him and began to climb the first steps, her right hand going to the banister, so that he was able to stop her by putting his own over it. Feeling trapped, she kept her eyes averted and didn't see the warmth fade from his. She only heard him say in a different tone, "Then when can I see you? I want to talk to you."

Acutely conscious of his closeness again, Laurel wondered wildly what use talking could be to them now—and why he had given her that smile that so encouraged every weakness in her. The time for talking and smiles was gone. It had ended with their ruined wedding day, and now any talking he wanted to do could be done with Renee, or some other girl friend. She at least wasn't going to be part of his harem at this late date.

Nonetheless, her hand had begun to tremble under his, echoing its warmth. If he couldn't tell that already, he would be able to soon, when the tremors spread and shook her whole body. If she didn't go now, it would be all too obvious what effect he still had on her, in spite of everything. Furious at the thought of that physical betrayal, she finally found the strength to pull herself free of his head. "No!" she said emphatically, and hurried up the stairs.

Watching her go, Morgan's face tightened. She was running away from him again, and it seemed to be becoming a habit, begun on their wedding day. In Paris his bitterness had finally been swallowed up by an even stronger emotion. But now that she kept refusing to give him any opportunity to talk to her, his prideful anger flared again. . .until it slowly gave way to an even stronger determination.. .

If Laurel didn't want to talk to him, Renee certainly did. At dinner the ploys that had always made him look at her with a dry blend of amusement and appreciation hadn't met with their usual success. But she was set on making him respond in the old way, so she went looking for him again. Setting aside the demitasse she'd been toying with while she assessed from under her lashes the rotund elderly man on the other end of the parlor sofa, she stood up and smoothed her red dress languorously over her hips with both hands. It was a gesture that left the man suitably impressed, and with a pleased smile Renee strolled out to look for Morgan.

She found him in the hall, but when she stood beside him, so close that her perfume was in his nostrils

and her hair against his shoulder and suggested softly, "Shall we find some place where we can be alone
at last, *mon cher*? I have much I wish to say to you."
His response infuriated her.

Lowering his eyes slowly from the staircase, he
looked at her as if his mind wasn't even on her, then
calmly ignored her invitation. "If you'll forgive me,
Renee, I'll say good-night to you now. I could use a
long walk after that drive up here."

And with those words he turned away, letting himself out the front door. It closed behind him, and
Renee, her face completely changed in seconds, spat
out something vituperative in French and swept furiously up the stairs to her room. Slamming the door
behind her, she flung herself onto the bed and pum-
meled it before she calmed down enough to consider
how to approach him tomorrow. But just in case she
might not have to wait that long, she made sure a
while later that she was wearing her favorite, and
most provocative, peignoir. Nonetheless, although
she listened and listened, she never heard the sound
of the connecting door she had so carefully left
unlocked.

Neither did Laurel, as she lay awake for hours in
her room at the end of the ell. She told herself she
didn't care what Morgan and Renee did. She told
herself she was too far away to hear an interior door.
She told herself basic discretion would make them
quiet anyway. During that long night she told herself
a thousand things, but none of them stopped her

from thrashing until the sheets and blankets were in a knot, so that even Limb, who ordinarily slept as though he were in hibernation, stirred at the foot of her bed and protested with a soft whine. At that, she forced herself to lie still rather than having to explain to any irate guests why a dog was disturbing their sleep. She didn't fall asleep until nearly dawn.

As a result, her fine skin was so colorless when she dragged herself from bed an hour later than even the scarlet sweater she put on didn't lend much illusion of warmth. She brushed a trace of soft color across her cheeks, but she still looked exactly like what she was—someone who has just passed a sleepless night—and knowing that did nothing to lift her spirits. Renee would probably look as sensational this morning as she had last night.

The thought depressed her, no matter how much she tried to tell herself that she didn't care how she looked to Morgan. As she fixed coffee and juice and heated last night's baking of croissants, her movements were slow and heavy. It might have helped if Abby had been there with her chatter and clatter for distraction, but like Betsy, she and Nate always came over to the inn about midmorning, since they stayed so late. So Laurel was left alone with no company but her thoughts and Limb, who with the best intentions in the world, could only sense her black mood and, for once, behave himself better than usual.

For a while, that was. Having set breakfast out in the dining room so the guests could serve themselves whenever they chose to get up, Laurel took her own roll and coffee over to a small table by the front windows, settling herself there while she tried to work up an interest in the morning paper. She wasn't very successful, but at least she was absorbed enough so that Limb had grounds for deciding she no longer needed to have him sit at her feet and stare soulfully up at her. He considered he was free to leave her side and go worry the edge of the hall carpet, just where it crossed the doorway—and just where Morgan, coming first to breakfast and distracted by the sight of Laurel alone at the far side of the room, tripped over him.

The puppy, although far more offended than hurt, announced their collision with a yelp that might have woken up several more guests and made Laurel drop her cup of coffee into her lap as her frayed nerves brought her leaping to her feet.

The coffee was still hot, and it soaked through her navy slacks almost instantly. Although she wasn't really burned, she was badly startled, and Morgan didn't help any.

He stooped to soothe Limb, so that the indiscriminate beast rolled over and paddled all four feet in the air in a ridiculous gesture of forgiveness and friendship. Then Morgan looked over to where Laurel was scrubbing furiously at her lap with a napkin. With a slight crooked smile on his face at Limb's exhibition, he said, "I'm sorry," and began to walk toward her with one hand out, as if to take the napkin and help.

Watching him come, Laurel felt something snap inside her. It was all just too much! How dared he look at her with that smile reflected in his mountain-blue eyes, so that they crinkled up at the corners in a way that would make any women melt? In fact, how dared he smile when she was covered with coffee, when it was all his fault? But worst of all, how dared he reach out for the napkin so that he could help her mop herself up—and she would feel his hands moving over her hips and thighs with only the wet fabric to protect her from his inflammatory touch, the touch that Renee must have enjoyed last night.

"You should be!" she snarled. "You damned well should be!"

Her voice had risen, but at first her tone didn't seem to register. He kept moving toward her with one bronze hand extended, and desperate to avoid him, she sprang behind the table and spat, "Don't you touch me!"

His hand dropped immediately to his side, and in his face it was as if the shutters had dropped, too, closing up the laughing light in his eyes.

"As you like," he said tautly, and something deep inside her writhed at his choice of words. If only everything were as she liked, there would be no need for her to flee from his touch or fight against her desperate yearning to feel it.

As if she could shout down those forbidden thoughts, she raged on, "Why couldn't you look where you were going, anyway?"

"I did look where I was going, only I wasn't expecting to find a dog in the center of the doorway," he returned, his face beginning to darken.

"Well, you didn't have to kick him for that!" she accused, hunting for something else to hurl at him in place of all the other accusations she couldn't express.

After a night nearly as restless as Laurel's, however, that comment was enough to make Morgan start losing his grip on the anger she kept stirring in him. In Paris months ago and again on the stairs last night, she'd refused to listen to him. And now she was standing there ranting like a fishwife—over a dog!

But in spite of the fact that it was the last thing he wanted to discuss, and that Limb was standing happily by his side, looking very little like an abused and cowering pup, Morgan defended himself. "I did not kick the dog," he denied, adding, "Although he has no business in a Hamilton hotel." Even while he spoke, he wondered why he was letting himself be dragged this far off the subject he wanted to talk about.

Apparently he really was here on business! Momentarily rocked in her turn by the official tone of his attack, Laurel returned faintly, "Oh, really?"

Morgan pressed home the point. "But then, I don't suppose the manager is aware of how much freedom he has to roam around here."

And that was another insult, suggesting that the

inn was slackly run! Laurel rallied hastily. "The manager knows perfectly well how much freedom my dog has or doesn't have," she announced arrogantly, looking down her nose in a way that Morgan had to challenge, even while Limb jumped up against his leg and he absentmindedly fondled the spaniel's ears.

"Then in that case I'm sure he wouldn't mind explaining to me why the standard company policy on pets isn't being followed here," he said coldly. "When may I see him?"

For a split second Laurel could remember with absolute clarity the roller-coaster ride her father had taken her on when she was ten. Her stomach felt the same way now. But she swallowed hard on the memory and on her sudden inexplicable wish to be just the employee he obviously assumed she was and made herself say with a fair imitation of calm, "You're seeing her right now."

"What?" His black eyebrows shot together.

"I *am* the manager of the inn."

"You can't be," he said flatly, and his disbelief restored her completely in some contradictory way.

"Well, I am. I've been in charge ever since the inn was only an abandoned building."

He glanced rapidly around the elegant dining room. "A derelict—this?"

"With antiquated wiring and plumbing, a leaking roof, next to no heat and no furniture," she confirmed, enjoying his amazement as she hadn't enjoyed anything since he'd arrived.

"But what do you know about wiring and plumbing?" he demanded, almost as though it was important that she not have abilities that he didn't know about.

"Not much," she admitted. "Those parts I contracted out."

"And the furnishings?"

"I found them in various places," she answered airily, knowing Abby would forgive her for taking sole credit, and aware that she was relishing his surprise more and more.

He shook his head, yet accepted the fact that she really had restored the old building. But that she should be completely in charge of running it was impossible. He was determined to prove it, although he couldn't have explained the connection between this and the marriage he really intended to talk about.

"Who handles your ordering?" he asked.

"I do, through the company."

"And your accounts?"

"I do."

"Who manages your staff—you *will* admit there is a staff here?" He was sounding increasingly exasperated.

"Of course." The more irked he got, the calmer she became. "Besides a girl from the village who comes in to help in the kitchen, I have Nate and Abby White. He handles the maintenance, and she works with me."

"That can't be all! Who's your chef?"

Standing there confronting him across the table as though she were a witness on the stand was silly, so Laurel sat down gracefully before she answered.

"I am," she replied coolly, and went him one better to add, "And also the wine steward."

Watching him stroke one sideburn absently in a gesture that she hadn't seen him use before, Laurel could sense him remembering last night's meal and the wines that had accompanied it. Idly she crossed her long legs and swung one foot while he continued to assimilate this new information. Obviously it wasn't particularly easy to do.

"I can't believe it," he muttered, and the tempo of their argument changed as he met her eyes to ask, "Did you always know—"

He broke off the question, but she recognized what he had been going to say: had she been able to do this right along, and he simply hadn't been aware of it? Somehow it was a sad question, revealing how little he had known her when he married her.

Both her first anger at him and her later pleasure in surprising him faded. She leaned toward him slightly. "No. Last summer I had a session of training at Cornell, and after that I took some cooking and wine courses in Paris," she explained, so he would know that at least their marriage hadn't been *that* ill-founded. And then an instant later she wished she hadn't, because her explanation reminded her of their brief meeting in August.

Her shortlived feeling of generosity evaporated,

and she leaped to her feet, sweeping up her newspaper and coffee cup so that she could get away from
him. Spinning on her heel, she turned toward the
kitchen, but he caught her left elbow.

"Wait! Don't go, Laurel. I have to talk to you."

"Well, I don't have to listen!" she flashed, and
tried to yank herself free of him. Nothing he had to
say could possibly interest her. The newspaper
dropped out from under her arm, and she abandoned
it, but his hold only slipped down from her elbow to
her hand. That he gripped firmly, while his lips
thinned again in irritation.

"Dammit, Laurel," he snapped, "I keep trying to
talk to you, and you keep running away!"

As he spoke he realized the hand he held was bare.
She felt him shift his fingers over hers and meet no
metal, only soft skin, and unconsciously she stopped
struggling. Raising her hand between them, he
looked full at it, and she saw a complicated expression pass over his face as he registered that she no
longer wore his ring—and hadn't for some time,
because there was no mark in the smooth skin.

Her gaze riveted on him now; she tried desperately
to fathom his reaction. Part of it was certainly anger,
she could tell; that hadn't faded from his face. Part
of it was shock, although she didn't know why he
should be shocked that she no longer labeled herself
as his wife, when he'd obviously never really wanted
to be married to her. But part of it—that couldn't be
dismay, could it?

If it was, it didn't show in his next words. "But then, I suppose I should have expected that, *Miss Andersen*," he said coldly. "After all, you started doing it on our wedding day, didn't you?"

He was glaring at her now with eyes that had turned to ice, and she could feel his rage from that day returning. Her own fury leaped to meet it. How dared he lay the blame for their separation at her door?

Her own eyes afire, she snapped, "Yes, I did, and I intend to keep on doing it!" She snatched her hand from his, and this time he made no effort to stop her. "We haven't had anything to say to each other since that day. But don't pretend it bothers you— After all, you can still talk to Renee. God knows, you had plenty to say to each other after our wedding!"

And there it was. Those few brief minutes...he remembered, and she had assumed.... He went completely still, all expression vanishing from his face. But her eyes kept on burning with the hurt and humiliation of that day, and color flamed across her cheekbones. Her breath was coming rapidly, so that she felt her scarlet sweater might flutter with agitation.

When it was clear that he had nothing to say, she ground out a bitter suggestion, "And since we've got that all straightened out, why don't you go have a nice chat with your girl friend right now? She's probably waiting for you to carry on with your rendezvous!"

She flung away from him so fast that her coffee cup skidded off the saucer and crashed to the floor, and that was the last straw. Her frayed nerves gave way. With a violent gesture, she threw the saucer after the cup, then blazed out the door to the kitchen. Behind her in the dining room the only sounds were the voices of the next guests who had come down for breakfast.

"Good morning, young man," one of them said, and another added, "Dropped your cup? Too bad. Here, let me give you a hand with the pieces before someone else comes in and steps on them."

If Morgan made any reply to this, it was inaudible to Laurel who had flown up the back stairs to her room and hurled herself on the bed.

It was a long time before she could think coherently. At first, twisting furiously, she just replayed their encounter over and over, tormenting herself with the longing and anger and bitterness she had felt in the course of those few minutes. Then she kept seeing the different expressions on Morgan's face. He had discovered sides to her that he hadn't known about, and she had finally confronted him with the fact that he and Renee were responsible for what happened on their wedding day. Laurel thumped the pillow. Arrogant as he was, that had been enough to anger him.

About to pound the pillow again, she clutched it instead as a perfectly coherent thought stood out suddenly in the jumble. Hadn't Morgan been angry—not just irritated that he'd misunderstood her role at the inn, but genuinely angry—before she mentioned Renee? Sitting up on the bed, she tucked the pillow under her chin and tried to figure that out, carefully reviewing what had happened when.

Yes! It was when he'd found her wedding ring gone that he'd looked really furious. Seeing again the cold glitter in his eyes and the hard planes of his face, she shivered a little. Even the anger he had displayed in his grandfather's office that first day hadn't seemed so fierce. He had certainly never looked at her like that in the few weeks before their wedding. Why on earth should he be so infuriated now about the ring?

Her forehead knitted in bewilderment. It didn't make any sense at all! He had married her in haste—and vice versa, she had to admit—without even knowing her well enough to be sure of what she could and couldn't do, and without even loving her enough to be willing to give up his lover. He had obviously managed perfectly well without her for the four months since she'd left him. Now he turned up at the inn to meet the same pliant girl friend, and got angry to find that his wife wasn't advertising the fact that her blasted annulment hadn't come through yet.

Suddenly she heaved the pillow away. He could only be so enraged because his twisted male pride made him insist she belonged to him. He'd never really wanted her for himself, but dog-in-the-manger fashion, he had to be sure she wasn't free to find another man to love her.

That had to be it. And this was the man whose touch she'd been afraid of? Why, his touch should have repelled her! How could she ever have loved him and cared that he didn't love her?

She sprang off the bed to go back downstairs and get to work without any more of this agonizing. The truth of the whole situation was simply that Morgan was like some childhood disease. Well, she'd had her illness, and now she was finally immune! She'd be able to ignore him from here on, she decided confidently.

At that moment Abby knocked at her door, and at Laurel's murmur looked in to say smilingly, "Morning, child. I was just checking to see that you hadn't crawled back into bed for another nap and forgotten us all."

"No," Laurel answered cheerfully. "I just came up to change my slacks—I'd spilled coffee all over them."

"Ugh." Abby made a sympathetic face at the wide stain across Laurel's lap. "Well, there's no real hurry. Come on down when you're ready, and I'll have a fresh cup set for you." And she left before Laurel noticed an intrigued look cross her face.

Renee wasn't having much success with Morgan, but she was still trying when Laurel came down the front stairs three minutes later. Wearing an expensive knit suit in soft tangerine that clung to all of her curves, Renee was sitting with Morgan on the front parlor sofa, so close her thigh lay along his. Laurel's abandoned newspaper, which he might have been trying to read, was folded carelessly in one hand, and he was looking at Renee with an unreadable expression while she made some point with a shrug and a sweep of her black lashes.

As she caught sight of them, Laurel's steps faltered for a split second. Then she carefully arranged her expression and came down the last few stairs into the parlor.

"Oh, good morning." She smiled pleasantly at them in her best innkeeper's manner. "I'm glad you two are getting to know each other. We always like our guests to enjoy meeting new friends."

She should have choked on the lies but she didn't, and she had a moment to be pleased with herself for that before the opening of the outer door drew her attention away from the pair on the sofa.

"Giles!" His bearded face poked around the door, and at the sound of her voice he broke into a broad grin. He came the rest of the way in, closing out the cold wind as she walked toward him.

"Good morning, fair damsel," he greeted her with his usual exuberance. Then he went a step further and wrapped her in a quick bear hug that lifted her clear off her feet. "That," he explained when he set her down, "is because I've finished the last movement of my new flute sonata."

"Congratulations!" she puffed, trying to get some air back into her lungs, temporarily conscious of nothing else but that basic problem, so she didn't notice Morgan come to his feet behind her.

Giles patted her shoulder encouragingly. "That's the girl!" he cheered her on with a teasing look. "One and two, in and out—keep trying and you'll have it in a bit." He dodged away when she poked at him.

But he didn't look in the least repentant, only announced, "And now I've come to carry you off to help me celebrate. How about running away for a lunch in North Conway that you don't have to cook? Abby and Betsy can hold the fort here."

Laurel hesitated, and heard Morgan snort with disgust behind her. Giles turned to look, and irresistibly she followed suit. The other two were standing at the parlor doorway, Renee with her arm linked possessively through Morgan's. The glance she gave them was cool and languid, as if only idle curiosity had drawn her to the sounds of Giles's boisterous arrival. The expression on Morgan's face was as dark and shuttered as an abandoned house, and he made no effort to detach Renee.

Giles seemed not to see anything remarkable about either of their expressions, however. "Good morning, good morning all," he hailed them jovially. "Help me talk this lady into treating herself to a break from the labors of innkeeping, and I promise you'll still be well cared for in her absence." He draped an arm around Laurel's slim shoulders, and she stood motionless between the two men, enormously conscious of their differences.

Both tall, they had contrasting body types, Giles

being barrel chested and sturdy, while Morgan was lean and powerful. Their usual expressions were markedly different, too, Giles's open and frank, Morgan's almost hooded by comparison. And as far as their personalities went—neither of them loved her, but Morgan had briefly let her think he did, and Giles was incapable of charades like that. Lifting her chin, she moved a step closer to him to indicate which man she preferred.

Ice blue again, Morgan's eyes registered her action, and there was a brief echoing silence. Renee just stared superciliously at Laurel, as if to ask why anyone would bother taking her out. Then Morgan spoke.

"Yes, of course," he said distantly. "I'm sure the inn can manage somehow without her, so running away shouldn't be hard for her to do."

To a casual listener, it would have sounded as if he were simply encouraging her to join Giles, but Laurel heard the undercurrents in his harsh voice and the double meaning in his words. He hadn't added "this time, either" to his sentence, but it was as plain to her as if he'd shouted the phrase. The faint color she'd acquired today ebbed, leaving her fair skin looking like ivory. But her eyes began to sparkle, and she linked her arm through Giles's in a gesture that was a deliberate imitation of Renee's.

"Well, in that case, Giles," she said brightly, "the runaway is yours. Lead me to your luncheon!"

Chuckling richly, he swung her away to get her

coat and tell Abby she was going. She went with her head high, refusing to look back at the two behind them. In a few minutes, though, when she was seated in Giles's Volvo, she unconsciously let out a long breath.

Reaching for the ignition, Giles paused and he turned to look at her.

"Who was that?"

"Which one?" she dodged.

"Not the feline woman with the tight orange fur and the sharp claws," he responded dryly. "I don't need to know who she is, because I can see for myself what she is. But who is he?"

She met his eyes now and dropped the pretense. Why should she pretend with Giles?

"That was my husband." She spoke as quietly as he had.

"Oh, my."

He sat back, and in spite of herself, her lips curved a tiny bit at those two expressive syllables. They were both silent for a moment. Then Giles spoke again, this time without looking at her.

"Do you want to go back?"

"No, please! Oh, Giles, let's go," she put an urgent hand on his sleeve, and he patted it consideringly.

"You're sure?"

"Yes. It would feel so good to get away. . . ."

"When did he come?"

"They both came last night."

She stressed the pronoun, and he slanted a startled look at her for confirmation. She nodded, and he agreed feelingly, "Yes, I can see why you'd like to get out for a while!"

Leaning forward, he started the car, letting it roar unevenly into life. But once it had settled into a slower idle, he still didn't pull away from the inn immediately. Hands on the wheel, he glanced at her again and asked matter-of-factly, "What can I do?"

She understood right away, and quick tears rushed to her eyes. She brushed them away—they were only nerves caused by too little sleep last night—and answered, "Just what you are doing, Giles—giving me a breather and helping me show him none of it matters anymore."

He threw her another look that comprehended even more than she realized as she added, "And thank you, Giles, more than I can say."

"Then don't try, my girl," he advised loftily, reverting to his usual cavalier manner, and she responded with a shaky laugh. As she burrowed in her pocket for a tissue, he drove out of the driveway of the Mountain View Inn with a flurry of gravel and a thoughtful expression.

CHAPTER NINE

IT WAS A LONG TIME before they came back. After
lunch they drove on past North Conway and deeper
into the White Mountains, which were just acquiring
their snow caps as winter drew on. But Giles took
Laurel places where beauty was seasonless, so that
she could enjoy the feeling of safety that comes with
crossing a river by a covered bridge, look into a
flume, through which pure icy water dropped over
granite cliffs like liquid lace, and search for the profile he promised she would find in the gray stone
ledges people called the Old Man of the Mountains.
She never was entirely sure she found it, but she
stopped trying when she remembered that Morgan's
face had looked like stone when they left.

It looked pretty much the same way when they returned. It was late afternoon—Abby and Betsy
would have dinner nearly done without her—by the
time Giles saw Laurel back into the inn. In fact, he
didn't just drop her at the door in the usual way, but
escorted her through the hall to her reception desk,
where he helped her take off her coat with a theatrical flourish. Flinging it grandly on a chair, he said,

"There you are, my girl, returned safe, sound and refreshed, just the way I promised. You see I know what's best for you!"

She chuckled at his tone, and he strode back to her, gathering her hands in his, so that they were completely engulfed. "And so, good evening, fair lady. Peggy's going ahead on her own, so I'll pick you up tomorrow at six for the premiere. That way we can get over there in time for me to have a last run-through of any problem areas before the concert. Agreed?"

"Agreed." She nodded smilingly, and before she had a chance to wonder why Peggy wasn't coming with them, he surprised her by kissing her full on the lips. It was only a brief contact, but it puzzled her. He hadn't tried kissing her again since that disastrous embrace they'd shared on the road to the lake. And she hadn't expected him to, either, now that they both knew each other's pasts.

She only had to wonder for a few seconds, though, because Morgan strode from the living room into the hall as soon as the front door closed on Giles. From the black scowl on his face, it was obvious he had seen the other man's graceful farewell to her, and Laurel speculated on whether Giles had deliberately been playing to an audience—and decided he had. Then Morgan cut off further speculation by grabbing her hand and yanking her into the still deserted dining room.

Caught off guard, Laurel went with him willy-nilly. The door swung closed behind them immediately, and Morgan blockaded it, towering in front of her, so that there was no question of her leaving that way unless he allowed her to. There was still the outside door, of course, and the one into the kitchen....

But then she decided it didn't matter anyway. Morgan Hamilton could be as enraged as he liked, and it wouldn't bother her in the least. Evidently he really was doing a management check on the inn, but otherwise she answered directly to Adam—at least for the foreseeable future—and even then she would never be answerable to Morgan in any way other than professional!

Drawing herself up to her full height, she met his angry stare and inquired coolly, ''And what, pray tell, is this all about?''

''I was going to ask you just that question,'' he grated, folding his arms across his chest. For a split second she thought how darkly attractive he looked in his crisp white shirt and Harris tweed sports coat, throwing his bronze skin into sharp relief, but she ruthlessly squashed the fancy. It didn't matter to her whether he was handsome or not—any more than his question mattered. She tilted her chin and didn't answer.

The silence seemed to vibrate, until he broke it to demand, ''Where have you been?''

''Out,'' she answered, and tore her eyes off him to look around the dining room. ''Oh, good,'' she murmured. ''Betsy has the tables set already. I should go help with dinner.''

She turned to leave him by that kitchen door, not as a retreat but as a triumphant withdrawal, and he surged away from the hall door to stop her before she could take a step. "Oh, no, you don't," he snapped, jerking her close so that she was pressed against his hard chest, reminding her of how tall he was. "Not again!"

"But I should help with things," she protested mildly to his necktie, wondering if her curls were tickling his chin.

"Damn dinner and damn the tables!" he roared, and she could feel the rumble of his shout. Then he lowered his voice with an effort at self-control that was almost palpable. "Where have you been?" he repeated in a carefully level tone.

"I don't really think that matters to you," she observed dispassionately.

"It bloody well does matter to me where my wife goes and who she's with!" His tone was anything but level again, and finally her voice began to rise, too.

"Well, then, why don't you ask your 'wife' that question someday?" she snarled, tipping her head back now so that she could meet his furious eyes with her own and match him glare for glare.

He chose not to hear her emphasis but fired back, "I am asking you, dammit. Little as it's ever seemed to matter to you, you are my wife!"

Pain shot through her, but like a soldier who keeps on fighting because he can't yet feel a mortal wound, she counterattacked bitterly, "Not in any way that counts!"

"That's right," he agreed, his ice-blue eyes dueling with her fiery gold. "You've taken off my ring, discarded my name, gone off entirely on your own without ever even having the guts to tell me to my face that you were leaving."

She drew a quick enraged breath to tell him—

But he cut her off. Raising his voice, he went on, "Yes, having jumped to your conclusions, and without bothering to give me the benefit of the doubt, or even a chance to speak for myself, *you* left *me*!"

Her eyes fell. Oh, God, how was he making her seem in the wrong? He had been the one with Renee in the library, hadn't he? Wasn't he just twisting it all to win this argument?

But now his fingers came up to her chin, and he forced her face back up toward his own. She searched his hard expression in confusion. It didn't alter as he ground out a savage conclusion, his breath hot on her lips. "So perhaps you're right, dear Laurel, and you're not my wife in any way that counts—not in loyalty and trust, certainly! But you're still my wife by law, and surely that gives me a right to some of the favors you're so willing to hand out elsewhere!"

And then the fierce anger in his face blurred out of her sight as he took her lips in a devastating kiss, holding her so tightly against the hard length of his body that there was nowhere she could turn her face to avoid him. She struggled wildly against him, pummeling his chest with both clenched fists, but he simply swept them into one strong hand and held them captive. The attack on her lips continued. Slowly and steadily he opened her mouth with his, and when he could taste her sweetness, her muffled protests began to die away as she was unbearably reminded of the last time he'd kissed her, that torturous night before the wedding. Then the memory faded along with everything else around them as he searched more deeply. The attack became a mutual surrender to passion.

She knew that outside of his embrace was only reeling darkness and clung to him now, no longer fighting against him—or herself. She gave herself up instead to the sensations only Morgan had ever aroused in her, and let the sweet hot tide spread throughout her trembling body. It seemed to flow down from the lips his own caressed, through her breast that swelled into the hand he raised to cup its trembling weight and down across her belly, until her hips and thighs melted beneath her and she felt herself begin to dissolve into him. So long she had yearned for this, so long—

The hall door opened behind them. A voice said cuttingly, "So this is how you spend your time waiting for me, *mon vieux*—practicing on the help, no?"

Dazedly Morgan lifted his lips from Laurel's and looked over his shoulder toward the door. "Renee," he said thickly, and to Laurel the sound of that name sliced brutally through the mist of desire like a searchlight through fog. That warm delicate mist evaporated, and she saw herself as if she were a stranger, a tousled pliant woman who clung mindlessly to the man who held her, even though she had every reason to detest him, simply because he aroused some chemical reaction in her body and she hadn't the self-control to resist him. That's how much of a fool she was—a weak desirous fool!

Tearing herself out of Morgan's arms, she stumbled without their support, but then recovered her balance as well as her sense and dealt him the fiercest slap she could.

"Child, what is it?" Abby asked anxiously as she erupted into the kitchen immediately after the pistol-shot sound of that slap.

Chest heaving, Laurel stood poised for an instant, turning her face, ravaged by anger, to Abby's kindly one, before she managed to choke out, "Him!" in tones of misery and loathing. Then she charged out the back door and vanished with a sob that was caused by rage at Morgan's base appeal to her desires.

Abby, left behind with the placid Betsy in a kitchen full of savory smells, glanced after Laurel, looked at the still swinging dining-room door with a slight smile on her round face and went back to preparing dinner.

On the far side of that door, however, Morgan and Renee faced each other across a space of about twelve feet. As the sound of Laurel's abrupt exit faded, the mark of her slap darkened on Morgan's lean cheek. Renee's angry black eyes fastened on it with satisfaction, and she stopped the hall door behind her with one heel, standing posed dramatically against it in her clinging silver dinner-dress.

"So," she snapped, "you have gotten what you deserve!"

He neither moved nor spoke, but the hard angles of his face sharpened in a way she had never seen before, and she realized abruptly that she had gone too far. Leaving the door, she swept gracefully over to him and laid her fingers across the scarlet cheek, crooning as she patted it gently, "Oh, no! I am wrong, and I ask your pardon, *mon cher*."

She smiled up at him penitently through her lashes and then looked sideways in the direction Laurel had gone, her expression sharpening. "It is she who deserves to be slapped," she hissed, "for trying to lure a wealthy man with her pathetic tricks—the common ignorant little slut!"

Her vituperative words seemed to echo, ugly in the air between them, and Morgan waited for a moment before he asked levelly, "Are you referring to my wife?"

Renee's jealousy was clearly overcome by her surprise as comprehension dawned. A ripple of satisfaction crossed her face at some secret thought, then vanished quickly. She almost purred her pleasure.

"I am sorry," she repeated easily. "I did not realize she was your wife. The hair is different now, no?" Laying her sleek head against his lapel, she toyed with one of his shirt buttons. "But when I saw how she treated you, I could not control my anger that she should behave so badly."

There was a brief heavy silence as she rubbed her cheek sensuously against the tweed of his jacket. Then he said expressionlessly, "I see," and removed her fingers from his shirtfront. Releasing them, he added punctiliously, "Excuse me, please," and walked away from her with his long even stride.

In a moment he had gone out the hall door and let it swing shut after him. Left behind, Renee snatched up a small vase of asters from the nearest table and heaved it with all her considerable strength at the far wall. It shattered, showering down to the floor in a heap of crystal shards that lay tangled among the flowers. Her feelings relieved, she swept out of the room, leaving the mess for Betsy to clean up.

Laurel didn't appear that night anywhere outside the kitchen, and both Renee and Morgan took note, but only the former with satisfaction. She managed to be invisible the following day as well, thanks to the back stairs that connected her room and the kitchen. Although she did her share of the cooking, she wheedled Abby into tending the registration desk, and Abby obliged without excessive commentary, which would have amazed Nate. She simply agreed with a smiling, "Of course, child; it's no bother," and asked no questions. But that could, of course, have been because she had already guessed most of the answers.

Laurel herself felt as though she had none. She was so confused by her response to Morgan's kiss that she lay awake for hours that night trying to comprehend how she could react so passionately to someone she despised. He had obviously been acting out of simple anger and possessiveness, and using his charge that she had never let him explain anything on their wedding day as a way to weaken her resistance. She didn't know what had got into her, letting him stir such a response in her. And she apparently wasn't going to be able to learn. All her thinking gave her little sleep and no answers, until at last she decided wearily that she might as well forget trying to figure it out. But if only she could also forget the piercing sweetness she had felt when Morgan's first angry kiss had been transformed into the brief shared surrender to desire....

THE NEXT NIGHT, when she began to dress to join Giles for the concert that would be the premiere of his Mountain Symphony, she found in her mirror a woman whose eyes were dull and smudged with sleeplessness and whose skin looked drawn and ghostly. Even her hair seemed to have lost its usual vitality, lying flat against her head. With one hand she made a halfhearted attempt to fluff the curls, but they sagged back limply into place.

All of a sudden she was disgusted with herself. Hadn't she any pride? What had happened yesterday—however it had happened—wasn't important to her. That kiss was meaningless; it had to be! What should be important to her was that a dear friend was taking her out tonight on an occasion that meant a great deal to him, and she owed it to him to look her absolute best—even if she was going to have to rush madly to make that miracle happen before Giles was due here to pick her up!

Stripping off the underwear she had dragged on dispiritedly, she shrugged into her robe and darted next door to the shared bathroom. In a surprisingly short time, a vigorous shower and shampoo had brought color back into her face and bounce to her hair. Bundling herself in her robe again, she wound a towel around her damp curls and barreled into the hall, without thinking to check first whether or not anyone else was nearby.

And Morgan was. Halfway down the corridor, near his own door, he looked up at the sound of the bathroom door being flung open and found her there, barefoot and damp.

"Laurel!" he exclaimed, and she jumped at his voice, then froze, wishing she could avoid him but strangely powerless to move.

He came toward her with that lean powerful stride of his, and she just watched him come, mesmerized. When he reached her, it seemed as though he were, too.

"I wanted to see you about yesterday—" he began forcefully, but then apparently forgot why. He broke off and simply stood there, hardly a hand's breadth away, looking at her.

It was almost as if yesterday's kiss had just happened, without Renee's interruption, as they stared at each other. Framed by coal-black lashes, his eyes were the pale blue gray of lake water on a hazy day, and she began to wonder dizzily if she were drowning in them as they clung to her and he absorbed every detail of her appearance. She could practically feel him take in everything, from the bare pink toes below her robe to the soggy towel that captured only half her curls, while the others straggled out below in wet little tendrils and the towel itself slid over one eye.

He lingered over the broad vee at her throat, where her clutching fingers hadn't caught the robe quite tightly enough, so that the swell of her breasts was visible, still faintly glistening with moisture. Finally he dragged his stare upward until it settled on her lips, half-parted by her uneven breathing. With hearing grown suddenly keen, she knew when his own breath began to come shortly. She even seemed to hear their two hearts starting to beat in rhythm. But neither of them spoke.

For Laurel, at least, it was as if she'd lost the ability, because she was all sensation. Speech, like reason, could have atrophied from disuse in the eternities they stood facing each other, when she could not have thought or said what held her there. Their quarrels, Renee, the cause of their ruined marriage—all that fled from her mind. The only thing she could do was feel, and what she felt was a creeping languorous warmth that spread delicately from the lips his eyes caressed, out and away until it reached the farthest corners of her being.

Perhaps Morgan felt it, too, because at last he began to move, to draw nearer to her warmth like a moth to a flame in that same unthinking fascination. But he seemed to come in slow motion, so that she saw each component gesture separately. She had ample time to avoid him if she could break the spell that held her still. She didn't try, however. She only stood poised for his embrace.

Then, an instant before it came, voices drifted along the hall, speaking of dinner and the evening, speaking of everything and nothing. And as though a silent enchanted spell had been broken, speech and reason returned to Laurel, and she realized what she was doing. She was letting desire overwhelm determination again, and on that thought she gasped, "No!" then twisted away into her own room, slamming the door behind her. Once Morgan knocked, only once, and without saying a word, but she ignored the sound, covering it and his retreating footsteps by banging drawers and screeching hangers along the closet bar.

When Giles arrived to pick her up an hour later, she had talked herself into being perfectly calm again—after all, this time she hadn't let Morgan succeed in undermining her resistance—except for the fierce bright color that flamed along her cheekbones, which only added the final touch to a vivid and spectacular outfit. Dressing as though she were putting on armor against any more devious attacks like that one in the hall, she set out to replace the image of her barefoot and defenseless against Morgan's magnetism with one that would be sophisticated and invulnerable.

Bringing out a gown she'd bought on the Riviera at the end of her stay in Europe, she put it on and smiled tightly at herself in the mirror. Demure pale blue silk, the dress began as a halter high on her throat with a wide neckband of sapphire velvet, then draped in a graceful cross over her bosom, gathered into a velvet waistband and flowed down over her hips to end in an uneven hem that frothed around her knees with every step. Crystal scintillated at her earlobes, and a length of velvet ribbon was threaded through her curls. The whole effect was delicate and fragile, like a porcelain figurine no one would dare touch.

The message was for Morgan Hamilton, whether he saw the dress or not, she thought resolutely, staring into the mirror. It said quite clearly that here, at least, was one woman who was not going to fall into his arms again! Then her expression lost its determination and became mischievous as she twisted, so that a little more of the dress showed in her reflection—or rather, a little less. As she turned and looked over one bare shoulder, her mirror revealed that the dress was completely backless, plunging from neckband to waist in a single dramatic swoop. And *that* was for Giles, the only man she'd dare wear an outfit like this for. He'd be appreciative and entertained, and if Morgan saw that, so much the better. It was about time he realized—

"Laurel!" Abby's voice floated up the back steps. "Giles is here to collect you for the concert."

"Abby, wait...."

Laurel walked to the top of the stairs and switched on the light, so that Abby blinked at the bottom. "What do you think?"

"Lovely, child! You look just like a fairy princess—"

She stopped abruptly as Laurel raised a delaying hand, then pirouetted very slowly to give her the full benefit of the back view as well as the front.

"Oh, my word!" Abby breathed, and her warm chuckle rose to Laurel. "I take back what I said about a princess—you look more like a movie star! Isn't it a good thing Giles will be standing up there conducting instead of you? Otherwise no one would hear the music."

The model-perfect hauteur of her pose crumbled as she smiled and called impulsively down the stairs, "Oh, Abby, I do love you!"

"I know, child," the comfortable reply came back up. "Now let me get back to serving dinner, and you go stop Giles from charging up and down the front hall as if the people at this concert were lions and he Daniel heading for their den!"

Laughing, Laurel turned out the light, and a minute later she was floating down the front steps. Giles, storming back from the far end of the hall, caught sight of her when she was halfway down and stopped dead, then strode over to extend his hand and help her grandly down the last few steps.

"Oh, my stars and garters," he murmured absurdly, keeping their linked hands high so that she could twirl for his inspection. Primly she did so, and as their hands loosened, he made a great show of winking and grinning wickedly. Then abruptly he schooled his mobile features into complete propriety, straightened his white tie, which sat oddly with the raffish beard, clicked his heels and intoned in a ridiculous accent, "Madam, your carriage awaits without. And might I say that your ladyship is looking particularly splendid tonight?"

"You may," she acquiesced on a gurgle of laughter. "Oh, Giles, you are wonderful!"

"I know," he agreed matter-of-factly in his usual tone, then added hollowly, "Let's hope the critics notice."

"They have to!" she stated firmly, and he slanted her a slight smile that broadened and became more intimate as he looked over her shoulder.

Without turning, she knew that Morgan had come into the hall, but she managed not to pivot and meet the stare she felt on her bare back. She left him to survey a considerable expanse of skin until Giles brought her coat from the hall closet and swung it elegantly around her and into place. Then he planted himself close in front of her and buttoned the coat carefully up to her chin, looking soulfully into her eyes all the time he did it. Only she was close enough to see the devilish glint in his gray eyes or hear the faint rumbling chuckle that made his starched shirt-front quiver.

When he was finally done, he extended his arm and she slid her hand into the crook of it.

"Madam?" he intoned.

"Yes, indeed, sir," she responded, and together they swept out the door, Giles still smiling to himself and Laurel congratulating herself. Not only had she somehow avoided kissing Morgan in the upstairs hall, but now she'd also refused to meet his eyes when she knew he was practically commanding her to do so!

Thanks to a triumphant champagne gala after the concert, they were very late getting back. Laurel drove the Volvo while Giles slouched beside her with his white tie pulled askew and his hair and beard rumpled, talking nonstop as he relived the entire evening. It was well past midnight when they finally pulled up in front of the inn, and Laurel—deciding with a private grin that this was not the time to wait for Giles to help her from the car—went around to his side and half encouraged him, half pried him from his seat. Swaying slightly, he pulled off his immaculate jacket and flung it over one shoulder, then draped the other arm heavily around her. As they lurched their way up the walk, he jubilantly sang the finale of his new symphony one more time.

She hadn't the heart to shush him, but as they reached the porch Laurel was wondering guiltily how many of her guests were being woken up. Then she realized the whole building was still ablaze with lights, and suddenly they were surrounded by a cheering crowd of townspeople and guests, all of whom had gone to the premiere. Giles was borne off to stand in front of the living-room fireplace and field eager comments and praise, gesturing jovially with a coffee cup in one hand. Laurel, still held loosely in the circle of his other arm, went smilingly with him, knowing how he was reveling in all this attention. Tonight's magnificent performance had certainly entitled him to wallow in it.

"It was superb, the most exciting concert I've been to in years!"

"Thank you, thank you—it was for me, too!"

"Your use of the brasses is marvelously innovative...."

"Lived here all my life, but that's the first time I've ever had the mountains *speak* to me...."

"How did you come up with that concept for a finale that sums up *all* the movements? It works perfectly here, but I haven't heard it done before."

"It's an idea I developed when I first conceived the whole symphony. I was trying to create a sense of the vast ages of the mountains and at the same time their underlying unity and renewal...."

It swirled around them both, an excited tide of congratulations and questions, and Giles bobbed happily as a cork on a flood. He wasn't entirely absorbed by it, though. Letting her eyes wander idly around the room from one enthusiastic face to another, Laurel's attention was caught by Peggy's bright head. Still in her plain black dress from the concert, so drab that her hair practically glowed above it, she must have got back from North Conway sometime before them and stopped by the inn on her way home.

On the edge of the group, she was chatting vivaciously with an attractive middle-aged man. Laurel couldn't catch any of their words, but she could see Peggy's hands move expressively, as busy as hummingbirds, and her companion throw back his head to laugh at something she said.

"As if you somehow spoke for the land and for all the rest of us as well...."

Laurel's eyes flickered toward Giles. He didn't seem conscious of it, but as if he couldn't help himself, he began to speak directly to Peggy, no matter who he was answering, while her male companion fell silent.

"Thank you." He put aside excitement and answered seriously. "I'm honored you felt that way. A composer can hope for it, but he can only know for sure that he speaks for himself—that he writes from his heart and soul, expressing everything he may not be able to find words for."

As if the action were beyond his volition, he met Peggy's look as he spoke, and unobtrusively Laurel began to slip away from his arm, trying to put a visible distance between them. Then a flash of movement caught her eye, and she identified Renee languidly crossing her legs as she sat on a settee at the far side of the room, at a distance calculated to show only a mild interest in Giles—and Laurel. The motion nicely displayed one of her best features, and smoothing her skirt over her knees, she smiled intimately up over her shoulder at Morgan, standing behind her so that she was between him and his wife. Then she turned back and looked directly at Laurel with a different sort of smile, one that was both challenging and complacent. Seeing it, Laurel knew for certain that even if Renee hadn't recognized Morgan's bride when she'd first checked in, she did now—and didn't care.

Morgan, too, was looking her way, but his expression was unreadable. An instant later he bent down to catch Renee's murmured phrase, and when he straightened again Laurel moved closer to Giles, after only a breath's hesitation, linking her arm with his.

It was a confident gesture, but the message in her eyes was an urgent plea, and she wondered if he would be able to see it. For a split second his own eyes moved in Peggy's direction once more. Then they met hers in a warm straight gaze, and he patted the hand on his arm possessively. A minute later she heard the front door close with a decided thump. When Laurel next looked for Peggy, the younger woman was gone.

Laurel didn't even hear the next several questions

and comments that flowed past her, intent as she was on looking as serenely untroubled as she could manage. Thanks to Giles's hand on hers, she was successful enough so that she didn't even blink when Renee rose sinuously and strolled to the living-room door, with Morgan slowly following suit. But it was hard not to flinch.

Passing near Laurel, Renee paused, so that she threw the differences between the two of them into sharp contrast, Laurel's copper-tinged curls and pastel dress almost overwhelmed by Renee's gleaming black hair and plunge-necked magenta satin. As she stood there, even their expressions were contrasting—Laurel's chin up and direct, Renee's sideways and seductive—but Morgan didn't betray any reaction to either. He simply walked out the door with his usual lithe stride, and Renee went after him, saying in a slightly husky voice that still managed to carry, "*Alors*, good night, all. We are going to bed." And on that thoroughly suggestive note, she swayed out of sight.

A while later even the most enthusiastic concert goers' momentum finally ran out, and when everyone else had gone Laurel saw Giles to the outer door. Complete exhaustion was beginning to catch up with him at last, and his face was paper white, with two deep holes for eyes.

Watching him drag his jacket behind him, she called an order softly after him. "Go home and sleep for a week, Giles! You've earned it."

He half raised one hand in a weary wave without turning, and she added, "And thank you again."

This time he turned, and he didn't ask what she was referring to.

"Anytime," he said with a grin, but the light from the porch didn't fall across his eyes.

"I only wish Peggy didn't think—"

"I do, too, but there it is." He shrugged and observed dispassionately, "No triumph is ever complete, is it?"

"Oh, Giles—"

"Never mind, princess," he cut her off. "If it's meant to, it will all come right somehow." And with another tired salute, he walked off into the darkness, leaving the Volvo to be claimed some other time.

Princess. . . . Her father had called her that when she was a child, and sudden tears stung Laurel's eyelids. Giles had probably been referring to his silly routine as footman when he picked her up—six hours ago that seemed like a thousand. Oh, why couldn't she have fallen in love with a man like him, instead of getting involved with someone who was probably upstairs with his lover right now? Sighing for Giles, or perhaps herself, Laurel swung the heavy door shut.

CHAPTER TEN

OVER THE NEXT FEW DAYS life at the inn returned to normal, as the excitement over Giles's symphony simmered down into a kind of steady local pride. To everyone's delight, the critics, too, were as enthusiastic as Laurel had predicted. As for Giles himself, after a day and a half when he was invisible, he took to coming by the inn nearly every evening to settle in the living room with his pipe and a cup of coffee, to chat with anyone who happened by.

That included an interesting procession of people as the guests came and went. But Morgan and Renee stayed, in spite of all of Laurel's urgent wishes to the contrary.

"He's using this place as a base of operations, and she's just hanging around waiting for him and complaining! You should have let me scare them off, child," Abby muttered in the kitchen more than once. She always glanced at Laurel as she did it, obviously hoping that permission would finally be forthcoming. But the response was always the same.

"You know all the reasons why we can't, and they haven't changed one bit," Laurel answered.

Although her answer came more and more slowly as she was increasingly tempted, Abby didn't comment on it. The interchanges always ended with her grunting a disappointed "Hrumph!" If she was privately pleased by any part of the situation, Laurel never guessed.

Laurel herself kept on playing the perfect innkeeper, no matter what she thought of some of her guests. She did, however, resolve that the best way to deal with her explosive reactions to Morgan was to avoid him completely, which she did by handling most of the inn's business from the kitchen, coaxing Abby into managing the desk out front again. That meant, of course, that she herself was in no position to watch all the goings-on and see that Morgan, too, was almost invisible, going out most days to survey other Hamilton inns in northern New England. When he did appear, the hard angles of his face began to look harder than ever, as if some fire were forging steel.

Renee was simply beginning to look furious. Whenever she stepped out of her room, she was dressed to kill—and nearly always discovered that the prey was somewhere else. And so, although she refused to leave, she stalked around the inn in a rapidly worsening temper, finding something new to complain about nearly every hour of the day. The only time her voice lost its fishwife edge and sank back into the customary purr was when Giles came up to the inn, setting off a series of elaborate ploys and subterfuges.

Charging in after dinner most evenings, he would start by dallying extravagantly with Laurel if she was available and Morgan anywhere within earshot. Then he would eventually stroll into Renee's orbit and soon have her moving in to sit pressed against him on the settee, gazing up at him through her sooty eyelashes and speaking to him in a voice too low for anyone else to hear. If—rarely—Morgan came by, Renee would twine herself around Giles like mistletoe. But Morgan was blind to all her efforts.

Finally one evening, when he had again cut through the room without giving her activities a glance, Renee unwound herself from Giles and followed the other man into the hall.

"Morgan!" Her voice rang behind him up the staircase, and he turned slowly to look down at her, his dark face impassive.

"We must talk, you and I."

Not a question, or even a statement. It had the ring of a command. His eyebrows rose, but he came back down the stairs and stood over her. She was right—they'd have to talk. Ignoring her clearly hadn't got the message across. Utterly preoccupied with Laurel ever since they'd arrived, he'd offered her only minimal politeness, but she couldn't seem to comprehend what that meant.

She evidently no longer comprehended Morgan himself, if she ever had, because she opened their conversation with an attack. "You are making a fool of me!" she accused haughtily.

His long upper lip twitched, but his answer was simply. "Is that possible?" he countered with quiet ambiguity.

She stared at him blankly, before several possible meanings of the remark occurred to her, and dark red color rushed into her face. It was not becoming.

Before she could fly at him, however, he had taken her elbow and expertly piloted her into the parlor, so that the rest of their conversation, at least, wouldn't be public.

As soon as he pushed the door closed behind them, she shook off his hand. But the gesture lost what violence it would have had a minute earlier, because the brief interruption had given Renee time to think, and where her own interests were concerned, she was no fool.

Now, free of Morgan's clasp, she moved to stand several feet away from him, her back partly to him, her head bent. This presented a touching profile of wounded womanhood, and when she spoke again her voice had dropped its stridency and taken on a wistful note.

"I see you so little," she sighed, "and I have waited so long!"

He made no answer, and she continued without looking at him, "When you first left me, I waited and waited—the weeks passed by, and still I waited. I thought to myself that you would come back, surely you would come, because you had not meant it when you said that everything between us was over."

She drew an audible shaken breath. "But you did not come, and I grew desperate. I tried to find you—"

One of Morgan's hands sliced the air impatiently but then became still again, and she went on.

"I called to your company, and at first they would not tell me. Then they said you were going from hotel to hotel and could not be reached. And finally I said that I had to deliver an urgent personal message to you, and they told me you were coming here."

So that was it. Morgan shook his head silently, scowling to himself in a way that didn't bode very well for company headquarters. Now Renee turned back and gazed at him pleadingly, prettily, as she came toward him again.

"And so I came here, too, to this—" she spread her hands expressively "—place, to see you—"

"Why?" The single syllable dropped into her monologue, and she lost her place.

"What?"

"I asked you why."

She shook her head sorrowfully and looked at him with the eyes of a lonely doe. "I have told you— because I had to see you again—"

"No." His interruption was very quiet and very definite. Searching his face, she found only hard bronze planes and a cold blue stare. Still she tried again, placing both hands beseechingly on his lapels.

"It has been so long since I have seen you, and I have waited so—"

He removed her hands and let them fall. "It won't work, Renee," he observed neutrally. "Why don't you tell me the real reason?"

The furious color swept back into her face, and it seemed to age her as it came, highlighting the coarsening texture of her skin and the deepening lines he'd never noticed before.

"*Salaud!*" she spat. "*Saligaud!*" And her hand flashed up across his cheek.

As soon as it connected, he caught it in a grip so hard she winced, as he had not done. She struggled, and the grip tightened further then slackened, and she was free, her other hand going automatically to her whitened wrist.

Morgan's own hand did not go to his cheek. A fraction of his mind noted with grim amusement that it wasn't the same one Laurel had smacked; he had apparently turned the other cheek. He stood motionless in front of Renee, and there was a glint in his eyes that made it extremely unlikely that she would slap him again.

"Why?" he repeated softly.

She eyed him with open resentment now but didn't dare do anything more than answer his question. "Because the lease on my apartment is running out," she admitted grudgingly, and then, as if such unaccustomed frankness freed her for more of the same, "Because I need money!"

Head flung back now, she glared at him defiantly. He met her stare. "But surely I wasn't your only bankable asset," he commented dryly, and saw her eyes flicker.

"Of course you were not! I only thought you might be my most...accommodating!" She hurled the insult at him, but he seemed entirely unaware of it, and her voice rose again. "I would not take your money now—" She raged on and lapsed into a torrent of gutter French. Before she had finished, Morgan was gone from the room.

Within an hour she was seated by the fire, cooing admiringly to another guest, a man twice her age. Her long nails patted his heavy cheek in mock displeasure, and as she softly murmured something, a fine dew of perspiration beaded his upper lip. Early the next evening, she left with him.

Alerted by Abby that she was leaving at last, Laurel wasn't able to resist the temptation to arrange her own comings and goings so that they would bring her past the parlor windows in time to see Renee's departure from the Mountain View Inn. In the wake of an elegant burgundy Lincoln, she wheeled her Porsche out of the driveway without even giving the inn a last contemptuous glance. For the first few yards Limb ran barking after her—something he'd never done with a guest's car before—and although she knew she couldn't let that become a habit, this time Laurel grinned to herself, because if the dog hadn't done it she might have!

Her smile fading slowly, she watched until Renee had disappeared around the bend in the road before

she let a small sigh escape her and turned away from
the window. Only then did she discover that Morgan
had come noiselessly to stand behind her and look
out the same window. Now, with her movement, she
found herself gazing right into his eyes, the gray blue
of clouds at dusk.

She held his stare, but her mind was beginning to
churn. She had barely seen him these past few days,
staying behind the scenes the way she'd been doing.
Abby had reported—although Laurel didn't ask—
that Morgan had been around very little, busy surveying the other inns. Now overwhelmingly conscious of his nearness, Laurel wondered urgently
whether that had occupied *all* his time. But he and
Renee couldn't have been meeting secretly, even
away from the inn, because during his absences her
presence had been so noticeable, thanks to her constant complaining.

Had he stopped seeing her, then, because of
Renee's flirtation with Giles? He'd been angry
enough, Laurel remembered hastily, when Giles
flirted with *her*, and she was only important to
Morgan because a piece of paper said she was his
wife. How much more it must have enraged him to
see his girl friend distracted by Giles's extravagant
courtship. And now that she had suddenly gone away
with yet another man, how miserably jealous he must
feel.

He was so close that she caught the faint tang of
his lime after-shave. His face was utterly impassive,

but the thought that he might really have been hurt by Renee sent a sharp pang through her. By rights she should have felt a sense of triumph and vindication. Renee was gone, and if it upset him to have her choose another man, then that was only a pale version of the distress she herself had known on their wedding day to have him choose another woman. Yet somehow all she felt now was angry pain. Her pulse began to race, like her mind, and so she lashed out, snapping like any hurt animal.

Still close enough to Morgan so that she could hear his even breathing, so that she longed to place her hands on his chest and let the corduroy fabric of his sports coat rise and fall under her fingers, she said caustically, "Dear, dear, we seem to have lost one of our most colorful guests. Aren't we fortunate that you're still here to make life worth living?"

His eyes held hers, but the color seemed to change, shifting from blank blue gray to a sapphire color that she had never seen before. Furiously, she wished that her taunt hadn't come out in quite those words. What if he had missed her tone and taken the words at face value?

Rushing into speech again to make herself perfectly clear, she added, "I trust you two at least had a touching farewell scene before this sad finale."

Now her sarcasm was unmistakable, and she threw it at him, even though it was like a dagger that went hilt first, pointing into her own heart. But instead of taking up her challenge and dueling with her until she forgot the pain of the moment in all the new blows, he simply gazed at her. His eyes lost their deeper color. His face changed in some subtle way, almost as if warm flesh were cooling again to ice, but otherwise he was completely motionless until she began to twist her fingers in the pockets of her skirt. When his answer finally came, it was totally unexpected.

"You should know," he returned harshly, "since you saw it for yourself."

With those words he left the room. She heard the outer door close decisively on him and he was gone into the darkness, quickly disappearing from view of her window. Her hands still, her eyes fixed, even her breathing practically arrested, she stood where he'd left her and tried to comprehend what he'd said.

She saw his farewell to Renee? She couldn't have! She had been careful to see them as little as possible—together or separately—and was able to count the few times it had happened. There was the night of the premiere, when Renee had announced she and Morgan were going to bed, and the time she had interrupted Morgan's kiss in the dining room.... With a kind of memory that had everything to do with sensation and nothing with intellect, Laurel could feel all over again the way that punishing kiss had melted into passion, and her skin was suddenly hot and flushed. She tried to shake off the remembered heat and concentrate. Before that, Morgan and Renee had come out into the hall together to see her leave with Giles for lunch in North Conway. That left only the afternoon they had both checked in...and the day she and Morgan were married.

Hardly conscious of what she was doing, Laurel sat down hard on the chair beneath the window. Morgan had just told her that he and Renee had parted that day in Adam's library. Everything else vanished from her mind.

Could Morgan have been telling the truth? Had he really said goodbye to Renee then? Distractedly Laurel wrapped her arms tightly around herself, clutching the hope to her. If it was true—if he hadn't been involved with Renee since their marriage.... Hope began to grow. What had he said when he'd first arrived at the inn and realized she were here? "I've looked so long." He hadn't finished the sentence, but it was indelibly printed on her mind. If he had been looking for her, didn't that mean...?

She was afraid to finish the thought. Then she remembered their kiss in the dining room. Surely that had been the embrace of two people passionately in love? She had been nearly swept away by the torrent of desire Morgan had stirred in her, and she knew the same flood tide had risen in him, too—they had clung together as if they were drowning!

Growing braver, she finally let herself admit she still loved Morgan. She loved him, and a feeling of relief swept over her. It had been a feeble sort of self-deception to deny it, and giving up the pretense was like dropping a heavy boulder. Released, she relaxed her arms and let them fall. She loved Morgan, and he

must care for her, too. She didn't need to deny
her heart and battle her body any longer. In spite
of all the hurt she'd felt because of the misunder-
standing over Renee, she could finally acknowledge her love for him for the first time since...
Paris.

At the name, her whole card house of happiness
came crashing down. Morgan had been seeing another woman at the café in Paris—and had tried to
deny it. He hadn't just lied to her before the wedding. He'd been trying to do it again then and could
just as well be doing it now. She couldn't trust anything he said.

Anger, pain and sick disappointment welled up inside her. She'd been a fool again. She'd let her heart
overrule her head, the way she'd always done where
Morgan was concerned. From the start she'd had
clues about the sort of man he was, but she'd ignored
them all until it was too late—ignored them because
she'd been swept away for the first time in her life by
all the magic and power of passion.

"It's on the back cover of the magazine—I think I
left it in here."

"Never mind. If it doesn't turn up, we can just buy
a new one."

Two guests were approaching the parlor door from
the living room, and Laurel dragged herself up off
the chair as if she were a thousand years old. Moving
to the hall door with steps that were actually un-
steady, she climbed the stairs to her room.

By MORNING she had made a decision. Since she couldn't ask Morgan to leave the inn, and since she didn't dare leave it herself as long as he was here to represent the company, she would simply have to be more careful than ever to avoid running into him. There could be no more of these shattering contacts! So far, every time they'd come face to face he'd left her shaken and confused, her mind awhirl and her body aching. Somehow she had managed to get by, but this last skirmish had been almost more than she could bear, building up her hopes and then razing them to the ground. She knew she couldn't stand that again, and her mirror gave proof of the fact, reflecting a face that was pinched with misery and strain.

Both Abby and Giles saw the effects, too, although Morgan had no such opportunity. Without comment, Abby continued handling the front desk and began coming earlier and staying later, so that she could take over virtually all direct contact with the guests and leave Laurel in the background. Giles kept coming to the inn most evenings, concentrating all his attention on Laurel and apparently unaware that Peggy—visiting regularly as well, as though she had to keep track of everything going on there—had taken to watching them both with angry eyes.

Once Laurel tried to explain it all to her. Catching Peggy on her way into the inn one evening, alone for a minute as she took off her coat in the front hall, Laurel set aside the flowers she'd been bringing to grace the parlor.

"Peggy, hello! How are you? Here, I'll put that in the closet for you."

"Thanks."

As a conversational opener, that exchange wasn't much to build on. Taking Peggy's heavy coat, Laurel gave up on small talk and tried a direct approach.

"Could I talk to you a minute, Peggy?"

"What about?"

Peggy's expression was suspicious, and when Laurel answered, "Giles," it went hard.

"No," she said flatly, and pulled a brush out of her pocket. Stepping past Laurel to the mirror on the other side of the hall, she began to fix her windblown hair. But even though her actions were obviously meant to show disinterest, she immediately spoke again, glancing at Laurel in the mirror.

"Why talk to me about him anyway?" she asked, as if she couldn't help it.

"Just because I wanted you to understand that Giles is only a friend of mine. The time he spends with me...."

Turning away from the hall closet, Laurel realized that she hadn't planned any way *to* explain it all. How could she ever tell Peggy that Giles was flirting with her just to keep her spirits up while her estranged husband was on the premises? Or that he had also flirted with her husband's girl friend to keep that impossible woman from driving everyone else to distraction with her complaints!

"Oh, I understand, all right!" Peggy cut in, swinging away from the mirror to glare at Laurel. Newly cut in a surprisingly sophisticated gamine mop, her red hair almost bristled with indignation, and her face flamed. "I understand fine! Giles is the handsomest, most talented man anywhere around here, and it's every woman for herself! He's nice, too, and polite, and you and that French pastry just fell all over yourselves when he paid you a little attention, so of course he had to keep on being nice. And in the meantime you two haven't even left him time to notice I'm alive!"

Laurel tried to interrupt, but Peggy just raised her voice and stormed on. "But at least she's gone now, and I'll show him I'm alive—I'm alive and *somebody* appreciates me!"

And without even giving Laurel time to wonder whether she dared hint that Giles certainly cared about her, Peggy tossed her head angrily and walked away into the living room—walked with a studied grace on the heels she'd just started wearing. Within minutes she was flirting madly with every man in the room, and Laurel overheard her tell someone later that she was hoping to arrange an audition with the New England Symphony Orchestra. Whether or not Giles knew what she was planning, Laurel couldn't tell, and Peggy wouldn't tell, confining herself after that to shooting Laurel furious glances whenever they passed—although she didn't stop coming to the inn.

That was that. As far as helping bring the two of them together by explaining what had been going on,

well, her effort had been a miserable failure. She
hadn't done any better for them than she had for
herself throughout her whole catastrophic relationship with Morgan. Yet still hating to feel she was a
barrier between the other two, she tried once more to
change her tactics and speak to Giles about Peggy.

They'd both taken the day off and driven over to
Mount Katahdin in Giles's car, because he wanted to
show her the state's tallest mountain, wrapped in
clouds and legends. She didn't get much of a look.
By the time they reached the mountain it had begun
to snow lightly, and Laurel could see only a dark gray
bulk against a lighter gray sky, a massive upsurge of
granite and pine. As they started home more slowly
than usual, she broke the companionable silence.

"Giles?"

"Mmm?" He shook off whatever he'd been thinking of and threw her an inquiring glance before returning his eyes to the road.

"You're a dear to be spending time with me like
this," she began.

"That's me," he said lightly. "Busy expiating my
sins with good deeds. Isn't it nice to know you're
helping me along the paths of virtue?"

She grinned as he had meant her to, and went on,
"And I'm grateful—"

"Hooey!"

"But I hate to be using up all the free time you
could be spending with Peggy."

"I wouldn't be doing that anyway," he said flatly.

"I have no intention of trying to tie her to me until she's had enough time to look over the rest of the world."

"But she's met dozens of men just at the inn this fall! Couldn't you at least give her some idea...!"

Her words trailed off as she realized his amiable face had taken on a set look. Instantly she knew she'd trespassed, but before she could apologize, he said expressionlessly, "If the time is ever right, I'll worry about that, thanks," and then softened the rebuff by adding, "But let me tell you the real reason I dragged you all the way over here to Katahdin. There's an Indian legend about the mountain that I'd like to try out on you, because I'm thinking about using it as the basis for some program music, now that the flute sonata is off to the printer's."

As he mentioned the mountain, his voice warmed to its usual tone, and Laurel, who had been feeling both gauche and snubbed a moment earlier, was thankful to let the subject drop and follow his lead.

"So tell me the story," she invited, "and I'll give you my inexpert opinion."

She settled herself deeper into her seat, and Giles looked down the road, gathering his thoughts before he spoke.

"In the times of legend," he began, and like any child Laurel was caught up by that ageless introduction, "long before the white men came, when Katahdin rose above the wigwams of the Abnaki, Kinaldo the warrior dreamed of a maiden. To his sister, young Winona, he described her as a beautiful woman whose face shone in the storm clouds when she called to him. And Winona was afraid that some-day this spirit woman would lure away her brother, as indeed did happen.''

Giles paused, and when he spoke again his deep voice grew deeper and took on the singsong rhythm of a born storyteller, so that the timeless enchant-ment started to spin around Laurel, and she was held spellbound.

"Hunting in the forest one day, Kinaldo found the steps of a child and followed their path, while a sweet voice whispered his name. To Katahdin, master of mountains, they went, and there she stood smiling before him, the maid of his dreams, dressed in light and great beauty." Unconsciously Giles's voice slowed, caressing the old words of his story, and Laurel knew he'd forgotten she was there.

"She beckoned Kinaldo and gladly he came, into the granite halls of Katahdin, forgetting home, family, and fear in her beauty. And when they had reached the highest of halls, before them Pamola, lord of the darkness and ruler of earth, was shaping men's lives like his arrows.

"He greeted his daughter, fair Lightning, and later her brothers, the Thunders, when in they rushed, unstrapping their noisy dark wings. Then all of them made Kinaldo welcome, showing him scenes of the death of men he could, with them, escape. Loving the maiden of light, whom he called Light-in-a-Cloud,

Kinaldo drank deep of the strong scarlet fluid they offered and lived there with them in great joy like the dawning of days.''

He paused again, and Laurel found she had woven her fingers together, clasping them. Her grip tightened as the tenor of the story changed.

''But at last came a time when a voice pierced his pleasures, the voice of Winona, his sister who grieved. Longing to see her, he vowed to be gone, and heeded not the great wrath of Pamola, who warned him that those who had drunk of the wine of Katahdin could not live long in the world of men. Tears in her eyes, his love said farewell, but promised at sunset the next day to claim him.

''The next day he was home in the forest of men, meeting his sister, a woman now grown with a babe in her arms. At last believing her brother had come, she told him the truth of his 'nights' in Katahdin— seven long years had passed since his leaving. Sadly he knew that Pamola spoke truly when he said that Kinaldo had done with all men. And at sunset a dark cloud rushed up from the west, while lightning flashed and the tall pines all swayed. But Kinaldo just waited till white arms reached down, as a spear of loved light struck the tree where he stood. Later his friends found his still form unscarred, but a banner of brilliance topped the peak of Katahdin.''

On the last line Giles's voice dropped and he fell silent. Laurel came very slowly back to the world of everyday things. Around her the Volvo took shape, picking its way through the snow, and when she could see Giles clearly again, he was holding out one of his big white handkerchiefs.

"It took me that way, too, when I first heard it," he said in his usual tone, and she managed a watery chuckle of agreement.

"It's so beautiful. . . ."

"I know." He picked up the sentence as she broke it off. "It's a good deal like other legends you can find around the world," he added thoughtfully, "and I suppose that's because we can all see something of ourselves in tales of love and separation."

She nodded silently, and they both shied away from talking about their particular reasons for finding themselves in the story of Kinaldo and his beloved.

Giles went on, "Anyway, ever since I first heard this one when I was a kid, I've had a yen to set it to music, if I could only begin to hear it in my mind. Now I think that's finally starting to happen. I can hear a mighty theme for Katahdin, heavy and solemn, and a lighter clearer melody—maybe in the woodwinds—for Light-in-a-Cloud, calling."

His voice rose, alive with enthusiasm, and he raked excited fingers through his hair until it stood up even more wildly than ever, while Laurel smiled sympathetically. All the rest of the long way home, he was hardly aware of the deteriorating weather around them, but drove much more sedately than usual simply because he was thinking out loud, deciding which of the brasses and drums could speak for the Thunders and how he could weave together the themes of Kinaldo, his love and the mountain in the finale. And so, although she helped him a little in developing his ideas, Laurel said nothing more about Peggy.

The whole situation was still thoroughly unsatisfactory, however, and the next evening Peggy herself made it plain how much she resented the way things were.

Morgan hadn't come in yet, so Laurel wasn't worried about running into him. She was sitting on the sofa with Giles, leafing through a stack of books he'd brought up to the inn, fired by her appreciation of the story of Kinaldo. Suddenly he dropped the one he'd been holding into his lap and looked at her with an arrested expression. Then he pushed the book aside and surged to his feet, grabbing her hand as he went. Forced to abandon her own book, Laurel protested laughingly, "Giles, what on earth—"

"Wait," he ordered mysteriously. "You'll see in a minute. I've just remembered something."

Baffled but intrigued, she let him urge her out into the hall and over to the closet that was tucked into the bend of the front stairs where they turned to go at right angles to the hall, rising almost to the second story before they turned back to their original direction. Releasing her hand, Giles swung open the closet door and with a sweep of his arm shoved aside the various coats hanging there, reaching up with his other hand to pull the string that turned on the overhead light. Peering in past his broad figure, Laurel was completely mystified. Then she followed his gaze and noticed the outline of a rectangle on the back wall of the closet, down low.

"What—"

"That, my girl," he interrupted her, eyes alight, "is the way into a hidden compartment. They were often built into houses of about this vintage, whenever there were three fireplaces arranged in a U shape the way they are here."

Running long sensitive fingers along the outline, he added, "They were probably used for storage and as drying rooms for fruit and flowers most of the time. But when I was a kid I used to think they must have been meant as refuges for the settlers in case of Indian attack." With a faint note of regret in his voice he admitted, "The truth is, though, that the Indian wars probably ended around here half a century before this place was put up."

Anyway the old fascination obviously still held, and Laurel found herself caught up in it, too. Crouched beside him now in the cramped space of the closet while most of her guests crowded curiously in behind them, attracted by the commotion, she slid her hands along the outline and came to a wider place in the crack so slight that only by touch would it be noticeable. While she was exploring it, Giles noticed her intent expression and leaned over to feel the same area.

"Hah!" he crowed. "You've got it! Now if we just pull here—"

He broke off, concentrating on easing out the panel covering the hole. With a screech of protest, it finally gave—probably for the first time in many years—and came away in his hands. Behind it, the thick darkness retreated slightly as light from the bulb in the closet fell partway into the hole. They could hear excited babblings behind them in the hall.

"Well, I'll be darned! Will you look at that?"

"Brrr! Looks spooky."

"How fascinating!"

Laurel agreed with all of them, but as a dry aged smell crept out past her it prickled her nostrils, and she sneezed.

Giles grinned, smelling it, too, but he only asked, "Do you have a flashlight anywhere handy?"

She blinked and sniffed, wrinkling her nose as she thought.

"Not here, I'm afraid, but I think there are a couple out in the barn. Shall I go get one?"

"No, let's not bother," he decided. "It's started to snow again, and even if you cut through the inside you'd freeze in those old passageways. Anyway, there's a fair amount of light going in from here."

Cocking one eyebrow, he grinned again and asked, "Want to go first?"

"Not me!" Her response was prompt, and his smile broadened. "You go right ahead and scout the way. I'll come along later."

"Fine spirit of adventure you have, my girl!" he teased, and she acknowledged the charge with a sheepish shrug, then scrambled out of the closet. The closet was claustrophobic enough, but that dark little space behind it looked even worse!

Not that it seemed to bother Giles one bit. He went squirming in and called back, his deep voice booming hollowly, "Marvelous! It's completely enclosed—it would make a perfect hideout."

That did it. As Laurel sat on the stairs, everyone else pressed forward eagerly. For now, even Peggy was too distracted to glower on her way by. In ones and twos they alternately squeezed in to join Giles in the tiny space behind the closet, coming out to blink in the light again and brush themselves off.

"That's a mighty interesting thing you've got there, ma'am," a silver-haired westerner commented to Laurel. "You ought to think about letting all your guests from now on have a look-see if they fancy finding out how one of these old places was put together."

She smiled in agreement, but when the last guest stumbled out and Giles shouted, "Laurel! You coming?" she called back cravenly, "Some other time."

She heard his rich laugh echo, and a minute later he reappeared before her in the hall. "Coward!" he taunted, combing the thick black cobwebs from his hair and beard.

"Hmm-mmm," she agreed, watching the process with interested revulsion. "Ugh!"

"It's not so bad now," he assured her. "We must have knocked down most of them."

She looked skeptical, but before she could say anything more he went off on a tangent. "Didn't one of those books you were looking at have a list of the early settlers who came into this area around the time of the Revolution?" he asked, and at her nod added, "We could check and see if there's any chance that some of those people might actually have built this old place."

Caught up in this new discovery, he strode off in the direction of the living room. The various guests straggled after him, comparing notes.

Left alone in the hall, Laurel went to pull the string and turn off the closet light, and realized Giles had left the panel to cover the cubbyhole leaning against the wall. She couldn't very well leave it like that—the pungent smell of that tiny chamber would get into the fabric of every coat in the closet—so she stepped inside to set it back in place. Kneeling, she found herself gazing into the recess.

How incredible to think that when the inn was young, Indian voices that told of Kinaldo might almost have echoed here. Did the settlers who had built the inn ever wonder about the Indians who had come before them? Or were they too desperately busy keeping body and soul together and bringing their different ways to this beautiful place? Did all the new Americans come in pride and triumph, or did some of them come to gain a brighter future when the old one had gone dark?

Without realizing it she had leaned farther and farther forward to peer into the cubbyhole. Now she
sank back on her heels. Going in there alone would
be crazy, but if she intended to make a practice of letting other guests explore the hole, she'd really need to
know more about it for herself. Glad that she was
wearing comfortable slacks, she took a deep breath
and wriggled forward into the darkness.

A moment later she rose to her feet and straightened cautiously. Finding that she could stand upright, she looked around her by the dim illumination
of the closet light, reflected dimly on the dust-
covered floor under her feet. All round her was
brick. It formed the floor and rose on every side until
it met just above her head. At first she was puzzled.
Then with an exclamation she realized how the
chamber was formed—and understood what Giles
had said about the three chimneys. These walls
around her were actually the inn's chimneys, serving
the fireplaces in the parlor, living room, and dining
room and coming together over her head to go out
through the roof in a single stack! For confirmation,
she touched the wall in front of her. It was warm;
there was a fire burning in the living room tonight, as
there was most nights.

So far she had been distracted by figuring out how
the tiny room worked, but now Laurel looked
around more closely, and once again her enthusiasm
started to wane. Whatever might once have been
stored here, now there was nothing. The carpet of

dust under her feet was thick and fine, a powder that made her eyes and nose react. It must have been laid down in infinitesimal layers over the long decades. Spiders had been busy too—long-gone ones, she hoped. Their webs still festooned the corners of the cubbyhole, in spite of what Giles had said, and they were coal black with age, thick and solid looking, hanging in dark drapes like the mourning robes for some ancient funeral. What was the old superstition about someone walking over your grave? She shuddered. The spiderwebs were too close for comfort. This really *was* a very small space!

On that thought she abruptly decided that the time had come to squirm her way back out of here—and just then the panel slipped into place over the hole, cutting off her exit and all her light as well, while the closet door clicked shut.

CHAPTER ELEVEN

FOR A MOMENT she was shocked into complete silence and immobility, and in that moment she heard footsteps retreating, a woman's steps, in high-heeled shoes.

"Wait!" she called. "Don't go! I'm still in here!"

But her voice seemed to bounce right back to her, and the footsteps faded into nothing. She was left surrounded by solid brick walls, cut off by two doors.

Without giving that realization time to sink in, she reached out to the walls so close on either side of her and braced herself, taking one full deep gulp of air to slow her breathing and the hurried beating of her heart. Then she crouched in the thick dust on the floor and started to feel for the edges of the panel. All she had to do was find it and knock it out.

Skimming her hands over the dry bricks, she finally found the place where they gave way to wood, old and rough and splintered on this side but welcome to her touch, and centered both palms on it, pushing as hard as she could. The panel didn't budge, so she leaned back and threw her weight forward on her hands. It still didn't move, and two more tries had no effect.

Dropping back on her heels, she took another deep breath. This time, however, the action wasn't very comforting. The air was already stale in the inky stifling darkness. Her plight would get worse, of course. If she couldn't get out of here, then she would eventually run out of air.

The thought galvanized her into shouting again. "Hey!" she cried, using every bit of volume she could muster. "I'm stuck in here! Help!" But still the dry old bricks around her seemed to drink in the sound.

Fighting down her fear, she bent forward to hammer on the panel at the same time as she shouted again. This time her voice was thinner. When she tried to get more air it was heavy with the dust she'd raised and caught in the back of her throat. She coughed until she was breathless. The only thing left to do then was to pound with both hands, again and again, while the rough wood under her fists caught and tore at her skin.

Even that effort was almost beyond her by the time the panel suddenly dropped away, and her last exhausted stroke carried her forward to fall onto the floor of the closet. Over the sound of her own lungs, drawing in deep welcome breaths of fresher air, she heard a harsh voice say, "For God's sake—Laurel!" She felt strong hands grip her shoulders and draw her forward, out of the cubbyhole at last, and then

Morgan was lifting her into his arms, elbowing the coats out of his way.

Around her the guests were murmuring sympathetically, finally attracted by the muffled noise of her hammering, as he had been on his way in.

"Lord, what a place to get trapped!"

"Worse than an elevator even."

"Poor girl!"

As soon as she caught her breath she stirred in Morgan's hold. "I'm all right. Put me down."

It came out in a dusty croak, though, and he didn't respond. Maybe he couldn't hear her over the other voices around them.

"Boy, I'd hate for that to be me!"

"But how could the panel get stuck on her like that? It wasn't that tight a fit."

That was Peggy's voice, and while Laurel tried to swallow so that she could get her own voice in better working order, both Morgan and Giles looked at the redhead. The arrested expression on both faces was surprisingly similar. Hot color rushed into Peggy's cheeks, but neither one spoke to her. Giles just said heartily to everyone else, "It's all right now, folks. She'll be fine," and Morgan turned toward the stairs with Laurel still in his arms. Encouraged by a gesture from Giles, everyone else began to drift back toward the living room, still talking.

"Put me down, please. I'm perfectly all right."

This time there were no other voices nearby, and her own came out sounding nearly normal.

"Yes, I imagine so," Morgan agreed equably, and began climbing the stairs.

"Then let me go. I can get upstairs by myself!"

He ignored the first part of that. "You probably could."

"So why carry me?" she demanded, trying not to notice how broad and solid the chest she lay against was.

"Because I feel like it."

There was no response possible to that, as he must have known, and danger flags went up in her mind. They'd reached the top of the stairs. As he turned down the hall toward her room she struggled in his hold, putting her hands out to fend him off and free herself. But he only tightened his grip, and as her hands rubbed along the rough tweed of his jacket she yelped "Ouch!" and raised one to survey it, discovering for the first time that the palm was scraped and raw. Both hands were stinging, in fact, a realization that distracted her until Morgan nudged her door open and walked into her room for the first time, still carrying her in his arms.

He laid her calmly in the center of the bed, and she would have bounced right off again, ordering him out, except that it was hard to do without using her hands. Anyway, Abby rushed in right behind them.

"Laurel, poor lamb! Are you all right?" she asked anxiously.

"Yes, of course, Abby. I'm fine, really."

She smiled reassuringly, but Abby was looking her

over with a worried frown. "Good Lord, child — your hands are a wreck! Let me—"

She was hurrying forward as she spoke, but halfway across the room she nearly collided with Morgan, who stepped between the two women.

"Thank you, but no," he said quietly, his broad back to Laurel "I'll look after her myself."

Abby's mouth opened again, but she shut it without speaking this time, looking up into the tall man's blue eyes. Nodding silently, she turned and left

Having finally worked her way to the edge of the bed and swung her feet over, Laurel went to stand up and found Morgan so close that she couldn't. Abby was gone. She'd shut the door behind her, and they were alone in the room.

Drawing back a little, she looked up and opened her mouth to tell Morgan to go, too—to leave—to get out.... But he was staring down at her, and her eyes met his with what seemed like a click; the words evaporated from her mind. She couldn't speak. It was almost as if he were hypnotizing her His blue gaze seemed to spread out and engulf her like lake water, rising around her and making movement too much trouble to bother with. Afloat in it, she saw him bend forward and catch her ankles, swinging them back onto the bed, but she didn't resist. He leaned one hip on the edge of the mattress as he sat down, brushing her tangled hair out of her eyes. When she didn't resist that, either, he gave her a sudden smile of approval.

"Now, let's get you cleaned up," he said, and she nodded slowly, as if the gesture were at his command.

She was still nodding when he stood up and walked away from her. Her eyes widened, but he wasn't leaving. Stopping at the basin on the far side of the room, he picked up her towel. In a minute he was back with a bar of mild soap, one end of the towel soaked in warm water.

Easing his weight onto the edge of the bed again, he reached over and washed her smudged and streaky face, wiping away the dust, while she watched him intently at that short distance. It seemed like such a long time since she'd really seen him, and she couldn't stop looking at him. One corner of his mouth flickered up into a slight smile, but he just continued his task and didn't meet her golden stare. When he was done, he brought the brush from the top of her chest of drawers and gently untangled the snarls in her hair, sliding long fingers into the curls to sort out the worst knots, while she tried not to shiver at his touch.

Her face and hair presentable again, he looked at her hands, taking each one separately in his own warm palms and turning them over to check the damage. It was considerable. She'd scuffed off a good deal of skin, and his lips tightened. Without comment, however, he left the room and took the towel, leaving her to think bemusedly about the way his hands had circled her wrists so easily. When he came back he was carrying the first-aid cream Abby kept in the kitchen, as well as a roll of gauze and the towel, wrung out in clean water. She watched him rather apprehensively, but when he settled beside her she couldn't see any iodine or alcohol and relaxed. He grinned then, producing a small plastic bottle of alcohol from his pocket, and she gave it a rueful look. The next few minutes were decidedly unpleasant, but finally he'd finished and both her hands were wrapped in gauze.

Setting aside all the first-aid supplies, he turned back to find her dubiously eyeing her makeshift white mittens. Yet she was reluctant to say anything and break the fragile bond that seemed to have been growing wordlessly between them.

But he must have read her mind. His eyes went from her bandaged hands to her filthy sweater and crumpled trousers. When his gaze came back to meet hers, there was a glimmer of laughter lurking there. Schooling it out of sight almost immediately, he walked over to the armoire, opened it and took out a soft flannel nightgown with long sleeves and lace at the neck.

Her eyes widened again until they were enormous in her face, and she lay on the bed practically paralyzed by surprise and something else she couldn't identify. He was looking at her now with a completely bland expression—and coming toward her with that nightgown.

Before she could decide what to do—sleep in her

clothes, call Abby for help, whatever—he was at the bed again and slipping a hand beneath her shoulders. He helped her easily into an upright position. Her mind was still dithering, but she hadn't managed to reach any decision before he slid one hand under the back of her sweater to unfasten her bra with a single neat twist of his fingers. Those fingers moved away again, leaving a warm trail across her skin, which quivered at his touch. Smoothly, but careful of her injured hands, he peeled both sweater and bra off her. Reflexively, her hands flew to shield her breasts while hot color surged into her face. But in almost the same motion he had picked up the nightgown and dropped it over her head.

She surfaced, embarrassed, from the froth of lace, and her eyes flew to his. He wasn't looking at her, only at the sleeve he held extended for her to put her arm through. Fumblingly she did, first that one, then the other, her eyes fixed on the open neck of his shirt, where a pulse had begun to beat more rapidly under his smooth bronze skin.

Suddenly she had to risk the bond, rushing into speech.

"I'm sorry. I didn't thank you for coming to the rescue," she blurted out, and he waved her apology away as she shrugged the nightgown into position on her shoulders. "I never imagined I could get stuck in there, or I wouldn't have tried it."

She was speaking rapidly, as if noise could some-how diffuse the intensity building between them, but it didn't stop him from reaching under the edge of the nightgown at her waist—although he must have heard her involuntary gasp of surprise as his hand touched her—and with the same economy of movement as before, unfastening the low-slung waistband of her trousers.

"It wasn't really all that bad," she explained hastily in a voice that was higher than usual. "I just wasn't sure how long it would be before someone noticed I was missing. . . ."

The glimmer appeared again in his eyes, only inches from hers, but he went calmly on to the next step, putting one arm around her and lifting slightly while the other hand slipped to the back of her trousers, hooked into them and her panties and peeled them away.

As he lowered her back to the bed, she frantically shoved the nightgown down over her hips. Her color deepened to crimson, the result of both embarrassment and some other more intense emotion. Morgan moved away to the foot of the bed before she could be sure whether the pulse at his throat was beating faster.

"I knew the air supply wouldn't last forever," she went on with a gulp, "and it was already getting pretty stale."

"I'm glad I heard you pounding," he said matter-of-factly at her feet, and raised her legs enough to slide the last of her clothes away. Turning slightly, he tossed them at the chair nearby, then looked back and met her eyes again.

Blue connected with gold. Gold wavered an instant, then steadied and held. Without having to see it, she knew that pulse would still be throbbing under his skin, and her own embarrassment seeped away, leaving only that other emotion, which she now recognized as desire.

They were alone in her room. Outside the snow was still falling lightly, but inside was shelter, and warmth, and intimacy. Whatever Morgan was, and whatever he had done, right now the past didn't seem important. Tonight he had brought her out of that stifling darkness and been kind to her, tending her hurts. He had undressed her, too, and now he stood at the edge of her bed, gazing at her with eyes gone the lambent blue of a very hot flame. Only a few feet and a length of fabric separated them from each other.

Their eyes still clung, and the air seemed to vibrate like a plucked string. She felt her own breathing accelerate and sensed the tension rising in Morgan. All other considerations faded from her mind. The only thing that mattered was this cord of desire that was drawing them toward each other. Spellbound by the need that quivered between them, she went to sit up and reach for him and, caught off guard by a jolt of pain, fell back heavily against her pillow, trying to stifle an involuntary groan.

She raised one bandaged hand to her other shoulder to rub away the stiffness that was rapidly setting in, then discovered she couldn't use the hand enough to do it and gave up. The delayed effects of battering that wooden panel as long as she had were beginning to be only too obvious. Her eyes, filled with pain, desire and frustration, flew again to Morgan.

He was standing at the edge of the bed, no longer leaning forward over it, and after a quick alarmed movement in her direction, he'd folded his arms across his chest when he realized what her trouble was. The flame was gone from his eyes. He was surveying her with a rueful twist to his lips.

"I'm sorry," she breathed, and his wry smile widened.

"So am I," he agreed softly, "but we should both have guessed it would happen to you. Since I can't help much more, I'll have to leave you alone to get on with recuperating."

There was a faint note of promise in his words, but she sighed to herself anyway. She knew she couldn't move enough to throw herself into his arms, and the discomfort had damped her desire somewhat, but she still ached for him, the way she always had.

He swung away from the bed, but instead of leaving immediately, he walked to the far side of the room with that lean-hipped stride that made her watch hungrily, then crouched at the fireplace. Poking the ashes harder than was necessary, he said over his shoulder, "But at least I can do one other practical thing for you. I can light a fire to keep you warm tonight."

Instantly she had the wayward thought that a fire

in the hearth was definitely second choice as a means of keeping warm, but somehow she didn't dare say so. She just watched as he laid the fire with characteristic smoothness and efficiency. All too soon it was blazing merrily, and he rose, the firelight red on his body, his face in the shadows.

Dimly she saw him turn toward her. He seemed to hesitate briefly, and her breathing faltered again, then speeded up as he came nearer, his face still shadowed. For a moment he towered over her. Fear and longing surged through her as he bent his head and kissed her gently on the lips. His own were cool at the contact, and as soon as they began to warm he removed them. Almost before she opened her eyes, he was gone, shutting the door quietly behind him.

"Thank you," she called softly, huskily.

For a long time she gazed at the closed door, then finally struggled under the covers and fell asleep in a matter of minutes.

IN THE MORNING she awakened stiff, practically unable to move. It was all she could do to reach for the phone by her bed and ring Abby.

The bell on the other end of the line seemed to ring forever, but finally a familiar voice mumbled hello, and Laurel gathered her forces.

"Abby, help!" she pleaded. "I'm so stiff from yesterday that I can't even get out of bed. I'll never make it downstairs to fix breakfast."

This time Abby came through clearly. "I'll come

right over, of course. I was just finishing my own breakfast anyway. Poor thing, how did you manage last night?"

Unwilling to give her all the details, Laurel merely replied, "Fine. Morgan bandaged me up, and I went right to sleep. But now it's all catching up with me, and I feel as though I've been over Niagara Falls in a barrel."

Abby's warm chuckle came over the line. "All right, child. You stay put, and I'll be right there."

She hung up, and Laurel wrestled her own receiver back onto the hook. Then she collapsed against the pillows, her mind going back to Abby's question about last night to consider just how she had managed. Morgan's fire was long dead, the ashes black on the hearth, and the cold light of morning filled her room, showing her, her discarded clothes lying across the chair and in a heap by the bed. They looked dissolute, somehow, and as she stared at them, slow color inched into her cheeks.

She had done it yet again. She had let Morgan get past her defenses with the most primitive weapon of all—desire. True, he'd rescued her from that airless little chamber and he'd tended her hurts as gently as her mother could have done. But then instead of leaving her alone like a gentleman, he'd stayed. She could have slept in her clothes—angrily she ignored the problem they would have presented to her today in this condition—but no, he'd stayed.

And she'd been too much of an idiot to resist.

She'd let him take off every stitch she was wearing and just lain there, an invitation to seduction. She squirmed in her bed, then grunted at the answering pain.

Oh, why had she ever decided to explore that wretched hole? None of this would have happened if it hadn't been for that impulse. She would never have been trapped there, and more importantly, Morgan would never have been the one to rescue her. She must have been more upset by the whole thing than she'd realized, and he'd benefited from her chaotic state of mind. Certainly, if she'd had her wits about her, she would at least have made him leave when he'd got her upstairs—she would have at least fended for herself from then on! In fact, she would have guessed just the sort of thing that was going to happen otherwise. . . .

Everything that *had* happened swarmed in confused images in her mind, looking worse by the second. He'd found her at a disadvantage and used the whole situation to light the bonfire that always flared between them when she was fool enough to let him anywhere near her. Flouncing indignantly, she almost welcomed the discomfort it produced. Thank heaven for last night's discomfort. Even he hadn't been barbarian enough to stay with her then!

Determinedly she squashed any memory of how disappointed she'd been when he left—or of his tenderness in handling her scrapes and bruises and the way he'd flinched at her pain as he applied the alcohol. And it was he who'd made the decision to leave, in the face of her evident regret, instead of staying to force the situation between them when she wasn't thinking clearly. But all those points were in Morgan's favor, and she ignored them, just as she'd been ignoring everything in his favor since their wedding day. Present physical pain and past mental misery weighed too heavily in the balance against him, so she stuck to her conviction that he was what her mind perceived, and not what her body believed. The battle between them was one her mind had to win, because the only thing on the other side was the force of raw desire.

By the time Abby brought her up a tray of breakfast, Laurel was in such a vile mood that even Abby wasn't able to break through, and while she coped with the inn with only Nate's and Betsy's help, Laurel lay all that morning in her bed, inert and refusing to see anyone else. The guests sent their best to her, Giles stopped by to ask how she was and Morgan knocked at her door—she knew his footsteps—but she wouldn't make the effort to get up and open it, and after a minute he went away.

Contradictorily, though, when Abby came up with a late lunch, Laurel was able to to sit up and willing to find out how things had been going with the inn.

"A little awkwardly, child," Abby admitted. "Nate's doing what he can to help inside, and everyone else is being patient with the confusion, but lunch definitely wasn't up to your standards, and as far as the desk goes—'' She shrugged expressively and finished, "Well, the only way I'd be sure right now how many people are even staying here would be to go and count the number of beds that have been slept in!''

Laurel grinned at the way she put it but replied repentantly, "Oh, Abby, I'm sorry! You shouldn't have to be coping with all this. Just help me into some clothes, and I'll come down with you right now.''

She went to throw off the covers, but Abby held them down.

"Oh, no you don't, Laurel," she said firmly. "After what happened to you, you're staying right where you are for at least the rest of the day, if I have to tie you to this bed!''

Laurel giggled at the fierce look that accompanied her words, but still tried once more. Once more Abby pinned the bedclothes down, then sat on them for good measure, perching on the edge of the bed.

"Seriously, child, take all of today off and don't try to work until you can move around comfortably again. Otherwise you're likely to wind up falling down the stairs or something even worse.''

There was some logic to that argument, and it made Laurel stop struggling. "Oh, all right," she conceded, while her muscles rejoiced and she tried not to feel guilty.

Abby confirmed her victory with a glance, then

stood up and grinned once more at Laurel. "Don't worry, child," she consoled her. "We haven't *completely* poisoned anyone yet!"

Laurel tried to reach the pillow behind her, so that she could retaliate for Abby's teasing, but it was too far away. Abby had discreetly retreated to the door, and she added from that safe distance, in a slightly more serious tone, "By the way, Laurel, Peggy Martin's here, and she's asking to see you—in fact, she's pacing around the hall downstairs, waiting to hear if you'll let her come up. What shall I tell her?"

"Did she say why she wanted to see me?" Laurel asked, puzzled.

"No, she wouldn't tell me a thing except that she absolutely had to see you right away."

Laurel could hear the quotation marks in Abby's rather dry tone and smiled. But why on earth. . . ?

"Oh, well, go ahead and send her up, Abby. If I can handle whatever it is from here, at least I'll be doing something useful!"

"Do whatever you like, child, but do it from right where you are," Abby admonished one more time, then left to fetch Peggy.

Alone for a minute, Laurel continued to wonder why the younger woman would want to see her now, when she'd been avoiding any direct contact between them for days—unless it had something to do with Giles. . . . With one bandaged hand, Laurel tried to tame her curls while she gathered her energy. If that was it, maybe this time she could convince Peggy she had no designs on Giles.

That was it, more or less, but for the first few startled moments Laurel couldn't have convinced Peggy of anything, because she couldn't figure out what the other woman was talking about.

The redhead came in like a whirlwind. Laurel heard her climb the stairs two at once before knocking on the door and coming in at the same time. Closing it, she stood against it with her hands behind her and her chin raised, rather as if Laurel were a firing squad, and spoke in a rapid breathless voice, as if she were giving a prepared speech and afraid of forgetting it if she didn't hurry.

"Laurel, I'm sorry! I just thought you'd be in there for a few minutes until you found your way out in the dark. I didn't know the panel would stick and you'd hurt yourself—"

"Only a bit," Laurel murmured mechanically, working out what Peggy was saying. *She* had shut the door of the hideout? With perfect clarity Laurel heard again the sound of high heels tapping away from the closet door—and leaving her in there.

Watching her tensely, Peggy rushed into speech again. "I'm sorry, truly I am!" she said, her eyes wide and dark with feeling. "I didn't have any idea—"

Her voice cracked, and tears spilled over to run down her cheeks, but she still stood pressed up against the door. "It—it was meant to be a joke!" she sobbed, then broke down completely.

Struggling to control her reaction to Peggy's "joke," Laurel was silent until her sobs began to taper off. By then she finally had her irritation under control.

"Tissue?" she offered quietly, pushing forward the box on the table by her bed.

Peggy nodded vigorously and left the door at last, knuckling her eyes like a child as she stumbled across the room. Taking tissue after tissue, she scrubbed her eyes and cheeks, blew her short nose determinedly, then sat on the bed, where Laurel patted an invitation.

Their eyes met, and they looked at each other for a long moment before Laurel smiled in encouragement. At that, Peggy's gaze dropped, and after an uncomfortable pause she muttered, "That was a lie. It wasn't a joke. I meant to upset you—but not to hurt you!"

Her eyes flicked up to Laurel's, giving her a glimpse of real regret before they fell away again and Peggy sighed deeply. Laurel stayed receptively silent.

"I came out in the hall, and that hole was still open, so I peeked to see if anyone was there," Peggy explained in a low voice. "And when I saw you—I was so miserable I just wanted to do something to you, too."

Shrugging unhappily, she made herself meet

Laurel's eyes again. "I guess it was an impulse, and I'd gone and done it before I even had time to think about it. But I honestly am sorry."

"Thank you," Laurel said, and at Peggy's questioning expression she added on a faint chuckle, "Not for shutting me in—I could have done without that—but for coming to apologize. That had to be hard to do."

Peggy's nod was rueful and energetic, and her eyes began to brighten. "It was! I felt like a lamb going to the slaughter—"

"You looked like it, too!" Laurel cut in laughingly.

"Except that I was more like a goat or something. But I had to come, because I'd been feeling really awful about it ever since they got you out." She paused and added, "Your hands looked so terrible!"

"Thanks!"

Laurel's tone was dry, but Peggy went on without noticing it. "And the stare Giles gave me— I suppose he guessed right away that it wasn't an accident." Head dejectedly bowed again, she began pleating the bedspread, adding almost absentmindedly, "And that man who carried you up here—Morgan? He did, too."

Laurel took a deep decisive breath; it was time she found the words to explain to Peggy. "You mean my husband?" she asked in a carefully matter-of-fact tone.

Peggy's red head came up with a jerk "Your—"

"Husband," Laurel finished for her, and watched bewilderment and hope dawn in Peggy's face. "We've had a lot of problems," she explained steadily, "so Giles has helped out and cheered me up when I was feeling low."

"Then he really is just a friend?" Peggy asked ingenuously, "and you're not—not—"

"Trying to steal him away from you?" Laurel answered in the sultry voice of a vamp that made Peggy giggle. "No, of course not," she added in her normal tone.

More and more Peggy's expression brightened, until the light suddenly went out again.

"But he still thinks I'm a child!" she wailed, springing off the bed. "Most of the time he treats me as if I were still about fifteen. You've seen how he is!"

Laurel had, of course, over and over again. But she also knew what Giles had admitted about his feelings for Peggy, who was now whirling around the room like a dervish.

"It makes me so mad!" she was fuming. "Here I've been in love with him since I don't know when. I even took up the flute and learned to play really well so I could be in his North Country Orchestra. I tried staying away from him so he'd stop seeing me the way I was years ago. I tried flirting with other men so he'd get jealous and realize I wasn't a child anymore, and *nothing's* worked! He's still behaving as if I were an *infant*!"

Struck by something, she abruptly stopped pacing. Her slim shoulders sagged as she added miserably, "And now he's probably going to do it for the rest of my life, thanks to my shutting you in that hole! At this rate, I might as well really try to get into the symphony tomorrow, instead of just setting up the audition to make him worry. Do you know, when I told him they were interested in me after listening to the tape I sent them, he didn't even react! He just kept playing the piece he's working on, then asked if I'd like to use his new flute sonata for the audition!"

She threw herself wretchedly into the chair, and Laurel decided that if Giles really did send Peggy away, it would only be because he had that pigheaded notion of letting her meet other men before he asked her to marry him. But if he would just see she'd already flirted with plenty of men and not felt the slightest spark of interest in any of them because of him! And if Peggy were just more certain he really did love her, so that she could do something about it for herself! Laurel teetered on the brink of telling Peggy what Giles really thought of her, then gave up the idea. A little interference was one thing, but something that direct would hardly be a little.

Peggy sighed gustily from her chair, and Laurel looked up to find the redhead standing up again.

"Oh, well, I suppose I might as well go practice. Giles said he could work with me one last time, and I guess that's better than not being with him at all. Maybe I should just set up auditions all over every-

where and have him help me for each one of them,"
she suggested with a faint smile.

Laurel grinned back sympathetically. "Anyway, I
really am sorry about being such a fool last night,
and before that too," Peggy added. "I apologize for
taking my frustrations out on you."

At the end of that graceful apology she gave Laurel
a last little nod and walked quietly out, and Laurel
was left to wish Giles would open his eyes and really
see her—see past the excitable girl to the woman inside and recognize that she was more than ready to
make her own decisions, about music, about her
career and especially about him. Then maybe at least
one relationship around here could work out.

CHAPTER TWELVE

IN THE MORNING, however, she began to doubt it. Laurel had just persuaded Abby over the phone that she was already downstairs and coping with breakfast on her own, when Giles appeared at the kitchen door.

"I thought you might be here," he commented when she responded to his knock. "Congratulations on being promoted to the walking wounded."

He smiled, giving her a casual salute, but as he came into the room she noticed his gray eyes were full of shadows—and behind him, still in the Volvo, was Peggy. She sat stiffly in the old car, and when she felt Laurel's gaze on her, managed only a subdued wave.

"I just stopped by to tell you we'll be in Boston for the day," Giles was saying. "Peggy's audition is at one, but we should be able to get back by late tonight. If anyone is looking for us in the meantime, tell them we're out launching her career."

"Giles, can't you—" Laurel began, but he anticipated the question and just shook his leonine head. Evidently he still hadn't changed his mind about making sure Peggy saw more of the world than just the corner he occupied, even though his plan must be getting harder and harder to stick to.

He swung away, a big man whose shoulders seemed to have lost their usual jaunty set, and she called after him, "Good luck! I hope everything works out the way it should...."

On her last words he glanced back, then gave her a wave and folded himself into the car, starting it with the usual noisy lurch and driving out of sight around the bend. Laurel, left alone in her kitchen, wondered sadly if Giles and Peggy would ever manage to sort out their relationship.

Not that she was doing any better herself. Her own relationship with Morgan had gone exactly nowhere. No matter how many times she gave in to the desire that drew her to him, she still despised her weakness afterward. Even if he really had told her the truth about saying goodbye to Renee on their wedding day, that didn't alter the fact that he'd been trying to lie to her in Paris. So, no matter how kind and gentle he might be, or—worse—how devastatingly appealing, she would just have to wait him out until he stopped camping at the inn, whatever his tangled reasons.

But he didn't go. Her hands had nearly healed, and Laurel was doing her full share of work around the inn, as well as avoiding Morgan again, who seemed to have withdrawn into himself since that night in her room. Then, for those few inflammatory minutes, they had been so close, and the next morning she had refused to see him. She had, however, caught a glimpse of him at dinner last night through the kitchen door as Abby went back and forth and been startled to see how grim he looked, sitting alone and intent. His hard jaw had been set, one hand carving designs in the tablecloth with his fork. Shivering suddenly at the sight, Laurel had an intuition that he wouldn't allow the situation between them to drift much longer. It was intolerable, which made Adam Hamilton's arrival very timely.

He came in on a flurry of snowflakes, and Laurel, looking up from her desk, hardly believed at first that he was actually there. Springing from her chair, she flew over to hug him. "Granda!"

"Hello, my dear." He kissed her cheek, and melting snow slid from him to her. Laughing, she mopped it up with her fingers. "I thought I remembered an old bargain between us—that we'd have Thanksgiving here together—so I gave in to an impulse and drove up to see if you had room for me."

"Oh, I'm so glad you did! Here, let me take those." Brushing snow off the coat and hat he gave her, she hung them in the closet and turned back to smile at him. "Letters are fine, but I've been wanting to show you everything! It looks so different from when you were here last."

Sweeping a look around the warm graceful hallway, Adam observed, "So I see," and his voice was so wryly amazed that she grinned.

"This time you won't have to go over to North Conway for your drink before dinner, either," she assured him. "I'll bring it to you in the dining room. And if I had to, I'd turn everyone else out to make space for you. But it just so happens our best room is empty—" A thought struck her, and she added, trying to keep the same offhand tone in her voice, "Oh, and Morgan will be right next door to you."

He had been drying his silver spectacles on a handkerchief, but at her words, Adam's gnarled hands stopped moving.

"Morgan?" he asked with an odd inflection, gazing at her keenly.

"Yes," she confirmed, and the strain in her voice was apparent. "He's been here for ten days now."

"I didn't realize that," Adam answered, perching the spectacles on his nose again. "I knew from the New York office that he was touring the chain on our management survey, but not that he'd decided to include the country inns." Tilting his head so the glasses would slip into their usual position, he added a shade stiffly, "We've been rather out of touch."

Then he put her hand in the crook of his arm and turned toward the desk. "Ten days," he repeated thoughtfully in his usual tone, patting her hand. "And how are things going, my dear?"

She stopped walking, knowing he wasn't referring to the inn. Meeting his eyes, she was searching for an answer when another voice cut into their conversation. "Granda!" Morgan changed direction to come and stand beside them, looking at his grandfather with eyes that had darkened with feeling. For a long moment the air between them was charged, and they almost seemed to be sizing each other up.

Finally Morgan spoke. "It's good to see you again, sir," he said.

"*Is* it?" Adam challenged, pushing his spectacles up again so that he could look piercingly at the younger man.

"Yes," Morgan answered quietly, and extended his hand. Adam gripped it tightly with his own, and watching them, Laurel had a quick fancy they were like old opponents who are surprised to discover that their constant quarrels have dissolved in the ties of friendship. For now even the tension between Morgan and herself was lost in the strangely heightened emotion of his meeting with his grandfather.

The clasp held, and so did their glances. "It's been five months, hasn't it?" Adam asked musingly, and keyed up as she was, Laurel caught the note of regret in his voice. But if Morgan had been surveying the Hamilton Hotels since she saw him in Paris, then why hadn't he met his grandfather face to face since the wedding?

Puzzled, she glanced at Adam, and suddenly she saw him as he would seem to Morgan after five months' separation, recognizing at least part of the reason for the intensity of emotion she could feel in her husband. Why, Adam really was an old man now. He was tall as his grandson, his gaze as sharp and observant as ever, but the hand in Morgan's had blue knotted veins she'd never noticed before, and the dimming of vitality she had worried about as Adam's assistant seemed even more noticeable now. Granda was like a dwindling fire, and that thought sent a pang through her, spurring her to action.

Putting her own hand on top of their linked ones and forcing away the thought that came at the contact—that these were two of the men she loved most in the world—she made her tone bright and sociable

"Well, then, why don't you two go sit in the living room and catch up with each other by the fire Nate just lighted in there?" she babbled, adding even while she hated the sound of her voice, "And I'll go work on dinner, so we can all have it together."

Dropping their hands, both men turned their heads to look at her with identically appalled expressions. She flushed, realizing she'd sounded like a cruise director as they caught each other's eye and chuckled together.

"Yes, Laurel," Morgan agreed with bland docility. "You go ahead, and we'll do just that."

Then he put an arm around his grandfather's shoulders, and they strolled away, leaving her wistfully conscious that for a brief moment they had all felt like a family, natural and at ease with each other. Just as they disappeared into the living room, Giles came in the front door, and she greeted him with something like relief at the distraction.

"Giles!"

"You rang, madam?" he responded absurdly.

"Come on in and tell me how Peggy's audition

went," she replied with a smile. "I haven't seen you since you got home."

He shut the door behind him, his broad shoulders turned away from her for a few seconds.

"It was superb." Turning back to her, he went on. "She insisted on getting there an hour too early and made herself so nervous that she dropped her music on the way in, turned pale as the paper and forgot to introduce the piece...."

A gleam of humor crossed his face at the memory, but as it faded Laurel thought she detected lines there that she had never seen before.

"And then she played like an angel," he finished, "with a clarity and brilliance that were all I could ever dream of."

"Giles, how marvelous!"

"It is, isn't it?" he agreed in an odd voice as he walked over to the potted chrysanthemum on the hall table and began absentmindedly pulling the petals off one flower. "She really *has* got the kind of talent that deserves a wider field than she could ever find around here."

Laurel wanted desperately to disagree with his unstated conclusion—to argue that it didn't mean he had to force Peggy out of his life to get her into that wider field—but while she was still hunting for words, he went on wonderingly, almost as if he'd forgotten she was there.

"But how can any one girl be such a bundle of contradictions? She went in there looking about ten and terrified, yet as soon as she started to play she displayed the kind of power and passion most people don't grow into in a lifetime...."

Taking a deep breath, Laurel walked over to stand on the other side of her abused chrysanthemum. "It's probably because she isn't a girl anymore," she suggested gently, "and hasn't been one for some time. She's a grown woman, old enough to make all her own decisions about her career."

Raising his head, he started to object. Even his beard seemed to bristle in contradiction, but she met his eyes squarely and went right on, "And old enough to play the music of the man she loves with every bit of the passion and brilliance you heard."

This time when she paused he just looked at her, and she watched disbelief and yearning war in his open face. With a slight smile she nodded, then said matter-of-factly, "I was just going to help work on dinner. Can you stay?"

"What?" he asked blankly. "Oh. Thanks, but no." And he walked to the door and out, without even noticing the trail of yellow petals falling from his hands.

Gathering them up, Laurel admitted to herself that she had interfered in his relationship with Peggy yet again, but at least this time it looked as though Giles would think about what she'd said. In the meantime, she had to think about dinner, and when it was ready she had to go into the dining room to eat with Adam and Morgan while Abby served them all.

Sitting down in the chair Morgan held for her, Laurel was unnervingly aware that this was the first time she had ever joined him for a meal at the inn. As a matter of fact, she hadn't even been in this room at the same time as him since the evening when he'd hauled her in here so furiously and kissed her so passionately. But that was no memory to dwell on!

Instead she responded to Adam's, "Well, my dear, what do you recommend from this tantalizing menu?"

He lifted one white eyebrow at the small chalkboard Abby had set near them, and Laurel answered demurely, "Everything, of course!"

He chuckled. "In that case, we'll obviously have to try everything." Turning to his grandson, he commented gruffly, "Morgan, if you and I order the two different choices for each course, then I'll be able to find out exactly what this newest inn of ours can do."

"Agreed," Morgan answered promptly.

At the same time Abby, coming back for their orders, cut in loyally, "Miracles, that's what. Not only can this girl bring an old place back from the edge of ruin, but then she can make herself the best chef in the state of Maine!"

Laurel colored at this partisan summary of her talents, but the meals Abby served with a flourish seemed to bear out her boast. Adam's *carpaccio*, thin slices of raw beef in watercress sauce, gave way to a delicate shrimp-crab *paupiette* on toast, while

Morgan had the oysters au gratin followed by spectacular braised venison that came with pureed chestnuts and wild rice with currant jelly. But if anyone had asked her which meal she herself was eating, Laurel couldn't have answered.

As if he were a roaring furnace and she a block of ice, she was conscious every second of Morgan's nearness as if their encounter in her room had happened only an hour ago. He ate with neat precision, teased Abby until she laughed like a teenager and held up his end of the somewhat stilted conversation that volleyed back and forth across the table. He also raised his wineglass in a silent toast as he finished his venison, looking across the table and into Laurel's eyes. His own crinkled at the corners in an intimate smile that was directed only at her and didn't touch his mobile lips. Staring into those eyes, Laurel gave only random answers when she was addressed and wondered hazily if he had any idea of his power. It felt as though they were alone again—

"How has the survey gone?" Adam asked abruptly.

"Fine." Morgan broke the link between them to look at Adam while he answered, and Laurel unconsciously took a deep breath, unaware that Adam's gaze had fixed on her. "The report on the hotels is in your office already, and the one on the inns should come through next week, as soon as my secretary in New York has it ready to go. I sent it on to her yesterday." Listening to him, Laurel got the strong impression that Morgan was on his mettle, striving to prove something to Adam.

Then he turned back to Laurel. "But if you'd like a summary right now: although all the inns appear to be well run, the one doing the most business and getting the best reputation is this one, in spite of its newness."

This time the smile touched his lips, and they quirked up lopsidedly in a way that made her pulse accelerate. Fleetingly she remembered his unflattering amazement at finding her in charge when he'd first arrived, and recognized this for a tacit apology. But she hadn't expected one from him.

"I'm not surprised," Adam announced, finishing his *crème brûlée*. "I make it a point to choose only the best."

It was a remark that could have had a couple of meanings, but he just beamed, and this time his smile included them both. Laying down his spoon, he added, "That was as good a meal as I've had anywhere, Laurel, and well worth waiting for!"

The twinkle in his eyes reminded her again of his last visit, when she hadn't been able to offer him more than coffee, and she grinned in response, collecting her wits to ask provocatively, "Then does that mean you won't be going off to North Conway?"

"Not unless you throw me out, my dear," he returned promptly, and she shook her head with a laughing affectionate look, while Morgan watched the comfortable byplay between them and pensively twirled the stem of his wineglass.

A minute later, though, Adam asked him another question about the survey, and while he answered Laurel's eyes dropped to his hand, resting on the table and toying with his glass. It was a strong hand, broad in the palm, with long blunt fingers that ended in short square nails. Fine silky black hair edged along the backs of those fingers, faint against the rich old-gold color of his skin, and spread across the back of his hand, past the brilliant white cuff and up his sleeve. Only a few days ago that hand had undressed her, unhooking her bra and waistband, sliding across her back, her belly, her hips and buttocks. . . .

Waves of heat lapped at her. She was melting, thawing—

"Well, my dear," Adam said genially, easing his chair back from the table a few inches and looking at her over the tops of his spectacles. "If you don't mind, I think I'd like to go back and sit by Nate's fire for a while before bed. Can you come and join me?"

Recalled to reality by his voice and thankful for the interruption, she yanked her gaze away from Morgan's hand and summoned up a smile for his grandfather, while the hot color ebbed from her cheeks and she prayed silently that her thoughts weren't written on her face. But Morgan's head was bent, and Adam had spoken matter-of-factly, as if he were completely unaware of the tension that vibrated between the other two. His old eyes were warm, too, and she wanted to agree. But Morgan would undoubtedly come with them, and how could she keep sitting calmly with him if her thoughts were going to be so totally undisciplined? Her pale gold eyes flickered from one man to the other.

"I should go help Abby fix the coffee—" she equivocated.

"I'll do it," Morgan interrupted unexpectedly. "I can give her a hand in the kitchen and then bring ours into the living room."

Laurel's eyes flew to him again. He'd never helped out in the kitchen before, but she knew Abby would welcome him now. Ever since the night he'd hauled her out of that wretched hole under the stairs, Abby's attitude toward him seemed to have changed.... Wondering why for the hundredth time, she searched his dark face, but it was unreadable.

"Fine," Adam agreed with pleasure. "We'll see you in a little while."

Standing slowly, he extended his arm to her again, and she slipped her hand into it. In a minute they were settled by the hearth, and Morgan had vanished into the kitchen. Laurel's thoughts compulsively followed him, however, and she remembered Limb was probably there, too, near the source of all food, as usual.

Following that train of thought, she asked abruptly, "Is there really a company regulation forbidding hotel managers to keep pets?"

"Why, no, there isn't. We've never had a problem come up that required us to make any kind of rule like that," he answered, pushing his spectacles up onto the thin bridge of his nose. "I know several of our managers have kept a pet of one sort or another for years and they'd simply been discreet about it. Why do you ask?"

Her eyes began to sparkle with sudden irritation. "Because I have a puppy here, and Morgan told me it was against company policy to have a pet."

"Now I wonder why he did that," Adam murmured thoughtfully. "With all his faults, I've never known him to lie." He looked at her through his glasses, so that his eyes were slightly magnified, and the ghost of a smile seemed to lurk there.

It didn't register with her, though. Her mind was racing, stopping and racing again.

Morgan *had* lied—but why over something as trivial as that, especially when he never passed the puppy without making it a point to speak to him and ruffle his ears? But whatever the reason, apparently it really was the first time Adam had heard of him lying. Perhaps he never lied to his grandfather, only to her? Perhaps he'd just never cared enough about her to tell her the truth.

Unconsciously she shook her head in exasperation. She didn't know the answers to her questions and she never had. Morgan had been an enigma to her from the start, and it looked as though he always would be. And she had had enough to last forever of the anger and tears, confusion and disruption he brought to her life! It was past time she gave up on the whole tangled situation and put him out of her thoughts for good. Then maybe she could finally forget those devastating physical responses even sitting near him always produced. She'd be better off going back to being the single-minded career woman she'd been when he first came on the scene!

And so, as Morgan approached the living room with a tray in his hands, he heard Laurel burst out impatiently, "Oh, isn't my annulment ever going to come through? You said the pre-court paperwork was all cleared up finally, and the waiting period would be over weeks ago—but I haven't heard!"

At the words he halted, putting down the tray on her desk with exaggerated care before it could slip from his fingers. Then he just stood, ebony head bowed, within sound but not sight of the other two.

"Laurel, my dear," Adam answered slowly, "I'm afraid I have a confession to make to you."

Even from where he stood, Morgan could hear her breath hiss in before his grandfather went on.

"Last June when you first asked me, I *did* get in touch with our family lawyer when he got home and had him look into the procedures for getting an annulment. He discovered that it's really very simple in Massachusetts—a matter of filing a twenty-five-dollar petition, waiting for it to be published in the papers for three weeks and then appearing before the judge, alone or with Morgan if he chooses to answer the court's summons. It's considerably easier than divorce, and Mr. Matthews was of the opinion that since you and Morgan have never lived together as man and wife, you could plead your consent to the marriage was obtained by fraud, as you didn't know the real situation."

Laurel was very still now, but Adam's sigh was audible, and so was the unfamiliar tone of his voice when he finally continued.

"And I've known all that for months, Laurel. Even last summer when you first came back from Europe, I knew it. But I've been delaying you ever since then, and I never let Mr. Matthews file the petition. That's the reason for the delay—not a hitch with the papers."

"But why ''

"I don't know," Adam answered in that unfamiliar voice, the tone of a person without purpose or direction—and he was a man who had never done a purposeless thing in his life. "I couldn't seem to make myself go through with it and cut all the official ties that made you one of us. I know that's exactly what you want to put an end to, at least as far as Morgan's concerned, but I suppose I didn't want to have it acknowledged once and for all that there wasn't any hope of the two of you working things out at last."

"But there isn't!" Laurel choked. "There isn't!" And on a rising note, "Oh, how could you? How could you interfere like that? Now I'll just have to do it for myself."

Shielded from her sight, Morgan heard the anger and determination in her voice and thought about letting her annul their marriage. When he picked up the tray again in a few minutes later, his face was expressionless, but his eyes had taken on an odd gleam.

THE SAME LOOK was still there when he knocked quietly at Laurel's door long after midnight. Finally falling into an uneasy sleep, she had been dreaming she was standing in a court of law, appearing before the judge. But somehow everything was changed. On the far side of the court, Morgan was appealing for the annulment, while she argued with the judge not to grant it. Morgan looked coldly over at her, and the judge gave an order that she be bound and gagged for interrupting the proceedings. When she rushed forward to the bench to protest one more time, it was Renee who laughed down at her, and then it was the woman Morgan had been with in Paris, staring at her. She drew back in horror, but they caught her from behind and bound a cloth across her mouth, so that she could only make desperate stifled cries while the judge banged repeatedly on the bench with her gavel.

But it wasn't a gavel. Opening her eyes, Laurel found her cheeks wet and the courtroom gone. Her room was filled with soft shadows from the last of the fire she had lighted for comfort when she came upstairs, and the sound from her dream went on until she finally realized someone was knocking at her door.

Dazedly she brushed a hand across her cheeks and slid from her bed, stumbling as she hurried to the door. What could be wrong? Was someone ill? Not a fire! Pale with fresh alarm and nightmare misery, she opened her door. When she saw Morgan standing outside, it was perfectly obvious he hadn't come about a fire, or illness, or anything else to do with the inn.

He stood in her doorway, and the look in his eyes was far from the cold stare she had just dreamed of seeing. She came entirely awake in an instant, meeting the hot blue flame in his eyes, the same flame she'd seen the night he'd undressed her and put her in her flannel nightgown. But the outrageous nightgown she now wore—one she'd bought an eternity ago for her trousseau—wasn't nearly as proper and unrevealing. As his gaze moved lingeringly down her body, and the heat rose inside her, she realized how little she had on. Although made out of several yards of ivory nylon, the gown was cut low across her breasts and slit up to the hip on each side. Worse yet, it was nearly transparent.

Devastatingly aware that Morgan could see the color rising in her face, she thrust away the dream memory of her longing for him and snapped, "What do you want?"

Before he answered, he moved his stare up to her face, then deliberately shifted it down again, so that she could feel it almost like a tangible pressure in the shadowed hollow between her breasts, making her breath come unevenly.

"You."

She should have laughed in his face then and slammed the door. But suddenly she didn't have the breath for laughing, and the door stayed open.

He met her eyes again and let her see the desire in his, flickering and leaping in the flame there. Mesmerized, she did so, and at the same time became exquisitely aware of his body. His usual tweed sports coat was gone, and with it his necktie. His shirt lay open at the throat and chest, so that she could see his pulse throb under the bronze skin and the beginnings of a tangle of curly black hair. If she leaned forward only a few inches, she could slip her fingers through the front of his shirt and across the hard warmth of his chest to twine them in that tangle. It would be fine and soft to her touch. . . .

Involuntarily she swayed toward him, but as she did so the corners of his mouth began to curve upward in a faint slow smile of satisfaction. As if that released her from the old spell of his making, she regained the power to speak and to move.

"No!" she hissed, and snatched at the door, swinging it with all her force. It would smash into the frame loudly enough to wake everyone at the inn, but she was beyond caring. But it didn't matter anyway, because the door never got that far. Morgan just shifted his position and slid one foot forward, so the door stopped right there with an impact that seemed to reverberate through her.

For a second she just clung to the edge of the door to regain her balance, not comprehending what had happened. Then a wave of wild anger—and fear—flooded her with energy. She had to get him away from her. She had to shut her door and keep him out of her room, out of her heart, out of her life! Letting the door go for now, she rushed forward through it and launched herself at him with her hands extended, palms out, throwing all her weight against him.

She hit his chest so hard that the force of it knocked him backward a foot or so, but it also unbalanced her and sent her stumbling forward, too. With reflexes twice as fast as hers, he recovered his balance first and surged forward, catching her tightly around the waist and bearing her before him until they were both inside her room. He set her down to push the door shut behind him.

"I'll scream!" she threatened breathlessly.

"Try it," he invited promptly. "Waking everyone here should do great things for the inn's reputation."

Knowing he was right, she glared at him furiously. "Damn you!" she muttered, but his only reaction was to cross his arms calmly over his chest.

It was like waving a red flag at a bull, a gesture that arrogant, and with an incoherent cry of frustration she flew at him again, pounding on his body with her fists. Grasping her wrists firmly, he held her at arm's length as she flailed. His continued calm infuriated her. He just stood there, holding her at bay, and she was tiring fast.

Her hands began to feel like leaden weights that she could no longer lift against him, and finally she fell back, her arms at her sides, her hair in her eyes, her chest heaving. Then he moved against a delayed counterstroke. As he stepped forward, her head jerked up so she could watch him warily. All he did, though, was walk toward her, his own arms lowered. But she gave ground in front of him anyway, retreating until she bumped into her chest of drawers and came to an abrupt halt, and Morgan, following her so closely that his breath fanned her face, took one more step and landed on her bare foot.

Both fury and desire evaporated for a moment. She yelped at the sudden pain and twisted away from him to double up and reach instinctively for her mashed toes, taking them in both hands and clutching them tightly.

That left her balancing on the other foot, however, and just as he said, "Laurel, I'm sorry!" she lurched against him. Jerking away as if his touch would scald her, she released her toes and crumpled to the floor, flexing her foot to restore sensation.

Dropping to a crouch in front of her, Morgan asked, "Are you all right? How bad is it?"

She didn't answer, and he said, "Let me see."

"No!" Her eyes opened, shining wetly, and she scowled at him.

"Don't be ridiculous," he snapped, and rested one knee on the floor as he reached forward.

Before she understood what he had in mind, he had gathered her hunched body into his arms and stood up with surprising ease in spite of his burden.

Three strides took him to the edge of her tumbled bed, and he deposited her there unceremoniously. Indignant, she uncurled and sat up, thrusting her feet over the side to hop down and escape him—this business of dropping her on beds had to stop—but, already kneeling back on his heels, he caught the bruised foot in his hands, effectively stopping her right where she was.

With a touch whose gentleness reminded her of the night he'd bathed her battered hands, he manipulated her foot, flexing the toes and pressing here and there to feel for anything broken. As his warm hands moved over her skin, it began to pick up warmth from him, while thoughts of pain and struggle and escape quickly faded from her mind. As it always had, physical contact with him seemed to hypnotize her until she was powerless to resist. Her body responded, and her mind fell silent, so that even the reason she had been trying to keep him from her room was unimportant.

His inspection finished at last, he murmured, "Nothing broken that I can find. I think you'll live." And on the final word he bent his head to press a kiss to the delicate skin on the inside of her ankle.

Laurel started involuntarily, and her nightgown fell away, dropping open along the slit high up on her thigh. Bemusedly, she felt as though his lips had sent tendrils of sensation winding their way up her bare leg to trace the branching of each and every nerve. He'd said she would live, and she felt his touch was bringing her to life. She had been a shell, a husk for so long, and the breath that simmered along her skin was giving her back the spark of life. Gently but inexorably, it spread through her while his hands and his lips followed the slim bare line of her leg. She caught fire gradually like a paper that sizzles around the edges until the flames finally reach the center and leap up high and strong, consuming it utterly.

When he found her knee and lifted it slightly to kiss the sensitive skin at the back of it, the flames leaped in her, and with an indistinct cry she reached for him. Eagerly, hastily, she bent and plunged her fingers into his hair, which gleamed like black silk in the firelight, tugged at the forelock that had dropped across his brow so that she could lift his face to hers. Head up, he simply looked at her, and such desire flickered there that she caught her breath before she met his mouth with her own.

At the contact her cry had its echo in his. Whispering her name on a sigh, he took the lips she offered and explored them with his own. When her lips parted willingly, he searched past the line of her teeth, probing with his tongue the softness she opened to him while they shared a single breath.

Releasing her leg, he came up onto his knees as his hands rose to cup her face, cradling it to his own, then tracing the smooth contours of her jaw with his thumb and running his fingertips gently along the flare of her cheekbones. Just when she thought she couldn't bear the piercing sweetness any longer, he lifted his mouth from hers to drop light kisses on her chin, her forehead, her cheeks, her quivering eyelids, while her own hands lost themselves in the thick dark curls at the nape of his neck.

But he only left her lips untended for a moment, returning to them quickly. While her tongue answered his, his hands slipped down the soft column of her throat, catching her fluttering pulse. Then they parted and followed the fine structure of her collarbone outward until he reached the straps of her nightgown. Murmuring against his mouth, she moved each shoulder forward slightly in turn, and he responded by sliding the silky fabric out and away, so that it dropped to lie shimmering at her waist in the firelight. Her breasts rose above the folds, gleaming softly as if they were carved of rosy pearl. But far softer than pearl, they trembled with her roughened breathing. Color flared into her face as she offered herself to him in longing and sudden shyness.

His thumbs, tangled in the fabric at her waist, moved in little circular caresses as he gazed at her beauty. The fire's reflection burned in his eyes, along with the flames of his own desire, which burned away her shyness. In a single powerful motion he rose to his feet and lifted her to him, leaving the nightgown behind so that she lay naked in his arms. Pressed convulsively to his hard chest, she used her hand to pull away his shirt, and when it was gone from between them she rubbed her face sensually in his mat of chest hair, scattering kisses everywhere she could reach, breathing in the hot sweet scent of his skin.

At her touch she felt the trembling begin deep inside him, quivering up his torso and through the arms that held her. As if he feared losing his hold on her, he bent and placed her gently on her bed, at the same time flinging aside the tumbled bedclothes so that she lay open to his eyes, her warm ivory flesh, each rounded curve caressed lingeringly by his gaze. Then with a stifled groan he dropped back onto his knees on the floor by the bed, so that his face was only a few inches above her and she could see the need and desire that racked him, altering the clean lines of his strong features. His blue eyes burned with a tenderness, too, that moved her almost unbearably. One hand flew to his cheek and hovered there, as if she would reassure him she was real and needed him as he needed her.

Turning his head, he kissed her hand, and as it sank away, followed it down, touching his lips to her wrist, forearm, elbow and the petal-soft skin inside her upper arm. When her arm came to rest on the bed again, he shifted his mouth across to the top of her breast, where he rained delicate kisses on the satiny, blue-veined flesh. His breath spread over her skin like a pool of welcome fire. Slowly, by infinitesimal degrees, he moved up the swell of her bosom until at last he reached its thrusting tremulous peak. There he dropped a ring of kisses. When she sighed and arched her back to his mouth, he took the velvet nipple between his lips and tugged at it with sweet insistence while his tongue flicked against its tip.

At that she cried out and turned into his arms, feeling them tighten around her and his face press between her breasts, the late-night roughness of his beard scratching her shivering skin. Her hands, locked behind his head so that she could clutch him to her, were buried deep in his hair. They trembled eagerly, and that same eagerness rocked her whole body. Responding to it, he lifted his head to place a kiss of promise on her breast and then released her, coming to his feet with that panther grace she loved so.

Stepping a pace or two away from the bed, he undressed rapidly, stripping off his crumpled shirt and tossing it aside, while her hungry gaze admired the smooth play of muscles across his lean torso. In a minute the rest of his clothing was gone as well, and he let his hands fall to his sides, standing before her naked in the gleaming firelight. Without haste, he offered himself to her eyes, and without shyness, she leaned on one elbow to survey the sheer masculine beauty of him.

His desire for her was as clear to her as her own for him, but for a while urgency was slowed to a sweet inevitability. Here in this timeless firelit room, there was no past and no future... only present. He was all men and she all women, as they acted out the elemental ritual of life.

Below the proud angle of his head, the tendoned column of his neck spread into a breadth of shoulder and chest, where the firelight caught on ridges of hard muscle and bone. His flat belly and narrow hips tapered down to lean flanks and straight legs, and there, too, the red glow flickered before vanishing into the darker patches of hair that shadowed his arms and legs and flowed down his chest.

When he came to her at last, she was throbbing with need. As he stretched the length of his body beside her, she reached for him urgently. Catching her in his arms, he drew her up onto his chest so that she lay across him, her white breasts pressed against his bronzed skin, where she could follow the outlines of his bones and sinews with eager hands and press busy kisses into the slight saltiness of his flesh. While she did that, his own hands slipped over the wings of her shoulders and traced her spine, curving over her buttocks to clasp her upper thighs against him.

Then with one fluid motion he rolled over, still holding her to him, so that she now lay beneath him and could feel the solidity of him as he pressed her into the yielding softness of the bed. One hand was pinned beneath her buttocks, and it stirred slowly, kneading her flesh until it seemed to melt in his clasp. The other he freed, shifting his weight to lean against her shoulder, so that he could arch his body over hers and explore teasingly beneath her breasts, along the curved rim of her navel and down into the shadowed depths of her desire, while she gasped in fiery delight and curved upward to his touch. Finally he slid one leg between hers, and they parted to receive him. A pang of pain and fulfillment. Then, as their heartbeats, breath and tangled limbs were shaken by a single driving force, they rose together to dizzying white heights of exploding joy. Her wild cry found its echo in his throat, and as one they soared into a burst of color and drifted down, consumed by its brilliance.

When she knew time and place again, she lay, her legs twined with Morgan's, her head cradled in the hollow of his shoulder, her cheek pressed against the damp warmth of his chest. She could hear his heartbeat slow gradually and his breath steadying at last as his fingers idly stirred among her tangled curls. Neither of them spoke. Their bodies were in perfect harmony, and so often they'd gone wrong with words. It was as if an instinctive pact held them silent.

For a timeless interlude they lay quietly in the firelight, flame and shadow dancing on the walls around them, and they were content just to be. Then some imp of mischief and desire stirred in her, and she trailed one hand airily over his body, alighting only for an instant on his dark eyebrows, his lips, which tried to kiss it, his throat, where a pulse began to pound wildly, the tender underside of the arm he'd flung over his head, the mat of hair on his chest, the shallow cup of his navel, his hard belly that tensed at her touch. . . .

Like a teasing butterfly her fingers roamed over him, assured by the pleasure he had given her, and as she tormented him she felt a rumbling chuckle begin deep in his chest. Then, pouncing, he caught that bold hand and used it to flip her on her back, where she lay laughing up at him, her golden eyes alight with joy. She tried to bring her other hand up to carry on where the first had been interrupted, but he trapped them both and pinned them against the mattress.

He had only one hand free now, but he used it to feather delicate strokes down her throat, up the summit of each breast, along the quivering flatness of her stomach and down to the satin tenderness inside each thigh. All laughter dying in her throat, she moaned at the wild ecstasy of his touch and arched herself into his body, eager for release. Instinctively they both paused, anticipating, until she gasped his name and his own breath tore in and out of his lungs. Then at last he came to her, and together they climbed to the tallest heights of passion, where they clung and cried out together, tumbling eventually into sleep.

CHAPTER THIRTEEN

WHEN SHE AWAKENED AGAIN it was early morning, and a cold white light was edging its way into her room. The fire on her hearth had gone out, but last night's enchantment still lingered, and she was filled with a singing warmth, surprised by joy and so happy she was almost afraid of it. Moving very carefully, she slipped out of Morgan's arms, wrapped around her from behind and heavy with sleep, so she could turn and study him. With the piercing eyes closed and the usually taut lips relaxed, his hard face had a gentleness that almost moved her to tears. Unable to resist touching him, she traced each of his straight brows with a delicate forefinger, then drew it down the bridge of his strong nose and across his mouth— and squealed in surprise when, without any warning, he caught the finger in his teeth and nibbled it. Then he set it free and captured her shoulders, pulling her until she lay stretched across his chest, her laughing face only inches from his.

"Thought you could catch me defenseless, did you?" he asked sternly, while his hands shifted inward on her shoulders, so that his thumbs could begin circling hypnotically on the tops of her breasts.

Trying to pretend indifference, she countered curiously, "Are you ever defenseless?"

"I haven't been allowed to be," he answered, his voice suddenly hard, and an odd pang of sorrow made her wriggle still closer to him, as if for comfort.

Her little burrowing movement seemed to bring him back to her from some distance, and his hands resumed their arrested motion. "But you do seem to have that effect on me," he admitted, looking deep into her eyes, the light she remembered from last night leaping again in his own. "I don't appear to have anything at all in the way of defenses against you."

"I'm glad," she breathed simply, and for a minute abandoned any pretense of resisting him, either. His lips were at her earlobe, her fingers twined into the hair on his chest, when she forced herself to go on, "But someone has to set out breakfast for the guests."

"Let Abby do it," he suggested cavalierly, and proceeded to explore the shell-like whorls of her ear with the tip of his tongue, making her shiver in his arms.

"I can't," she murmured unsteadily. "She's not due here until nine o'clock, and by then everyone will have starved."

"Not us," he asserted, moving down to bite the side of her neck and illustrate his point. "We can dine on each other, and they can eat cake."

She giggled breathlessly, but struggled back to the subject. "They can't," she replied. "We've only got croissants, and they need to be reheated. And then there's the coffee and juice. . . . "

His mouth was skimming along her collarbone, and she forgot what she'd been saying by the time he reached her breasts, which had been crushed against his chest. He began scribing fiery circles on them with his tongue.

"I could do it." His voice was slightly muffled.

"What?" she asked blankly, having lost track of everything but the way his caresses seemed to be making her melt.

He chuckled richly and pulled his head back to repeat more clearly, "I could take care of breakfast."

"You?" Astonishment made her concentrate, and she peered at him in surprise, trying to focus on the amused dark face now so close to hers.

"Yes, me," he reiterated. "I'm perfectly capable of heating, boiling and pouring out the various parts of this breakfast you're so worried about. I'm not just another pretty face, you know," he added, scowling ferociously as her expression of amazement made it plain that she'd never considered he might have any domestic talents whatsoever.

She laughed aloud at his absurd comment but still looked uncertain. In an entirely different tone he tacked on, "Meanwhile, you can wait for me here in bed." She gazed at him, and he let her read the desire and promise in his eyes, until color washed quickly up into her face. To hide it, she bent her head into the hollow between his neck and shoulder.

"I take it my offer's accepted," he observed, running his hands over her back from shoulder blades to buttocks and then rolling her gently onto the far side of the bed so he could slide free and stand up. As he left her, she sighed with regret, and he leaned over to brush kisses along the full length of her torso from collarbone to hips as he stood naked by her bed, his own desire evident. Then he drew the rumpled bedclothes up and covered her to her pointed chin, kissing closed the wide gold eyes.

When she opened them again, he was in the middle of the room, still barefoot and shirtless but fastening his pants around his narrow waist. She watched with interest, and he grinned at her intentness, then suggested tongue in cheek, "Why don't I relight the fire before I go, so you won't get cold before I'm back?"

Catching the double entendre, she made a face at him, and he laughed, bending to pick up the poker and stir the ashes for coals. Finding a few, he dropped to one knee and blew on them, tucking crumpled bits of paper and small scraps of kindling into the hesitant heat. Finally they began to flicker into renewed life, and he turned slightly to ask over his shoulder, "When shall we tell Adam?"

"Tell him what?" she repeated absently, her attention on the sensuous play of muscles across his bare back.

His answer was a fraction late in coming, and when it did it came in an odd tone, accompanied by uneven laughter. ''That the annulment is off,'' he said, and she missed the uncharacteristic hesitancy in his voice. She missed it because she only heard his words, and misinterpreted them—misinterpreted them because her joy was so new that she couldn't really believe in it yet.

She gasped involuntarily at the word ''annulment,'' as if it were a splash of icy cold water across her warm body. Her annulment.... Only last night she had told Adam she would take care of it herself. And it would probably have been easy. Because it was unconsummated, she could have argued that their marriage had never been a real one, that she had accepted his proposal without really understanding the sort of man he was. But now she had made love to him and forgotten everything else. Now there could be no easy annulment, only a divorce that he might or might not choose to contest.

Shivering suddenly, she looked over to see a stranger kneeling half-naked in her room. He had said the annulment was off? She tried to recreate his words, but his tone eluded her. Deafened by her own fears, she was left to guess—had that been triumph in his voice? Having found out somehow that she meant to apply for an annulment, had he set out deliberately last night to see that she couldn't leave him so easily? While she lay deliriously happy in his arms, had he been cold-bloodedly carrying out a plan to make sure she couldn't readily escape his possession?

"Get out," she choked through teeth that literally chattered.

"What?" He was on his feet and turned to her, his expression disbelieving.

"Get out!" she repeated, clenching her jaw until it ached, so that her chattering teeth wouldn't disrupt her words.

But still he didn't seem to understand her. Her voice began to rise, and now she couldn't control her teeth or her limbs. She shook all over. "Get out of here! Go!"

"Laurel, for God's sake...."

Irresistibly he started toward her to take her in his arms again, to hold her until the perfect understanding between their bodies echoed in their minds, to kiss her until whatever was going wrong would be right.

But she writhed away from him. "Don't touch me! Don't ever touch me again!"

His hand dropped to his side. His eyes seemed to turn to ice, and his heart went numb with the cold of love withdrawn. He knew this bitter chill—knew it and had never meant to risk feeling it again. Picking up his clothes in silence, he let himself out of her room and closed the door behind him with hard finality.

His fire quickly dwindled on the hearth. Shaking with grief and revulsion, Laurel watched it and wished she, too, could just fade away. When it was dead, she cried for it in great wrenching sobs that seemed torn from her body.

She was a long time getting downstairs to see to breakfast, but when she finally reached the dining room, several of the guests were just finishing their meals. Piled plates and cups on her tray indicated the others had already eaten. Perhaps Abby had come early and taken care of everything? She murmured an absent response to several hearty good-mornings, hoping no one could read in her face how she really felt, and went into the kitchen to look for Abby.

But Morgan must have made breakfast after all. The kitchen was in considerably more disorder than usual, and Limb was happily finishing up what looked like the extra croissants. He wagged sociably at Laurel but looked behind her to see what else Morgan might offer. There was no sign of him now, anymore than there was of Abby, and Laurel's tight muscles relaxed. She tensed again as the extension phone on the wall rang.

"Hello?" she answered hoarsely.

"Laurel, it's Abby." The familiar voice came on the line, subtly soothing at first, before she added, "Have you looked out the window yet this morning?"

"Why, no," Laurel admitted, knowing she couldn't explain why it hadn't even occurred to her.

"Well, do," Abby instructed, and Laurel set the receiver on the table and walked over to pull the kitchen curtains across and stare out—at a blank and howling whiteness. For a minute she did just that—stared—and the scene drove everything else temporarily to the back of her mind.

Hurrying back on the phone, she picked it up and said concisely, "Wow!"

A mile down the road, Abby chuckled. "Mmm," she agreed. "It's a little early in the season for this sort of thing, but apparently Mother Nature decided to pay us back for the mild winter we had last year! At any rate, it snowed all night and doesn't show any signs of letting up yet, so I don't think we're going to be getting over there."

"What does an innkeeper do around here when it snows like this?"

"Very little, actually," Abby answered comfortably. "There's isn't much that needs doing, and even if there were, you probably couldn't get at it.

"The plows have gone out, but they were a bit late realizing this one meant business, so they won't be around to us for a while. This isn't a main road. We don't usually get done until they've taken care of more urgent things. But they'll be along eventually. In the meantime just sit tight. Were any of the guests planning to leave?"

"A couple, I think," Laurel answered, counting Morgan in. He would probably leave as fast as possible now, and she should be glad of it. The next time she saw him would be in a divorce court—

"Well, encourage them to stay where they are," Abby advised. "If they try to get out, they'll probably only find themselves stuck in the plow's way, and then we'll all be snowed in just that much longer.''

Laurel felt reprieved, but before the feeling could sink in, the significance of Abby's words caught up with her. "Snowed in." She had coped with snowstorms before, but never one that made her its prisoner. At home they'd occasionally had to wait a few hours to be plowed out, but this sounded as if it might possibly be days! If she were a child, that might be fun. But she was an adult, and responsible for seeing that everyone staying at the inn was warm and dry and fed—all without Betsy, Abby and Nate! The weight seemed to fall on her slim shoulders like a rock. But Abby was still speaking.

"Now, didn't Nate just bring in a whole stock of food and such?" she was asking matter-of-factly, and Laurel focused on the question.

"Yes," she said slowly. "Yes, he did, didn't he? So we're well supplied with staples." Relief lightened her voice still more as she went on, "Come to think of it, he brought in everything for the Thanksgiving holiday already, because I wanted to make sure I wouldn't forget something at the last minute."

"So you see, things really are still under control," Abby teased gently. Sheepishly, Laurel let out her breath in a loud melodramatic sigh. Abby chuckled, then returned to practical matters. "All right, now, you should be all set for food for at least four or five days—"

"Four or five *days*!"

"Not that it's likely to be that long—so that's no problem. The furnace has a full tank of oil—" Abby's voice sank thoughtfully as she took inventory aloud "—the power's still on and the phone lines haven't gone down—"

"Yes," she concluded briskly, "you really are lucky. Everything's in fine shape to ride out a bit of a storm."

Hanging up the phone a minute later, with the last of Abby's encouragement ringing in her ears, Laurel still wasn't entirely convinced. But checking the register on her desk, she reminded herself that she only had seven guests—not all that many mouths to feed, and certainly no one from the village would be likely to stop by for a meal! Nevertheless, for the next half hour or so she prowled around the kitchen and pantry, reassuring herself that there really was plenty of food. Then she realized she'd been subconsciously reminded of the doomed Donner party, trapped in the snow on the far side of the continent more than a hundred years earlier, and was able to smile wryly at herself. She and her guests were hardly likely to be reduced to cannibalism, in spite of Morgan's suggestive nibbling this morning. . . .

A stab of pain so strong that she winced made her force her thoughts away from the joy she'd felt then. She hurried out of the kitchen to see how everyone was faring. Almost all her guests had gathered in the living room, where someone had already started a bright cheery fire. A few people stood looking idly out into the storm, while others were sitting comfortably, talking. Morgan and Adam were on the far side of the room, but she just gave Adam a strained smile, refusing to go close enough to hear what they were saying. Only one man was standing impatiently in front of the television set, listening to the weather forecast and slapping his hand irritably against his thigh.

A minute later the broadcast ended, and he strode over to Laurel, who was now speaking to a pleasant middle-aged couple. "Excuse me, Miss Andersen," he said at her elbow, and she turned away from her other guests with a brief apology.

"Yes, Mr. Greene?"

"According to the forecast, we're in for another storm after this one—" the hand was slapping his leg again, and his color was high with annoyance "—so if I'm going to get on to Augusta for my appointment in the capitol tomorrow, I've got to start trying now. If I could have my bill, please?"

"Yes, of course," she answered politely, "but the road hasn't been opened yet by the snowplow—"

"And may not be for hours yet," he interrupted her. "I don't dare wait for it, so I'll have to check out now." She hesitated, but there was really nothing she could do to prevent a guest from leaving.

Ten minutes later he brought his suitcase downstairs, and Laurel led him through the inside passageway to the barn. It took both of them to force the sliding door open far enough so that his Chrysler could squeeze out. Then he had to fight his way back outside to help her drag the door closed again. Just before it finally slid into place, she shouted through the narrowing gap, "Good luck!"

The words were torn away from her mouth by the wind, but he must have understood. He lifted one gloved hand in acknowledgement, then vanished. Catching her breath, she leaned against the inside of the door and watched a cloud of steam form around her. Listening intently, she tried to pick out the car's engine in the howling storm. Faintly she heard it and, satisfied, raced back to the warmth of her kitchen. Even the heavy parka she'd pulled on over her sweater and wool slacks wasn't anywhere near warm enough for this weather.

Trying not to think that if one guest could leave, then so could another, she was nearly through preparing a hot corn chowder when she heard a commotion at the front door, audible even over the tremendous whistling wind. Wiping her hands on her kitchen smock, she hurried through the dining room to the hall.

But no one else was leaving; instead, Mr. Greene had come back. Looking more like a snowman than a human being, he was standing tiredly just inside the door, while Morgan and another man forced it closed. It took their combined strength, but finally they slammed it shut. The snowflakes in the hall settled lazily when the wind ceased. As willing hands brushed the snow off him, Mr. Greene met her concerned look.

"I should have listened to you, Miss Andersen," he said thinly, his face white. "I only got about a half a mile before the car was hopelessly stuck. I tried to dig it out, but it was in a drift almost to the tops of the wheels, and I didn't have the energy to get it out."

Wearily he tugged off his gloves and added, brushing snow off his forehead, "It's taken me this long just to fight my way back here. Will you take me in again?"

"Of course!" she assured him hastily, and reached out to lay her fingers on his white cheek. "Forgive me, but can you feel that?"

"Barely, but yes, I can," he answered and smiled faintly, recognizing her worry. "No frostbite there, or anywhere else, I think. But I'm certainly glad this inn wasn't any farther down the road."

"So am I," she agreed for his sake, while someone helped him off with his coat and muffler. Taking them, she told him, "I'll hang these in the kitchen to dry."

Nodding, he looked at the puddle forming around his feet. "May I give you my boots, too?" he asked, "and borrow a mop to take care of the mess I'm making here?"

"Yes, to the one and no to the other," she returned firmly. "I'll take the boots willingly, but that puddle can wait a bit. I'll tend to it later, but right now I'd be a lot happier if you would just go sit by the fire until you thaw out and let me bring you some of the hot soup I've been making.''

Tugging off his wet boots, he handed them to her and admitted, ''That sounds much too good for me to argue with.''

''Good.'' She gave him a warm smile, and he let himself be led docilely away to the fireside while she headed back to the kitchen. Ten minutes later, while Mr. Greene's clothes steamed quietly near the stove, she brought him a bowl of the soup—and noticed as she crossed the hall that the puddle was gone.

That sort of thing happened a good deal in the next two days. When something needed to be done, it seemed to get down, whether or not Laurel had time to attend to it. Although the snow tapered off, the huge wing plows couldn't get through to them, thanks to Mr. Greene's car, snowed under in the middle of the road. The inn was still cut off. By phone Laurel was able to tell the road crews that their situation wasn't urgent and that they would see to digging out the car when the weather cleared a bit. But even though she was managing without any help from Abby and Nate or Betsy, so that she rarely sat down and seemed to see people at a distance, everything somehow continued to run smoothly.

Deciding to regard being snowbound as an adventure, her guests joined in, persuading her not to worry about offering them a choice of meals. They quietly began serving themselves buffet style, as well as seeing to their own rooms. But there were still a hundred chores to be done every day, and Laurel knew she was coping with only a scant half of them. Finally, the second evening, she realized Morgan was responsible for taking care of the other half.

Without fanfare, he was shoveling the porch and driveway every few hours, so the drifting snow couldn't blow in too deeply to be moved. He was checking the roof for the weight of snow on it and beating snow off the bushes around the building so they wouldn't be crushed. He was splitting and hauling wood from the shed by the barn, so the fire, which seemed to help keep up all their spirits, wouldn't go out on the main hearth. And, she gradually noticed, he was doing more of the other chores than she could count—all this in spite of the fact that they hadn't spoken directly to each other since the morning when she'd told him to get out of her room and out of her life.

Every minute of the day when she wasn't totally involved with the problem of keeping the inn going, she was thinking of him, telling herself a thousand times a day that she *had* been right to drive Morgan from her. But it felt so wrong that a thousand times a day she blessed the snow that kept him from going away forever. Every night she dreamed of him, waking alone in her big bed to find her pillow damp and her body aching. Eventually, she knew, the snow would be cleared and she would have to watch him leave, but for now there was at least a tiny remaining bond between them.

"Morgan, wait, please."

She stopped him on the stairs that evening, coming to stand below him and gaze up over the banister. This was where he had stopped her that first night he had come to the inn, she remembered. But then he had looked at her so warmly, and now his face was a cold dark mask. Standing four steps up from her, he seemed to tower almost oppressively over her.

"Yes?" he asked coolly.

"I wanted—" Her voice cracked unexpectedly, and she had to clear her throat to try again. "I wanted to thank you..." she began awkwardly and paused.

"Why?" he prompted dispassionately.

"For helping out so much."

He shrugged his broad shoulders. "Adam and I agreed the company owed its newest manager whatever assistance we could come up with in a crisis. Since I'm considerably heartier than he is, I'm the one providing it."

He made it sound entirely impersonal, and she felt herself shrivel. Not only was their wretched marriage over, but so was any pretense of friendliness between them. "Well, thanks, anyway," she said past the lump in her throat, and with a negligent gesture of one hand that seemed to sweep away her gratitude— and her—he went on up the stairs.

Behind her, the front door swung open, and she

dashed away hot tears she couldn't have rationalized. Turning, she found Peggy brushing a few snowflakes off her quilted parka and pants.

"Hello!" The younger woman's tone was cheery. Her cheeks were red from the cold, but her eyes seemed as shadowed as Laurel knew her own must be. "Half the village is still snowed in, but I wanted to see some different faces, so I borrowed dad's snowmobile to come looking for company—"

Her gaze flickered involuntarily toward the door of the living room, where people laughed and chatted, but she dragged it back. "I suppose you heard me from a mile away!" she said brightly.

"Well, no, I didn't," Laurel admitted, "but then I wasn't really listening." Her voice came out hoarse, but she added more warmly, "It's nice to see our first outsider, though, however she comes!"

At her words, Peggy's pretended good spirits evaporated. "Then Giles isn't here," she concluded, and Laurel had to nod. Peggy's small triangular face seemed to become pinched before her very eyes, and the younger woman said miserably, "I knew he probably wouldn't be—he wouldn't think of using a snowmobile, and he'd rather compose than bother hiking out on snowshoes. But I just wanted to see him so badly—"

Her voice was husky, but she went on, as if she had to talk to someone. "I got a call from Boston, and on the basis of my first audition they've offered me a final one, before the conductor as well as the application committee. I guess I wanted to tell Giles, and ask him outright if he'd rather I stayed here. But I suppose it's hopeless, anyway.'' She shrugged, her shoulders drooping.

"Lately he hasn't even been teasing me anymore. I never thought I'd welcome that, but it would be better than nothing. . . .''

Her voice faded away, and the two women stood looking at each other unhappily. Finally, Laurel broke the silence, remembering something.

"I don't know if it would be any help,'' she began diffidently, but at the faintly hopeful look in Peggy's eyes, she went on, "but the last time Giles was here he left a folder of some music he said he'd just picked up at the printer's. I haven't looked to see what it is, but maybe it's something you could return to him? Then at least you'd have another reason to see him—''

"I would, wouldn't I?'' Peggy agreed, the hope growing stronger. "Where is it, Laurel?''

Frowning, Laurel tried to think where it was she'd seen the folder last. "I think it's still in the parlor, on the table there,'' she decided. "I haven't been very good these past few days about putting things away.''

Peggy managed a smile of understanding and walked into the parlor, while Laurel sat on the lowest step, still too chilled by Morgan's coldness to go any farther.

A minute later Peggy erupted out of the parlor.

"Laurel!" she cried, skidding to a stop in front of her. "Look at this!"

She waved the open folder containing Giles's music under Laurel's nose but didn't hold it still long enough for Laurel to focus on the heading at the top of the page. "What is it?"

"It's the flute sonata, and it's dedicated to me!" Peggy told her, with a face like sunrise. "My copy was one of the originals, and it didn't have any dedication!"

"Well, that's nice—"

"Don't you see?" Peggy interrupted her, clutching the folder to her. "Remember how he said one time that he used his music to say what he couldn't put into words? Isn't this saying something?" She twirled around the hall on tiptoe before halting again in front of Laurel. "Oh, Laurel, don't you think—"

She broke off the sentence as if she didn't dare finish it, and Laurel stood up. Giles, she decided, had sacrificed both himself and Peggy for long enough. "I think you've better take your snowmobile and return Giles's sonata," she said firmly.

Thinking of Giles's report on Peggy's audition, she went one better to add, "After all, what could be more appropriate than it being returned by the woman he told me played it with a passion and genius that were all he ever dreamed of?"

She gave Peggy a meaningful look, and after a moment's dawning wonder and joy, Peggy gave her a hug that nearly crushed her. The door slammed, and then a roar that should have awakened the dead confirmed that she was taking Laurel's advice. As the unholy sound faded off toward the lake, Laurel found herself smiling faintly at the thought that Giles would hear his beloved long before he saw her—but no wonder he wouldn't have a snowmobile of his own!

LATE THAT NIGHT it began to snow again, and the storm Mr. Greene had heard about was upon them at last. And if the first storm had been impressive, this one was awe inspiring. Laurel heard it all night through her restless sleep. No matter how determinedly she burrowed under the covers, she couldn't escape the sound of the wind. Easily blizzard force, it howled and groaned and tore at the inn, rattling her windows and shrieking down her chimney so that even with the damper closed, a cloud of ashes flew around the room.

When morning came, it was still snowing, and only a slight lightening of the sky confirmed that it was daytime. Whipped by the wind, the flakes seemed to rise as often as fall, blowing sideways as well. Every outside landmark had disappeared into enormous drifts, and sky and earth were both a sullen grayish white, so that even to look out a window was frightening, because it caused such a feeling of disorientation. Uneasily, Laurel remembered reading about a "whiteout," and realized this whirling maelstrom of snow must be one.

Abby's voice on the phone that morning was faint and punctuated with crackles and hisses that came along the line. "Laurel, are you there?" she asked, and Laurel knew she was shouting.

"Yes," she called back, "but I can barely hear you!"

"I know. I'll holler, but we probably only have a few minutes before the line goes. Is everything all right?"

"Yes! We have lots of food still, and everyone's fine!"

"If the power goes off...." Abby's voice faded away, and Laurel tightened her grip on the receiver as if that would increase its volume.

"What?" she shouted, and Abby came back, but faintly.

"Not working yet. Nate says he's sorry, but at least there's the fireplaces, and you can make do with the lanterns in the barn. There's plenty of kerosene for them anyway."

"What did you—"

"Stove is gas, so you can cook anyway, and the food will certainly keep cold in the snow, if not in the barn passage. But don't let the pipes freeze.... If you have any real trouble, get word to Giles somehow—he's got a CB radio...."

"Abby, how—" Laurel began, and stopped as she realized all she could hear on the line was a sort of sizzling noise. Then that vanished, too, and the phone was dead in her hand.

Putting it slowly back on the hook, she just stood there, taking stock. Actually, Abby was right; things did seem to be in pretty good shape. Now that Mr. Greene's appointment in Augusta was no longer an issue, none of her guests, mostly retired couples, seemed to have anywhere they'd rather be than at a country inn, snowed in. They still had plenty of food. Everyone was well, and the power hadn't failed—

But even as she thought that, the light overhead flickered, glowed, flickered again and went out.

"Damn!" she muttered fervently, wishing she'd never tempted fate by counting the inn's blessings. The power lines must be on the same poles as the phone lines.

There was at least a pale snow light coming in from outdoors, but her eyes were adjusting slowly to the gloom, and she was still standing motionless when she heard someone open the kitchen door. Morgan's called, "Laurel?"

"Right here," she answered from beside the door, and felt him jump. Instinctively she put her hands out and touched his hard chest. It was irrationally reassuring, but she let her hands fall hastily. "I was just deciding what to do first," she said.

"Light would seem to be the first priority," he responded as coolly as the last time they'd spoken. "Is there a flashlight in here anywhere?"

"Yes," she answered briskly, stung by his tone. "I made a point of bringing one in after I—"

She stopped, wanting to avoid any reference to the

cubbyhole and the ensuing intimacy between them. Turning away, she groped her way across the kitchen, rummaging noisily in a far drawer while he waited at the door.

"Here it is!" She disentangled the flashlight from a welter of note pads, string, pencils and pens and switched it on so that the gloom receded a little around the pale cone of light.

"Good." Morgan's tone was businesslike, and he took the flashlight from her hand without touching her fingers—a fact she noted unhappily. She'd fought so often and so desperately to avoid contact with him, but now he seemed almost to recoil from touching her. Gratingly in her ears, she heard her own voice saying, "Don't touch me!" But surely he hadn't taken her so literally! But he was already striding out through the passage that led to the barn, and snatching up her parka, she hurried after him.

When she got there, he was already filling a lantern from the kerosene tank Nate kept handy, and when he had it lighted he slipped the chimney into place and held up the lantern to look intently around the shadowy barn. On the far side a line of cars filled the old horse stalls, and Laurel realized for the first time that Nate must have been moving them around before the snow began. Her boxy little Rabbit now sat incongruously beside Morgan's sleek Corvette, and at the sight of them she had a sudden urge to laugh—and to cry. But she didn't have time for either.

Morgan was striding over to a massive gray piece of machinery.

"There it is," he exclaimed, more to himself than her. "I thought Nate said there was a generator."

Laurel looked at it now with recognition, but then something Abby had tried to say on the phone clicked into place. "There is," she agreed ruefully, "but it doesn't work. It ran perfectly in the tests when it was first delivered, but ever since then, Nate's been fiddling with it, trying to make it go again."

Morgan's mouth tightened, and she suddenly remembered his relationship to the company. She rushed to Nate's defense—and her own. "We never dreamed we'd need it this soon! And besides, Nate just hasn't had enough time to spend on it—he does so much around here. You should know that now—"

She broke off, biting her lip. She had tried yesterday to thank him for taking over Nate's work, and he'd brushed her aside. She hadn't meant to refer to it again. But he barely seemed to notice. Going back to the group of lanterns set neatly on a shelf, he was filling one after another. Following silently, she picked them up as he finished, juggling them carefully to avoid spilling the fuel. Then, still in silence, they went back to the kitchen, where they lighted the rest of the lanterns before setting them down in various rooms. When that was done, she fixed breakfast, thankful for a gas stove at least, while he went around and lighted a fire in each of the inn's hearths, now their only source of heat.

When she heard his steps overhead in her room, she tried not to remember the last time he'd stood by that fireplace, tried not to see the expression that had come into his eyes at her words. But the image seemed etched in her mind, and hot tears slipped down her cold cheeks. Thinking that she never used to cry before Morgan came into her life, she wiped them away. When the roads were finally cleared, he would leave, and she would only see him that one last time in court. Then the whole tragic mess of their marriage would be over, and she could try to forget he ever existed. It was all very clearly laid out in front of her, so why was she being such an idiot, standing here sobbing heartbrokenly because he treated her with chilling politeness now?

CHAPTER FOURTEEN

HE TREATED HER THE SAME WAY all that day, as they
worked side by side and harder than ever to keep the
inn lighted and decently warm. In spite of the help of
other guests, most of the effort still fell to them.
Even as they shared it, however, he went on avoiding
any accidental contact with her and spoke to her only
when it was absolutely necessary. By evening, they
were both pale with fatigue and strain.

After an early supper of hearty beef stew, most of
the guests voted for bed as the warmest place to be,
so Laurel rounded up and distributed every spare
blanket in the inn, while Morgan heated bricks in one
of the fireplaces and wrapped them in rags, to be
used as foot warmers. Then, one by one, the guests
climbed the stairs with their lanterns and vanished,
until only Adam, Morgan and Laurel were left.

Glancing at the other two without meeting their
eyes, Morgan said abruptly, "We're going to need a
lot more wood to keep this place from freezing
tonight. I'll go split some." And turning on his heel,
he left rapidly, apparently eager to avoid them—or
her, Laurel corrected herself.

"Well, my dear, we seem to be on our own," Adam observed as the sound of Morgan's footsteps faded away. He sighed and added, "But since I don't feel up to tackling those stairs yet, and the fire in the living room is still very inviting, I think I'll sit up for a while. Can you come and join me? I've hardly seen you since the snow and I arrived."

He ended on a light note, but her gaze flew to his face. She had heard that sigh and—a good deal more disconcerting—Adam's confession that the stairs were a problem for him. Never having known him to admit to any limitations before, she studied him worriedly, remembering that when he'd first arrived she and Morgan had been struck by his age. Now she realized that although he was smiling at her over his spectacles, his color was bad. A cold fear twisted in her stomach.

"Yes, of course I can," she answered, making her tone as light as his with an effort. "I can't think of one more errand that has to be done right now, so I'll reward myself with some time by the fire with you."

She slid her hand into the crook of his arm in the usual way. They walked into the other room together, but she noticed his stride seemed less energetic than it ordinarily was. When she had poked the fire and settled beside him, though, he smiled at her and began to talk about the inn. Trying to keep her concern for him out of her expression, she answered his first quick questions. But the next ones came more slowly, and he seemed to be paying less attention to her responses, too. Finally he shook off his abstraction and gave her a candid stare.

"My dear, I really want to talk about something else," he admitted, and she nodded.

"All right," she agreed, registering the fact that he was still looking at her in that intent way.

"I know Sophie would have liked you for a grand-daughter," he murmured, then added more briskly at her puzzled expression. "But that wasn't what I wanted to talk to you about."

Taking her hand in his, he added, "What I want to talk about is Morgan, and what I have to say is in the nature of an explanation and a confession."

The hand in his stirred, but he didn't release it. "No, my dear," he said, responding to her instinctive movement of withdrawal, "I'm going to ask you to hear me out, please."

The seriousness of his tone decided her, and seeing this, he patted her hand, as if to thank her for staying with him. He didn't speak again immediately. When he did, he started in the middle of things, looking at her musingly.

"I've wondered ever since then if I should have told you about Morgan's background that very first day, before I persuaded you to accept his dinner invitation."

He paused, shifting his gaze toward the emptiness at the far side of the room. At her indistinct murmur, his thoughtful attitude changed to one of self-reproach. "But then, of course, I would have had to admit right away that I was partly responsible for the streak of wildness in him, and accepting blame hasn't ever been easy for me to do.''

A scathing note came into his voice as he added, ''If only I'd been as good at that as I was at empire building, we would never have come to the pass we did!''

Understanding his tone but not the topic, Laurel could only think to lace her slim fingers tightly through his gnarled ones. It seemed to bring his attention back to her, though, and he managed a slight crooked smile. ''But none of this makes any sense to you yet, does it, Laurel?''

She shook her head, and he backtracked far enough so that she gradually began to understand him, as he looked into the fire and turned into the past.

''I should never have let Simon marry Vanessa,'' he said despairingly. ''That was the first and worst mistake. But she was beautiful then, and when I got around to noticing what was happening I started badly by trying to forbid him to see her. I told him it was because she was so much more sophisticated than he was, but that just made him all the more determined to be with her. And he was right—that wasn't my real reason for objecting to her.''

Adam tightened his grip on her fingers, and his voice changed, gaining force and bitterness. ''The truth was that even as young as she was then, she was silly and shallow and corrupt. But before he found it out my only son had married her in Europe, and before Morgan was even a year old, she'd made Simon the laughingstock of the Continent with her affairs. But a divorce wasn't her style, either—she preferred to keep a hold on Simon's bank account, and she specialized in using Morgan to do it."

He paused as if to steady himself, but the rage and contempt did not abate as he went on. "Knowing that Simon would never tell a court all the vile details of their life together, she taunted him with the threat that in a divorce proceeding, she'd be given custody of the boy, and then if Simon didn't cooperate financially she'd refuse to let him see his son."

Sickened, Laurel drew a deep breath and let it out again before he added, "It was after one of their flaming rows, when she pried Morgan screaming out of his father's arms, that Simon was killed driving into an abutment when he was too drunk and heartsick to handle the car on wet pavement. What she told Morgan, though, was that it was his fault."

Adam's voice cracked on the last sentence, and he fell silent. Laurel, following Adam's mesmerized gaze into the flames, could almost envision the whole scene there. She sat numbly beside him, feeling as if she had been turned to stone by the touch of so much remembered pain and grief. Somehow she had never imagined Morgan as a child, perhaps because her contacts with the man had so preoccupied her. But now he appeared unbearably clearly in her mind's eye, a sturdy little boy with dark eyebrows and vulnerable eyes, who didn't know yet that people could lie just to hurt each other.

For a long while his image stood before her, and probably before Adam as well, while around them the only sounds were the quiet crackling of the fire and the ticking of the clock, the sighing of the wind and the muffled noise of Morgan's maul in the wood-shed.

Eventually, however, Adam spoke again, tiredness evident in his tone. "After the funeral, Vanessa squandered Simon's estate, supposedly to support Morgan, and for the next six years she hauled him around behind her like luggage as she went from lover to lover. Finally one of them objected to having the boy underfoot, and at that his devoted mother packed him up and shipped him home to the States to live with her sister."

With his free hand Adam pushed the spectacles wearily upward on the bridge of his nose. "There wasn't any harm in Angela, at least," he conceded, "but she was an incredibly silly woman, and she spoiled him rotten to make up for his mother's neglect. By the time he finally came to me at eigh-teen, when Angela died, Sophie was gone, too, and my corporate empire was built, so I had time at last to notice what a mess we'd all made of his life."

The bitter self-condemnation was back in his voice, and Laurel clung to him in silent pity and fear—pity for a younger Adam who could do any-thing except guarantee happiness for the people he loved, and fear for the old one beside her who was racked by the pain of his own words. He didn't stop yet, though. It was as if, having started, he couldn't halt the floodtide of regrets until they had all ebbed away and he was left drained and empty.

"Ever since then, I've tried to straighten it all out by offering him the training and responsibilities Simon never had a chance at, because I was too busy to notice my own son needed a place in my life. And although we fought each other almost every step of the way, over my methods and his life-style, Morgan's proved to be superbly capable."

A brief note of pride lightened his tired voice, but then it faded as he glanced absently down at their linked hands. "Perhaps I should have left well—or bad—enough alone at that point," he went on slowly, "but it stuck in my throat to see him racketing around Europe just the way his father was doing when Vanessa got her claws into him. Even though he has good reason to loathe her, he makes a point of seeing her whenever he's in Paris. But instead of crediting him with a certain compassion and common sense, I kept expecting him to let her draw him into her destructive orbit.

"I suppose I was afraid he'd eventually make the same kind of disastrous marriage as his father, so I tried to force his hand. When he came back from Biarritz last spring, I told him he had to marry some-one I approved of, or I'd make his cousin, Paul, the head of the company after me."

For the first time since he'd started speaking, Adam looked fully into Laurel's eyes, and his own expressed something she'd never seen there in the three years she'd known him. Prompted by that look, she remembered Morgan's return from Europe and the raised voices she'd heard from his grandfather's office before he'd burst out the door and invited her to dinner. And she finally began to understand her marriage.

"Then when he asked me out to dinner that first evening," she recalled in a toneless voice, "it was just because he had to find someone to marry or lose his chance at control of the company."

Adam's answer seemed to come from a long way off, but she could now put a name to the odd expression on his face—apology.

"Yes, my dear, it was," he confirmed quietly, "and I was delighted, because I'd thought for months that you were just the sort of woman he needed. Knowing how he usually reacted when I issued an ultimatum, I simply put you in his path before I did it and hoped for the best."

Sighing he added, "I thought I had it, too, until you told me his mistress was with him in the library—"

"He told her goodbye," Laurel cut in, still without expression.

"I know that now. I'd guessed almost immediately, but he finally told me after you went upstairs the night I arrived," Adam agreed, surprised. "But when did you find out?"

"Morgan told me about a week after he came up here.'

"Then why—" Adam began on a rising note, like someone who sees hope where all seemed lost. Then he interrupted himself. "My dear, I'm sorry again. I have no right to ask that."

"What does Morgan's mother look like?" she asked suddenly, ignoring Adam's last words.

His face grew dark. "I can hardly tell you that objectively," he grated. "To me, she will always look like the woman who killed my son. But I suppose to someone else—to all too many men—she still looks like an haute-couture mannequin, all current fashion and bright colors and blond hair. After all, she's not fifty-five yet. It isn't until you're close enough to see her eyes and hear her voice that you discover she's as hard and dead inside as a mannequin."

Sliding her fingers out of Adam's, Laurel clenched both her hands together in her lap, shut her eyes and wished that she, too, were hard and dead inside. If she were, then she wouldn't mind sitting here, learning too late that he really hadn't been trying to lie to her about his "date" in Paris! She bowed her head and listened to the wind blowing outside, feeling as though it were sighing through a great aching hollow inside her as well.

Last spring Morgan had set out to marry her out of anger. It wasn't a noble motive—thoughtless and arrogant at best—and she had been right to wonder at the time why a man like that had suddenly dropped out of his usual social circles and chosen her. He probably wouldn't have if he hadn't been looking for a way to defy Adam. Learning the truth at last certainly didn't inflate her ego.

But weighed against that first careless cruelty was so much else. Her knuckles whitened as she remembered what he had done since then, and how she had misinterpreted, misunderstood and misjudged him again and again. Seeing him first with Renee and then with his mother, she had immediately assumed the worst of him, assumed he was lying over and over again. Hadn't he accused her once of lacking loyalty and trust? Yet he had still come to find her, had still looked at her with warmth and desire, had still tried to salvage their relationship.

And she had held him off and put down what she felt for him to simple lust, refusing to believe her body could understand him better than her mind. She'd always feared the way her love for him overwhelmed her reason, and now she knew that what she'd done was to snatch eagerly at every excuse to deny that dangerous feeling. That, too, he'd tolerated, leaving her time to get to know him better, and when he finally forced the issue by coming to her room three nights ago, she had been hypocrite enough to love him all night with her body and then deny him by day with her mind, misjudging him one final time. Her fingernails sank deep into her palms, and she heard again the ugliness of her own voice hissing, "Don't touch me!"

He had looked at her with an oddly defenseless expression, unable to believe it was true, and then gone away, withdrawing completely into himself before he had even physically left the room. Every contact between them since had made it clear that she had finally managed to destroy his feelings for her. Somehow, improbably, in spite of a bad start to their relationship, he had fallen in love with her, and she had responded with doubt, suspicion and distrust, always looking for the fool's gold in their marriage. Finally she had made it out of real gold. Now she knew the truth, and now it was too late.

"Laurel." Adam's weary voice reached into the echoing emptiness inside her, and she opened her eyes. "My dear, I'm sorry," he said quietly. "Sorry for my own sake that it hasn't worked out, and deeply sorry for yours that I put you through all this unhappiness."

"No," she said, her own voice thick with unshed tears. Somehow it seemed important that he should know what she meant, and she unclenched her stiffened hands with an effort, to place them over his. "I'm not sorry. I have been sometimes, but only because I never understood it all before. Now I won't ever regret what you did, only what I did myself."

Their eyes locked in a long look of love and compassion, and Laurel bent forward to place a kiss on Adam's thin cheek. But the skin her lips touched was clammy. Startled, she drew back enough to look closely at him, remembering what he had said earlier about not attempting the stairs. His face was bluish and haggard. A fine sheen of perspiration shone all over it. "Granda, are you all right?" she asked anxiously.

"I will be, my dear," he answered, but with difficulty.

"Can I get you anything?" she all but pleaded, kneeling in front of him, still holding his hands, fear in her pale face.

"Perhaps the medicine by my bed," he managed, and she leaped to her feet.

"I'll have it in just a second," she promised, darting out of the room.

She was halfway up the stairs when she heard a heavy thud, and knew in an instant that Adam had fallen. But at least the fear of anticipation had ended. She was faced with fearful reality.

"Morgan!" At the foot of the stairs, she paused only long enough for that single urgent shout. Then she was back in the living room.

Adam lay in front of the sofa where they had sat together, crumpled and motionless, his tall figure appearing shrunken. But Laurel, dropping to her knees beside him, had only a second to develop that impression, because she was in action immediately, working as smoothly as if she were a machine designed just for this purpose. With remote-computerlike clarity her mind ticked off the steps she must take.

Slipping an arm around his shoulders, she drew his body over until he lay on his back, flat on the floor, at the same time calling his name. But there was no answer, as she had feared there wouldn't be, and no breath warmed her cheek when she held it near his lips. Putting one hand at the nape of his neck and the other on his forehead, she lifted him until his head tipped back, checking then to see that nothing was choking him. Then she brushed her fingers across his throat and settled them firmly in the hollows where his pulse should have been. But it wasn't.

For an instant she closed her eyes, and a wordless prayer flashed through her mind. Then she bent again, sealing Adam's nose and pressing her mouth to his, so she could blow four quick breaths into his lungs and watch to see his chest rise and fall. She checked for his pulse again. Again it wasn't there, and she was half-aware of hot tears sliding down her cheeks.

But she didn't have time to wipe them away. Adam's jacket had fallen away from his chest. She used both hands to open his shirt, yanking the buttons off instead of taking precious time to unfasten them. When she had his chest bare, Morgan's hands came onto it from the far side where he had come to kneel, his face drawn and intent.

Without any more delay than a flashing glance of question and answer between them, he ran his fingers along Adam's rib cage until he found the sharp point of the breastbone and measured swiftly up from this lower part of the sternum in finger widths. Locking his hands together, he placed one on top of the other

over Adam's still heart and shifted forward, keeping
his elbows locked so that his weight on the sternum
forced it down to drive the blood through Adam's
body. Back on his heels again, he released the
pressure and counted, "One," before leaning forward to repeat the process.

When he reached five, she had slipped one hand
back under Adam's neck and sealed his nose again
giving him her own breath, squeezing it in between
Morgan's compressions of the chest. At the count of
five the next time she did the same, bending to offer
the "kiss of life," and they began the cycle again,
working together with the smoothness of a practiced
rescue team and the strength of loving desperation.

Above and around them, worried voices began to
murmur as the guests responded, too, to the sound of
Adam's fall and Laurel's shout. Fully occupied with
his counting, Morgan had to ignore them, but between breaths for Adam, Laurel was able to say a little. Blessing Abby for her last messages before the
phone went out, she remembered how they could get
help.

"Giles Thomas— at the bottom of the hill—has a
CB radio. He can send for help if we get word to
him," she explained hastily to the ring of concerned
faces above her.

"I'll go." One of the faces came down to her level;
Sam Greene crouched beside her. He waited for her
to breathe for Adam again, and when she looked up,
waved away her gratitude.

"Glad to help," he said briefly. "Besides, it won't be as hard as getting back from my car was, if you have an old pair of skis lying around anywhere." He ended on a questioning note.

As she gave Adam more air, her mind raced. Raising her head, she told him, "In the barn, I think— back corner, behind the last car."

"Good. I should be able to find them pretty easily."

"I don't think there are any poles—" She broke off to bend over Adam, and Sam stood up.

"No problem," he assured her. "I can manage without. Give me a minute to pull my clothes on, then I'll take one of the lanterns and be off. It should only take me another few minutes to find the skis and get down the hill on them." Between breaths she looked at him thankfully as he promised, "We'll be able to call for help, don't worry." A reassuring smile, and he left, sending two of the other men ahead to the barn.

When he was gone, time warped for Laurel and Morgan. They were conscious of it only in counted seconds and measured breaths as they knelt together over Adam's fallen body, checking periodically to see if his own heart had taken over. They had changed positions four times, for the little relief it offered, when the terrible silence they worked in was finally interrupted by the roar of an approaching engine. Both of them jumped as if their tired bodies had been jerked by the same string, and they looked up, Laurel white-faced and Morgan with sweat streaming down. Their eyes met anxiously; his blinked as a stinging drop ran into one. Mechanically she wiped his forehead and whispered, "Is it help?"

It was. One of the women who had stood helplessly by ran to the door, and a minute later two men from the village, trained in C.P.R., were kneeling beside him, checking for Adam's pulse.

"Good work," one of them said. "The heart hasn't started up again for itself, but we can take over for you now and hold him until the ambulance squad gets here."

"They'll drive as far as the road's plowed," the other man cut in to explain, "and then come the rest of the way on one of the other snowmobiles out there."

Wearily Morgan nodded for them both, and at the end of the next count cycle, fresh hands replaced his. Fresh lungs took over for Laurel, too, and they dragged themselves out of the way, leaning against the far settle, too breathless for the moment to move.

It was less than ten minutes later that an ambulance team of three men took over working on Adam, calling "Stand clear!" and using electric paddles to jolt his heart into picking up the rhythm for itself. Then he was moved onto a stretcher and wrapped warmly, to be carried by snowmobile trailer to the waiting ambulance for the trip to the community hospital in Bridgton.

When they were ready to go, Morgan hauled himself to his feet and asked, "May I go with you?"

"Sorry, but no." One of the ambulance men threw him a quick compassionate glance that took in his expression, set with strain and grief, but he shook his head.

"We haven't got the room, Mac. We'll relay word from the hospital, but that's the best we can offer. In the meantime, why don't you get back to that CB so we can let you know that way?"

Stiffly Morgan nodded, but as Adam was carried out the door and into a night that was now crystal clear and getting rapidly colder, Laurel could see the tears that ran silently down her husband's angular cheeks. Watching love twist that hard face, her own throat closed suddenly and her eyes filled again as she pulled herself to her feet.

"Morgan—" she began. But her voice was husky with emotion, and he didn't hear it, turning away to find the heavy jacket he'd ripped off to work on Adam. Someone handed it to him with a word of hope, while one of the women gave her a quick comforting hug.

"I'm sure he'll be all right, dear. You two worked wonders, and now he's in the hands of the experts."

Laurel could only manage a grateful look in response. By the time she reached Morgan's side, he was nearly at the outer door.

"Morgan, wait!" This time urgency made her voice audible. "I'm coming with you."

He turned to look at her, his face a mask of worry,

and at first she thought he was going to say no. Then as she met his eyes, he nodded slowly.

"All right."

"I'll get my parka and be right back."

Drawing fresh energy from somewhere, she hurriedly gathered up boots and parka, cap and gloves.

"Must you go out in that cold?" The motherly woman who'd offered reassurance was anxious now.

"Yes, Jo, she must." Her husband put an arm around her and answered for Laurel. "It's important to them both to hear Mr. Hamilton's reached the hospital safely." He gave Laurel a steady smile from kind brown eyes and added, "He will, of course, but meanwhile you two do what you have to. We'll all be going back to bed, so everything will be fine here."

He patted her shoulder encouragingly, then led his wife away. In a minute the subdued guests began climbing the stairs, lanterns in hand, while a solitary one passed through the front door and out into the night.

Outside, Morgan spoke only once. As they stepped off the porch into powdery snow that rose nearly to their knees, he said, "Follow in my footsteps and I'll break a path for you." He had turned away almost before she'd agreed.

She did as he ordered, though, thankful for the slight advantage his steps gave her as they made their way down toward the lake. Before, this always had been a short pleasant walk, but now it seemed to go on forever. They struggled through a moonlit world of silver and shadow, in silence except for the steamy explosions of their breath, coming faster and harder with each difficult step. By the time the lights of Giles's boathouse finally came into sight, they were both gasping.

For Laurel it was almost more than she could manage to climb the stairs, but Morgan somehow hurried heavily up them. Light flooded out the doorway in response to his knock, and then Giles was drawing him in while Peggy rushed to help Laurel up the last few steps.

Inside, she propped herself exhaustedly against the nearest wall as Peggy brushed the snow off her and knelt to tug her boots off. Peeling off the outer layers of Laurel's clothes, she shepherded her into the studio to a chair by the wood stove, where heat lapped out in golden waves.

"Now just sit there and bake yourself," she commanded, "while I go pour you a cup of hot soup."

Laurel nodded, but all of her attention was fixed on Morgan. Still snowy and booted, he leaned on his hands over the CB radio on Giles's desk, while the other man sat in front of it and fiddled delicately with the knobs and Sam Greene watched intently from the far side. Coming back from the kitchen, Peggy set a steaming cup near Laurel and touched her shoulder sympathetically, but didn't try to draw her attention away from Morgan, who seemed to be willing the radio to work with an almost tangible power.

"Hang on," Giles muttered. "We had them just a minute ago."

"New Suncook Rescue Squad here," a voice suddenly boomed out, making them all jump. "What's the news at the hospital?"

Laurel caught her breath, waiting for the answer to that question, and a few feet away from her she could see Morgan's knuckles suddenly whiten. Inside her own body she seemed to feel his muscles tense as they waited. At first there was no sound at all. Then a burst of static grated across their nerves, bringing Laurel back to her feet. She moved to join the others, huddled around the radio.

Another silence, and then in the middle of a second explosion of static, a few disjointed words faded in and out. "Trip was.... Patient...." The faraway voice faded entirely as static took over again.

Across the desk from her, Morgan closed his eyes; he pounded the wood with one fist in an outburst of frustration. Responding as if on cue, the voice came back immediately.

"Giles? You still there?" it asked, and they all drew closer as Giles picked up the microphone.

"Right here, Tom."

"Did you copy that?"

"Negative—too far away."

"Well, the news isn't much, since they just got through to Bridgton—" two feet away from her,

Morgan stopped breathing, and Laurel felt the sus-
pension ''—but he stood the trip and they're working
on him in the emergency right now.''

His dark head bent so that his face was hidden,
Morgan breathed again, while Peggy murmured,
''Thank heaven.'' Instinctively Laurel laid her own
hand on top of the bronze one that rested palm upward on the desk. For an instant Morgan's fingers
stirred around hers, so quickly she almost thought
she'd imagined the brief contact. Then his hand
slipped away, and he walked to the far side of the
room, standing with his back to the others to look
out the window toward the snow-covered lake below.

''Got it,'' Giles was answering in his deep voice.
''Thanks, Tom. We'll stay in touch with you in case
anything more comes through.''

''Ten-four. Over.''

The radio went quiet, and Giles put down the
microphone as Sam Greene said, ''Well, that certainly is good news, isn't it?''

He glanced Morgan's direction, but got no response. Clearing her throat, Laurel answered instead. ''Yes, it is,'' she confirmed. ''Now that he's at
the hospital, the most dangerous part of it all is. . .
over.''

Her voice cracked a little on the last word, and
Giles stood up to wrap her in a comforting bear hug.
''I'm glad,'' he said simply. ''We all know how much
you care about him.''

Nodding mutely, she returned his hug and tried not

to wish it had been Morgan who offered comfort so easily.

But Giles was speaking again, and in a deliberately brisk tone of voice. Turning to Peggy and dropping an arm around her slim shoulders, he said portentously, "And now, young woman—"

"Yes, my lord and master?" Peggy's reply was honeyed, and the changed vocabulary and tone of their teasing brought Laurel's mind back from the silent figure at the window.

"Since I have no intention of letting you disturb the gods much later than this with that infernal snowmobile of yours, you'd better be off home." Giles scowled sternly, then shuddered in exaggerated fear. "Besides, I don't care to offend my future father-in-law by having him think I've detained his only child against her will."

"Never that," Peggy answered softly on a tiny breath of laughter, and for a moment they met each other's eyes, oblivious to everyone in the room.

Watching them, Laurel knew how much everything had changed for them at last. If only she and Morgan were looking at each other with that sort of open delight—or even openly sharing the worry over Adam. Without volition, she began to move toward the tall man on the far side of the room, but Morgan still stood looking down at the cold lake, his back toward her. She'd probably imagined that answering touch of his hand. She'd forfeited that kind of communion when she drove him away from her. Torn, she sank back into her chair and with groping fingers picked up the mug of soup Peggy had left for her.

Her slight movements broke the transfixed tableau. With a last smile that was an embrace in itself, Peggy left Giles's side and went to collect the scarlet snowmobile suit that hung near the wood stove, pulling it on while Giles gave Laurel a look that was as observant as it was kind. He took in the wearily boneless way she sat and the pinched pallor of her face before his eyes flickered to Morgan and back.

"Laurel..." his bass voice rumbled as he hunkered down by her chair.

"Mmm?"

She looked up from the mug in her hands, and he suggested gently, "Why don't you let Peggy give you a lift back up the hill on the snowmobile? I don't think Morgan's going to want to leave the CB yet, but he and Sam can walk up in the morning. In the meantime you can get some rest."

She nodded tiredly, and in two minutes she and Peggy were off, a pair of bulky figures lumbering out the door. Giles had kissed Peggy soundly and given Laurel a last encouraging squeeze. Sam Greene had said good-night to them both. But Morgan had only lifted a hand to acknowledge their going, still standing in the shadows, so that Laurel couldn't read his expression. She kept trying, though, even after they were out in the arctic night. Even as the snowmobile's roar rose around them, she kept seeing him in her mind. When they reached the top of the hill she slid numbly off the seat behind Peggy.

"Thanks, Peg." She mustered up a slight smile and started to turn away.

"Laurel, wait a moment—please."

Peggy's voice caught her, and she looked back. "I wanted to tell you—I returned Giles's music... and told him I'd never play again if he sent me away." Even by moonlight Laurel could see the expression on her small face, laughing and guilty and defiant. "It was an awful piece of blackmail," she admitted, "but it worked! He finally agreed that if we take the North Country Orchestra on tour next year, I can see the world without losing him."

Slipping off the snowmobile, she flung her arms around Laurel, adding in a rush, "And I just wanted to thank you for everything! Giles told me what you said about me being ready to make my own decisions, and that it finally got through to him." In a laughing parenthesis, she added, "Even though I do still keep catching him looking at me with a sort of surprised expression! But oh, Laurel, thank you so much! I just hope—"

Automatically Laurel shook her head a little, and Peggy broke off her torrent of words. For a moment they just looked at each other. Peggy tightened her hold briefly, then released Laurel. Silently she climbed back onto the snowmobile and far from silently, roared away.

Laurel barely noticed the racket. Entering the quiet inn, she groped her way upstairs to her room, to fall asleep near the welcoming warmth of the fire some-one had built for her and carefully banked on the hearth.

CHAPTER FIFTEEN

Nevertheless, because the outside temperature kept plummeting, her room was cold when she woke up several hours later. She opened her eyes and looked around, her breath steaming. On the hearth, her fire was only a dim red glow, a glow easily outshone by the icy brilliance that glistened across the floor from her two windows. Outside, the full moon poured its light over a still world of eerie white beauty, snow carved into fantastic forms by the wind's knife. Laurel slipped out of bed, pulling on her heavy woolen robe to go gaze at the sculpture.

She had to hold her breath to keep frost flowers from forming on the windowpanes so that she could look out. But when she did, it seemed to her that the cold was so intense that the very air had solidified into a perfect crystalline sphere that would shatter at the slightest movement. Then it did. At the far edge of the meadow below her windows, something stirred, and she leaned forward, trying to identify the moving shape. It detached itself from the trees, and she recognized Morgan, coming back up from the lake without waiting for morning.

Everything else seemed to fade away as she watched him, his dark bulk silhouetted against the unearthly radiance of the moonlit snow. He seemed like a figure in a dream, but a few hours earlier he had been real and immediate as they knelt together over Adam, and in perfect unison, fought to save someone they both loved. They had been so close to each other then that it seemed she could almost hear his muscles straining with the effort of compressing Adam's chest, heard his breathing grow labored with the strain, seen the sweat streak his tired face and felt in her own muscles the weight of weariness building up in his. For the first time since she'd driven him away from her room, he had let her stay near him, accepting her help out of necessity. For the first time since then, he'd shown emotion, and she had seen the difficult tears scald down his cheeks—although for Adam, not for her and their ruined happiness.

But then he had turned away from her in Giles's studio, pulled back from that moment of contact and gone to stand alone and isolated at the window, instead of letting her share the worry and tension while they waited for more news from Bridgton. The unhappiness she had felt seemed to foreshadow the grief that lay ahead of her if they were divorced and he left her forever. She had killed his love by not believing in him. He would walk out of her life, as he had just walked out of her sight.

She blinked away a cloud of tears, realizing abruptly that he shouldn't have disappeared. He had still been too far away to pass into the lee of the building, so he had to be somewhere in the meadow. Yet no tall shadow stretched across the snow, and a faint unease began to feather down her spine, pushing aside sorrow. She saw him again as he had looked a few minutes earlier, and now she knew he had been moving strangely. All of his usual lithe grace seemed to have been replaced by a stiff lumbering quality that even his heavy clothing couldn't be responsible for. As she saw that bearlike shamble again in memory, Laurel raised both hands slowly to her lips. Something was terribly wrong.

An instant later, she had spun away from the empty snowscape outside and stripped off both robe and nightgown without even noticing the room's chill, scrambled into her long underwear and heavy stockings, wool slacks and sweaters and stamped her way into her boots. Then she dashed down the back stairs and out of doors, snatching up coat, cap and gloves as she raced through the kitchen. Beyond the back door, the cold was so extreme that it seemed to be sucking the air from her lungs, and Laurel gasped involuntarily. But still there was no sign of Morgan except for the narrow track their footsteps had beaten in the snow hours earlier.

Trying to ignore the lurch of her heart as she gazed at that empty track, Laurel tucked her mouth and nose into the collar of her jacket and leaped off the porch to follow it, stumbling across the meadow. Around her, even the silver beauty of the night seemed sinister, watching impassively as she struggled through it to find the man she loved. And when she finally did, the icy cold was a feral predator, a snow leopard crouched to kill. Morgan was indeed at the bottom of the meadow, but he had fallen in the deep snow and lay there, motionless.

"Morgan!" His name came out of her collar muffled; he didn't seem to hear it at all. "Morgan!" Freeing her lips as she hurried closer, calling him again, the word a frightened explosion of steam.

At first it seemed as though he still hadn't heard her, but at last he raised his head slightly and looked in her direction. "Wha'?"

She tried to slow her uneven breathing, to calm the panic she'd felt when he didn't answer, to keep the frigid air from searing her lungs like fire. "I was worried about you—I just came out to see that you were all right."

"'m fine. Perf'ly a'ri," he mumbled, peering at her as if he could barely see her. But the moonlight was still streaming across the snow, light enough for her to have read a newspaper by it. She couldn't read his face, though. It seemed stiff and blank, and fear began to rise in her again.

"Morgan, come on," she pleaded. "Don't stop now. It's too cold to be out here anymore. You've got to get inside!"

She tried to take his arm, but he shook her off clumsily. "Wai'—gotta tell you. Granda—"

And her first fear was joined by a second.

But after an agonizing pause when he seemed to gather his thoughts very slowly, he finished, "'s okay. Stable. Taking him...Portland."

Inside her was a deep thankfulness, but there was still Morgan himself to worry about. Peeling off one glove, she raised her bare fingers to his pale cheek. It was so cold it numbed her hand almost immediately, and it had an odd glossy look to it, catching the moonlight in nearly the same way that the snow did. His skin vibrated under her touch, the movement coming in waves, and she realized what his bulky clothing had hidden at first—his whole body was shaken by violent shivering that started at his feet and shuddered up from there. And his indistinct speech—fearfully, she remembered that that drunken quality was another symptom of advanced hypothermia.

"Please!"

The urgent note in her voice slowly penetrated his sluggish brain, and with an effort he focused on her again.

"Don' cry, Laurel."

"Then come inside!" she choked as tears cooled rapidly on her cheeks.

"A' ri'," he slurred, letting his hand drop limply. "Jus' don' cry."

"I won't," she promised, tugging on her own glove. "Let me help you up."

"I c'n do it—I'm fine," he objected. But when she slid an arm under his shoulder he leaned heavily on her. Somehow he got to his feet, and they turned toward the inn.

They made slow wavering progress, Laurel silent with the effort and concentration, Morgan occasionally mumbling something indistinct. Twice they stumbled, and once he went down on his knees in the unbroken snow beside the narrow track.

"You go on ahea'." He stopped thrashing in the heavy powder and raised his head to peer at her. "'m tired. Jus' gonna have a nap 'fore I come, too." On the last word his eyes shut, and his head sank.

"No!" The word flicked around him like whiplash, but he didn't respond. "You can't! I won't leave you!"

She struggled over to him and sank to her own knees to force his head up from the snow, so that he couldn't droop peacefully into a final sleep. "Get up! GET UP!"

Her voice cracked on the violence of the command, but it got through to him. Opening his eyes at last, he looked at her with recognition. "Why?" he asked mildly.

"Because you have to! You've got to come inside!"

He still seemed to be watching her with nothing more than idle curiosity, unconvinced, and in utter desperation she flew at him, flailing in the snow as she tugged and yanked at him. He didn't budge at first. She was as ineffective as a single snowflake, until her strength began to fail.

"You have to come with me!" she gasped in desperation one more time, and somehow that finally galvanized him.

With a sudden burst of energy, he surged to his feet, and she staggered up beside him, putting her arm around him again.

"A'ri'," he agreed resignedly, and then gave her his rare sweet smile, docilely letting her lead his wandering feet the rest of the way back to the inn.

Urging him up the back porch steps, she pushed open the kitchen door and guided him inside, nudging the door closed behind them. She left him leaning against it while she ran ahead. There was a hot bright fire still burning in each of the three downstairs fireplaces, but the one in the living room was the largest and the hottest, so she set aside the fire screen and dragged a wing chair over to it, then brought Morgan in.

In the firelight he looked like the ghost of snowstorms past, a lean powdery figure, pale and swaying slightly as the uncontrollable shivering still racked him. Even in the warmth and shelter of the room, there was something shadowy and insubstantial about him, and that fact drove her into action again, even as she refused to let herself recognize the fear that he wasn't safe yet. Peeling off her own gloves, she used them to flick the loose snow from his clothing. Sitting him in the chair, she raced off again with a hasty word of explanation over her shoulder, while he gazed unseeingly at the fire.

In a couple of minutes she came back with blankets dragged from her bed and, since his clothes seemed reasonably dry, tucked them tightly around him as he was, trying to make them stay in position in spite of the shudders that had him moving continuously. But it didn't work. The blankets kept slipping away, and his shivering didn't diminish, so she ran to the kitchen for the kettle she'd set on the gas stove. With hands that shook, she fixed him a mug of strong coffee, liberally adding cream and sugar. When it was ready, she hurried back to the living room, pasting an optimistic smile onto her lips. Maybe this would help.

But it didn't do any more good than the fire or the blankets.

"Morgan...." She said his name as she came near, but again she had to repeat it several times before he reacted. Then finally he raised his head unsteadily, trying to control the shivering, and looked toward her with blue eyes that seemed opaque and blind. A cold fist seemed to squeeze her heart, but she forced herself to say calmly, "I brought you a warm cup of coffee. Please drink it."

Her voice broke, but slowly he lifted shaking hands, still wearing the gloves she'd forgotten to take from him, and groped for the mug. She put it into his stiffened fingers and bent them around it; he brought it awkwardly to his lips. But it clattered against his teeth and slipped out of his slack grip, dumping the coffee in his lap before it fell to the floor and rolled away. Dropping his hands, he sank back into lethargy, closing his eyes.

Laurel let it go, too. With a stifled cry of distress she knelt by his chair, trying to brush away the liquid from his clothes and wind the blanket around him again. But his involuntary shaking hampered her efforts. Panic-stricken, she knew she'd failed. She had brought him from the arctic cold of the outdoors to the moderate warmth inside the inn, but that wasn't enough. He was still in danger unless she could warm him—and quickly. Bowing her head to rest it on the arm of his chair, she forced herself to breathe deeply and slowly, trying to concentrate.

She could wake some of the guests again—but what good would it do? They could only offer the same ideas she'd tried. The fire hadn't warmed Morgan enough, nor had the blankets or the coffee. What else was there? Ordinarily, the inn would have had warm water available, and she could have put him in a tepid bath until the water brought his body temperature back to normal. But without power, she'd have to heat the water on the gas stove, a few panfuls at a time. And in the meantime Morgan would continue to shudder like this, so that his whole body was convulsed. If she really had destroyed all his love for her, then she would have to lose him to divorce. But to lose him to exposure would be much more terrible, because it would be utterly final.

Then she was on her feet again, putting the fire screen back in front of the fire for the rest of the night, before she bent over Morgan, setting her hands on his shoulders where the tremors still vibrated.

"Morgan," she called in a voice of fear and love and resolution. "Morgan—please listen to me."

His eyelids with their heavy fringe of lashes quivered slightly, before they rose as she said his name a third time. Cloudily he looked her way. Then his eyes began to drift shut again, as if he were slipping away from her to some far place. Shaking him, she called him back.

"Morgan, you can't stay here! You have to stand up, because I can't carry you and you've got to come with me."

She made her tone commanding, and slowly, infinitely slowly, he began to respond to it. His eyes opened a bit more; his head lifted.

"Good!" From some deep reservoir she drew vitality to put in her voice. "Now let me help you...."

Shifting sideways until she faced the same way he did, she put one arm around his shoulders and encircled his waist with the other.

"Here we go!" she announced in the bright voice of a nursery nanny, and thought fleetingly of the small boy who had been Morgan and who had never known any more of a mother than a hired nanny. Her throat closed so that she couldn't speak again, but she leaned forward and put all her strength into her arms, and weakly Morgan tried to heave himself out of the chair.

Somehow, between them, they made it. When he stood unsteadily beside her, Laurel didn't dare stop. Keeping her right arm tightly around his waist and her shoulder under his for support, she wadded up the blankets under her left arm and matched her steps to his faltering ones, urging him up the stairs, along the hall and finally into the room that she'd left so hastily when she went out to look for him.

Banked on the hearth, her fire was still giving off some heat, and leaving him momentarily, she built it up until it burned with a hot bright flame. When its warmth began to lap across the floor in rippling waves, she brought Morgan to stand shivering in front of it, while she spread the blankets over her bed again. Then she stripped off her own jacket and cap, tossing them aside as she turned to him.

Standing on tiptoes, she pulled off his gloves, the old hunting cap of Nate's that Morgan had been using and unzipped his wool jacket, slipping it off his shoulders and down to drop at his feet. Under it he wore a heavy wool sweater, a flannel shirt and lighter turtleneck, but at these temperatures even that hadn't been enough to protect him from the dangers of struggling back up through the snow when he was already exhausted. Layer by layer, she took it all off him, and feebly he cooperated without question, awkwardly ducking his head or extending his arms when she asked.

When he was stripped to the waist, she paused. But his pants were soaked with cold coffee, and even in the red glow of the firelight, his skin had lost its usual bronzy sheen, looking pallid and almost shrunken; when her fingers brushed over his chest he felt chilled and bloodless. For a minute he seemed to become aware of her. His head turned her way, and his blue eyes almost focused, while a faint flicker of expression crossed his face. Then an avalanche of shivering swept over his body, and he seemed to withdraw again, becoming only a lethargic robot once more.

That decided her. She crouched at his feet, quickly unlacing his boots. While she held one at a time, he stepped out of them at her urging, and she peeled off his socks as well, revealing feet that were blue with cold. Then she reached up to his waistband, fumbling with the unfamiliar fastenings and resolutely ignoring the idiotic color she could feel rising into her cheeks. But it didn't matter anyway, because undressing Morgan right now couldn't mean anything.

Finally he stood naked in the firelight, and now she couldn't stop herself from contrasting this moment to the last time she had seen him this way. Then he had been a perfect male animal, so beautiful and confident that the desire she'd felt had left her weak and trembling. But now he was vulnerable, weak and trembling himself—not a dream, or a hero, or an idol, not some fairy-tale prince but only an ordinary mortal—and all she had ever wanted. Love surged through her with almost choking strength, replacing desire with the undemanding will to cherish, to nurture and nourish.

Taking his cold hand in hers with ineffable tenderness, she led him to her bed, sitting him on it and helping him swing his long legs up under the blankets. Then she covered him and stepped away to shuck off all her own clothing, letting it fall behind her as she came back to slip into bed beside him. Twining her warm arms and legs around his frozen body, she fitted herself into him from head to toe without the least retreat from the shock of his chilled flesh against her. She molded herself to touch him as much as possible, cradling him against her breast. While his shudders shook them both, she offered him the heat of her own body as the most elemental gift of all.

For a long time the waves of shuddering came, vibrating through his lean frame while she tightened her hold to keep him safe against her. His shallow breathing fanned across her breast as he lay with his head in the hollow of her shoulder. But eventually the shivers grew less violent and less frequent, and his breathing grew deeper and steadier as his body warmed to hers, beginning to give back heat for heat. The fear she had felt for him faded harmlessly away. Lulled by the rhythm of their breathing, she fell asleep.

SHE AWAKENED GENTLY as the fire burned low and the first faint lightening of the sky began. Morgan's dark head stirred against her breast; she felt a drop of moisture on her skin. Her hand rose to his angular cheek, and another tear slid down to her fingers. Gently she brushed it away, and he turned to kiss her fingertips.

"I thought I'd lost you both," he said into her hand, his voice low and harsher than ever. "The only two people I ever dared to love."

"Not me," she answered brokenly, tightening her arms around him convulsively, as if by clinging to each other they could keep away loneliness, and change and time—time, which had made Adam seventy years old and subject to a heart attack. A few drops spilled over to run down her cheeks, too, and she raised fingers wet with Morgan's tears to wipe away her own.

For now she drew back from speaking about her love for this man in her arms, swallowing hard to add, "And not granda, either."

On her last words Morgan lifted his head, raising himself beside her so that he could touch a kiss to each damp eyelid before he leaned back against the headboard.

"No, they seemed to think that transferring him to the cardiac-care unit in Portland was more of a safety measure than a necessity now."

"When did you learn C.P.R.?" she asked him huskily, determined to make herself talk about it without any more fear.

"About a week after the first time I saw Adam taking one of those nitroglycerin tablets," he answered. "And you?"

Her response came more slowly. "My father trained us all after our mother died of a heart attack when I was fourteen. He said he couldn't change the past, but he might be able to change the future."

Her voice cracked again on the last word, because suddenly her father's face was before her, gray with grief when he promised his children that they would never again have to stand by completely helpless when a heart faltered. And she hadn't. With Morgan beside her, she had worked until they had pulled Adam back from the shadows—but now she curled into Morgan's body and dissolved into scalding tears again, while his arms came around her and he whispered words of comfort.

Overcome now by the grief that she had held back for so long, she huddled against his broad chest and wept for her parents, for Adam and his Sophie, for every couple whose love is curtailed by death. While the sobs shook her, she came to understand the inescapable sorrow: that all love must end in separation. She knew now that she and Morgan would escape the nearer separation of denying their love, but they, too, would be parted one day. And so she cried for the oldest of griefs, the grief of mortality.

As her tears began to ease, she heard, faint but clear and true from the parlor, the grandfather clock in the corner of the room chime six times. Adam had made a ritual of winding that clock for her every day since he'd come to join them at the inn, and when she heard it strike Laurel felt her cheeks grow damp again. This time, though, her tears seemed cool and fresh, and she was able to smile at Morgan through the mist. Dimly she could see on his face the certainty that lighted her own. Like his clock, Adam, too, would go on.

And now around her shoulders were Morgan's arms. Under her cheek his heart beat with comforting steadiness. They lay in each other's embrace. No divorce would part them now, and the final mortal parting was far into the future. Here and now, they had each other. Here and now, there was life to affirm.

She moved against his chest, and in a homely comforting little gesture, he stretched out one hand to get her a tissue from the box on the bedside table. The other arm stayed wound loosely around her as she sat up, but when she went to scrub away the tearstains on her cheeks he stopped her, turning her face to him. She looked at him with eyes reminiscent of liquid gold of coins underwater, and tenderly he stroked away her tears with one long finger. When he was through, he drew her head down to him and gave her a gentle kiss that spoke an understanding and a vow.

''I love you,'' he said very quietly, and she realized he had never risked saying those three dangerous words before. But that danger was over now for both of them, and she answered him not in words but in actions.

He released her, and she slipped down beside him

in the deep soft bed, turning to reach for him with hands that were almost afraid to touch their happiness. He came eagerly into her arms, and she clung to him for a long time before she could bear to loosen her hold enough to run her fingers over the clean strong lines of him. Storm and sorrow behind them at last, they could touch with a sense of awe and wonder and delight that was even stronger than when they'd first given each other the freedom of their bodies a few nights and a lifetime ago.

Seeing him with her hands, almost as if love were indeed blind, she explored the planes and angles of his face, tracing his eyebrows and nose and lips, following his jawline to his ears. Then she curved her palm around the back of his head and slipped it down through the short curls at his nape, while he tried to cover her face with tiny kisses. Her hands went on with their delicate exploration, marveling at the strength and grace of a man's body as she learned the structure of his shoulders, his arms, his chest.

She traveled lower, too, mapping out his narrow hips and smooth hard flanks. But now the nature of his kisses changed. His lips left her forehead, where his breath had fanned her curls as lightly as a moth's wing, and suddenly returned to her lips. His breath was coming harder. For an instant she felt it on her cheek. Then it was lost in her own breath as he took her mouth with his.

It was a kiss unlike any they had shared before. This was a kiss of both passion and promise, and as she opened her lips to him, she felt as though the last barriers between them had fallen. Faint and far, in some distant corner of her mind, a single line of poetry echoed like a silvery trumpet call to victory: "My true-love hath my heart, and I have his. . . ."

Through their lips the exchange was made—of heart, of mind, of spirit—and with their mingled breath she made a small sound of joy and welcome. Then the poem faded from her thoughts, and with it went the fear of the last hours, the misunderstandings of the days and weeks before, and the pain of the months since she'd married Morgan Hamilton. Only the joy was left, a towering bonfire of incandescent joy.

She felt it flame through him, too, at her touch, felt it in the renewed power and vitality that were everywhere her eager hands went as they swept over the taut muscles of his arms, the hard framework of his rib cage, the lean strength of his thighs. He was quiveringly alive beneath her fingers, and the same trembling began in her as he lowered her gently back against the pillows. Her hands fell away from him, but before they dropped to her sides, he caught first one and then the other, to press a kiss to the inside of each wrist, his lips firm on her racing pulse.

Then he set aside the rumpled sheet, pulling it gently from her so that she lay completely uncovered to his eyes in the dawn light. Before she could be chilled, the heat of his mouth was on her body as he bent to kiss her arms, her shoulders, her breasts, belly, hips and thighs. His breath fanned gently across her skin like the warm spring winds that bring life, and she felt his presence in every cell of her being as she offered herself to his quickening lips.

Each kiss had a quality of homage, but there was passion, too, and passion rose in her to meet his. It ran in her veins that throbbed beneath his touch, rode on her breath that gasped in time to his movements and sang in her cries that welcomed him. It filled her and emptied her at once, so that she drew him to her wildly until their two bodies arched and melted into one and all the distance that had ever been between them was gone. That distance would not reappear, and for now they were fused together, welded in each other's embrace, melting, searing, soaring like a rising meteor until, like the meteor, they were consumed.

Much later, as she lay against his chest, listening to the rumble of his voice murmuring endearments, she finally found her voice. Raising her head, she put soft fingers across his lips and in the silence said, "I'm sorry."

Above her hand his eyes darkened, and she added quickly, "Sorry for being blind and pigheaded and distrustful—"

His eyes returned to a clear light blue and crinkled at the corners. Freeing his lips, he cut in with mock severity, "At the same time that you were being infuriating, enchanting and utterly desirable."

He punctuated each adjective with a stern kiss but

set the last one improbably on the tip of her nose, and they left the exalted heights of love for its delightful plains. She giggled, then tried to finish her confession. "But I misjudged you so horribly!"

"And apologized so beautifully a little while ago," he observed thoughtfully. "I think I'm going to insist on quite a few more of those apologies before I forgive you completely."

He gave her a meaningful look and grinned at the luminous smile she gave him. She burrowed against him, and he turned to fold her in his arms.

It was quite a while before either of them spoke again. But finally, when she lay with her head pillowed against his shoulder, he said quietly, "I'll be apologizing, too, because you weren't entirely wrong in what you thought about my relationship with Renee."

Her fingers stopped moving idly in the silky hair on his chest, and he laid a hand over them, as if to hold her so she couldn't withdraw again. But this time, with newfound wisdom, she only waited to hear him out.

"I meant to marry you from the moment I asked you to dinner that first day," he began slowly. "And that's the first apology I owe you, because at that point you were only a means to an end for me. I don't know of any way I can make this sound better than cold-blooded, but Adam had said I had to marry or lose the company I'd trained for years to run, and I was so angry—"

"That you simply chose the first woman you met," she finished quietly for him, adding as he turned his head to give her a look of surprise and regret, "I heard you arguing that day but didn't understand what it meant until last night, when granda told me you had reacted just the way he'd hoped you would."

For a moment Morgan was utterly still. Even his pulse seemed arrested under her hand. Then he began to laugh, a soft, rich, full laugh of amusement and admiration. "I should have known!" he said. "For years I've watched him maneuver people into doing whatever was best for them, whether they knew it or not. But he made me so angry that day that I never realized he was doing the same thing to me. Having found me the perfect wife, he was making sure I married her, even if I didn't know yet how perfect she was."

He gave her a quick hard kiss, and the small regret of knowing he had originally come to her in anger evaporated. He wasn't done speaking, though, and when he went on the laughter had faded from his voice.

"Even on our wedding day, I still didn't realize what I had. Right up until Renee waylaid me in the library and started making plans for us to go on seeing each other, I suppose I'd been thinking of you in one compartment of my life and her in another, assuming nothing had really changed. That's the other apology I owe you."

Raising her left hand from his chest, he looked absently at the bare fingers, his black eyebrows arched in remembered surprise. "But then I discovered I'd meant what I said in church about 'cleaving to you only,' so I unwound Renee from my neck and said goodbye. Three days later I had to do it again, because she didn't believe me, and she wasn't overly pleased with me either time—" his tone went very dry, and Laurel had a quick vivid picture of Renee's displeasure "—but I wasn't in the mood to care, because she didn't seem important. You were the only thing on my mind, even if I still didn't know why."

He fell silent, and she put in sadly, "And before you could find out, I'd seen Renee with you and assumed the worst, because I had never really been able to believe you cared. I loved you so much it terrified me, but you'd never said in so many words that you loved me."

"I didn't find out I loved you until that day in Paris, either," he agreed. "When you vanished, I was wild—told myself it was just because you had embarrassed me publicly. I didn't give a damn. I'd go back to my old pursuits, and to hell with heading the company—to hell with you."

Remembered anger echoed in his voice, but his arms pulled her closer, and he laid his cheek on her hair as he added ruefully, "And I couldn't figure out why everything I did was boring and flat and pointless. Not until I caught sight of you across that café did it all dawn on me, and then I couldn't make you stay to hear me out.

"I came back to the States and checked in with the company. I still wasn't ready to make my peace with Adam after the quarrel we had when you left, so I was operating out of the New York offices. But I did find out from his office that there'd been some kind of delay in installing Paul as president—"

"Like the supposed delay in getting my annulment?" she asked on a whisper of a laugh.

His answering chuckle rumbled. "Exactly like that, it seems. And I also discovered through a secretary's convenient carelessness with some files that you were still working for the company in some capacity. After that, it was only a matter of time for me to work my way through each hotel, running that damned survey, while I looked for you."

He held her away from him for a moment. "And it wouldn't have taken me so long if I'd had any idea my wife was a master innkeeper. I didn't think to look here until I'd come up empty at every hotel in the chain. By then, the inns were my last chance, and this was almost the last one."

The old despair shadowed his face; his hold on her tightened. With perfect clarity she remembered how tired he had looked the night he'd finally reached the Mountain View Inn. But she had ignored the signs, because Renee had come before him. Tenderly now she slipped her fingers along the angle of his cheek in the gesture she had wanted to make then.

His thoughts must have been paralleling hers, because when he spoke again it was to say disgustedly, "And then, when I finally found you, Renee found me. Here I was, trying to get close enough to you to tell you how much I loved you, and here she was, trying to get close enough to me to have me renew the lease on her apartment—and worst of all, there you were with your composer."

His tone made it perfectly clear what he thought of Giles's role in her life. "And dear friend," she added with smiling emphasis on the last word. "He was just helping me cope with having Renee around."

Morgan made a small appeased sound, and she smiled again. Then her expression grew serious. "I wouldn't have needed all that help, of course, if I hadn't believed Renee was still sleeping with you."

"She made it easy for you to think so," he pointed out as an extenuating circumstance.

"But you told me she wasn't, and I didn't believe you," she admitted with difficulty, her voice catching on the words. "It scared me so, loving you, that I was looking for ways to stop it and go back to just being the coolly rational career woman. But I didn't know that was the problem for a long time. I just kept looking for reasons why I should stop caring about you. Even after Renee was gone—"

She pulled away from him, and he let her go, but when she turned her face away, he reached out with one strong hand and turned it back to him, looking at her tenderly as he held her chin between his fingers.

The tears that were close to the surface welled up again, but she had to finish. "Even after she was gone, I told myself everything was still just as bad, because you'd still tried to lie to me about the woman I saw you with in Paris. I still couldn't trust you."

Hearing again what she had taken for the beginning of a lie, he looked away across the room for a long minute while she huddled beside him, and when he turned back to her his expression was a study. "It took me a long time to deal with that," he remembered. "With the way you jumped to such a conclusion, with the irony of your thinking that I'd lie about being with my mother. She's the reason that every time you turned away from me, I tried to convince myself I didn't love you, either. There really wasn't any such thing as love; I thought I'd learned. She's why I hadn't ever dared to care for anyone before and wouldn't even for you if I'd seen you coming —and you thought she was a connection I'd lie to cover up."

He searched her face, and she made herself meet his eyes, apology and appeal in her own. One last time Vanessa's image rose before him, but the shadow she'd cast over his entire life seemed to dissipate now, fading away until he saw only Laurel's face, saw her looking at him with regret and love and hope. Unsteadily he laughed. All of their confessions had been made.

Against his lips she whispered, "Even when my mind misunderstood, my heart always knew who and what you were. That's why I had to fight so hard whenever you came near me—my body wanted you, but my mind didn't know why."

"You should have listened to your body more."

"I will now."

The words were a promise and an invitation, but before he accepted it, he cupped her face in both his hands and looked at her with such a flame of love in his eyes that she felt she might melt right then. Yet what he said seemed irrelevant at first.

"Do you know the mythological origin of your name?"

She nodded her head very slightly. "After a great battle the Greeks used to make a crown of laurel leaves and give it to the victor." Softly she whispered, "Hail, victor!"

"Hail, victor!" he replied, and as his lips closed on hers she remembered Giles's words: "No triumph is ever complete."

But he was wrong.

Discover the new and unique

Harlequin Category-Romance Specials!

Regency Romance
A DEBT OF HONOR
Mollie Ashton

THE FAIRFAX BREW
Sara Orwig

Gothic Romance
THE SATYR RING
Alison Quinn

THE RAVENS
OF ROCKHURST
Marian Martin

Romantic Suspense
THE SEVENTH GATE
Dolores Holliday

THE GOBLIN TREE
Robyn Anzelon

A new and exciting world of romance reading

Harlequin Category-Romance Specials

Begin a long love affair with

SUPERROMANCE.
Accept LOVE BEYOND DESIRE, **FREE.**

Complete and mail the coupon below, today!

- -